ODIN'S BETRAYAL

DONOVAN COOK

Boldwood

First published in Great Britain in 2023 by Boldwood Books Ltd.

Cover Design by Head Design

Cover Photography: Shutterstock

A CIP catalogue record for this book is available from the British Library.

Paperback ISBN 978-1-80483-814-3

Large Print ISBN 978-1-80483-810-5

Hardback ISBN 978-1-80483-809-9

Ebook ISBN 978-1-80483-807-5

Kindle ISBN 978-1-80483-808-2

Audio CD ISBN 978-1-80483-815-0

MP3 CD ISBN 978-1-80483-812-9

Digital audio download ISBN 978-1-80483-806-8

Boldwood Books Ltd
23 Bowerdean Street
London SW6 3TN
www.boldwoodbooks.com

To my readers, none of this would have been possible without you.

CHARACTERS

<u>FRANKS</u>

Charles – son of Torkel and grandson of Sven the Boar
Gerold – slave
Bishop Bernard – bishop of Paderborn
Duke Liudolf – duke of Saxony
Lothar – chatelain of Hügelburg
Prince Louis – son of Emperor Louis I and future king of East
Francia

<u>DANES</u>

Sven the Boar – former jarl of Ribe, grandfather of Charles
Thora – former shield maiden
Sigge – young warrior from Hedeby, nephew of Ketil
Torkel – son of Sven the Boar and father of Charles
Jarl Bjarni – jarl of Ribe and brother of Sven
Oleg – hirdman of Jarl Bjarni, former hirdman of Sven the Boar

Amund and Egil – Danish warriors of Hedeby

Ketil – uncle of Sigge and friend of Jarl Torgeir, jarl of Hedeby

Oda – wife of Arnbjorg

Rollo – son of Arnbjorg

HISTORICAL NOTE

After three years of civil war over who would be the next emperor of Francia, the surviving sons of Emperor Louis I (also known as Louis the Pious) signed the Treaty of Verdun in AD 843. The Frankish Empire was divided into three kingdoms, Charles II (Charles the Bald) received West Francia, Lothar I received Middle Francia and Louis II (Louis the German) received East Francia. But the peace brought by the Treaty of Verdun was fragile and did not prevent the brothers from coveting each other's kingdoms. In AD 854, King Louis II seized his opportunity and sent his son, Louis the Younger, to invade Aquitaine in West Francia after a group of nobles opposed the rule of Charles II and appealed to Louis II for help.

Meanwhile, in Denmark, Francia's troublesome neighbour to the north, King Horik was struggling to control his rebellious jarls who were eager to take advantage of Francia's inner turmoil and raid her fertile lands. King Horik had signed a peace treaty with Emperor Louis I in AD 834, and was desperate to avoid a war with the mighty Frankish Empire. But this did not prevent some of his jarls from raiding in Francia, which strained the relationship between King Horik and the three Frankish kings.

DENMARK AND
EAST FRANCIA
AD 850

n

DENMARK

Jelling ★

• Ribe

Hedeby

Sven the Boar's raid
in AD 834

Hügelburg •

Elbe

×

Bremen

Weser

EAST FRANCIA

SAXONY

OSTPHALIA

WESTPHALIA

Ehresburg
★

PROLOGUE

AD 834, OFF THE COAST OF NORTHERN FRANCIA

Sven the Boar rubbed the Mjöllnir pendant around his neck as he stared at the small Frankish army between him and his two ships hauled up on the beach. Behind him stood his eighty men and the women and children they had taken as captives from the farms they had been raiding over the last few days, and the carts filled with whatever plunder they had found. The money from selling the captives would make him richer than the king of Denmark. Sven let go of the pendant as the clouds drifted in the blue sky above, the summer sun soaking the tunic he wore under his *brynja* in sweat. He knew Odin would not help him. The All-Father was a bastard and would kill Sven just to amuse himself.

'Jarl Sven, what do we do?' Arnbjorg, his champion and one of his hirdmen, towered over him. Sven was shorter than most men, but he had broad shoulders and a barrel-like chest. His arms were the size of most men's legs, and his legs were even thicker. Sven's head was shaved, and he had convinced himself it had nothing to do with losing his hair, even though he had only seen twenty-seven winters. He had a raven tattoo on his scalp, something he had done so that Odin could always find him. His blue eyes were full of violence and his red beard was neatly combed with three thick braids, each one with a golden ring tied at the end. The ring in the middle had belonged to Sven's father, the other two to two of his brothers. Sven had killed all three of them to become the jarl of Ribe, a large trading town in Denmark.

Sven glanced at his remaining brother, Bjarni, wondering why the larger man was so unusually quiet, before turning his attention back to the Frankish army. Behind the small army, a nobleman wearing a tunic as green as the first grass in the spring and a cloak fastened by a large golden brooch sat on a white horse. His dark hair and beard were short and tidy, while dark eyes scrutinised Sven. The Frank had more men than Sven, but most of them were part of the levy: local farmers and men of fighting age who were summoned to defend their lands when needed. They had round shields and spears, a few even had swords, but none wore any armour apart from the helmets on their heads. Sven wasn't too worried about them; they were usually the first ones to run. But he was concerned about the thirty or so household warriors. Like his hirdmen, these were elite fighters, and all wore chain mail and helmets. They had round shields and spears like the levy, but these warriors all had either swords or axes. Sven glanced over the Franks' heads towards his ships and saw the men he had left to guard them lying dead as their blood seeped into the sand. His heart pounded in his chest as he searched for Torkel, his son of nine winters. He had left the boy with the ships, believing he would be safer there than with him during the raids, but there was no sign of him amongst the dead men. Sven took a deep breath as he fought to calm his nerves. The boy was smart; he would be hiding somewhere.

Sven glanced at the forest not far from the shoreline, unable to ignore the unease he felt, and wondered if there were more men hidden amongst the trees. He had not wanted to beach his ships here. He had raided here the previous summer and did not like to raid the same place twice. But his brother and some of his men had convinced him to do it.

'Jarl Sven?' Arnbjorg tried again.

A growl escaped from Sven's throat as he put his helmet back on his head, feeling the heat of the metal against his bare scalp. He gripped his Dane axe as his men prepared themselves for the fight. 'Orm, take your group and protect the captives and the plunder,' Sven ordered, not bothering to look back to see if Orm did what he asked. His eyes never left the Franks. Sven saw the smile on the nobleman's face, before glancing at Bjarni. He was still surprised by how quiet his younger brother was as one of his men handed him his shield.

Sven struck the rim of his shield with his axe and heard his men do the same behind him. The sound echoed around them like thunder and he smiled when some of the women they had captured cried out. In front of them, the Franks were forming a shield wall with the household warriors in the centre and the levy spread out on either side of them. The Frankish lord stayed on his horse behind his troops, the large animal pawing the beach as Sven spat in disgust at the leader who would not fight with his men.

The Danish warriors formed their own line, which stood forty men wide and two men deep, with Arnbjorg on Sven's left and Bjarni on his right. Sven lifted his head to the clouds, looking for a sign from the gods, but saw nothing to tell him of his fate. He shrugged and, with a glance to either side of him, punched his Dane axe into the air.

'Odin!' he roared, and charged at the Franks, his men keeping pace with him as they screamed their own war cries.

The Franks held their line with the nobleman sitting silently on his horse as his more experienced warriors called the orders. The household warriors stood strong, their faces grim, but Sven saw the spears wavering from the levy forces. He knew they would break as soon as his men struck.

They were about five paces from the Franks, close enough to see the whites of their eyes, when Sven shouted. '*Svinfylking!*'

Sven expected his brother to come in closer on his right, just as Arnbjorg was doing on his left, while the rest of his men fell back to form an arrow point that would punch through the Franks' wall. But then Bjarni cried out and fell. Sven had seen no bows, nor had he heard any arrows, so this caught him and his men by surprise.

But he had no time to think about that as he barged into the large warrior facing him. The force of their charge broke through the Frankish men, splitting their line and allowing Sven and his hirdmen to get behind them. The nobleman's horse whined and took a few steps back as Sven swung his axe and split the helmet and skull of the man in front of him. To his side, Arnbjorg caved a man's head in with the rim of his shield before cutting an arm off another. Sven lifted his shield to block a spear thrust and as soon as the spear point lodged into his shield, he turned it and chopped down hard with his Dane axe. The Frankish warrior tried to block the blow with his shield and Sven's axe caught the top of it, tilting it back onto the Frank's shoulder. The man screamed as the axe blade cut through the rim of his shield and broke his collarbone. But before Sven could free his axe from the shield, he heard a new noise. A noise he was hoping not to hear, but also expected. Sven freed his axe from the Frank's shield and looked towards the forest to see the small Frankish cavalry force erupting from the trees. Growling, he looked for his brother but could not see Bjarni amongst the fighting men and remembered he had fallen just before they reached the Franks. Sven knew Odin was laughing at him then. He could hear it in the hooves of the horses as they galloped towards his men, most of them too busy fighting the Franks to notice the new threat approaching their rear. He turned to the dark-haired nobleman astride his powerful steed, who smiled as he saw the same thing Sven had seen. That the Danes were about to lose. Sven gritted his teeth, determined not to go to Valhalla empty-handed.

'Odin!' Sven roared, and charged at the Frankish lord, who saw the threat and yanked on the reins of his horse. But the animal, already nervous from all the blood and violence, refused to obey its master. Instead, it reared up on its hind legs and threw the nobleman off. Sven grinned, feeling that Odin was with him for the first time since they had come across the Franks on the beach. He lifted his Dane axe to kill the nobleman, who was desperately trying to free his sword from its scabbard. But before Sven could bring the axe down, he sensed a spear coming from his right. He deflected the spear point with the haft of his axe and punched the Frankish warrior in the chest with the rim of his shield. There was a crack as the man's ribs broke and the Frank collapsed, his eyes filled with panic as he struggled to breathe. Ignoring the dying warrior, Sven turned to the Frankish nobleman and chopped down with his large axe. The richly dressed Frank rolled out of the way of Sven's axe and managed to free his sword from its scabbard before stabbing at Sven. Sven blocked the blow with his shield and was about to swing his Dane axe at the man's head when the cavalry struck, the shock wave rippling through his men and causing him to pause. Some of Sven's men had seen the threat and had turned to face the charging horses. But the small cavalry force tore through them, and all Sven could do was watch in dismay as his men were maimed or slaughtered. The air was filled with the blood and cries of his men as the horsemen stabbed down with their spears, skewering the Danes and trampling over their corpses. Eyes wide and nostrils flared, Sven turned back to the Frankish nobleman and saw the sneer on his face.

'Jarl, what do we do?' Arnbjorg asked. There was no fear in his voice, only uncertainty. The same uncertainty Sven saw in the faces of the few men close enough to look at him.

Sven glared at the nobleman, feeling the anger of his defeat engulf him. 'We fight!' he roared, and charged at the arrogant man, whose sneer was replaced by panic. One of the nobleman's house warriors tried to get between Sven and his lord, but Sven sliced through his leg with his Dane axe before the warrior could do anything and, as he rushed past, punched at the nobleman with the rim of his shield. The nobleman stepped to the side, dodging the shield, but couldn't avoid the axe head as Sven jabbed with it. The blow caught him on the shoulder, spinning him around and causing him to drop his sword as he fell. Sven stood over the man while grinding his teeth. Odin had turned his back on him, but Sven was determined to kill this rich bastard and lifted his axe for the killing blow, grinning as the nobleman's face paled. He did not hear Arnbjorg's warning, though, and only knew of the horse charging at him as the beast thundered into him. Sven was sent sprawling to the ground, his helmet almost falling off, and somehow avoided being trampled on. He rolled to his feet, his head swimming as he dropped his shield, but he still had his axe and that was all he needed to kill the Frankish turd. Standing between them was the horse which had run him over, the animal pawing at the ground as the warrior on top pointed his spear at him. Sven clenched his teeth as he fixed his helmet and took a step forward when he heard his champion cry out. He turned in time to see two Frankish horsemen drive their spears through Arnbjorg's chest, the sharp spear points breaking through the links of his *brynja* and tearing through his lungs. Arnbjorg swung his Dane axe, breaking both spears and killing one horseman. But another came from behind and speared the large warrior through the neck. There was an explosion of blood as Arnbjorg's eyes bulged before he dropped to his knees and sat there gurgling while blood pumped out of his neck.

Looking around, Sven saw his men fighting a desperate battle against their enemy, but the Franks had the upper hand. Most of his men were injured or dead and those still standing would not last much longer. His heart sank as a group of the Frankish cavalry killed his men guarding their captives, the women and children screaming as they fled the bloody violence on the beach. Sven knew the battle was lost and there was nothing else he could do but find a way to save the rest of his men. He glanced at Arnbjorg, still on his knees, but with his eyes devoid of life and *brynja* reddened by his blood. Sven had no time to mourn the loss of his friend or his brother, that would have to come later. First, he had to get off this beach with the rest of his men. Looking at his two ships and praying to Odin that his son was hiding in one of them, he shouted, 'On me! *Skjaldborg!*'

Those who could, rushed to his side, linking their shields together to form a small shield wall. Sven stood in the centre, with no shield and his axe gripped in both hands as the Frankish cavalry surrounded them. His men glanced around nervously as the Franks formed their own line behind the cavalry.

'It's over,' the Frankish lord said, holding on to his shoulder as he glared at Sven. 'You've lost.' Sven knew enough Frankish to understand the nobleman's words. From behind the Franks, Bjarni struggled to his feet, his forehead bloody. Sven was relieved that his brother was still alive. He looked back at the sneering nobleman, gripping his axe and wondering if he could get past the horses and still kill the bastard. But then rejected the idea as he knew all of his men would be killed. As well as Torkel, his only son.

'It's only over when the Norns decide so,' he responded in Danish, not caring if the nobleman understood him or not. The Norns were the three sisters who lived beneath Yggdrasill, the mighty tree that connected the nine realms, and controlled the fate of all men. They would decide if it was over or not. Sven glanced at his brother again, willing the bastard to attack the nobleman from behind. If they could kill him, then the rest of the Franks might flee and they could still get home. But Bjarni just stood there, staring at them like a dumb ox.

One of the horsemen translated Sven's words for the nobleman, who smiled. He said something to the man beside him, who turned to the trees and whistled two sharp notes. Sven felt the shiver run down his spine as he saw the sneer on the nobleman's face. He knew what was about to happen and prayed to Odin that he was wrong. But the All-Father was a chaos-loving bastard who must have been laughing at Sven as a horseman came from the trees. It took all of Sven's strength not to collapse to his knees.

'No,' he muttered when he saw the short red-headed boy astride the horse, held tightly by the Frankish warrior behind him. As they got closer, Sven saw the fear in his son's blue eyes and the tear streaks on his cheeks. He gripped his axe, his knuckles turning white, before glaring at the Frankish nobleman. The nobleman smiled back, but it was a smile filled with malice. Sven felt the unease amongst his remaining warriors as they all saw the son of their jarl held captive. He sensed some of their eyes on him, but Sven ignored them as he continued to glare at the Frank. The horseman holding his son galloped past Bjarni, who barely reacted, and Sven heard one of his men ask why Bjarni did not rescue the boy. Sven would have wondered that too if his mind wasn't filled with images of him slaughtering all the Franks and burning their kingdom to the ground. But he knew that would never happen, and the next words spoken by the Frankish nobleman confirmed that.

'This is the last time your filth will harass my lands. This I swear by the Almighty God, our Lord in heaven.' The horsemen parted to allow the nobleman to come closer, but the two on either side of him kept their spears levelled at Sven.

Sven hawked and spat at the bastard's feet. 'Your weak god has never protected you before. What makes you think he will do so now?'

The nobleman glanced at Sven's son and laughed as the horseman holding Torkel pulled a knife from his belt and pressed it against Torkel's throat. Sven felt his blood go cold as his son tried to pull away from the knife. He looked at Bjarni, but his younger brother just stood there, his face strangely calm, and Sven's head swam as he struggled to make sense of it. 'Because God has given me your only son. Sven the Boar, as dumb as the animal you are named after.'

Sven heard the words and felt his hands trembling. What would his wife say when he returned without their son? Sven felt his legs go weak and dropped his axe as he collapsed to his knees.

'Not my son. Anything but my son. Take my ships or me,' he pleaded before he could stop himself. He heard the gasps from his men, but he did not care. He could not lose his son.

'Pathetic,' the nobleman sneered. 'And to think you terrorised my lands for so long.' The Frankish warriors laughed, but Sven ignored them as he stared at his boy. He saw fresh tears run down the boy's cheeks as he too understood what was happening. 'Look at me,' the nobleman said.

Sven kept his eyes on his son, willing the boy to be strong. One horseman came forward and struck Sven on the head with the butt of his spear. 'Look at my prince when he addresses you, heathen!'

Sven's head snapped to the side as his ears rang. His men tensed beside him, and Sven held his hand up to stop them from doing anything. He looked at the nobleman, gritting his teeth and wanting nothing more than to launch himself at the arrogant worm and rip his head off his shoulders.

The prince must have seen the fire in his eyes because he smiled. 'Try that, and your son dies,' the prince said, and the horseman pressed the knife harder against Torkel's neck. The boy paled as Sven felt his throat restrict. 'Take your ships and what's left of your men. Leave these shores and never return. Your son will be my hostage to ensure your compliance.' The prince leaned in closer, and Sven resisted the urge to headbutt him. 'I will make sure to turn your son into a good Christian so that he's better than you heathen worms. But I promise you, if I ever see your ships or any other that look like yours again, I will slit his throat myself.' He locked eyes with Sven, and Sven saw the steel in them. 'Do you understand?'

Sven looked at his son and then back at the dark-haired prince. He did not trust himself to speak, not with the anger threatening to erupt inside of him, so instead, he nodded. His men shuffled on their feet, and Sven could sense the uncertainty in them as they did not understand the prince's words, but saw how they affected him. He hoped that none of them was dumb enough to attack the prince and cause the death of his son.

The Frank smiled as he adjusted his cloak. 'Good. I will allow you to say your farewells to your boy, but by sunset I want you, your godless men and your ships gone from my shore.' He did not wait for a response as he turned and walked away, signalling to the horseman to let the boy down.

As soon as Torkel's feet touched the ground, he ran towards his father, who took his helmet off. Sven grabbed his son and embraced him as tears ran down his cheeks and soaked into his beard. He glared at the Frankish horsemen as they came closer, their spears pointing at Sven as if daring him to try and run off with his son. Sven had to resist the urge to do just that. He knew he and his men would be cut down before they reached his ships. But what really stopped him was the fact that Torkel might be killed as well. After a while, Sven pulled away from his son and without taking his eyes off the boy, he said to his men. 'Get the ships ready. We'll be leaving soon.'

'But we don't have enough men for all the ships,' one of his warriors said.

Sven felt his anger threaten to take over and fought hard to stay calm for his son's sake. 'Then burn one and prepare the other.'

The man hesitated. 'Which one?'

'By Odin, ask me one more question and I'll burn you with the ship!'

The man ran off to do what his jarl asked him, while Sven tried to absorb as much of his son's image as he could.

'I have to stay, don't I?' his son asked. Sven nodded. Torkel had always been smart. He got that from his mother because all Sven knew was fighting. His son squared his shoulders and tried to look strong. 'Then that's what path the Norns have decided for me.'

Sven felt proud of the strength his son was showing and anger at the gods for doing this to him. But he did his best to stay calm as he took the Mjöllnir pendant from his neck and handed it to his son. The hammer pendant was about the size of his thumb and made from ivory of the tusked seal from the north. It was beautifully carved with swirls and patterns and had belonged to Sven's father. Sven had worn it since the day he had slain the old bastard. Perhaps that was why this was happening. His son took the pendant from him and Sven saw him fighting back the tears. 'Stay strong, Torkel. The gods will watch over you and I swear by Odin, no matter what that Frankish bastard says, I will come back for you.'

Torkel nodded but said nothing. Sven wanted to say something else, but he had never been good with words. So the two of them just sat there, staring at each other as his men prepared one ship and burnt the other.

'Jarl, the ship is ready,' one of Sven's men said behind him. Sven nodded and glanced at the sun. They still had a while to go until sunset, but he saw no point in dragging this out for longer than necessary. Bjarni walked past them, his hand covering the cut on his forehead. He hesitated as he neared Sven, but then walked away without saying anything or even looking at Torkel. Sven frowned, wondering why Bjarni did not say farewell to his nephew. Perhaps the blow he had taken to his head had muddled his senses. But Sven decided not to think about that as he looked at his son again. He gave Torkel one last hug and then he took his axe and stood up, his legs weak with emotion.

'Farewell, Father, tell Mother I will think of her,' his son said, and Sven felt the dread in his chest at having to tell his wife.

'Be strong, Torkel, and don't show these bastards any fear. And remember, just because you are smaller doesn't mean you are weaker. Fight harder and be more aggressive.'

The boy nodded and Sven gave the young prince one last glance before he walked to his ship. As he climbed on board, he looked at his dead warriors littering the beach and Arnbjorg's body sitting there, as if waiting for the Valkyries to take him to Odin's great hall. Sven thought about the women and children in Ribe who would be left without husbands and fathers and ground his teeth. His remaining men were silent as they pushed the ship out into the water and rowed her away while Sven watched as his son, surrounded by the Franks, grew smaller in the distance. He felt his anger build up inside of him, suffocating him and threatening to boil over as he gripped the side of his ship and clenched his teeth. His hand went to the Mjöllnir pendant around his neck before he remembered he had given it to his son, so instead he rubbed the head of his Dane axe as he made an oath to Odin.

Because Sven knew he had been betrayed.

1

'There he is!'

'Get him!'

Charles heard the voices and ran. He did not need to look behind him to see who it was. He knew already. They had been picking on him since the day he and his father had arrived in Hügelburg, a small fortified town near the outskirts of the Frankish kingdom. That was five years ago. Back then, they had all been small boys and the worst they could do to the red-headed boy was call him names. But now that they were older, the abuse had gone from verbal to physical and there was nothing Charles could do about it. Not only because there were six of them, but also because he was smaller than them all, even though they were all roughly the same age. That was one of the reasons that the boys enjoyed picking on him.

Charles ran down the street to the only place where he felt he would be safe. It wasn't his house. The small, run-down building barely offered any protection against the weather, and if his father was home, then he would only expect Charles to fight the boys. He glanced at the tall tower sticking out over the roofs of the houses as he ran, its bell silent but calling to him. Charles did not want to look behind him to see how close his pursuers were, but he knew they were near. He could hear it from their excited shouting, like hunting dogs about to catch a fox.

'We're going to get you, piglet!' one of the boys shouted. Charles recognised the voice as Drogo's. He was the leader of the group and bigger than them all.

'Yeah, piglet. We're going to make you squeal!' He heard the boys laugh as Gunthar, Drogo's cousin, shouted this. Gunthar was younger than Charles by a year, but already bigger than him.

Charles kept his blue eyes on the tower in the centre of the town and did not see the baker walk out of his bakery, carrying a tray full of freshly baked cakes for the market. 'Watch out!' the baker shouted as Charles narrowly avoided barging into him, but could do nothing as the tray sailed through the air, the cakes flying every-where. Stray dogs appeared out of nowhere, eager for a free meal and getting between Charles and his pursuers, as the baker waved a fist at him. 'I'll tell your father about this!'

'Thank you, God,' he whispered as he turned the corner and saw the church on the other side of the market square, which was very busy today as Duke Liudolf, the duke of Saxony, had come to visit their small town. His heart raced in his chest and Charles smiled, thinking he was going to make it. But he did not see the little boy who had freed himself from his mother's grip and was running away from her, laughing at his own little game. Charles flew through the air as he tripped over the boy and landed hard, his ears filled with the boy's cries and his mother's screams.

'My son! You little bastard!'

Charles shook his head, not sure if he was the little bastard or if the woman was talking about her son who sat on the ground crying as a lump started to form on his head. But Charles had other prob-lems, as six shadows loomed over him.

'So you like picking on smaller children?' He heard the sneer in Drogo's voice. Charles looked up and saw the boys standing around him, all of them looking smug, and Drogo with a small cake in his hand. He looked between their legs and saw the church. It was so close, but for some reason, God had decided that today he would not reach it.

'I think we should teach him a lesson,' Euric said. He was Drogo's best friend and just a bit shorter than the boy. They had been the first two who had started picking on Charles, and the others had joined their ranks as they grew older. There was also Pepin, who had been Charles's friend until the previous year. The others had picked on him as well because he had befriended the short red-headed boy. But he had never got it as bad as Charles. His father was an important man, and Pepin had a beautiful sister. Last year rumours had started that Pepin's sister and Drogo were to be married when they were old enough. That was when Pepin turned and joined Charles's tormentors.

'I agree. We don't like boys who think they can pick on those smaller than them,' Drogo said, and Charles could only stare at him, dumbfounded. The others laughed, including Pepin, which turned Charles's shock into anger. It didn't help when the young boy's mother chipped in.

'Aye, you boys show that little bastard!'

His father's voice came to him, saying something he would always say when Charles complained about being picked on. *Just because you are smaller, doesn't mean you are weaker. You just need to fight harder and be more aggressive. Then they will see it's not so much fun to pick on you.*

Charles clenched his fists. He was tired of running, tired of constantly having to look over his shoulder and wondering when Drogo and his friends were going to jump him. His father was smaller than most of the men Charles had ever met, but he was one of the greatest warriors in East Francia. Louis II, the king of East Francia, had even honoured his father after he had fought for him during the civil war between King Louis and his brothers. So if his father could be such a great warrior, then so could he. Charles ground his teeth as he remembered all the times these boys had humiliated him in front of others. He felt his heart beating hard in his chest and the heat spread through his limbs. As his vision turned red, Charles decided that this time he was not going to just sit here and take the beating.

Before the other boys knew what was happening, Charles launched himself at Drogo. The tall boy was about to take a bite of the cake when Charles punched him in the face. The cake squashed in his mouth as Drogo's head snapped back before he started choking on a piece of the cake which had lodged in his throat.

'Fuck!' Gunthar had time to shout before Charles turned and kicked him between the legs. Gunthar's feet lifted off the ground, his eyes bulging out of his skull, and then he collapsed, crying as he cupped his crotch. Charles turned and was about to punch the next boy when he saw it was his old friend Pepin. He hesitated for half a breath and that was enough time for Euric to strike. The blow caught Charles on the side of the head and before Charles could react, Pepin punched him in the nose. White pain tore through his skull, but it was nothing compared to the stabbing pain he felt in his chest that his once best friend was the one who had punched him.

Charles struggled to stay on his feet while the voice of the woman whose son he had tripped over drowned out the beating of his heart.

'Get the little bastard!' she yelled, as the rest of the townspeople in the market square added their voices to hers. It seemed to Charles that the whole town wanted him to be beaten up.

Charles's vision was blurred. Somehow he blocked Euric's punch, but before he could do anything else, another boy tackled him to the ground. The boy landed on top of Charles and no matter how hard he tried, he could not get the larger boy off him. The blood from his nose ran back down his throat, almost choking him as the boy punched him on top of his head. Charles's head swam from the blow as he tried to remember the words of his father. He tried to be more aggressive, but there was nothing he could do as the boy punched him again.

'Stop! He's mine!' Charles heard Drogo's voice and knew things were only going to get worse for him. He looked up and, though his vision was still blurred, saw the tall boy's bloody mouth. 'This time, you're going to get it!' Drogo growled and was about to kick Charles when a powerful voice stilled all the noise in the market square.

'Enough!'

All heads turned towards the church and to the old man standing there, his face stern and eyes judging. He wore a black cassock with a purple cincture around his waist and a large golden cross hung from his neck. Bishop Bernard. The townspeople, who moments ago had been baying for blood, quickly crossed themselves and got back to doing what they were supposed to while the mother of the small boy glared at Charles before collecting her child and standing to the side. The boys around Charles – apart from Gunthar, who was still rolling around on the ground – looked at Drogo, all of them uncertain of what to do. Drogo glanced at Charles, and Charles thought he was going to kick him anyway, when the bishop said: 'Drogo, if you kick that boy, then I'll ask God to turn you into a toad!'

Bishop Bernard was not a large man, and neither was he young any more. His shoulders were stooped, his tonsure grey, and his face heavily lined. But the old priest had sharp eyes and a powerful voice from many years of studying and giving sermons in churches all over the Frankish kingdom. And those sharp eyes were focused on Drogo as the tall boy stood over Charles, his leg still raised. Charles did not know if Bishop Bernard could do that, but neither did Drogo nor the boys around him. Drogo glanced at Charles again, causing him to tense, and then at his friends.

'Boy, if you don't listen to the bishop, then I will flay the skin off your backside!'

They all turned to the new voice and Charles saw armed men walking into the square. It was the town's guard, led by Drogo's father, Lothar. The man was big, bigger than most Charles had ever seen. He had dark hair and bright eyes filled with violence. His scarred hand was on the hilt of his sword, while the other swung casually by his side. Charles had heard Drogo boast about how his father had once fought off twenty Danes with his bare hands, and it was hard not to believe the story. A handful of men followed the huge warrior and Charles saw his father amongst them, looking like a dwarf as he walked beside Drogo's father. But Charles's father looked no less confident as his broad shoulders were relaxed and his blue eyes bored. Drogo hesitated for a heartbeat as Charles looked away from his father.

'Boy, do not make me repeat myself!' Drogo's father threatened. Charles heard the frustrated sigh as Drogo stepped away, but not before spitting in Charles's face.

'You better watch your back, piglet,' Drogo whispered to him as the other boys helped Gunthar to his feet. They left the market square and disappeared behind some of the houses.

'Lothar, do not be so hard on your son. He was only helping after that little bastard knocked over my poor little boy,' the mother of the small boy said, pointing at her poor little boy who was smiling as he chewed on the remains of the cake Drogo had started.

'And he made me drop my cakes!' the baker protested. 'Spent all morning baking them and they've all been eaten by the dogs!'

'Your boy seems fine to me.' Charles heard his father's voice and cringed at the strange accent he had. It was another reason they always picked on Charles. The other boys thought his father sounded funny and would constantly imitate him while beating Charles.

'Well, your little barbarian bastard could have killed him!' The woman jabbed her finger at Charles.

'Enough!' Lothar ended the argument. 'I don't care what happened! My job is to protect the town from raiders, not deal with childish fights! Torkel, deal with your boy. If I have to deal with one more problem caused by him, then you'll both be sent to the prisons!'

'Aye,' Charles heard his father say with no urgency in his voice and a lopsided smile on his face. Charles knew his father did not fear Lothar, despite the difference in height between the two men.

'Don't—' Drogo's father started before he was interrupted.

'Lothar! Lothar!'

Charles looked up as a warrior ran towards them, his face flushed from the effort.

'What?' Lothar's face creased as he struggled to contain his frustration.

'There's a messenger for you. He's waiting in the fort.' The man stood straight, despite breathing heavily from his run. Charles couldn't help but glance at the old wooden fort on top of the large hill which had been built a long time ago to protect the kingdom from the heathen tribes to the east. Over time, a small town, with a large stone church and a market square directly opposite it, had grown around the hill and was named Hügelburg, which meant fort on a hill. Tall wooden walls surrounded the town and the fort and was garrisoned by less than a hundred warriors. Duke Liudolf had appointed Lothar as the guardian of the fort and the town, the chatelain, and Charles's father was his second in command.

'He can wait. I'm dealing with something here.'

'I'm sorry, Lothar. But the man said it was urgent.'

Drogo's father raised his eyebrows and glanced at Torkel, who wasn't paying attention. Charles heard the whispers of the towns-people as they all wondered what this urgent message was.

'Fine.' Lothar turned to Charles's father. 'Deal with this.' He pointed at Charles. 'And remember what I said.' With that, he turned and followed the warrior back to the fort.

Charles saw his father look at Bishop Bernard and nod before turning to the other warriors with him. 'Come on, boys. Back to your posts. There's nothing to do here.'

'But what about him?' the woman protested, pointing at Charles. 'Lothar said you had to deal with it.' Charles gritted his teeth at constantly being referred to as it.

Torkel turned to the woman, again not looking at his son. Charles wasn't sure what to think of that. 'And I did,' his father said, and walked off before the woman could respond.

'And my cakes?' the baker asked.

'You fed the dogs. You did God's work today,' Torkel shouted as he walked away, the warriors laughing as the baker gaped.

Charles watched his father leave the square, feeling hurt that he had not even checked up on him. He felt the tears build up in his eyes when a hand touched his shoulder. Looking up, Charles saw the kind smile of the bishop.

'Come, let's get you cleaned up.' Bishop Bernard helped Charles to his feet. The woman and the baker still stood there, both of them glaring at him. 'It is not your place to judge the boy,' Bishop Bernard said to them. 'Now leave him alone and be sure that God will ask for his penance.'

The baker just shook his head and walked away, muttering to himself, while the woman looked like she wanted to say something but then decided against it. She grabbed her son, who was licking his fingers after finishing the cake, and dragged him away.

Bishop Bernard led Charles to the church, the two of them walking in silence as Charles ignored the glances from the people in the market. As they entered the large stone building, the bishop signalled something to one of the priests. It took Charles's eyes a short while to adjust to the dark light in the church, even though there were plenty of candles burning and stained windows on the walls. They walked past the rows of old wooden benches and glanced at the paintings of Christ and the Virgin mother which adorned the walls, before they sat on a bench near the front of the church, below the statue of Christ on the cross. Charles wondered if the old bishop had brought him here on purpose as the young priest returned with a bucket of water and a cloth. Charles nodded his thanks and looked at the water, surprised by his reflection. His nose was bloody and both his eyes had red rings around them. There was also a mark on his head where he had been punched. Charles had expected to look worse, as he normally did when those boys got hold of him. But then, he guessed if it hadn't been for Bishop Bernard, then he would have done.

'Thank you,' he muttered as he dipped the cloth in the water and started wiping the blood from his face, wincing at the pain in his nose.

The bishop smiled. 'It's not me you should thank, young man.'

Charles looked at the old priest, seeing the warm smile on his wrinkled face. 'I doubt Lothar would have stopped his son from kicking me, even with my father there.' Charles wondered if his father would have stopped the boys.

Bishop Bernard chuckled. 'I do not mean that oaf, though I suspect you are right. He is ever jealous of your father.'

Charles frowned. 'Lothar's jealous of my father?'

'Oh yes, but don't tell anyone that I told you that.' The old priest smiled a mischievous smile, but Charles still did not understand.

'But why? He is huge and a great warrior. Everyone keeps saying that.'

'There's no doubting Lothar's fighting ability. He has kept this town safe for many years, but your father was one of the king's *scarae*. And then there was the training incident when your father first arrived.'

'What training incident?'

Bishop Bernard raised his eyebrows as he realised he had said too much. 'That is not important.' He looked at the statue of Christ, but Charles saw the smile in the corner of his mouth.

'Then who should I be thanking?' Charles asked when he realised that Bishop Bernard would say nothing more.

The old priest smiled and nodded towards the statue of Christ. Charles looked at it, seeing the sadness in the eyes of Jesus. He wondered if Jesus ever thought He sacrificed Himself for no reason. Charles had seen no evidence that men had learnt from the lesson that He was trying to teach them. Especially not Drogo and his friends. 'Here I was, just minding my own business when I suddenly had the urge to go outside. Strange really, I never enjoy going out during this time of the day. The weather is too hot and the people too many. They are so loud.' The bishop pulled a funny face.

Charles couldn't help but smile at the man whose job it was to save people, but here he was complaining about them. 'Would have been nice if He sent you out sooner.'

Bishop Bernard chuckled. 'Then what would you have learnt?'

'To run faster.'

The bishop chuckled again and they sat in silence for a while as Charles wiped the rest of the blood off his face.

'Why are you in Hügelburg?' The bishop spent most of his time in Ehresburg, the capital of Saxony, but he often came to Hügelburg to give sermons. Charles always enjoyed it when the bishop came to town as the old priest had known his father for a long time and would often tell Charles stories of his younger days when they were not discussing religion or praying.

The bishop waved a hand at Charles. 'I'm here with Duke Liudolf on some important business. Nothing too interesting.'

Charles nodded and then looked at the bloody cloth in his hands. 'I don't understand why they have to pick on me. Just because my father is not a Frank and I have no mother. Why is that a reason for them to attack me almost every day?'

Bishop Bernard looked at Charles. 'We often attack what we fear before that fear can defeat us.'

Charles frowned. 'They don't fear me, they hate me.'

'Same thing, really.' The old priest looked at the statue of Christ again. 'The Romans feared Jesus. They hated the influence He had on the people and so they crucified Him.'

Charles had heard the story many times before, but wondered what it had to do with him. 'But I'm not the son of God.'

'No, but you are the son of a Dane. And the people of this town learnt a long time ago to fear the Danes.'

Charles frowned again. 'My father's a good Christian.'

'Yes. But to the people here, including Lothar, who has spent many years fighting the heathens from the north, he is still a Dane.'

'Then why did my father choose to come to Hügelburg?'

Bishop Bernard shrugged. 'Perhaps you must ask him that.'

'He never tells me anything.'

'Well, there is one thing I do know about your father.' Bishop Bernard smiled when he saw Charles frown. 'He's very proud of you.'

'I don't think so, especially not after what happened today.'

Charles took a deep breath. 'My father might be a great warrior, but I will never be. Not like him anyway.'

To his surprise, the old priest chuckled. 'Trust me, Charles, there will never be another warrior like your father, or his father, and we should thank God for that.'

'You know of my grandfather?'

'Only by reputation, but I suspect he's another reason so many people here dislike your father. Sven the Boar was an evil man, known to do vile things to good Christians.'

Charles looked at his hands, remembering how good it had felt when he punched Drogo in the face. He could still see the boy choking on his cake and wondered if he had a part of his grandfather in him. He felt his cheeks burn at the thought and then looked at the statue of Christ, wondering if God was judging him. 'My father never talks about him. And every time I ask, he gets upset.'

'It's a hard story for your father to tell, but I'm sure when the time comes, he will.'

'You know my father's story?'

'Young Charles, I am the one who baptised your father, just like I baptised you. Now come, let's pray and then you go home. Your father will be waiting.'

* * *

Lothar stormed into his office, irritated at how the day had turned out so far. He never understood why the duke had sent that bastard Dane and his son to Hügelburg, but both of them had been a constant pain in his arse since they had arrived. Lothar reminded himself to tell his son to beat up the little runt in a quieter place next time. He stopped as he saw a thin man wearing a cloak standing in front of his desk, his back to Lothar whose scarred hand went to the hilt of his sword.

'That won't be necessary, Lothar,' the man said in a soft voice.

'Who are you, and what do you want?'

'I have a message for you from your master.' The man turned around and looked at Lothar with narrowed eyes.

Lothar raised an eyebrow. 'My master?'

'From the west.'

Lothar gasped when he realised whom the man spoke of. King Charles of West Francia. For many years, the king of West Francia had been paying Lothar to keep the borders of East Francia weak instead of protecting them as Duke Liudolf wanted. Especially recently, as King Louis had sent his son to attack West Francia. Lothar shot across the room and grabbed the thin man by the neck and lifted him up. The man's eyes bulged as he struggled to free himself from Lothar's powerful grip. 'What are you doing here? Do you want people to know the truth about me?'

The man slapped Lothar's hand and Lothar let him go. He gasped for air as he landed on the ground and rubbed his neck before he glared at Lothar. 'Don't worry, nobody saw me but the man I sent to fetch you, and he will be dead before sunset. But the message I was sent to deliver is too important to write down.'

Lothar growled at the man. 'What's this message?'

The man straightened, still rubbing his neck. 'There's a boy, about ten years old. You need to find him.'

'And who is this boy? What does he look like?' Lothar crossed his arms across his large chest.

The man shrugged. 'I don't know.'

'So how am I supposed to find this boy?'

'His father's a warrior. He would have come here a few years ago with a small boy.'

Lothar smiled, feeling that his day might just be getting better because he knew exactly who the man was talking about. Torkel and his bastard son. 'You want me to kill the boy?'

The man shook his head. 'No, your master wants him alive. He could be useful if the east decides to invade the west.'

'Fine.'

'There's one more thing,' the man said, and Lothar frowned at him. 'There is a cross. I don't know what it looks like, but I've been told you'll know it when you see it. You need to find that cross. According to our source, the boy's father might have it.'

'What's so important about the cross?'

'That's not your concern. You must find this boy and the cross. Men will arrive in a few days to take both to the west.'

Lothar nodded, not really caring about that. He only cared about one thing. 'And what about the father?'

The man stared at Lothar as if the question was inconvenient. 'The father's not important. Do what you want with him.'

Lothar smiled again as he rubbed his hands together. His day had just got a lot better. 'Consider it done.'

2

That evening, Charles sat with his father at the table, watching as he took his wooden spoon and stirred the stew before lifting some of it into his mouth. Praying with Bishop Bernard had calmed his mind, and not for the first time Charles wondered if he should follow the path of God and become a priest instead of training to be a warrior. He looked at his father again and wondered what he would make of it.

It was late evening, and even though the sun was still out, it was dark in their small house. They had a lantern on the table to provide light while they ate, and a few other candles scattered around the room, but that never seemed enough. Charles and his father lived in a two-storey house, which was poorly maintained as his father was too busy with his duties to look after it. None of the townspeople were prepared to help them because his father was a Dane and the people of Hügelburg didn't like Danes, even if they were Christians. On the ground floor was a tiny kitchen where their housekeeper would prepare their meals, and a dining area which consisted of the small and uneven table they were sitting at and a few chairs. The rest of the room was bare apart from a few smaller tables. There were no bookshelves or cabinets like you might find in other houses. Neither were they any benches for guests, as they never had any. On the second floor was one bedroom, which Charles shared with his father. Like the first floor, there wasn't much in that room, only two thin mattresses and two chests where they kept the few clothes they owned. Charles thought about the grandness of the church and how being there made him feel more at home than he did in this house with its cracked walls and leaking roof.

'You're not eating?' his father asked in the Danish tongue. Something Charles hated, but his father insisted he learn the language.

'I'm not hungry,' he responded in Frankish. His father looked at him, his wooden spoon hovering over his bowl. As usual, Charles struggled to see what his father was thinking behind his blue eyes.

'Is it because of today?' His father spooned more of the stew into his mouth, frowning as he chewed. Their housekeeper was not a skilled cook, but at least they had food and she kept their small house tidy. Though Charles knew the woman did not like them and was sure he saw her spit in their food once. But she had no husband or any other family to support her and she needed the money his father paid her. Bishop Bernard had told Charles that her husband had died fighting the Danes. He stared at his stew and couldn't blame her for spitting in it, although he prayed she didn't.

'I'm sorry if I disappointed you, Father.' Charles swallowed down his nerves. To his surprise, his father smiled.

'You did not disappoint me, son. I thought you did well today.' He ate more stew before pointing his spoon at Charles. 'You should have seen Lothar's face when he saw what you did to his son. By God, I had to try hard not to laugh.' He chuckled at the thought.

Charles was stunned. 'But I lost! They beat me, as always!' He felt his frustration take hold of him, which was not helped by his father smiling.

'Yes, you lost. But you hurt two of them,' his father said. 'And not just that, you hurt their leader. You made him look bad.'

Charles did not understand. 'But that only made him angry. Next time, he'll beat me up even worse.'

Torkel shrugged. 'Perhaps. Or perhaps one of the other boys might decide that he will be a better leader.'

'Or they'll just hurt me even more next time. I'm not a fighter, not like you, Father.' Charles's shoulders sagged as he pushed his bowl with the stew away.

His father stared at him for a short while, before saying, 'The only reason you lost was because you hesitated. If you had punched that boy, then you would have evened the odds a bit more.' Again, Torkel pointed the wooden spoon at him. 'Remember what I keep telling you, you need to be more ferocious than them. You need to make them think twice before they want to pick on you again.'

'You saw the fight?'

Torkel stared at him as if trying to work out what to say before he sighed. 'From a distance. Lothar and I were doing an inspection of the town's walls.'

'And you didn't think to help me?' Charles felt himself getting angry and he knew what his father was going to say even before he said it.

'You need to learn to defend yourself, son. I can't always protect you.'

Charles nodded and thought back to the fight. 'But that was Pepin. He used to be my friend.'

'Used to be. And he didn't seem too concerned about punching you.' His father pointed at Charles's bruised eyes. 'Never hesitate in a fight, son. In battle, that will kill you.' The flame in the lantern fluttered, almost as if it agreed with Torkel.

Charles knew his father was right about Pepin. He still could not believe his one-time friend was the one who had punched him in the face. 'But I'm not like you.'

His father sighed and then smiled. 'No, you are better than me. I am a Dane trying to fit in with people who hate me because of things my father and his kin did. You were born here. You are one of them.'

'Tell them that. They treat me as an outcast.'

'Only because they don't know what you are capable of yet.'

Charles frowned at his father. 'What am I capable of?'

'How should I know? That's for God to show you.'

The response caught Charles off guard and, after a moment's silence, they both started laughing.

'You never talk about your father,' Charles said when they finally stopped. He saw his father's face darken and wished he had kept quiet.

'I don't really remember him.' Torkel spooned more stew into his mouth. 'I was about your age when he gave me up.'

'But why did he?'

His father's eyes misted over and Charles guessed he was thinking of the past. 'I don't really know.'

Charles felt his father was lying to him and was about to press him for the truth when their front door burst open. Charles cried out in shock as nine armed men stormed into their house.

'Fucking bastards!' Charles's father shouted as he lifted the table and threw it at the men, the lantern and bowls of stew flying through the air before crashing against the wall. Charles yelped at the sudden violence and was surprised by his father's instant reaction. It was as if he had expected it to happen.

'Kill the Danish pig!' one man shouted before the table struck him, knocking him and two other men down. The voice sounded familiar to Charles, but in his panic he could not place it, as his father, armed only with his wooden spoon and still wearing his chain mail, placed himself between Charles and the attackers.

'Run!' his father shouted as a man jumped over his fallen comrades, his sword in hand. Charles saw it was one of the town's warriors, still in his uniform. He just had enough time to see that all the men who had invaded their home were the town's soldiers, but he had no time to wonder about it because his father launched himself at the attacking man and shoulder-barged him before his feet even touched the ground. Charles's father grabbed the chair Charles had been sitting on only moments ago and smashed another warrior in the head. The chair burst into splinters as the man collapsed, his helmet dented and blood running down his face. Charles stared open-mouthed at the man's eyes, surprised at how devoid of life they were. 'Charles! Run!' his father shouted again as another soldier attacked, stabbing at his father's stomach with his sword. Charles's father twisted out of the way and grabbed the soldier's sword arm, at the same time jabbing the wooden spoon into the man's eye. The soldier's shriek tore Charles from his trance and he almost vomited when he saw the wooden spoon sticking out of the man's eye socket, blood and eye goo leaking down his cheek. Charles's father ripped the sword from the man's grip and stabbed him through the neck. The remaining eye bulged as the man choked on the iron in his throat. Charles's father pulled the sword free, almost severing the man's head, and launched himself at the remaining soldiers, who hesitated now that he had a weapon. Charles had never seen his father fight before and it was hard for him to recognise the man he saw in front of him. His father was vicious and uncompromising. These were men he had spoken to earlier in the day, men he had shared ale and food with. Men he had fought alongside for many years, yet now he was slaughtering them as if they were nothing to him. Charles's father roared as he stabbed one man through the chest and stomped on another's

knee, breaking the leg and slicing the man's throat as he collapsed
to the ground. Blood sprayed through the air, drenching Charles as
he stood frozen to the spot. The stench of blood and death, something Charles had never smelt before, replaced the smell of the
stew, and he felt the bile rising in his stomach.

The table lifted as the men beneath it pushed it off of them and
got to their feet. Charles recognised Lothar and his heart thumped
hard in his chest as the large man sneaked up on his father while he
was fighting off two men.

'Father, behind you!' Charles screamed, his high-pitched voice
tearing through the sound of violence in their small house. All eyes
turned on him, angry faces glaring at him and filled with hatred.
Charles felt a fear he had never felt before. He had thought he was
afraid when Drogo and his friends had chased him, but that was
nothing compared to this. Without realising, his bladder gave way
and Charles pissed himself.

'Run, Charles!' his father shouted before launching himself at
Lothar.

But Lothar sensed the attack and got out of the way. He cut with
his sword, the blade almost too fast for Charles to see as it struck
his father's back. Charles cried out as his father arched backward
before falling to the ground, but to Charles's surprise, his father
jumped to his feet straight away and deflected the stab from Lothar,
before ducking under the larger man's arm and punching him in
the ribs. Lothar grunted and bent over, but then tried to elbow
Charles's father in the head. But Charles's father was not there any
more. He had rushed past and sliced another soldier's chest open as
the man stood there, his mouth agape. One of the men standing
beside Lothar was about to rush at Charles's father when Lothar
stopped him.

'No! The pig's mine. Get the boy!'

The soldier looked at Charles and sneered as he started stalking towards him. Charles would have pissed himself there if he hadn't done so already. He knew he should turn and run, but he could not. His feet were stuck to the ground as if he were a tree with its deep roots, and all he could do was watch as the woodsmen came to chop him down. Two other soldiers joined the first, the three of them fanning out so that Charles could not escape. But Charles was not thinking of that. He was not thinking about the layout of their small house, nor remembering the back door just behind him. He was like a lamb, his mind blank as the wolves came for him.

'For God's sake, run, boy!' Charles's father roared as he launched himself at the men, his speed catching everyone by surprise. Lothar swung his sword, trying to slice his head off, but Charles's father ducked under the blade. Another soldier stabbed with his sword, the blade just catching his father, but he barely reacted to it as he kicked one man in the back and stabbed another through the neck. As the first man fell to the ground, his father rushed forward and stomped on his head, denting the helmet and crushing the man's skull. Charles heard the crunching noise and saw the explosion of blood and brains from under the helmet. He felt more bile rising in his throat, but when he looked up at his father, all thoughts of vomiting were forgotten. He had never seen his father's blue eyes so full of rage. For a moment, Charles thought his father was going to strike him, but then he turned and faced the remaining men.

Charles stood behind his father and looked at the three men, Lothar and two others, as they stood glaring at them. 'Your time's up, Dane. Today you die,' Lothar growled.

'And who is going to kill me? You?' His father laughed, which surprised Charles. He saw his father bleeding from his side where a few of the links in his chain mail were broken, but it did not seem to bother him. The two men on either side of Lothar spread out and lifted their swords, while the large warrior sneered at them.

'To think, King Louis let you protect his family.' Lothar spat. 'It's disgusting that he let you be so close to them.'

'Well, he needed a real man to protect his family.'

Charles wondered why his father was taunting these men. Surely, they should be finding a peaceful solution. Charles would apologise to Drogo for punching him if it meant that they would be left in peace. He was about to say so when his father grabbed the candle on a small table near them and jabbed it in the face of the man to his left, while the one on his right lunged at him. Charles cried out at the sudden violence as the man with the candle in his face shrieked. His father parried the other man's lunge and was about to punch him when Lothar tackled him to the ground. Before his father could do anything, the huge warrior got on top of him and punched him in the face. The remaining soldier was about to make his way to Charles when Charles spotted something behind them. He raised his hand and pointed at the flames which were slowly spreading up the wall of their house.

'Fire,' he tried to say, but it came out as nothing more than a whisper. But the soldier still glanced over his shoulder and saw what he was pointing at.

'Fire!' he cried.

Lothar looked at the flames, and that gave Charles's father the chance he needed. He stabbed up with his sword and Lothar grunted, his eyes wide as he stared at Charles. 'Fucking pig,' he muttered before he collapsed. Charles's father rolled the large man off of him and struggled to his feet.

He faced the remaining soldier, who now looked uncertain, his eyes darting between Charles's father and the spreading flames. In the end, he decided he did not want to face either and ran out of the door. Charles's father wasted no time. He rushed to the corner of the house and, with the sword, he lifted one floorboard.

'Father, what are you doing?' Charles managed, unsure of why his father was not taking him out of the house. He watched as his father retrieved something from the ground before he turned to Charles.

'Come, son. We need to get you out of here.'

'Me? What about you?' Charles felt the tears streaming down his face. He was not sure what was happening, but just knew it would not be good.

His father did not respond. He did not have time to, as Lothar, his face pale and side bleeding heavily, sneaked up behind him with a knife in his hand and stabbed him in the back. Charles screamed and his father turned, Lothar's knife still in his back, and rammed his sword up into the large man's skull. Lothar's eyes bulged as the blade pierced through his skull and lifted the helmet off of his head. Charles's father stepped out of the way as Lothar collapsed. He grimaced as he pulled the knife out of his back and dropped it to the ground before he grabbed Charles and dragged him out of the back door, which led straight to the town wall and was near the eastern gate. It was also known as the Trader's Gate as it led straight to the market square and was the gate the traders had to use if they wanted to enter the town. His father led him towards the gate, his face pale as blood leaked from the wound on his back and soaked his trousers.

'Father,' Charles started, but his father shushed him.

As they neared the gate, his father pressed Charles against the wall and motioned for him to be quiet. Charles nodded as his father sneaked towards the gate, leaning on the wall for support. A few moments later, Charles heard a clash of weapons and a man scream. He trembled as his fear took hold of him. Surely, no man could fight with the injuries his father had sustained, but then his father returned, his pale face covered with fresh blood. He knelt in front of Charles, grimacing, and handed Charles the package he had taken from the ground in the house.

Charles took it from his father and realised it was a small leather pouch. But Charles was too afraid to wonder what was inside and why it was so important. He looked at his father and saw the pain in his eyes.

'Son, listen to me.' The words struggled to come out, but his father continued in the Danish tongue. 'You must do exactly what I say. Your life depends on it.'

Charles could not make sense of what his father was telling him. *Why only my life?*

'Head north,' his father continued, coughing up blood as he spoke. 'Go to Denmark—'

'Denmark?' Charles interrupted his father. A fresh wave of fear washed over him. Denmark was the land of their enemy, the heathens intent on killing them all. Why did he need to go there?

His father nodded. 'Yes, Denmark. Do not fear, son, you know the language and you are a smart boy. You'll be fine.'

'But why?'

His father tilted his head and listened. Charles could hear the townspeople shouting and dogs barking in the distance. The fire was growing and people would be rushing to make sure it didn't spread to the other houses. The church bells had also started ringing, which gave Charles an idea.

'Bishop Bernard. We could go to him. He will help us. He will make everything OK. God is with him.'

But his father only shook his head. 'No, you cannot go to him. You need to get out of Francia. Believe me, son, I know this is difficult to understand, but you are no longer safe in the kingdom.'

'Why?' Charles did not understand. His head swam as he tried to make sense of everything. 'I'll apologise to Drogo and Gunthar. I'll clean their weapons after sword practice.'

'No!' his father barked at him, spitting blood in his face, but then softened his voice when he saw the fear in Charles's eyes. 'Son, it has nothing to do with that. Just trust me, that is all I ask of you.' His father coughed out more blood. In the distance, they heard angry voices. 'We don't have much time. Now listen to me.' Charles nodded, so his father continued. 'Go to Denmark and find a town called Ribe, it's a large trading town on the east coast. Find my father, he's jarl there.'

Charles felt his heart skip a beat. Bishop Bernard had said enough to Charles to make him understand his grandfather was a man to be feared, not run to for help. 'But I don't know how to get to Denmark.' Charles felt the tears starting to build up in his eyes. He didn't understand why his father could not come with him.

His father glanced over his shoulder at the angry voices that were getting closer before he turned back to Charles. 'Just remember everything I taught you about surviving in the forest and keep heading north. You're a smart boy, my son, you'll be fine. And God will keep you safe.' Charles nodded, not wanting to tell his father that he did not remember anything from their hunting trips. Charles had never been interested in hunting or living in the forest so he had not paid any attention. 'Give the pouch to my father. He will keep you safe. God will make sure of it.'

'But he's a heathen.'

'Yes, but God will watch over you.' His father smiled and Charles saw the blood on his teeth. 'Now, what did I tell you to do?'

Charles repeated his father's instructions, his hands shaking as the pouch suddenly felt much heavier. 'But what about you, Father?'

His father smiled, but Charles saw the tear run down his cheek. 'This will be the last time we see each other, my son.' Charles felt like someone had kicked him in the chest as new tears streamed down his cheeks.

'No.'

His father cupped his face and thumbed the tears away,

smudging his cheek with blood. 'Don't cry, my son. This is the path God has laid out for me. I always knew this day might come, that they would come after us. I tried to prepare you as well as I could, to teach you how to survive on your own.' He smiled as the screams of the people got closer. 'I am ready for God's judgement.' Charles's father glanced over his shoulder again. 'I will give you time to get away. Remember, get to Denmark. Do not trust anyone.'

Charles nodded, unable to speak or make sense of what his father was saying because of the tears running down his face and choking him. His body felt numb, and if he hadn't already been crouching, he would have collapsed. His father was the only family he had ever known, and he could not cope with the thought of losing him. He did not know how to deal with life without his father's strength to guide him.

'Good. Now go while I deal with these bastards. God be with you, my son.'

'And you, Father,' Charles managed, and saw his father grimace as he stood up with a sword in each hand. Charles had not noticed the second sword until now. His father led him to the gate and Charles saw two bodies slumped up against the wall. One had his throat slit, while the other's chest was stained red around the wound in his chest.

His father crouched down, his face pale, and grabbed Charles by the shoulders. 'I'm proud of you, and I know your mother is also.' Before Charles could say anything, his father pushed him away. 'Now run, my son. Run like the devil's minions are chasing you. Trust in God and you will be fine.' With that, he turned and faced the soldiers who were gathering on the road. To Charles, it looked like most of the town's fighting men.

'There they are!' someone shouted.

Torkel stood up straight and grimaced in pain. 'Run, Charles, and don't look back.'

Charles hesitated, not wanting to leave his father. But when he saw the glare from his eyes, he turned and ran as fast as his young legs could carry him. Over the wind rushing through his ears and the choking sound of his crying, he heard his father's voice.

'I am Torkel! Son of Sven the Boar! Slayer of Danes, Norse and any who stood in front of me! Come and fight me, you cowards!'

3

HEDEBY, A LARGE TRADING TOWN SOUTH OF DENMARK

The old man wandered up to the northern gate of Hedeby and stopped. He was shorter than most men, his stooped shoulders wide and stomach round as what was muscle a long time ago had now turned to fat. His skin was blotchy and red, his nose round and veiny, a result of a lifetime of heavy drinking. His dirty hair, which was a bright red once, but now duller and mixed with grey and dirt, was long and only grew around the side of his head, leaving him with a large bald patch on top of his head. An old tattoo of a raven, barely visible through the layers of dirt, covered much of his bald head. He had a bushy beard, which, like his hair, was once bright red, but was now dull with grey and dirt. He wore no shoes, only a tunic and trousers, which were both filled with holes and dirty. But the old man did not care about any of this. He had seen almost fifty winters and cursed the gods every day for not letting him die.

Standing in the middle of the road, he stared at the earth-bank walls with the wooden palisade on top as a voice from his past wondered what it would take to capture this town. He shook his head, chasing the voice away, not only because he didn't want to hear it, but also because he knew it was foolish. The earthen wall was the height of three men, the sides steep enough so you couldn't just run up them like on a hill. And if you managed that, then you would have to deal with the wooden wall, which was over two men tall. Behind this wall was a wooden platform from where the defenders could throw spears or shoot arrows at you. But before you could get to the walls, you had to find a way over the two defensive ditches which surrounded the town. Both ditches were too wide to jump and shallow enough not to kill you if you fell in, but deep enough to make it impossible to climb out if you avoided the wooden stakes. The old man grunted. There was no way to take this town by land and nor by sea. He looked east, towards the bay, and in his mind he saw the two walls which had been built on the water. To sail into the town, you had to go through the gate, which was only wide enough for two large ships. But both gates had towers filled with men carrying spears and bows and arrows which they could rain down on any who dared to attack the town. The old man looked at the gates in front of him again and sighed. The town was large enough for him to be lost in, but unfortunately, not large enough to lose himself in.

'Out of the way, you fool!'

The old man was dragged out of his reverie to see a horse staring at him. He frowned, thinking the horse had spoken to him until he spotted the lean face of the trader sitting on the cart behind the horse.

'Get out of the way, you old drunk! Some of us have places to be!'

The old man raised a hand in apology and stepped aside so the cart could go past. He did not look up as the trader passed, but it did not surprise him when the man spat at him. He wiped the spit off his cheek with the back of his hand and walked with a slight limp in his left leg towards the town in search of a tavern. The old man spotted the two warriors guarding the gate and sighed. He recognised them from before, but did not know their names. Most of the warriors in Hedeby paid him no attention, but these two had a vicious streak that made his mouth go dry every time he saw them.

'You still live then?' one of the guards greeted the old man as he walked through the gates. The old man grunted his response as another guard wrinkled his nose at him. Both men looked like they could be brothers with their light-coloured hair and similar appearances. But the one who spoke had a scar on his lip where his moustache could not grow, while the other had dark brown eyes, filled with malice.

'Only Odin knows how that stink does not kill you, old man.'

'Aye, I don't understand why you have to keep coming back to bother the folk of Hedeby with your smell,' the first guard added, waving his hand in front of his face.

The old man stared at his feet as he mumbled an apology.

'Just get moving. You're stinking up the place.' The warrior kicked the old man on the backside and almost sent him sprawling to the ground. That he stayed on his feet seemed to annoy the warrior, who took a step towards the old man. He lifted his spear and jabbed at the old man with the butt. This time, the old man fell to the ground. He grimaced at the pain in his shoulder, but kept his eyes down and made no attempt to get up. He knew they would only knock him over again. These young warriors, looking so grand in their *brynjas* and helmets, with their swords and axes on their hips and spears in their hands, thought they could do anything. Just like he had once done. The warrior jabbed at his stomach with the butt of his spear, laughing as his stomach wobbled. 'Whose food did you steal to get so fat?' The warrior jabbed harder, causing the old man to grunt, which only made the two warriors laugh more. The old man felt the eyes of the townspeople on him, but he kept his gaze fixed on the boots of the man tormenting him. He knew none of the people would help him. None of the traders leaving the town before sunset would tell the warriors to stop. So the old man just sat there and waited for them to get bored. The gods had done a lot worse to him, so he could take this.

'Make him squeal like the pig he is,' the brown-eyed warrior shouted, his hand on his stomach as he laughed.

'You heard him.' The warrior standing over the old man jabbed him in the stomach again. 'Squeal like a pig.'

Children gathered around, all of them pointing at the old man and laughing at his suffering. The old man's face burnt with shame, but there was nothing he could do.

'All right, enough, you two. Let the old bastard go.' The old man looked up and saw Ketil, one of the jarl's warriors. The warrior was a few winters younger than him, but much taller with broad shoulders and dark hair, which he kept in a topknot. His dark beard was adorned with golden finger rings and a long braid which came down to his chest. 'You've had your fun. Now let the bastard go find a tavern and drink what little wits he has left away.'

The warrior standing over him took a step away. 'Was getting bored anyway.'

'No, you weren't. You just don't want Ketil to kick your arse,' the other warrior joked.

'I'll kick both your arses if you don't get back to guarding that gate,' Ketil threatened, his face stern but with no steel in his voice. 'And you,' Ketil reached into his pouch and threw a few gold coins to the old man, 'get out of here before I change my mind.'

The old man gathered the coins and struggled to his feet while grimacing at the pain in his knees. He glanced at Ketil's face and saw the hard eyes and the new grey hairs which highlighted his black hair. Nodding his thanks, he walked to his favourite tavern.

'Why didn't you let them kill the dwarf?' one boy asked Ketil.

'Because that dwarf used to be someone once.' Ketil's response reached his ears and the old man dropped his head before he turned the corner.

A while later, after the sun had set and the stars glowed in the night sky, the old man was stumbling down the street with a jug of ale in one hand while the other hand helped him lean against the walls of the houses. He was mumbling an old war song to himself, although he could not remember who had taught him the song or who it was about, as his faded memory guided him towards his destination. He raised the jug to his lips to take another sip of his ale when he sensed a presence behind him. The old man turned, swaying slightly, and saw a man with broad shoulders and a sword on his hip. He had drunk too much to see clearly enough to recognise the man or the sneer on his face. The old man stepped to the side to get out of the man's way and frowned when the man did not move.

'F... forgive m... me if I have disturbed your rest,' he muttered, unsure if the words came out clearly. But still, the man did not move or respond. Thinking that perhaps he was imagining things, the old man took another swig of his ale and turned to walk away when something knocked him over. The jug slipped from his hand and its contents spilled over the ground. 'No!' he cried out, not for himself but for the ale he had spent his last coin on. In the dim night sky, he saw two figures looming over him. 'I... I...'

'Stop muttering, you old drunk!' a familiar voice sneered, but the old man's ale-fuelled mind could not place it.

'Aye, time for you to squeal like a pig,' the other man said, and the old man's eyes widened as he realised who they were. 'Get to your feet. Let's see if you're really as good as Ketil said you were.'

'I... I...' the old man muttered again, but did not stand up. His hands trembled in anticipation of what was to come and he kept his eyes fixed on their boots, not wanting to aggravate the two warriors more.

'I think all that ale dulled his wits.' The warrior with the scarred lip laughed. 'Now get up!' He kicked the old man in the side. 'I'll not fight a man who is on the ground.'

The old man grunted from the kick and held his side as he shook his head. He would have prayed to the gods if he believed they listened to him, but he was sure that Odin had sent these two to torment him even more.

The brown-eyed man had had enough and grabbed the old man by his threadbare tunic and hauled him to his feet, ripping the tunic. 'By the gods, you smell worse than the swine.' He pulled his face away from the stink.

The old man swayed on his feet and kept his eyes low. He did not even think of running away. They would catch him easily, and he knew it would only make it more exciting for them. He had learnt a long time ago the path of least resistance was usually the best for him. His attackers would get bored quickly and leave him alone. Besides, the pain from the beating would cover the pain of what he had done. He thought of his wife as the first punch landed, rocking his head to the side, but he stayed on his feet because of his short and stocky frame. He would have felt his cheek smart if it had not been for all the ale he had drunk.

The warrior shook his hand, grimacing. 'By Thor, he has a thick skull!' The other warrior laughed, which only angered this one more. This time he kicked the old man in the chest and, as the old man stumbled back, he struck him on the side of the head with his elbow. Legs wobbling, the old man fell against the wall, but not to the ground. And neither did he look up at the two sneering faces as both men started pummelling him. He instinctively raised his hands to protect his head, which only made the two warriors target his midriff.

The old man collapsed as a blow caught him in the ribs and took his breath away. He curled into a ball, anticipating what was about to happen as the two warriors started kicking him, both men grunting with effort. After a short while, they stepped back, panting. The scarred-lipped man leaned against the wall.

'He's a tough old bastard.'

'Aye,' the other agreed, wiping the sweat from his face. 'A pity his jug's empty, could do with a drink now. Come on, I'm bored. Thought he'd put up more of a fight.'

The scarred warrior spat on the old man as he lay on the ground, bruised and bloody, his gaze fixed on their boots. 'Especially after what Ketil told us about him.'

'Odin knows Ketil's an old fool too.' The brown-eyed warrior laughed as the two men walked off.

The old man stayed where he was, still curled up in a ball. He tasted the blood on his lips but made no effort to wipe it away. He did not feel any pain, his body numbed by all the ale he had drunk before, but as he lay there, an image of his wife, her eyes wide in shock and her mouth open, came to him. 'I'm sorry,' he mumbled as the world went dark around him.

* * *

Cold water splashed over him, dragging the old man from his deep, dreamless sleep.

'What the—' he spluttered as children laughed. The old man opened his eyes and saw a group of them standing around him, a few of them with sticks in their hands. He also saw a woman with broad shoulders and wide-ish hips standing over him with a bucket in her hands. Blue eyes glared at him before she blew a strand of her light-coloured hair out of her face.

'Still alive then?'

'Do it again, Thora,' one child said as he handed her another bucket filled with water.

'Yes, do it again. He smells,' another added.

Thora turned to the children. 'No, leave the old man alone. Go and play somewhere else.' She chased the children away.

'But Thora,' the boy who had handed her the second bucket started.

'But Thora me again, and I'll kick yours. Now go before I throw this bucket over you!' she threatened the children, who laughed as they ran away. She then turned and emptied the bucket over the old man's head.

'What the—' he cried out again, coughing as some of the water went down his throat.

'They're right, you stink. When was the last time you had a bath?' Her nose creased as she picked up the first bucket.

The old man stared at her with dull eyes, seeing her handsome face and her long hair braided. 'I...'

Thora shook her head. 'Never mind, it's dumb of me to think that you would remember.' She looked at him with her stern eyes. 'So what happened to you then, old man?'

The old man glanced towards the gate before answering. 'I made some new friends.'

Thora stared at him, seeing his bruised face and cut lip. His face was already covered with old scars, and each time she saw him, he seemed to have new ones. 'Maybe you should stop trying to make friends. Odin knows one day one of them will kill you.'

The old man waved a dirty hand at her. 'Odin makes sure they don't. He enjoys my suffering.'

Thora shook her head, not wanting to have this conversation again. 'So, what brings you back to Hedeby?'

The old man sat up and wiped his long, dirty hair out of his face. He picked at some old food in his beard and popped it in his mouth without thinking. Thora grimaced, but he paid no attention to that. 'The usual.'

Thora nodded and then sighed. 'Trying to find some work so you can pay for all the ale you try to kill yourself with.'

The old man nodded. He looked at the basket filled with vegetables by Thora's feet and rubbed his stomach as it growled. He couldn't remember the last time he had eaten, but was sure it was a few days ago. Some food he had stolen from a group of travellers as they slept.

'If you didn't stink so much, then I would have invited you for some food,' Thora said, seeing what he was looking at, but then she shook her head and threw the two buckets at the old man so she could pick up her basket of vegetables. 'Come on then, but you stay outside.'

The old man nodded his thanks and struggled to his feet. He grimaced at the pain in his chest and back. His back was from age, that much he knew, and he guessed his chest was hurting because of the beating he had taken the previous night. Then there were his knees, which protested as he picked up the buckets and limped after Thora. People glanced at him as they walked past, a few even crossing the road to avoid him. But he did not care. He had stopped caring about what others thought of him a long time ago.

'Every time you leave, we think it's the last time we will see you, and yet you always come back,' Thora said as they walked towards her house.

'Told you, Odin does not want me dead. He wants me to suffer.'

'For what?'

The old man glanced at her, but could not read her face. 'You know for what.'

Thora sighed. 'Aye, so you keep saying.'

'How's your father?' the old man asked before she could say what he knew she would.

'Dead,' Thora responded. The response caught the old man off guard and he stopped, not sure he had heard Thora properly. She stopped as well and looked at him. 'Died a few weeks back.'

'I...' The old man struggled to find the words.

'He was old, and the Norns decided it was his time.'

The old man saw the tears building up in her eyes and regretted asking. He also felt the sadness in his own chest.

'He asked about you before he went. I think he wanted to see you again. He was trying to hold out, but we never know when you will show up, or if you even will.'

'I'm sorry. He was a good man. Better than me.'

'Aye, he was,' Thora said and walked off.

The old man watched her for a short while and then followed. Shortly after, they reached the house that had belonged to her father. A house the old man knew well. It looked just like the others around it. Small and built out of wood. It had a door and a slanted roof with a smoke hole. Thora's house was one of many on this street near the edge of Hedeby. She stopped outside of her house and pointed to the side of it.

'You can drop the buckets there. There's some water in the barrel behind the house to clean yourself.'

The old man nodded and looked around at the other houses, seeing how others stared at him. 'Did you bury your father?'

Thora stopped by her door and, without turning, responded. 'Clean yourself up and I'll take you to his grave.'

The old man did what he was told after she went into her house. He put the buckets down and found the large barrel where she said it would be. He looked at his reflection and wondered when he had got so old. His heavily lined face was bruised, his left eye slightly swollen and his mouth covered in dried blood. And his nose was more bulbous and veiny than he remembered. His red beard had faded and there were more grey hairs in it than the last time he had seen himself. The same with his hair, although he kept his head at an angle so he could not see the large bald patch on the top. His blue eyes, once so bright, were now dull, which matched the large dark circles around them. The old man shook his head and dunked it into the water. The coldness cleared the fog away, which he regretted because it made him remember things he didn't want to.

'Well, you still stink, but at least you look better.' Thora walked up to him and handed him an old tunic.

The old man looked at his own and saw the large rip, although he was not sure where that had come from. He nodded his thanks and removed the old tunic and put the new one on. He was glad her father had been a large man, otherwise his tunic would not have fit him.

'Come, let's go. It's not far from here.'

They walked in silence to the area outside of the town where they buried the dead, the old man not knowing what to say and also knowing Thora was not interested. As they left the houses behind, a young warrior approached them.

'By Frigg, not him as well.' Thora shook her head.

The old man saw the young warrior, with his broad shoulders and confident walk, and averted his gaze so he could not see the friendly smile on the man's face.

'Good morning, Thora,' the young warrior said. 'You escorting the drunk out of town?' He laughed at his own joke.

Thora shook her head. 'No, Sigge. I'm taking him to my father's grave.'

'Mind if I join you?'

The old man hoped Thora would say no, but she didn't. 'Not that I have much of a choice.'

'If you just point me to your father's grave,' the old man said, his eyes fixed on the ground. He did not feel comfortable in the presence of the young warrior.

'You sure?' Thora asked, and the old man nodded. She pointed him to a fresh mound not too far from them and the old man nodded his thanks and walked away without looking at her.

'I never understood why your father remained friends with that old bastard,' Sigge said, still within earshot of the old man.

Thora sighed. 'He used to say he's a reminder not to go against those who have more power than you.'

'Like the gods?'

'And kings.'

4

Charles opened his eyes and frowned as he stared at his surroundings. Instead of lying on his thin mattress and seeing the thick wooden beams of the small room he shared with his father, he was under a bush. He squinted as the sunbeam which broke through the branches blinded him and as he breathed in he smelt the damp soil and the green leaves. Birds were singing as they greeted the new day, their chirping almost deafening in the quiet of the forest.

'Where am I?' He dug out the stone which had been poking into his back. But as he asked the question, an image of a burning house came to him. His father leaning against the town wall, his face pale and blood leaking from his mouth. 'Father.' Charles's breath caught in his throat as he remembered his father by the gate, a sword in each hand and ordering him to run. He had run as fast as he could and for as long as his short legs could take him. But in the end, exhaustion had taken over and Charles had tripped over a root he had not seen in the dying light of the day. He had hit the ground hard and just lay there sobbing. Eventually, he saw the bush and crawled under it. He was too tired to think about anyone chasing him or of the large animals he had been warned about before, but in that moment the bush had looked safe, like God's hand protecting him as he grieved for his father.

Charles felt the sting on his knee and when he looked, he saw his trousers had ripped and the skin was scraped off. He took a deep breath, feeling more alone than he had ever done in his short life. Charles felt something in his tunic and pulled out the pouch his father had given to him and could not stop the snot and tears as he squeezed the pouch in his small hands. He had no home now and worse still, no father. Charles wanted to pray to God, to ask him why this had happened as his tears choked him. But he could not think of the words he needed to say and, in the end, just sat there and cried for his father. And then he remembered the one person he still had. Bishop Bernard. Charles could go to him. His father had told him not to, but Charles had nowhere else to go, no one else to turn to. He wiped the tears from his eyes and the snot from his nose, wincing at the pain before remembering being punched in the nose the day before. Charles was certain the bishop would help him despite what his father had said, and after putting the pouch back in his tunic, he crawled out from underneath the bush.

Charles stared at the trees as birds sung from their branches. He heard tits, sparrows and finches, all of them greeting the new day with their different songs. Looking at the ground, he saw fresh deer tracks and wondered how the animal had moved past without him noticing it. But as he looked around, taking in the sights and the smells of the forest, he realised one thing. He did not know where he was or how to get back to the town. Charles tried to get his bearings and tried to remember what his father had taught him, when he heard the church bells ringing for the morning prayer.

'Thank you.' Charles looked to the heavens as if God himself were ringing the church bells and ran towards the sounds of the bells. Soon, he saw the walls of the town and the gate where he had fled from. He stopped, his heart in his throat as he shook his head to clear the image of his father telling him to run. Hands trembling, he spotted the two guards on either side of the gate, their faces hard while their eyes scrutinised any who walked past. Charles knew those two men and wondered if they would let him in, but then his father's voice came to him.

Trust no one.

Charles had to find a way in. He stood by the edge of a tree, dejected as he tried to think of something, when a small scruffy dog ran up to one of the guards. The man was too busy looking at those who were entering the town to notice the dog lifting its leg and pissing on him.

'Little bastard!' he screamed and tried to kick the little dog. But the dog was too fast as it ran away, the irritated guard chasing after it. The second guard clutched his stomach and laughed at his companion. For the second time that morning, Charles felt that the Almighty was guiding him. He ran towards the gates as fast as he could and slipped in before the guard came to his senses.

Once inside, Charles's heart beat so hard he thought it might break out of his chest while his hands shook with fear. Especially when he saw the large red stain on the road. Charles did not know how much blood there was in a person's body, but that stain seemed too large to belong to one person. There was a lump in his throat as he wondered if his father's blood was part of that stain. *It must be*, he thought. He had seen how badly his father had been injured before he fled through the gate. Charles's chest tightened at the guilt of leaving his father to die, but what could he have done? He was a small boy, smaller than everyone his age, and not only that, he was the worst student in their sword lessons. If he had stayed to help his father, then both of them would have died. And besides, he told himself to ease the pain of his guilt, his father had told him to run.

The church bells sounded again, dragging Charles away from his thoughts and reminding him of why he had sneaked back into Hügelburg. He had to get to the church, which was in the centre of the town. Charles swallowed down his fear. All he had to do was to go past all the houses and cross the market square without being spotted by anyone who knew him, which was most of the town because of his father.

'Please, Father Almighty, protect me as I try to reach your church,' Charles whispered, and walked towards the church. He stayed off the main road and used the smaller streets between the houses. The boys who tormented him all lived on the north side of the town, so there was no reason for them to be here. But he still gripped the small wooden cross around his neck as he hoped that none of his neighbours would spot him. He wasn't sure how they would react to seeing him.

Charles made his way past the houses, all the while praying that no one tried to stop him. As he rounded the corner of one house, there was a loud noise behind him. The blood froze in his veins as he turned around and saw a large hound straining at the rope tied around its neck as it barked at him. He crossed himself as he thanked God the hound was tied up because he knew he could never outrun it, before carrying on until he reached the square.

That was when he saw an even bigger challenge. Charles pressed his back against the wall of a house as he wondered how he was going to get past the busy market. It was still early in the day and most of the stalls had not been set up yet, but there were still plenty of people about, including Duke Liudolf's warriors, all of them looking grim. They looked like they had not slept all night, and Charles wondered if the warriors were searching for him as they walked around the square, glaring at people with their hands on the hilts of their swords. The townspeople did their best to avoid the angry warriors, but a few could not get out of the way fast enough and earned an angry rebuke or shove. The baker Charles had almost run into the day before stood outside his small bakery, glancing nervously at the warriors as his hands fidgeted with the edge of his apron. And near his bakery were the very boys Charles was most desperate to avoid. They were sitting around a barrel, with Gunthar on top, and all of them staring at the ground. Drogo was not with them, which made Charles more nervous. But as Charles looked at the boys who had been tormenting him for years, he realised they were not angry, and neither did it seem like they were plotting their revenge against him. He frowned as he realised they were sad. Pepin was crying and even the others had red eyes. For a moment, Charles wanted to walk over to them and apologise. Perhaps they would forgive him and they could all be friends. That was what God said in the Bible. To forgive your enemy. But as he thought that, he remembered his tender nose and bruised face. Charles shook his head at his own naivety. These boys would never forgive him, especially not now. Then another thought struck Charles. Pepin's father was not a warrior, but theirs were. He thought back to the blood stain by the town gate and wondered if any of their fathers had died fighting his. He knew that if that was the case and he approached them, then the beating he would get would be worse than anything they had ever done to him before. Especially if Drogo got hold of him. Charles could still see the image of Lothar, Drogo's father, standing there, his eyes wide as his father's sword skewered his skull. No, Charles needed to avoid them as much as he needed to avoid the warriors walking around the square. He looked away from them as he plotted his path to the church and saw one warrior with the right side of his face bruised, and wondered if his father had done that. For a moment, he wished his father had and then felt ashamed. Violence was never the answer. That was what the Bible taught them.

Charles glanced at the church, the cross on the bell tower

calling to him like a beacon, and wondered how he was going to get to it. The boys were too busy sulking by the barrel to notice him, but all it took was for one of them to look up and spot him. The warriors were the bigger concern. They were clearly searching the market, but most of them looked tired and Charles thought that might help him. As would the fact that he had spent most of his young life sneaking around and trying to avoid those who wanted to harm him. This was one of the few times he was glad that he was so short, because it meant that it was easier for him to hide. He gripped the wooden cross he wore around his neck and prayed for protection before setting off.

Charles kept himself low as he sprinted to the first stall. The trader had his back to it as he discussed the weather with another trader, both men nervous about the heavy clouds on the horizon.

'Won't sell much if those clouds decide to empty themselves over our heads,' the trader said as Charles ducked behind the stall. He did not look up to see if he was spotted. He had learnt it was best not to. Instead, he searched for his next target. He spotted an empty stall about fifteen paces away, the trader nowhere to be seen. With a quick glance to make sure none of the warriors were looking his way, Charles darted towards it. His heart pounded in his chest as he went straight for the stall and reached it with no one shouting his name or grabbing him. Charles ducked beneath the stall and waited for his heart to calm down. As he searched for his next target, he saw an old trader berating his slave, a dark-haired boy, about sixteen years old, on his knees, picking what looked like broken pottery off the ground. The trader struck the slave with his cane and the slave clenched his teeth, but did not flinch. Charles felt bad for him. No man should be treated like a dog. Just then, the slave looked up and the two of them locked eyes. The slave frowned and tilted his head as he stared at Charles, who was holding his breath and praying he did not point him out. But to his relief the slave looked away and got back to picking up the broken pottery as the trader turned and walked away. Charles slowly let go of the breath he was holding and decided he needed to move on. He had been sitting under the stall for too long.

Charles searched for another empty stall, and his heart sank when he saw none. The market square was getting busier as people rushed to it to avoid the rain they were certain would come. Charles knew his only option now was to walk to the church. He glanced at the church again. He was not far from it and was certain that if he kept his head down and avoided bumping into people, then he could make it. With a deep breath and another quick prayer, Charles sneaked out from under the stall and headed towards the church. As he walked through the square, he saw the small boy, with a large lump on his head, whom he had tripped over the day before. The boy looked at him and Charles almost froze. But the boy only smiled and waved at him, which caught Charles by surprise. Because of this, he did not notice the warrior he bumped into.

'Watch it, you—' the warrior started, but then stopped as he saw who had bumped into him. 'Charles,' he hissed, quickly glancing around him.

Charles's wide eyes darted around as he tried to find somewhere to run to. But the warrior grabbed him by his shoulder.

Keeping his voice low, the warrior asked, 'What in God's name are you doing here?'

Charles was stunned by the question. He opened his mouth to respond, but no words came out. He stared at the warrior, seeing the reddish beard and hair under his helmet. The strained brown eyes suddenly became familiar, and Charles recognised the man who had been one of his father's staunch friends. One of the few who would come to their house to share food and drinks with his father. Eomar. But Charles was not sure if he should be relieved to see the red-headed warrior.

'What are you doing here?' Eomar asked again, his eyes still darting in all directions.

'I... I...' Charles started, but couldn't get the words out.

'It's not safe for you in the town any more, boy. You need to leave now. Do not waste your father's sacrifice.'

Charles looked up at the warrior as his heart thumped in his chest. 'My father?'

Eomar shook his head. 'He fought bravely, killed more than a handful of men, but his injuries were too much. I'm sorry, Charles, but you can't be here. You must leave.'

Charles felt the heaviness in his chest and the tears running down his face as he thought of his father. *Why did this have to happen*, he wondered as he glanced at the church.

Eomar must have understood what Charles wanted because he shoved him in the church's direction and hissed behind him: 'Be quick. Next time, you might not be so lucky.'

Charles sprinted for the church, throwing all caution to the wind. Eomar was right. If that had been any other warrior, then Charles surely would have shared the same fate his father had. He reached the church doors and glanced behind him, seeing Eomar talk to another warrior and waving his hand in the opposite direction of the church. He sent a silent prayer to God, thanking him that his father had one true friend in this town, before he slipped through the doors.

The usual comfort he found in the church was not there, and Charles could not understand why. He glanced at the tall columns which supported the roof, seeing the candles flutter. The richly decorated windows filled with images from the Bible did nothing to calm his nerves, neither did the familiar smell of candle wax. Charles looked around and knew he needed to find the bishop without being spotted. All the priests here knew him, but Charles was not sure how they would react if they saw him. Sticking to the walls where the light of the candles could not reach, he sneaked around to the back of the church, which was surprisingly quiet. None of the priests were there, and neither were there many towns-people inside. Even old lady Hiltrude, who had been coming to the church every day since her husband had passed the previous winter. Charles found this odd and wondered if it had anything to do with what had happened the previous night. He had not seen what was left of his house, or the damage the fire had done to the other houses around. Charles doubted he had the strength to go back there as he neared the back of the church and heard two voices talking to each other. He stopped and listened intently as he tried to recognise them. One belonged to the bishop, and the other sounded familiar, but Charles wasn't sure whom it belonged to. Both sounded annoyed, though. Charles crept closer, needing to see whom the bishop was talking to and why both men were angry.

Staying low, he stuck his head around the corner and saw the bishop, still wearing the same robe he had the previous day, his face tired and eyes rimmed red. The man he was talking to stood almost a head taller than the old priest. He had broad shoulders and thick limbs, his brown hair short and tidy, just like his matching beard. Charles knew the man, although he rarely saw him. Duke Liudolf, duke of Saxony, and an old friend of his father.

The duke's face was red, and he waved his arm in the air as he spoke to the bishop. 'What was that idiot thinking?'

'I don't know,' the bishop responded, rubbing his forehead. Charles had never seen the man looking so tired or frail. 'He received a message yesterday. Must have decided to act upon it.'

'What message?' The duke scowled.

'I don't know.' The bishop rubbed his hands nervously.

'You should have stopped him,' the duke rebuked the bishop.

The bishop scowled and stood tall, reminding Charles of the man he knew. 'He is not my man. He is yours! If anyone should have stopped him, it was you!'

'Yes, yes, you are right.' The duke tried to calm the bishop with his hands. 'The idiot. We had Torkel and his son where we needed them.'

Charles frowned, wondering what the duke meant by that.

'Where's the boy?' the duke asked.

'We don't know.' The bishop shrugged, looking old and frail again. 'He escaped while his father fought off the men sent to stop them. I sent my most trusted men into the forest to look for the boy, but they couldn't find him.'

'We need to find that boy!' The duke slammed the wall in frustration. The noise startled Charles, who had been holding his breath as he listened to their conversation and he yelped before he could stop himself. 'Who's there?' the duke shouted as both men turned in his direction.

'Charles?' the bishop shouted, his eyes widening at seeing him before Charles could hide behind the corner. 'Charles, come here!'

Charles's breath caught in his throat as he panicked. His father had been right, he could not trust the bishop. He had made a mistake coming to the church and now he needed to find a way out of the town. And this time without his father there to help.

5

Charles hid under the same stall he had hidden under before and watched as Bishop Bernard and Duke Liudolf stood by the entrance to the church, both men scowling as they tried to find him amongst the people filling the market square. But Charles was confident they wouldn't find him. He wasn't good at many things, but he was good at hiding. He only wished he was as confident about getting out of the town again. Charles doubted he'd be as lucky again to have a dog distract the guards so he could slip out. *But then what?* His father told him to go to Denmark, to find his grandfather. Charles gripped the pouch his father had given him. He did not know where Denmark was. He knew it was in the north, but then he did not really know which way north was.

Charles looked towards the gate he had entered from. That was the eastern gate, so if he left through that gate, then he only needed to turn left. That should take him north. He frowned. Or did he need to turn right? Charles wanted to scream in frustration as the tears rolled down his cheeks again. He wished he had paid more attention to his father when he had tried to teach him these things while they were hunting. But Charles had never been interested in hunting or fighting. More than that, though, he wished his father was still alive. Charles hugged his knees as he sobbed, unable to stop his emotions from taking over him.

'Are you all right?' Charles heard the strange-accented voice and almost screamed in fright. He opened his eyes and saw the slave from before sitting in front of him under the stall. He panicked, his eyes darting to the sides as he tried to find a way out. 'It's all right, I'm not going to hurt you,' the slave said. 'But I'm guessing you are hiding from them?' The slave pointed towards the church.

Still gripping the pouch, Charles peeked out from under the stall and saw the duke and the bishop talking to Eomar. He couldn't hear what they were saying, but it looked like neither the bishop nor the duke were happy with the warrior. Charles looked back at the slave and nodded, not able to speak because of the raw emotions still in him.

'What did you do? It must have been something bad to anger them so much.' The slave smiled.

'I... I... punched a boy,' Charles responded, still struggling to understand how that could have caused all of this.

The slave frowned. 'You punched a boy?'

Charles nodded and glanced towards the church again. Eomar was gone and so was the bishop, but Duke Liudolf was still outside the church, his face dark as he scanned the market. He turned back to the slave again. 'I think they killed my father.'

'Because you punched a boy?' The slave frowned again.

Charles nodded and then shrugged. He wasn't really sure any more.

'Does this have anything to do with the fire that happened last night?'

Charles nodded again.

'And the big fight?'

Again, Charles could only nod.

'They say one of the duke's men turned against everyone. That he was a Dane and that he wanted to kill the duke. Killed over twenty men.'

Charles's eyes widened, and he thought of the bloodstain by the gate. 'Th... they attacked us first.'

The slave looked at him for a few heartbeats. 'So you're a Dane?'

Charles shook his head, paused and then shrugged. 'My father is... was a Dane, but my mother was a Frank.' He felt the pang in his heart when he said 'was' and struggled to keep the tears from flowing. The slave nodded, and Charles looked at the pouch in his hands. 'Did my father really kill twenty men?'

The slave shook his head. 'Most likely a lot less. People like to exaggerate. But he killed a lot of warriors. No one seems upset that he's dead, though.'

Charles nodded as he swallowed back the tears. He did not want to cry in front of the slave. 'Because they didn't like him.'

They sat in silence for a short while, listening to the townspeople as they walked past and discussed what had happened the previous night and the approaching dark clouds. The traders were more concerned about the clouds. 'My name's Gerold.' The slave smiled at him.

Charles tried to smile back, but struggled. He looked at Gerold again, seeing his short black hair and the small scar on the left temple. But other than that, the boy looked like everyone else and Charles imagined it was easy for him to blend into a crowd. 'I'm Charles.'

'Nice to meet you, Charles.' Gerold looked toward his master's stall. The trader was discussing his wares with a potential buyer. He had a big toothy grin on his face as he showed a beautifully decorated vase to the woman. But she did not seem interested and, with a gentle shake of her head, she walked off to another stall selling jewellery. The trader's smile quickly turned into an angry scowl.

'Looks like I'm in for a beating again,' Gerold said, with a hint of frustration in his voice.

'He beats you often?' Charles frowned as he looked at the trader.

'You never beat your slaves?'

'We never had slaves.'

Gerold shrugged. 'A few times a day, but he's getting old so the beatings aren't as hard as they used to be.' Charles nodded, and before he could say anything to that, Gerold pointed at the church. 'Looks like it's safe for you to go.'

Charles peeked out from under the stall and saw the duke was gone. He looked around the market square and saw most of the warriors had left as well. Perhaps they were looking around the streets for him.

'Where are you going?' Gerold asked him.

Charles stared at the slave, wondering if he could trust him. He guessed he could. No one would believe a slave, anyway. 'To Denmark, but I'm not sure how to get there.'

Gerold gave him a big grin. 'Well, it seems God is on your side. We leave for Denmark in the evening.'

'Really?' Charles smiled, again believing that God was watching over him.

Gerold nodded, still smiling. 'If we're careful, I can hide you in my master's cart.'

'Won't I be spotted?'

Gerold shook his head. 'My master never looks at the cart. He thinks he's above that, and the guards know him well, so they never check it when we leave.'

Charles thought about it for a short while. He felt the weight of the pouch in his hands, the pouch he had to give to his grandfather, and realised it was his only hope of getting out of here and to Denmark. He smiled and nodded at Gerold, who smiled back.

'Good. You can stay under here. The trader who used it died in the fire last night, so he won't be needing it today.'

Charles's chest tightened with guilt and he wondered if any other people had died in the fire. He decided not to ask, but that he would pray and ask God for forgiveness as soon as he could.

'Come to our stall when you see me packing up. By then my master will be in the tavern spending the few coins he will make today.' Charles nodded and Gerold slipped from under the stall as silently as he had entered and made his way to his master. The old trader shouted at the slave and smacked him on the back of his head, but Gerold barely reacted and got to doing what his master had told him to.

Charles sat there for a while, not sure of what to do. He didn't want to stay under the stall, even if Gerold told him he would be fine. There were too many people walking around, not to mention the dogs, which might alert people. Luckily for Charles, he knew the perfect place to hide. He had used it many times to avoid his bullies. The thought of them made him wonder if they were still sitting by the barrel, but he couldn't see them from where he was.

Charles tucked the pouch into his tunic and kissed the wooden cross he wore around his neck for luck. When the path seemed clear, he sneaked out from under the stall and made his way to the back of the church. As before, he kept his head low and made sure not to move too fast as to draw attention to himself. When he neared the church, Charles hesitated for a heartbeat. He glanced around, but saw no sign of the duke or the bishop. Feeling that it was safe, he darted around the corner and followed the wall of the church until he reached the rear. There, he found the old oak tree with high branches that nobody could reach. But Charles had found a way to scale the church wall and reach the first branch. Because he was small, he could creep along the branch to the trunk and from there climb up higher and be hidden from anyone below.

Charles often climbed this tree when he was avoiding Drogo and his friends and would spend his time listening to the priests sing. He quickly scaled up the wall, his fingertips hurting as they gripped the stone until he reached the first branch of the oak tree. He then reached out and grabbed the branch before pulling himself onto it. The branch swayed, but Charles wasn't afraid. He knew it would hold his weight as he crawled along it to the trunk and climbed up a few more branches until he decided he was high enough not to be seen. There, he spent the rest of the day hiding away and watching as the priests rushed past while performing their duties. At some point, one of the younger priests arrived with a girl, the two of them constantly glancing around. Charles wondered what they were up to and then understood when they kissed each other. The young priest pressed the girl up against the wall and struggled to lift her dress, which only made the girl giggle. Charles turned away, not wanting to see the young priest sin behind the church, and prayed to drown out the noises of their lovemaking. Luckily, it didn't last long and Charles was soon left on his own. He tried not to think about what had happened, but his mind kept going back to his fight with Drogo. Charles still did not understand why that would cause Lothar and the others to attack their house, or what that had to do with the message the bishop had mentioned to the duke. Charles wondered what they had done with his father's body. His father might have been born a Dane, but he had been a good Christian who regularly attended church and said all of his prayers. He deserved a proper Christian burial, but somehow Charles doubted his father would get that.

'I promise, Father, one day I'll give you the funeral you deserve,' Charles whispered as he clutched the pouch his father had given him. He could feel what felt like two crosses inside, one large and the other small, but Charles could not bring himself to look inside.

The day passed slowly as Charles sat in the tree, singing songs as he tried to distract himself from his thoughts. The dark clouds still hung over Hügelburg, but despite the occasional thunder, no rain fell. Something Charles was glad for, as he didn't want to be in the tree while it rained. Finally, as the sun started its descent, the church bell rang to signal it was time for vespers and Charles guessed it was time to meet Gerold. He climbed down to the lower branch and from there he crept along until he reached the wall. The light was fading, and it was harder for him to see, but Charles had done this often enough not to need any light. Quietly, he made his way to the front of the church, trying not to look at the spot where the young priest had sinned, and peeked around the corner. The market square was filled with the traders' carts as they packed up their stalls. Some made their way to the eastern gate, while others went to the warehouses where they would pay some men to look after their wares for the night. He saw Gerold by his master's stall, the old man nowhere to be seen. The slave was packing up, but was constantly looking around as if he was searching for someone. Charles checked the rest of the square again and was about to go towards Gerold when he heard the shout from behind him.

'It's the piglet! Get him!'

Charles recognised Drogo's voice. His heart seemed to stop as he grabbed the pouch tucked away in his tunic and sprinted towards Gerold. Gerold must have heard the commotion because he suddenly looked his way and frowned. Seeing the boys chasing Charles, he beckoned for him to run faster. Charles was almost by Gerold's cart but wasn't sure how far behind him the other boys were. He could not feel their breaths on him and, as he reached Gerold, the slave lifted the tarp covering the cart. Charles jumped into the cart and hid behind the pottery and vases, his body trembling as his heart raced in his chest. He heard the other boys run past and then stop. Charles held his breath, covering his mouth with his hand, afraid Drogo and his friends would hear him.

'Where did he go?' Drogo asked Gerold.

'He went that way,' Gerold responded, keeping his voice respectful, and Charles heard them run away.

A few heartbeats later, the tarp covering Charles and the pottery was pulled to the side and Gerold's face appeared. 'You have many friends, I see. Don't worry, I sent them along the street. By the time they realise, we should be gone.' He looked up. 'My master is coming and from the way he's swaying, I guess he has no coin left. Stay low. We'll be leaving soon.' Charles nodded and when Gerold covered him again with the cloth, he thanked God for the slave's help.

'Ish everything... *hic*... ready?' the old trader asked, his voice slurring from all the drink.

'Yes, master.'

'G... good, let'sh get going. Pah, my pouch is empty. Ushelesh shit you are. If you did what you were told, inshtead of always dishappearing, then we'd have more coin.'

'Yes, master. Please forgive me.'

'Pah! Just get to your place.'

Charles felt the cart shake as someone got on it. There was a snapping sound, and then the horse whined before the cart started moving. Charles wondered who was steering and hoped it wasn't the trader. From the sound of his voice, he was very drunk. The cart suddenly swayed to the side.

'Bashtard horshe!' the trader shouted. Charles crossed himself and prayed that the trader did not kill him with his drunkenness. But the cart straightened, and they headed for what Charles guessed was the eastern gate. He tried to make himself comfortable, knowing he might be stuck in the cart for a while.

The cart stopped with a jolt, and Charles almost knocked the pottery over. He heard something sloshing around inside a few of the barrels, but had no time to wonder what was inside when he heard the voice of a guard by the gate.

'Leaving so soon?'

'Aye... *hic*... gonna go where they hash more money. *Hic*. Hadsh enough of this pissh-poor town.'

The guards laughed, and then one of them asked. 'What you got in the back?'

'Whatsh it got to do wish you?'

Charles held his breath and hoped that Gerold had been correct about the guards never checking the trader's cart.

'Looking for a fugitive. Just need to make sure he's not hiding in any of the carts leaving the town.' Charles's hands started sweating as his heart tried to rip out of his chest.

'Does this have anything to do with the fire last night and the fight in the street?'

'Shhhut up, slave! Well, does it?'

There was a brief silence before the guard responded. 'Aye, a Danish scum tried to kill the duke. Pretended to be one of us so he could get close to the duke, but Lothar, God rest his soul, saw through the pig.'

Charles felt sick and hoped he wouldn't vomit. His father never would have killed the duke. They had been friends for as long as Charles could remember.

'Thought you killed the Dane?' It was Gerold's voice.

'Nosey for a slave, aren't you?' A brief pause and then: 'Aye, but we're looking for his son. He was spotted inside the church trying to finish what his father had tried.'

Charles's head spun, and he was worried that he was going to pass out. How could they think he was there to kill the duke? Maybe he shouldn't have run, maybe he should have stayed and explained everything. Then they would have understood it was a mistake. He wanted to jump out of the cart and scream at the guards. Tell them it was not true, that his father didn't want to kill the duke, and neither did he. They wanted to kill his father.

'That'sh all very intereshting, but there'sh nobody in my cart. My shlave'sh too dumb to help shomeone eshcape.'

The guards laughed and then the cart started moving as Charles still struggled with his thoughts. Was that really what the people believed? They never liked his father, but to think that he was trying to kill the duke. And how was he supposed to kill the duke? He was only a small boy. Charles wanted to cry as he gripped the pouch, feeling the contents digging into his small hands. He wanted to tell them they were all wrong. But as the cart trudged along the path away from the town, his exhaustion took over him and he fell asleep.

Charles woke up the next morning, sore and confused. He had fallen asleep in an awkward position and his neck was aching and his right arm was numb. Sunlight streamed through the holes in the tarp, allowing Charles to finally see what was in the cart. There were clay pots and bowls, all different sizes and shapes. Some of them even depicting stories from the Bible with bright colours. Charles recognised Noah's ark on one vase and saw an image of a short man facing a giant which he guessed was David and Goliath. He also saw large barrels filled with wine and a locked chest, which was smaller than the one he had had in his room. Charles wondered what was inside it when his stomach rumbled. He rubbed it and licked his lips, remembering that he had eaten nothing for almost two days, nor drunk anything.

The cart wasn't moving, and Charles guessed they had stopped for the night. He was not sure what time of the day it was, but he knew the sun was out. That much he could tell. Charles debated with himself whether he should wait for Gerold to bring him something to eat, assuming the slave remembered about him, or whether he should try to sneak out and find some food. His stomach growled again and Charles groaned silently as the hunger pains bit into his stomach. He decided not to wait to see if Gerold was going to bring him food. He crept to the side of the cart and slowly lifted the tarp so he could peek out.

Charles saw a campfire with a small pot sitting on the embers and licked his lips as he wondered what was inside. Most likely porridge, which he didn't like, but Charles was so hungry that he would eat it. He looked around the small clearing and saw neither Gerold nor the trader. Charles briefly wondered where they were when his stomach rumbled again. He hoped they were somewhere else because he could not wait any longer. He needed to eat. Another quick glance around and he was about to jump out of the cart when he heard the trader's voice behind him.

'Well, what do we have here?'

6

Charles froze as a firm hand gripped his shoulder and spun him around. Staring at him were two dark eyes filled with malice and an ugly sneer, with a few teeth missing.

'Who are you and what are you doing in my cart?' the trader asked, his face creased in an angry scowl. 'Are you trying to steal from me?' He shook Charles as he carried on talking, not allowing him to get any words in. 'Do you know what I do to those who try to steal from me? Gerold! Gerold! Where are you, you useless shit!'

Charles's eyes darted around, trying to find the slave the trader was calling for. He hoped Gerold would explain to the trader why he was hiding in his cart.

'Gerold! Get here now or I'll flog you again!'

Gerold walked into the clearing, his arms filled with sticks for the fire and a frown on his face. But the frown quickly turned into shock when he saw Charles standing there with the trader's hand gripping his shoulder. His mouth opened to say something, but then it quickly closed when he saw the glare from the trader.

'Where were you? You were supposed to watch the cart while I took a piss!'

'Forgive me, master. I thought I'd get some more wood for the fire.' Gerold dipped his head, but Charles thought he saw the slave's jaw clench.

'Well, luckily for you, I caught this little thief before he could steal something.' The trader shook Charles again, so hard this time that Charles felt his teeth rattling in his mouth.

'I... I... am not a th... thief!' he cried, and the trader stopped shaking him.

'Not a thief, hey? Then what were you doing sneaking around in my cart?'

'I... I...' Charles glanced at Gerold, but saw no support from the slave. 'I was hiding.'

'Hiding? Hiding fro...' The trader's eyes widened as he remembered something. 'You're the boy the guards at the town gate were looking for?' He looked at his slave, pointing a finger at him. 'And you helped him! That's why you were asking so many questions.' He laughed when Gerold raised his eyebrows. 'Aye, you thought I'd be too drunk to remember. Boy, I've been drinking since before your dad had any hair on his balls!'

'Forgive me, master. The boy was being chased by others and I helped him.' His brown eyes flicked towards Charles and then back to his feet. 'I did not know who he was.'

'Well, what's the little bastard doing in my cart?' The trader shook Charles again. Charles glanced over his shoulder at the trees behind him and thought about running, but then the trader gripped his shoulder tighter.

'He said he needed to get to Denmark. I thought as we were going the same way, he could hide in the cart. I only wanted to help the boy, master, nothing more.'

The trader's face went dark red. 'And what if the guards checked my cart?'

'They have never before, so I thought it was safe enough.'

The trader glared at his slave for a short while. 'You could have told the guards about him hiding in the cart.'

Gerold shook his head. 'I didn't want you to get into trouble.'

'Pah.' The trader hawked and spat. 'More like you didn't want to get yourself into trouble.' He looked at Charles again. 'What's your name, boy?'

'Charles, sir.'

'Hmm, not very Danish, is it?' The trader glanced at Gerold again as he dropped the sticks by the fire and added a few to the flames.

'I'm not Danish.'

'But your father was.'

The sentence still felt like a kick to the gut for Charles and he felt the tears threatening to come, so he just nodded.

'Why did he want to kill the duke?'

'He... he didn't.' Charles still couldn't understand why people thought this. 'They were friends.'

'Is that so?' The trader rubbed his stubbly chin. 'That's not what the people in the tavern were saying. Your father wasn't much liked in the town. Many are glad he is dead.' He smiled as the tears erupted from Charles's eyes.

'They were friends,' Charles repeated, not knowing what else to say as he swallowed back his tears. He glanced at Gerold. The slave was stirring the contents of the pot, but with his head tilted their way.

'Well, there's no way a weakling like you could ever kill the duke, so they probably lied about your father as well.' The trader licked his teeth and stared at Charles with a raised eyebrow. 'You want to go to Denmark?'

Charles nodded.

'Why?' The trader leaned in closer, his dark eyes studying Charles. 'It's a dangerous place for one as young as you. They love nothing more than sacrificing Christian children to their heathen gods.'

Charles opened his mouth to respond, but then thought better of it. *Trust no one*, his father's voice came to him. 'That's my business.' He tried to sound strong, but knew he failed.

The old trader smiled. 'Aye, so it is. How you gonna pay me?'

Charles's eyes went wide. 'Pay you?'

'Aye, pay me, boy. I'm not some jumped-up priest. My aid isn't free.' The trader's eyes fell on the bulge in Charles's tunic and lit up.

'I... I... have no... nothing to pay with.'

'Don't lie to me, boy.' His hand flicked out and, before Charles could react, he grabbed the pouch that Charles had been hiding in his tunic. Charles yelped as the trader smiled. 'What do we have here?' He opened the pouch and his eyes lit up even more. Reaching into the pouch, the trader pulled out a large golden cross.

Charles gasped as he took in the object, which was bigger than his hand and thicker than his fingers. Small gems, all of them different colours, rimmed the cross and shone brightly in the morning sun. In the middle of the cross was an emblem Charles recognised, but had never known whom it belonged to. His eyes widened when he saw the large red ruby, almost as big as Charles's eye, which was above the emblem. Even Gerold stopped what he was doing as he stared open-mouthed at the cross.

'Well, well, well, what's this then?' the trader asked with a toothy grin, his eyes already seeing his rich retirement.

'Give it back!' Charles somehow found some steel in his voice, which only amused the trader.

'Why?'

'It... it belonged to my mother.'

'Your mother, you say?' The trader glanced at Gerold. 'And where's your mother?'

Charles lowered his head. 'She's dead. Died a long time ago.'

'God bless her sweet soul,' the trader said insincerely. 'Now what else is in here?' He fished out a second object, the one Charles had believed was a smaller cross. Both he and the trader frowned as they stared at what looked to be a hammer pendant. It looked like it was made of bone, but Charles had never seen bone so white. It was bigger than his thumb and decorated with markings he did not recognise. But it seemed the trader did as he smiled. 'Well, this should cost quite a bit where we are going.' He put both items back into the pouch and tied it to his belt. 'This will cover the ride, but you'll still need to work for your food.' The trader sneered and pointed towards Gerold. 'Now go help that useless bastard.'

Charles stood his ground and stared at the trader. 'Give me back the cross!'

The trader slapped Charles across the face, the sting of it bringing fresh tears to Charles's eyes. 'Do as I say, boy, or I'll take you back to the town and hand you over to the duke with this pretty cross you stole.'

'I did not steal it.'

'And who do you think is going to believe you?' The trader cackled. 'Now do as I say!'

Charles glared at the trader for a short while and then meekly looked at his feet and shuffled towards the slave. He rubbed his cheek as it burnt from the slap and sat down next to Gerold.

'I'm sorry,' Gerold said.

Charles glared at him. 'You could have helped me!' He quickly glanced at the trader, but the man was busy going through his cart.

Gerold scowled at him. 'And what could I have done?' he hissed. 'I'm a slave, if you've forgotten.'

Charles felt his cheeks go red. He had forgotten. 'I'm sorry.'

Gerold sighed. 'Just keep your head down, and you'll be fine. Once we get to Denmark, I'll help you escape.'

Charles frowned. 'Escape?'

'You really think he's just going to let you go now?'

'I...' Charles looked at the trader as the man walked around his cart, muttering to himself. 'But...' He then looked at Gerold. 'Is that what happened to you?'

To his surprise, Gerold laughed, loud enough for even the trader to hear.

'What are you two shits laughing about? Get my breakfast ready!'

Gerold got back to stirring the porridge in the pot before responding, 'My old man sold me to one man who then sold me to this bastard.'

'Your father sold you?' Charles's eyes widened, unable to believe a man would sell his own child.

'Aye.' Gerold gritted his teeth. 'Got into a lot of debt because of his drinking, so the bastard sold me to pay the moneylenders. Although, last I heard, he never did. Took the coin he got for me and went straight to the tavern and drank it away.'

Charles did not know how to respond to that, so he kept quiet. But he could not stop wondering what it was like to be sold by your own father. He thought of his father, which threatened to bring more tears, so he tried to focus on the chores Gerold had given him. He had to feed the horse, which was old, but gentle. It stared at him with its big, glassy eyes and Charles thought about jumping on the beast and riding away. But he quickly forgot about the idea. He still didn't know how to get to Denmark. On top of that, the trader had the pouch with the cross and the other pendant he had never seen before. Charles did not know what it meant and wondered if it had anything to do with his grandfather.

The trader sat by the fire and took the bowl from the slave. He frowned at the contents before he started eating the porridge as Gerold rolled up his master's sleeping mat and tied it up with string before bringing it to the cart.

'Where did you get that cross from?' Gerold asked after he had placed the sleeping mat in the back of the cart.

'I didn't steal it.' Charles scowled.

'I know,' Gerold smiled, 'you said it belonged to your mother.'

Charles nodded.

'But you looked surprised to see it.'

Charles glanced at the trader, who was still eating his porridge. 'I've only ever seen it once, and that was a long time ago.' Charles remembered the day a few years back when he had sneaked into the house late at night after hiding in his tree all day long. His father was sitting in the kitchen. It had been one of the few times Charles had seen his father drunk. In his hand was the cross, which he was rubbing with his finger as he drank and cried. Charles had tried to sneak to their room, but his father had spotted him. He had thought his father would be mad, but he had shown Charles the cross and told him it had belonged to his mother. The next morning, the cross was gone and Charles hadn't seen it since.

Gerold nodded and said, 'Well, I doubt you'll ever see it again.' He turned around and walked towards the trader who had finished his breakfast and, after throwing the bowl on the ground, stood up and walked towards the trees to relieve himself. 'Come,' Gerold called. 'If you want to eat, then you'll have to be quick about it.'

Charles's stomach rumbled, reminding him he was still hungry, and he rushed after the slave. They ate the porridge in silence, both boys gobbling it down. It helped that it wasn't warm any more, but Charles was surprised at how tasty it was.

'You learn to cook well if you want to avoid a beating,' Gerold said when he saw Charles's reaction.

Once they had finished their porridge, Charles helped Gerold clean the pot and load the rest of their stuff onto the cart. Gerold poured some water over the fire to kill the flames as the trader appeared from behind the trees, pulling his trousers up.

'Let's go,' he said as he climbed onto the cart. Charles was about to do the same when the trader glared at him. 'What do you think you're doing?'

'I...' Charles started and then glanced at Gerold, who stood at the back of the cart and shook his head. Charles let go of the cart and walked to the back. The trader glared at him as he took the reins and his small whip, but said nothing. He snapped the whip at the horse, which slowly started walking back to the road.

'Slaves don't ride on the cart,' Gerold explained to Charles. 'We have to walk behind it, out of sight.'

'But I'm not a slave.' Charles looked at the back of the trader's head with its bald patch.

Gerold smiled. 'As far as the old bastard's concerned, you are now.'

Charles grabbed the small wooden cross around his neck and prayed that it was not true. He also prayed for his father's soul and asked God to protect him from the evils of the road.

'You can keep doing that, but God has never bothered answering me,' Gerold said, seeing what Charles was doing.

They travelled the road north, or so Charles thought. At first, he tried to keep track of where they were going, but his mind soon went back to what had happened and he lost himself in his thoughts. He wasn't sure how he felt about leaving Hügelburg. It was the only home he had ever known as he could not remember where they had lived before. But Charles had never been happy about living in Hügelburg. The people were always mean to him and then there were Drogo and his friends who would always pick on Charles and beat him up. Still, there was a part of him that would miss the small town, especially the church where he had spent most of his time. And then there was the part that was glad that he'd never have to see Drogo and the other boys again.

The road they were travelling on looked well used, but it was quiet that day. Occasionally, they would meet another trader going the opposite way and the two carts would stop so the traders could exchange news. Charles was glad for these moments as they gave him a chance to sit down and rest. He was not used to walking such long distances, and his feet and legs were aching. He marvelled at how the walk did not seem to affect Gerold, who would lean against the cart every time they stopped and listen to the conversation.

While they travelled, Gerold told Charles of all the places they had visited. From the giant cities in the west to the savage lands in the east and north. He described places Charles was sure were not real, including a church so big you could put an entire village inside and it still would not be full. Charles hoped this church was real and that he would one day see it. Gerold explained how the trader collected wine in the west of Francia and then travelled east to sell the wine and buy other things like pottery and jewellery. This, with whatever wine he had left, he took north to Denmark and traded for fur, ivory and amber, which he would then sell in the west. To Charles's young mind, this all seemed very complicated, and he wondered out loud about why the trader didn't just stay in one place and sell wine.

'Because if you take the wine to where they don't make it, you can sell it for more,' the trader responded, his ears sharper than Charles had realised.

As the sun waned, the trader moved the cart off the road and found a spot near the forest for them to camp. He stopped the cart and, without looking at them, said, 'You know what to do.'

'Yes, master,' Gerold responded. He collected a small axe from the back of the cart and went into the forest to collect wood for the fire. Charles was about to follow when the trader stopped him.

'No, you stay here. I'm not letting you out of my sight.'

Charles glanced at Gerold as he disappeared amongst the trees, and then nodded and returned to the cart. He sat with his back against it and rubbed his legs, glad that the walk was over. His shoes were worn out and there were a few new holes in the soles. He had needed new shoes for a while now and was going to ask his father for a pair. But that would not happen now. Charles felt the knot in his throat again and tried to distract himself by thinking about his grandfather. He had no idea what the man was like, or if he even still lived. His father had never spoken of him, but in his mind, he imagined a tall and strong warrior with an evil laugh and blood-stained clothing. The skulls of Christians by his feet and a necklace of finger bones around his neck. Charles shook his head to clear it of that image. The trader moved along the cart and grunted as he sat down. There was a jingling noise, like a set of keys and a lock unlocking. Charles guessed the trader was opening the chest he had seen in the cart and wondered what was inside as the trader muttered to himself.

A short while later, Gerold returned, carrying the wood he had chopped for the fire. Charles watched as he neatly piled the wood up and got the fire started. Once Gerold was satisfied that the wood was burning, he walked to the cart and retrieved a bow and some arrows.

Charles frowned and wondered why Gerold never used the bow to kill the trader, but before the thought could finish, he berated himself for his sinful thoughts as Gerold disappeared back into the forest. This left Charles on his own with the trader again, who was still sitting on the cart and doing something in the chest. Charles watched as the clouds drifted over his head and listened to the birds as they sang from the trees. Nearby, he could hear a bee buzzing and looked around to find it, but he could not. The smell of the fire reached him and reminded Charles of the fire in the town as he had fled. He tried to distract himself from the memories and then remembered it was evening. That meant it was time for vespers. He tried to work out which way was east, but gave up. He closed his eyes and whispered the words Bishop Bernard had taught him, hoping praying would calm his mind, but as he prayed, he kept seeing the bishop and the duke talking in the church.

He was halfway through when the trader kicked his leg. 'Wake up, boy! This is no time to sleep.'

Charles opened his eyes, annoyed that he could not finish his prayer, but the trader did not seem to care.

'Can you cook?' he asked. Charles shook his head. 'Pah, what use are you, then?' The trader scratched his chin, determined to find something for Charles to do. 'Go sit by the fire, make sure it doesn't die out.'

'Yes, sir.' Charles stood up and walked to the fire. He sat down in front of it and wondered what he was supposed to do. There were a few branches lying next to the fire, but it was burning strong and so Charles didn't think he needed to do anything. Instead, he just sat there, staring at the flames and trying to keep the images of his house burning out of his mind.

Gerold returned, carrying a rabbit with an arrow sticking out of its back. Again, he said nothing to Charles nor even looked at him while he used his knife to remove the arrow and skin the rabbit. Charles felt the bile rise in his stomach when Gerold pulled the skin free from the rabbit's corpse and remembered people in the town saying that the Danes liked to skin children alive and sacrifice them to their gods. He shook his head to get rid of the image, and Gerold frowned at him.

'What's the matter with you?'

Before Charles could answer, he spotted movement in the trees behind Gerold. At first, he thought it was a deer because it stood too tall to be a boar or fox. Then, to his surprise, a man walked out of the trees. He wore dirty clothes, but had new shoes on his feet and an old sword in his hand. Charles did not need to see his broad shoulders to tell the man had been a warrior once. He had lived amongst warriors his whole life and knew how to recognise them. Three more men came out of the trees, all of them looking dangerous and with knives in their hands.

Gerold turned around and jumped to his feet. He levelled his bloody knife at the newcomers, which only made them laugh.

'Who are you?' the trader asked from the cart, his voice wavering.

'Ne'er mind who we are,' the man with the sword responded, his voice rough.

'Please, we want no trouble. You are more than welcome to share our fire and food. I can send my slave to hunt for more.' The trader smiled his best smile as he closed the chest and climbed out of the cart.

The men looked at each other and smiled, but Charles thought those smiles weren't friendly.

'Where you going?' one of the bandits asked, pointing his knife at the trader.

The trader gulped, but kept his smile on his face. 'North, to trade in Denmark.'

'Denmark, hey?' The bandit leader looked at his companions. 'Why would you want to trade with those God-hating swines?' He circled around to get a better look at what was in the cart.

Gerold moved, so that he stood between Charles and the other two men, his knife still levelled at them.

'Tell your slave to drop his knife, or I'll cut his hand off!'

'Gerold, you idiot, do as the man says!' the trader barked at him. Gerold lowered his knife, but still gripped it tightly.

'So, old man. Why are you trading with the Danes?' the man asked again, his face turning into a scowl.

The trader hesitated for a moment before answering. 'They have good quality furs and amber. And they love our wine and jewellery.'

'So you have wine and jewellery in that cart of yours?'

Behind them, Charles heard the third man climb into the cart and rummage around.

The trader shook his head. 'No, no jewellery. Only wine.'

The bandit leader shot forward and grabbed the trader by his tunic as he sneered at him. 'Do not lie to me, old man. I don't like liars.'

The trader's face paled as the second man took a step towards Gerold to make sure he didn't protect his master. But Gerold just stood his ground. Charles trembled as images of that night came to him again. His heart was beating so fast that Charles was struggling to breathe. His legs felt weak and Charles had to fight not to collapse on the ground.

'I'm not lying, I swear to the Almighty.' The trader's hands were quivering as the smile fell from his face. The man holding him by his tunic looked at his companion on the cart.

'Plenty of pots and vases. A few barrels filled with wine,' he smiled, 'and a juicy-looking chest that's locked.'

'What's in the chest?'

The trader stuttered in fear, but got the words out. 'No... nothing im... portant.'

The bandit sighed and shook his head. 'Do you know what I hate more than liars?' The trader shook his head. 'Men who deal with those bastard Danes who killed my wife and took my boys!' He plunged his sword into the stomach of the trader, who gasped in shock. Charles's panic took hold of him and before the trader dropped to the ground, he turned and fled.

7

'Don't like the look of 'em clouds.' The old fisherman looked at the heavy clouds on the horizon, the thunder rumbling like a giant's hungry stomach. He glanced over his shoulder, his jaw muscles working as he tried to work out if he could make it back to land before Thor's fury caught them.

The old drunk looked up from the net he was working on, his face bruised and lip cut from the beating he had taken. His eyes flicked between the dark clouds and the fisherman, whose son had joined him by the tiller. Both men were thin, their faces worn and skin leathery from spending their entire lives out at sea. The old fisherman was missing a few teeth and was a sour bastard, but he did not mind. The man gave him regular employment on his fishing boat and always paid him what was owed. And more importantly, he asked no questions. The rest of the crew, four men in total, had stopped what they were doing, all of them staring at the clouds and rubbing the Mjöllnir pendants around their necks. Lightning flashed from the clouds and the old drunk felt the blood stirring in his veins. He glanced at the fisherman again, seeing the man shake his head and pull on the tiller. His son rushed along the ship and untied the sail. One man helped him, while the rest secured the net and the barrels filled with the fish they had caught. The drunk helped, but not with the same vigour as the others, as he kept glancing at the fast-approaching clouds. He knew as well as them they would never outrun the storm. Rán, the giantess of the seas, wanted more men for her hall and she was sending her daughters to collect them. Thunder ripped through the air as lightning flashed and the clouds released a dark wall of rain. The wind picked up and the fisherman's son and his help struggled to control the sail which threatened to split.

'Out of the way, you old fool!' the fisherman's son shouted as he rushed past to tie a rope which had come loose. The drunk stepped to the side, his eyes on the fisherman, who took some coins out of the pouch tied to his belt and threw them into the darkening water. He smiled. If the man thought that would calm the bitch of the seas, then he was mistaken. He turned to the coming storm again, feeling the wind tug at his thin tunic and straggly hair. A few coins would not calm Rán. She wanted blood, and the gods wanted him. Perhaps Odin had decided that he had suffered enough, but did not want him in Valhalla with his ancestors, so instead the All-Father was giving him to Rán.

'What are you doing?' one of the crew shouted as the old drunk grabbed hold of the tack line and climbed onto the gunwale, his heart beating hard in his chest. But he ignored the man, and the rest of them as they all gaped at him.

The first fat raindrop fell on his face as the drunk looked up into the sky and thumped his chest. 'Here I am! You old bastard! Come and get me if you have the balls!'

'Are you mad?' the fisherman's son screamed as he struggled to hold on to the rope of the sail.

'Kill the fat fool,' another of the crew shouted as the rain lashed down on them and the sky darkened, but he ignored them all as he bared his teeth at the clouds. These men would never harm him. He was a cursed man and his death would only curse them. That's why the old fisherman shouted at his crew to be silent. The men obeyed as they held on to anything they could find as more lightning flashed around them, illuminating the sky and revealing the white-capped waves which rose over the drunk's head. Rán's daughters coming for him. But he did not care about any of this as he laughed into the gale. The heavy rain soaked him in an instant and plastered his thin hair to his face, but he paid no attention to any of this as he screamed into the storm.

'Is that all you've got?' He thumped his chest again. 'Come and get me! Here I am!' The old man let go of the tack line and spread his arms wide. 'Odin! Come and get me, you one-eyed whoreson!'

'You mad bastard! You'll kill us all!' the old fisherman shouted as he fought to control the tiller, his face creased with effort. The rest of the crew cowered in the midship, all of them gripping the Mjöllnir pendants around their necks and praying to Thor to protect them.

The old drunk laughed, his arms still wide. 'Come and get me!'

A lightning bolt erupted from the clouds above them, the thunder almost deafening. He watched the bolt, convinced it was coming for him, but then it twisted away and struck the water. The water lit up, blinding him and causing him to arch backwards. His feet slipped on the wet gunwale and his heart stopped as he fell. For a moment, he thought the gods had listened to him and had come to take him, but then he hit the deck of the ship.

'Is that all you've got, you ginger bastard?' The drunk lay on the deck, waving a fist at the black clouds. As if in response, the cloud lit up again, and the thunder rumbled. The old man laughed.

'That's it. Come and get me!' he roared as the lightning flashed once more.

* * *

Charles sat by the tree, his hands tied in front of him, his eyes closed and his lips moving as he prayed. He had barely made it to the trees before he was grabbed from behind and thrown to the ground. The bandit had then tied his hands and left him there, while the others took Gerold's knife from him and tied his hands up as well.

'I don't know why you insist on doing that,' Gerold said, sitting beside him, his hands also tied. 'Neither God nor any of his angels will come down here and save us.'

Charles opened his eyes and frowned at the slave. 'I know.' Although he hoped something like that would happen. He looked at the bandits as they looted through the trader's cart, kicking the side panels and searching under it.

'They're looking for hidden compartments,' Gerold explained while watching the bandits.

'How do you know?' Charles asked.

Gerold shrugged. 'That's what I would do. Many traders have hidden compartments to hide their coins from bandits and greedy soldiers.'

Charles frowned and guessed it made sense. His father had a hidden place in their house where he had concealed the pouch with his mother's cross and the other strange pendant. 'Did your master have one?' he asked as he wondered about the pouch. He could not see it on any of the bandits and wondered where it was.

'No, the old man was a fool and a drunk. Whatever coin he earned was normally gone before we left the town.' Gerold leaned back against the tree and closed his eyes.

Charles gripped the small wooden cross around his neck and tried to find the same courage his father had possessed, but he could not stop the quiver in his stomach. The only thing that calmed him was praying, so he closed his eyes and recited the same prayer as before.

'I already told you, there's no point.' Gerold looked at the blue sky through the trees. 'He's not sending anyone to help us.'

'You don't believe in God?'

'I do, but I learnt a long time ago that God is too busy to concern himself with the likes of us.'

Charles frowned and tried to think of what the priests in the church would say. 'That's why He sent his son, Jesus Christ, to look after us and to shepherd us away from evil.' Charles smiled, proud of himself for thinking of that, but Gerold barked a laugh which caused the bandits to look at them and his smile to falter.

'Shut up, you two,' the bandit guarding them shouted and then went back to eyeing up the barrels of wine. He was about the same age as Gerold, but was shorter and thinner than the slave.

'And where is our great shepherd?' Gerold asked, a hint of hardness in his eyes. 'Will He come bursting through those trees with His flock of battle-hardened sheep and rescue us from these men?' He waved his hand at the bandits. The one guarding them glanced over his shoulder at them, but said nothing.

Gerold's sudden anger surprised Charles, and he bit his lip as he tried to find the right words to calm his new friend. But he was not as skilled as the priests. Charles lowered his head. Perhaps he was not meant to be a priest either, just like he was not meant to be a warrior. Perhaps a slave was the only thing he could ever be. If he survived this.

'I'm sorry,' Gerold said, surprising him again. Charles looked at the slave and tried to stop his lip from quivering. 'Many nights I have prayed for God to take me away from my life so I would not have to be a servant to a master that cared nothing for me. There were nights when I even asked God to kill me. But night after night, prayer after prayer, God stayed quiet and so did His son.' Gerold sighed and looked up at the sky again. A small bird sat on the branch above them, tilting its head as if it was studying them. 'After a while, I just decided that God and His son were too busy to hear my prayers.'

Charles thought about that and guessed he understood. There had been many times when he felt like God was not listening to him. 'Bishop Bernard always says that God works in mysterious ways. That even though it might not seem like He is listening to us, He is watching us and, if we stay faithful, then He will respond to our prayers. But not always in the way we expect Him to. He might not have taken you away from slavery, but He gave you the strength to endure it.'

Gerold smiled. 'Perhaps you're right.'

Charles smiled, pleased he had found a way to get through to Gerold. Perhaps he could still become a priest. But then another thought made him frown once more. 'I wish God could give us a way to escape, though.' He lifted his tied hands.

Gerold looked at the bandits and smiled as they gave up on their search for hidden loot and opened the barrels filled with wine from the south of Francia. 'The blood of Christ will come to our aid.'

Charles tilted his head and frowned as he tried to understand what Gerold meant by that. He followed his friend's gaze and saw the bandits filling their cups with wine and guzzling it down, the red wine running down their cheeks. 'What do you mean?'

Gerold glanced at him, still smiling. 'Just wait and see.'

The bandits spent the rest of the day drinking their way through the dead trader's wine stock. As the sun moved along the skyline, Charles felt his eyes growing heavy. He tried to stay awake so he could see what Gerold meant, but soon his body slumped to the ground and he fell asleep.

A hand startled him awake and his heart raced as another covered his mouth. Eyes wide, he saw Gerold's face close to his, the firelight sparkling in his dark eyes. Slowly, Gerold removed the hand and brought a finger to his own lips. Charles nodded and then looked at the bandits. All of them were passed out around a small fire that was struggling to stay alive. Shattered vases littered the ground around them and Charles scowled, wondering how he had slept through all of this. At his side, Gerold slowly got to his feet and signalled for Charles to be quiet. Charles nodded and watched as Gerold crept towards the snoring bandits. He picked up a piece of broken vase and cut the rope around his hands. Charles expected him to come and cut his hands free so they could flee, but then frowned when Gerold turned his back to him and went towards the bandits. Moving more silently than Charles thought was possible, the slave leaned over the young bandit who was supposed to be guarding them. As quick as lightning, Gerold covered the bandit's mouth with one hand and stabbed him in the neck with the shard. Blood sprayed over Gerold as he pulled the shard out and stabbed again. The bandit's legs thrashed wildly, but Gerold was too strong for him. Charles covered his mouth with his hands, his eyes wide at the sudden violence as Gerold discarded the broken shard and pulled the knife from the bandit's belt. Gripping the knife in his right hand, he moved from bandit to bandit, killing them quietly before he crept over to Charles. The stench of the blood on the slave's face and clothing reminded Charles of that night and he could not stop the shiver which ran down his spine.

Gerold cut the ropes around Charles's wrist. 'Let's get away from here.'

Charles nodded, too afraid to speak, and got to his feet. They were about to sneak into the darkness when Charles's hand went to his tunic. He stopped, Gerold almost barging into him, and turned around. 'The pouch.'

'Forget about it,' Gerold hissed. 'We need to go now.'

'No.' Charles shook his head. 'It's all I have left of my family.'

'You'll live without it. I have nothing of my family and I'm fine,' Gerold retorted and then sighed, sensing the effect his words had on Charles, who was fighting back the tears. 'Fine. Stay here.'

Charles nodded and hid behind the tree as Gerold sneaked back into the camp and searched the bodies of the dead bandits for the pouch. His heart sank when Gerold shook his head. He wondered where the pouch could have gone and then gasped as he realised something. Gerold realised the same thing as he jumped to his feet and scanned the surrounding trees. One bandit was missing. The slave glanced at the cart and then ducked low as he crept towards it. Charles held his breath while gripping the wooden cross around his neck and prayed as he hugged the tree he was hiding behind.

Gerold was a few paces away from the cart when the bandit leader walked out of the trees, still pulling his trousers up. Charles wanted to cry out as the bandit stopped and took in the scene by the fire. All his men were slain and the slave they had captured was standing near the cart, staring at him with a bloody knife in his hand.

'You little mutt!' The bandit swayed slightly as he pulled his sword from his belt. But in his drunken state, he had not finished tying up his pants, and they dropped to his ankles, tripping him up. Gerold reacted instantly, and darted over to the fallen bandit, knife ready to plunge into his back. Charles watched, eyes wide, as at the last moment the bandit rolled onto his back and grabbed Gerold's hands before the knife could take his life. He was bigger than the thin slave, and despite being drunk, easily threw Gerold off him. Gerold quickly rolled to his feet and launched himself at the bandit again, not wanting to give the man a chance to get to his feet. The bandit grabbed his sword and stabbed it at Gerold, who had to twist out of the way or risk being skewered, and this gave the bandit time to get to his feet. 'You sneaky fuck! I knew we should have killed you!' The bandit bared his teeth at Gerold, who was crouched low with the knife in front of him. The bandit held his trousers up with his left hand and rushed at Gerold, who jumped back to avoid his stomach being cut open. Before he could attack, the bandit turned and stabbed at him. Again, Gerold was forced to jump back to avoid the sword. To Charles, it looked like Gerold was no match for the bandit, who, while still swaying from all the wine he had drunk, cut and stabbed at the dark-haired slave. Gerold twisted out of the way and stepped back, doing everything he could to avoid the bandit's sword. He tried to stab at the bandit's exposed side, but the drunken man turned and batted the knife away with his sword and then turned the blade to stab at him. As Gerold jumped back, his foot caught on something Charles could not see and he fell on his back. The bandit sneered at him.

'Die, you worthless worm!'

Before the bandit could stab down with his sword, Gerold rolled out of the way and kicked his leg. The man dropped to his knees and Gerold was up in a flash, before launching himself at the bandit. The man turned as the slave barged into him and they rolled around on the ground. Charles held his breath as a voice in his head told him to run, but he could not. Gerold had gone back to get his pouch. If it hadn't been for that, then they would have been far away by now. His heart raced in his chest as he searched for something he could use to help his new friend. His eyes fell on a large stick, but then Charles hesitated. He knew he should help the slave, but he couldn't get himself to grab the stick. Charles looked up and gasped when he saw the two of them had stopped rolling around. The bandit was on top, but neither of them seemed to move. The stick trembled in Charles's hand as indecision gripped him. Again, the voice in his head told him to run and Charles was about to obey when he heard.

'Are you going to just stand there or help get this stinking oaf off of me?'

8

Charles stared at the two bodies on the ground, one lying on top of the other, unsure if he had really heard Gerold. But then he saw Gerold's hand move from under the bandit's body in the dim firelight.

'Thanks for the help,' Gerold groaned as he heaved the heavy body off of him. He sat up and ran his trembling hand through his short hair while staring at the bandit leader he had killed.

'I... I...' Charles stood frozen, his eyes fixed on the hilt of the knife sticking out of the bandit's chest. He gripped the wooden cross around his neck and looked up at the starry night.

'What are you doing?'

'I'm thanking the Lord,' Charles said as Gerold pulled the knife out of the dead man's chest and cleaned it.

Gerold scowled. 'Why?'

'Because He helped you kill the bandit.'

Gerold shook his head. 'The knife helped me kill the bastard.' Before Charles could respond, Gerold bent down and plucked something from the bandit's belt. 'There's a town, not far from here. My master,' Gerold glanced at the body of the dead trader, 'my former master and I usually stop there on our way to Denmark. We should go there.'

'No!' Charles covered his mouth as the word came out louder than intended. Gerold looked at him with a raised eyebrow. 'My father said I must get to Denmark, that I'm not safe in Francia.'

'You can find someone in the town to take you to Denmark.'

Charles bit his lower lip as he stared at Gerold. He had already disobeyed his father by going back to Hügelburg and that had almost not ended well for him. Now he was determined to do what his father had said. 'My grandfather is a rich man, he can pay you.' Charles guessed that was true.

Gerold frowned. 'Pay me?' He looked at the cart as Charles nodded and after a short while he sighed and handed Charles the pouch he had been holding. 'Fine, I'll take you to Denmark. It's probably not safe for me here either now.'

'Thank you,' Charles said and then grimaced as he held the sticky pouch in his hands. 'It's covered in blood.'

'So am I.' Gerold pulled off his tunic, revealing a thin torso covered in scars, and walked to the cart. Charles stared at him open-mouthed, wondering if the scars had been caused by Gerold's master beating him. Gerold found another tunic in the cart and pulled it over his head before he grabbed a flask and a small bag filled with some food.

'What are you doing?' Charles asked as Gerold started freeing the horse from the cart.

'We need food, water. And it's a long way to walk, so we'll need the horse.'

Charles frowned as he scratched his head. He guessed that made sense, especially now that the trader was dead. 'But why don't we just take the cart?'

'The cart will slow us down and draw too much attention. With the horse, we can move faster and stay off the main road if we need to.'

Charles frowned again and guessed that Gerold was right. He glanced at the dead bodies and the broken shards of pottery. 'How did you know this would happen?'

Gerold stopped what he was doing and looked at Charles. 'Know what would happen?'

'That they would drink so much?' Charles pointed at the dead bandits.

'I knew they would drink so much because they didn't look like men who could go into taverns. And we had a lot of wine.' He shrugged. 'It was easy to guess what would happen next.'

Charles scratched his head. 'But why couldn't they go to taverns?'

'Because they're outlaws. The town soldiers would kill them as soon as they reached the gates.' Gerold undid the buckles of the horse's harness and threw it to the ground as Charles still stood there, holding the sticky pouch in his hands and looking at the dead bodies. Until a few days ago, he had never seen a person die so bloodily. He had seen a few hangings. His father had always encouraged him to go so he could witness the justice of the Almighty. But that was nothing compared to all the violence he had witnessed recently. 'Let's go, we don't want to be here when a bear shows up.' Without waiting for a response, Gerold turned and led the horse away.

Charles felt his heart skip a beat at the thought of a large bear wandering into the clearing before he rushed after Gerold.

They walked back to the main road, Gerold using the moonlight to find his way. Charles stayed close and did his best to hide his fear, but he could do nothing about his trembling body. In his mind, every shadow hid a monster or another bandit, waiting to pounce on him. Every rustling leaf was something sneaking up on them. He constantly glanced over his shoulder, trying to spot the evil hiding from them and on more than one occasion he bumped into Gerold, who would stop to get his bearings.

'Watch where you're going!'

'S... sorry.' Charles glanced around, hiding his shaking hands behind his back so Gerold didn't see them. He did not want the slave to think he was weak. But then a noise above his head made him scream, and before he could stop himself, he rushed to Gerold and wrapped his arms around him.

'It's just an owl,' Gerold said as he freed himself from Charles's grip.

'How do you know?' Charles asked, his jaw trembling.

'Because I spent many nights sleeping amongst the trees. Trust me, there's nothing out there more dangerous than what we have already faced.'

Charles tried to believe the dark-haired boy, but he had too many stories of children being carried off into the night by Satan's monsters, never to be seen again. His hand clutched the wooden cross around his neck and he squeezed it so hard, he felt it dig into the palm of his hand. Gerold sighed.

'You're not very brave, are you?'

Charles shook his head, unable to look the older boy in the eyes.

Gerold sighed again. 'How old are you? Six, seven?'

Charles shook his head. 'Nine.'

'Nine?' Gerold raised an eyebrow. 'You're too short to be nine.'

Charles could only shrug. 'I am short, and so was my father.'

'I thought Danes were supposed to be big, like giant demons from hell.'

Charles shrugged again. Apart from his father, he had never seen any Danes, so he didn't know. But he had heard the stories about them around the town. Big, hairy beasts with horns on their heads, and blood drooling from their mouths. The flames of hell could be seen in their evil eyes, a sign of where they came from. 'My father was no demon. He was a good Christian.'

'He was a Dane.' There was an edge to Gerold's voice which caught Charles by surprise, but it also ignited the spark inside him. He straightened his back and glared at the slave.

'My father was a good man and a good Christian. If you say otherwise, then I'll...'

'Then you'll what?' Gerold smirked. Charles opened his mouth to speak, but the spark had gone. Gerold knelt down and put his hand on Charles's shoulder. 'You need to stop being afraid. This world will chew you up if you don't show strength. Now get on the horse, we'll move faster that way.' Gerold wrinkled his nose as he helped Charles mount the mare. 'You also need a wash, you reek.'

Charles nodded, but said nothing. He knew he stank, as did the clothes he wore, but he had not found a chance or place to clean himself since his father died. He thought about what Gerold had said as he led them along the road, using the moon and stars to guide them. Gerold was just a slave, but he had shown strength when the bandits attacked them. And that had saved them. His father had also shown strength, but he was dead. He stared at the back of Gerold's head, his hands gripping the mane of the horse so he wouldn't fall off, and felt the sticky pouch against his skin in his tunic. Perhaps Gerold was right. It was time he stopped being afraid.

They travelled in silence for the next few days after Gerold had found a stream where Charles could clean himself and his clothes. Gerold had also cleaned the blood off his face and arms from the bandits he had killed. Throughout their journey north, Gerold kept them off the main road when it was busy, afraid that word might have spread about the death of his master. But the few people they came across paid no attention to them. At night, they would find a place to make camp and Gerold would hunt for rabbits while Charles prepared the fire. Charles tried not to be afraid when he was alone in the clearing, wondering what demons hid in the shadows, but he was always relieved when Gerold returned. The landscape around them changed little, although Charles noticed there were fewer farmsteads the closer they got to Denmark. He also saw a few fort towns, like Hügelburg, in the distance, which they avoided.

Charles wasn't sure when they entered Denmark, but after a few days, Gerold became more tense. His body was more rigid, and his head kept moving side to side as if he was looking for a threat. They met many travellers heading south towards Francia, most of them looking like traders, but they all ignored the two boys and their horse.

'Welcome to Hedeby, the trading jewel of the Danes,' Gerold said with some scorn when they reached the large town with its high walls and busy port. Charles could not keep his mouth closed as he stared wide-eyed at the large earth-mound wall with the tall wooden palisade on top of it. The road they were on was packed with travellers and carts, disgruntled traders complaining about having to wait so long to enter while children ran around, chasing each other with wooden swords.

'See, they teach them from a young age to be killers,' Gerold said as he glared at the boys not much older than Charles.

Charles looked at them and thought about how similar they were to the boys he grew up with. They too would run around with wooden weapons, pretending to fight the Danes, which usually meant him. He wondered if these boys were pretending to fight the Franks.

'Aye, when they're not stabbing you, they're stealing your money with their high taxes,' an old man on a cart beside them said while staring at them with a raised eyebrow.

Gerold glanced at the man and then looked away, hoping to avoid conversation.

'What are you two boys doing travelling here alone? God knows it's not a safe place for two helpless Franks.' The old man scratched his wrinkled cheek.

Charles looked at Gerold, wondering if he should tell the old man. Perhaps he might know of his grandfather and could help them. He was about to say something when Gerold responded.

'Our business is none of yours, old man.' Gerold put his hand on the hilt of the knife he had taken from the bandit.

The trader sat up straight, his face pale, and whipped his horse so they moved away from Charles and Gerold.

'Why did you do that?' Charles asked.

Gerold glanced at him, his eyes hard. 'That man knew my master. If his memory had been sharper, then our journey would end here. And trust me, the Danes are very creative with how they kill people.'

Charles looked at the trader as he forced his cart past others, ignoring the complaints sent his way.

They made their way to the gate in silence after that. Gerold kept his head low, while Charles sat up straight on the horse as he tried to take in as much of the town as possible. It was a lot bigger than Hügelburg, the walls almost three times as high. The noise of all the people was deafening and his ears started hurting from hearing so many people talking and shouting to each other, everyone jostling for their place in the line as they approached the gate. He recognised the Danish tongue and Frankish, but was surprised to hear other languages he did not know. The sky was filled with white birds and a few large black ones, most of them flying over the port, which he could not see. Charles crinkled his nose at the smell of horseshit, mixed in with other unpleasant smells he did not want to think about. He had been told the

Danes were filthy people and guessed that was what he could smell.

Gerold tensed his shoulders as they reached the gate and Charles could almost hear him grind his teeth as he looked up and saw the men in the tower looking down at them, their eyes hard. He also saw the two guards on either side of the gate as they passed through. They were big men, much larger than his father, their chests wide and shoulders broad. Both men had a large spear in one hand and a shield in the other, with swords at their waists. They wore metal-linked vests which went halfway down their thighs and covered most of their arms. Large rings of silver and gold adorned their wrists, while both men wore pendants similar to the one that was in Charles's pouch, just not as big or beautiful. Long hair stuck out from under their helmets while long beards covered their necks. Charles shivered at the thought of these large warriors attacking his town.

One warrior glanced at them and raised an eyebrow before turning his attention to the cart behind them.

'Were you scared?' Charles couldn't help but ask as they passed through the gate and Gerold released the breath he had been holding.

Gerold looked at him from over his shoulder. 'Shut up.' He turned his attention to the surrounding houses. Charles followed his gaze and saw the long street that seemed to disappear in the distance, with small wooden houses on either side. They weren't touching each other, like the ones in Hügelburg, and were more rectangular than square and neither were they built high up. The roofs were slanted and made of reeds or hay, and Charles saw smoke coming out of the top of the houses. The houses had no windows either, and Charles wondered how they got any light inside. Countless people wandered around the streets, the noise of them all hurting his ears. Women were carrying baskets filled with vegetables, sometimes with young children in tow. Or sometimes in groups, laughing as they whispered to each other. Men, long-haired and bearded, either lounged around and eyed everyone up or walked to their destinations, calling out greetings to those they knew.

'How will we find anyone in this place?' Charles saw a woman throw a bone out of her door. Two large dogs rushed towards it and growled at each other as they both grabbed the ends. The dogs started tugging at it, each hound refusing to give up its meal, while some men cheered and placed bets. Gerold led the horse along the street, away from the fighting dogs. Charles turned his head to see which dog would win, but then they went around a corner and the dogs disappeared. Two boys rushed out from between two houses and almost barged into them.

'Watch it!' Gerold said, glaring at the two light-haired boys who looked a few years younger than Charles. They reminded him of the boys who picked on him, and he found himself not liking them. The boys stared at Gerold, frowning as they didn't understand what he had said, before one whispered to the other and they ran away. 'Let's go.' Gerold pulled the horse along.

'Where are we going?' Charles asked, his head constantly turning as he tried to take in as much as he could. He saw a thin man, his clothing of poor quality and his hair cut short, rushing past and carrying two buckets of water, and another like him, but this one was following a woman while carrying a pig carcass over his shoulders.

'To the market. Perhaps there we can find some information about your grandfather.'

Charles guessed that made sense. His father had always told him that traders were the best source of news in the kingdom. 'How do you know where the market is?'

'It's not my first time here.' Gerold kept his head low and led them towards the market and as they passed one street, Charles thought he saw a building that looked like a church.

'Wait!'

'What?' Gerold turned, his hand on the hilt of his knife.

'I think I saw a church.'

'So?'

Charles frowned. 'Why would they have a church here? I thought the Danes hated Christians?'

Gerold shrugged. 'Perhaps so they could lure the Christians here and then it's easier for them to kill them.'

'That can't be true.' Charles scowled.

'How do you know? You said it yourself. They hate Christians.' Without waiting for a response, Gerold led them away. Charles looked back in the church's direction and frowned. He didn't want to think that Gerold was right, but then why else would they have a church here?

Somehow, they made it to the market square, although Charles wasn't sure how. He had tried to follow the path Gerold took, but there were so many turns and many of the houses looked the same and his head was soon swimming. But then the market took his breath away. It was much larger than the one in his home town, although that wasn't really his home any more. Stalls spread out as far as he could see, all of them selling different things. There were stalls with jewellery, some adorned with large gems and some with amber. Another stall had weapons Charles had never seen before, knives and swords with curved blades and one that made him scratch his head as he could not imagine fighting with a stick that had a large spiked ball on a chain. He also saw a stall selling furs from animals he could not think were real, so strange were the colours and the patterns on them. It wasn't just the thing the traders sold that caught his attention, but the traders themselves. He recognised Franks, with their short hair and trimmed beards, others he guessed were Danes because of their long hair and beards. And then there were strange men, their skin unnaturally dark and bodies more delicate than the large Danes around them. These men had thick curly beards and wore what looked like large cloths wrapped around their heads. Their tunics, longer than those of the Franks and the Danes, were brightly coloured, and they all wore many rings on their fingers. Charles gaped at these strange men who spoke a language he did not understand, as the noise of the traders shouting almost made his ears bleed. Even the mare was skittish under him, but Gerold seemed undisturbed as he scanned the market, his eyebrows drawn together.

'Who are you looking for?' Charles almost had to shout.

Gerold glanced at him. 'Nobody. Just making sure there's no one here who could recognise me.'

'Do you think they might?'

'No, I'm a slave.' Gerold shook his head. 'But we need to be careful.'

Charles looked at the sea of stalls in front of him, his heart racing in his chest as more people than he had ever seen in one place milled around, talking and bartering with the traders. Somewhere a vase broke, the shattering sound silencing those around as they turned to see what had happened. The trader berated the old fat drunk who stood next to the stall, swaying as he held his hand up in an apology, his thin hair dirty and loose, his bald head with a strange marking on it. Two warriors made their way to the drunk, who seemed to sense them approaching as he never looked up from his feet, but turned and walked away. The people around took a step away from him, their faces turned away and grimacing. Something about the old drunk bothered Charles, but he quickly forgot about it as he turned his attention back to the vast market and rubbed the wooden cross around his neck.

God Almighty, please help me find my grandfather.

9

Charles sat in the barn, rubbing his eyes as his stomach rumbled. The morning sun was peeking through the gaps in the roof and gave Charles enough light to look around the place where they had been sleeping for the last two nights. A horse whined and another shook its head as Gerold still lay on his back, his eyes closed. Charles's stomach growled again, reminding him they had not eaten for almost a day. The food they had brought with them had run out the previous morning and they had no coin to buy more. Gerold had suggested stealing food, but Charles refused. They might be in the land of the Danes, but God was still watching them and Charles did not want to sin.

He fished out the stained leather pouch from his tunic. The blood had dried now and left its mark on the pouch. A reminder for him to be more careful. Charles opened the pouch and peered inside, seeing the gold cross glinting in the dim light. He took it out and marvelled at its beauty as he ran his thumb over the small gems, which were set around the edge of the cross. But his eyes were fixed on the large ruby in the centre of the cross. Charles had never seen a gem so big or beautiful and wondered if his mother was as beautiful. He had asked his father about her many times, but he would only ever say that she died when Charles was very young and nothing more. Charles frowned as he looked at the emblem stamped on the golden cross below the ruby. It was a cross with a diamond in the centre and, at first, Charles thought it was a compass, but the letters on the end of each arm were wrong. The north arm had the letter R, the east arm had S, the south had L and the west had K.

'Do you know what that means?' Gerold asked, startling Charles who had not heard him sit up.

Charles almost dropped the cross and had to take deep breaths to calm his heart before it ripped out of his chest. When he had calmed himself, he looked at the emblem on the cross again and shook his head. 'No.' He frowned. 'It looks familiar, like I've seen it before, but I don't know. Perhaps my mother's name?' he wondered out loud.

'What was your mother's name?'

Charles looked at Gerold, seeing how his dark eyes studied him. 'I don't know. My father never told me.' He lowered his head, embarrassed by that.

'I don't remember much of my mother, only that she had dark hair,' Gerold said as he tried to comfort Charles. 'Perhaps your grandfather will know?'

Charles shook his head again. 'My father was taken from my grandfather when he was a small boy.'

Gerold nodded as if he understood and then picked some straw out of his hair. 'I'm sure God will guide us to the answer.'

Charles tried to feel the same positivity his friend had, but he couldn't. The events of the last few days were getting to him, and he struggled to make sense of it all. He tried to pray, but every time he closed his eyes, he saw his father kneeling in front of him, covered in blood, and his face grimacing with pain. And then he would see the old drunk from the market. They had not seen him again, but he kept coming to Charles's mind. The thought of the short, fat man made Charles dig out the other item in the pouch. It looked like a hammer and was about half his palm in size. He stared at the swirls and other patterns carved on the pendant and wondered what they meant.

'They call it the Mjöllnir,' Gerold said as he leaned over Charles's shoulder.

'Mjöllnir?' Charles repeated. The word sounded comfortable in his mouth, like he was meant to say it. But then he could speak in the Danish tongue.

'It's a symbol for one of their gods. The Danes believe wearing it will protect them from evil.'

Charles thought about that. 'Just like we wear the cross.'

Gerold shrugged. 'Perhaps. Your father never told you about it?'

'He never told me anything about their gods.'

'They were his gods once.'

Charles stared at the Mjöllnir in his left hand and then at the cross in his right hand. 'But he gave them up and became a Christian.'

Gerold shrugged as he stood up and stretched. Their mare stared at them, her tail swinging around before she lowered her head.

When they first arrived, Charles and Gerold had spent the entire day asking anyone who would talk to them about his grand-father, but no one had heard of a Jarl Sven from Ribe. At the end of the day, exhausted and hungry, they had met the owner of the barn, who had agreed to let them sleep inside and even feed their horse. Gerold did not trust the man and believed he was going to ask for their horse as payment, but Charles had agreed anyway. He needed to sleep. The second day had gone much the same as the first, but worse as they had run out of food. Gerold wouldn't ask the stall owner for food and Charles wouldn't steal, so they just went hungry.

Charles's stomach growled again as he put the cross and the Mjöllnir back in the pouch and tucked it into his tunic. 'I hope we can find some food today.'

'I'm sure we will. I think today will be a good day.' Gerold smiled and the two of them left the barn. Their horse looked up as they walked out and then shook its head before it went back to munching on the straw.

They spent the morning visiting the taverns around the market and asking about Charles's grandfather and food. But neither was forthcoming and, by midday, Charles was starving and down. He walked around the market, his head low and hand on his stomach. Gerold kept behind him, staying silent, but Charles felt his constant presence. He did not understand how the lack of food was not bothering Gerold. Perhaps starvation was something Gerold was used to. Charles was slowly getting used to the sounds of the market. The noise was still too loud, but it didn't send his heart racing any more. He even stopped staring at the strange men Gerold had said were from lands far to the east. But now he wondered why they were in Hedeby and how they got here.

'What's got you looking so down?' An old voice startled Charles. He looked up and saw three old men sitting on a bench outside the latest tavern they had visited, their backs to the wall. They all looked older than the bishop, their hair grey and their beards down to their stomachs. One man was missing his leg and had a walking stick leaning against the wall beside him. And all three old men were staring at them.

'Nothing,' Charles responded in the Danish tongue, feeling nervous under their scrutiny.

'Been watching you, we have. The last two days, you and your friend. Walking around here and bothering people,' one of the old men said, his wrinkled face stern. He had a head full of long grey hair and his thick arms still looked strong despite his age. He also had an ugly scar over his right eye which Charles tried not to look at.

'That boy's not his friend. He's a thrall. It's as obvious as Odin's missing eye.'

Charles glanced over his shoulder at Gerold behind him and saw the dark-haired boy clenching his jaw. He wondered if Gerold understood what the old man had said.

'Aye,' the one-legged man said. 'But the young 'un's no thrall. No Dane either, either of them.'

The bald man sitting next to the one-legged man scowled at him. His beard was longer than the others and had a large Mjöllnir tied to the end. 'The gods know you lot can talk nonsense.' He turned his attention back to Charles. 'Where you from, boy?'

Charles tugged at his trousers and wondered if he should respond while the old men waited, although impatiently.

'Come on, boy. We'll be dead soon, so you better answer quickly.' The other two laughed.

'We're from Francia, to the south.' Charles heard Gerold hiss behind him, but decided not to look at him.

'Francia, you say.' The bald man stroked his beard, his old eyes scrutinising Charles and taking in his short and thin frame and red hair. 'How come you speak our tongue?'

'You call that speaking,' the old man with the scar said. 'It's like he's stabbing my ears with his tongue.'

'Quiet, you old fool. You can barely hear anything anyway.'

'Who you calling old? I'm younger than you.'

'No, you're not.'

'How do you know?'

The bald man was about to respond, his mouth already open to reveal several missing teeth, but then he frowned and turned his attention back to Charles. 'How do you speak our tongue?' The other old man smiled in satisfaction while the one-legged one shook his head.

'We should go,' Gerold whispered behind him, but Charles ignored him.

'My father taught me. He was a Dane.'

The old men glanced at each other, and then the one-legged man asked Charles, 'What are you doing here, then?' He raised his bushy eyebrows.

'I'm looking for my grandfather. Before he... died, my father told me to find him.'

The bald man scratched his head. 'And who is your grandfather?'

Charles thought about the Mjöllnir pendant in the pouch. 'He's a mighty jarl in the north. Jarl Sven of Ribe.'

The three old men looked at each other as if some silent communication was happening between them, before the scarred one said, 'Sorry, boy. There is no Jarl Sven of Ribe.'

'Aye, Jarl Bjarni rules there. Did he not have a brother once called Sven?' The bald man glanced at the other two.

The scarred man shook his head. 'No. Odin knows I've never heard of Jarl Sven of Ribe.'

The one-legged man's face went dark as he waved his hand at the man next to him. 'That's because your head's as muddled as a young boy's after he fell into a barrel of ale.' He stared at Charles, his eyes hard. 'The gods know I'll never forget that boar-headed swine shit.' He hawked and spat and raised his stump. 'Cost me my leg, that bastard.'

The scarred man next to him raised an eyebrow. 'Thought you lost your leg in a raid?'

'Aye. A raid led by Sven the Boar, may Odin piss in his skull.'

Charles struggled to keep up with what the old men were

arguing about, but he understood that the one-legged man knew his grandfather. He took a deep breath. 'Do you know where he is?'

'Who?'

'My grandfather.'

The one-legged man scowled at Charles and then turned his head away. The bald man beside him answered in a gentle tone. 'Sorry, lad. If there ever was a Jarl Sven of Ribe, there isn't one now.'

Charles stared at the old man, fighting back tears as the words raged in his head like a storm. 'Are you sure? My father said—'

'Your father lied to you, boy! Jarl Sven,' the one-legged man spat after he said the name, 'died a miserable fool a long time ago.'

'Ebbe!' the bald man said.

'What? The boy needs to know the truth. He's been wandering around like a *draugr* looking for something that isn't real!'

Charles fought back the tears as he tried to swallow the knot in his throat. 'Th... thank you. May God be with you.' He turned and walked away, Gerold behind him.

'What did he just say?' Ebbe asked.

'He called you an old sour bastard.'

Charles lost himself in his mind as he drifted past the market stalls and the people going about their business. Had his father really lied to him? Charles did not understand why he would. But then, his father had rarely spoken about his grandfather. The pouch felt heavy in his tunic, and Charles wanted to throw it away, but it was the only thing he had left of his family, of a mother he never knew. He paid no attention to where he was going, his head down and his teary eyes fixed on his feet as they transported him along.

'Perhaps your father did not know? You said yourself he lived in Francia most of his life.'

Gerold's voice broke Charles from his trance and when he looked up, he saw the small wooden church in front of him. It was like God had guided him there. Ignoring Gerold, he walked towards it and stopped in front of the open door.

'Charles?' Gerold called him. Charles looked at the slave and then entered the church. Inside was cold and dark, and Charles couldn't suppress the shiver that ran through him. He felt Gerold's presence behind him, but didn't look as he made his way to the front of the church. It differed greatly from the one in Hügelburg. There were plenty of burning torches on the walls and candles burning by the altar, but the church was still dark. He did not feel the same sense of calmness he did when he entered his own church. Charles held the wooden cross around his neck as he stared up at the statue of Jesus hanging on the cross. It was smaller than the one back home and not as beautiful. This one was crudely carved out of wood and Charles struggled to make out the features on His face. He tried to picture the face of the Jesus statue back home, but all he saw was his father's face, pleading for him to run. He shook his head and tried again, but again the same image came to him. Charles felt the knot in his throat, and he tried to swallow it down, but it refused to go as his eyes teared up. His hands shook as he clenched his fist. This church was not like the church back home. He did not feel safe here. He did not feel the warmth of God. All he felt was alone and cold. Abandoned by everyone and left to fend for himself. To find a grandfather who might not even be alive any more. Charles dropped to his knees as tears ran down his cheeks. Gerold took half a step forward and raised his hand, but then thought better of it and took a step back, leaving Charles to his grief. Charles's shoulders shuddered as he cried, his father's face in his mind. He wanted to go home, back to his father. But that was not his home any more and his father was not there to keep him safe either. And then there was Bishop Bernard, a man he had thought he could trust. But the bishop had lied to him, and it was possible his father had too.

Your father lied to you, boy! The old man's voice rang in his ears.

'He did not lie to me!' Charles screamed and stormed out of the church.

Gerold, who had been studying the church, was caught by surprise as Charles sped away. 'Charles! Stop!'

But Charles did not hear Gerold as he ran out of the doors and, blinded by the sunlight, ran into a woman he had not seen.

'By Frigg, watch where you're going!' she shouted as Charles fell to the ground and Gerold came running after him.

Charles shook his head and stared at the woman he had run into before frowning at her stunned expression. She had light-coloured hair, her face was pretty, and she looked old enough to be his mother. Her shoulders were quite broad, as were her hips, and she had a scar over her left eyebrow. Sharp blue eyes scrutinised him in return before the woman straightened her dress.

'You should watch where you are running. You could have hurt someone.'

'I... I'm sorry.' Charles lowered his head. He was aware of Gerold standing there, but didn't look at him.

'Never mind that,' the woman said. 'I've been looking for you and... your friend.'

Charles looked at the woman and saw her scowling at Gerold, who was glaring at her in return.

'You were looking for me? Why?' His heart raced in his chest and Charles wondered if they were in trouble. But he couldn't understand why they would be.

'What does she want?' Gerold asked in Frankish with a hard edge in his voice.

'She was looking for us.' Charles stared at the woman, who glanced at the church and then looked at him again, looking almost angelic.

'Why?'

Charles frowned, his heart still racing away. 'Why?'

The woman sighed as she crossed her arms. 'You've been asking around for someone.'

'Say nothing,' Gerold hissed, and Charles wondered if he understood what the woman was saying. But he still listened and kept quiet, waiting to see what the woman would do.

'By the gods, don't play dumb with me. I heard you in the market asking around.'

Charles nodded, too nervous now to speak.

'Who are you looking for?'

'My... my grandfather.' Charles looked at his hands, remembering what the old men had told him. 'But he's dead. Or not real.' He felt the tears welling up again.

'What's his name?'

'Doesn't matter.'

Gerold stood behind him, his eyes fixed on the woman and his hand hovering near the knife tucked into his belt. The woman saw that and shook her head before she knelt down.

'What's his name?' Her voice was gentler this time.

Charles looked at her and saw the kindness in her eyes. 'Sven. His name was Sven.'

She nodded. 'Sven the Boar?'

Charles raised his eyebrows, not sure how she knew that. He glanced at Gerold behind him, but Gerold only shrugged while still glaring at the woman. 'How do you...?'

The woman held out her hand for him. 'Come, there's someone you should meet.'

'Who?' Charles frowned.

'Someone,' she chewed on her bottom lip, 'someone who knew your grandfather once.'

'I already met the one-legged man.' Charles puffed his cheeks out.

But the woman only smiled. 'Not that old fool. Come.'

Charles looked at her and then at Gerold, who shook his head. He glanced at the church where he had ended up and now he had met this woman who claimed she could help him. Perhaps this was a sign from God. His heart racing in his chest again, Charles took the woman's hand, surprised by her strong grip, and stood up.

'Good.' She smiled. 'Now follow me. And tell your friend not to look so sour. The people here don't trust that.'

'What's she saying?'

'That you should smile.'

Gerold grunted, but ignored the advice as the woman led them away from the market. Charles wanted to ask her about the man she was taking them to meet, but when he looked at her, he saw her purse her lips and frown like she was struggling with some thought. Gerold just followed behind, but his eyes were always darting around, like he was trying to see everything. Soon they came to a crossroads, and the woman stopped. She took a deep breath and then turned to face him and her wrinkled forehead made his hands go clammy.

'Frigg, help me,' she said as she put her hand on Charles's shoulder. He tensed, but then she led him around the corner where he saw the old drunk with a bruised face and cut lip sitting against the wall, a jug in his hand. The same drunk they had seen in the market when they first arrived. The man stank. Charles grimaced as he could smell him from where he stood.

'God Almighty,' Gerold said behind him, while waving his hand in front of his face.

The old man was bald, apart from the ring of long dirty hair which circled his head. It looked like it had been red at some point but now was mostly grey. Charles now saw that the marking on the man's head was a picture of what could have been a bird, but it was faded and hidden under dirt, so it was hard for him to see. His clothes were dirty and torn, with large sweat patches under his arms, and his bare feet black with dirt. Dull red eyes looked up at him as the old man took a deep gulp of whatever was in the jug. Golden liquid ran down the sides of his mouth and into his beard, which was the same colour as his hair and just as dirty.

The woman sighed. 'Meet your grandfather, Sven the Boar. Or what's left of him.'

Sven frowned, his ale-muddled brain making it hard to understand
what Thora had just said. He stared at the small boy with his short
red hair, narrow shoulders and slim body. But it was not this that
caused his breath to catch in the back of his throat. It was the boy's
blue eyes and small nose, and the way his jaw was rounded. Even
the faded bruises reminded him of a face he had not seen for a very
long time. One he never thought he would see again. He struggled
to breathe as his mind drifted back to that day on the Frankish
coast, so many winters ago.

'Sven!' Thora said, but Sven ignored her as he saw his son disappear in the distance. 'Sven!' She tried again, this time kicking him in
the leg.

The vision disappeared and Sven saw the boy standing in
front of him. Another appeared by his side and again Sven
frowned as he took in the second boy. This one was older, almost
a man, but not quite. He was slim, but wiry, his arms tense as he
glared at Sven with dark eyes. His dark hair was short, like the
young boy's, and Sven noticed some straw sticking out. His
clothing was different, though. The tunic he wore was too small

and thin, with a few holes which had been badly patched up. His trousers were the same and, like the boy, he wore no shoes. But this one brought no flashback to Sven. If anything, he reminded Sven of a thrall. Sven glared at Thora. 'What, in Odin's name, do you want now?'

Thora straightened and put her hands on her hips. 'I want you to acknowledge the boy!'

Sven looked at the boy again with his wide eyes and trembling chin. 'Why?' He took another gulp of ale from the jug and realised it was empty. 'Thor's balls.' He threw the jug on the ground.

'You'll have to forgive the old fool. He's as polite as the beast he's named after.'

Sven waved a dismissive hand at her and then looked around for another jug of ale. He was sure he had one more. Or was that a different day he was thinking about? He scratched his head and then realised they were still staring at him. 'What?'

'Are you really my grandfather?' the boy asked, his voice timid and irritating.

'No,' Sven responded before Thora could say anything. He was about to say something else when Thora kicked him again. 'Ow!'

'By Freya, I wish it wasn't true, lad. But yes,' Thora said.

'But...' The boy scratched the back of his neck as he struggled with some thoughts in his head. The older boy just stared at Sven, his face unreadable. 'But my father said you were a great warrior.'

Sven hawked and spat. 'Your father's an idiot.'

There was a spark in the young boy's eyes, so quick Sven almost missed it before tears replaced it. 'He was your son.'

'My son died a long time ago.'

'Sven!' Thora kicked him again before she turned to the boy. 'Forgive him. The gods turned their backs on him and so he turned his back on everyone else.' She glared at Sven before softening her face and looking at the boy again. 'Where is your father?'

'He... he...' The boy swallowed back the tears and then: 'He died. They killed him.'

Sven felt the stab in his chest, but showed nothing on his face as he glowered at the young boy. Thora glanced at him, her eyebrows drawn together, before she turned back to the red-headed boy.

'And he told you to find your grandfather?'

The boy looked up sharply, confused, but nodded.

'I heard what you told Ebbe and his friends,' she explained.

The boy frowned as he thought about it and glanced at the older one beside him, who shrugged. 'He told me to give this to his father. Said he would understand.' The boy fished out a leather pouch from his tunic and handed it to Thora, who held it out for Sven to take.

Sven stared at the pouch, seeing the bloodstain which brought another memory to him. He blinked rapidly to clear his vision and then glanced at Thora before taking the pouch. It wasn't heavy, and he wondered how much ale he could get for whatever was inside.

'Don't even think about it!' Thora scolded him and he stuck his tongue out at her, before opening the pouch and seeing what was inside.

Again, the breath caught in the back of his throat when he saw the Mjöllnir pendant he had not seen for a long time. He fished it out and stared at it, remembering how he had taken it from his father's corpse and then how he had given it to Torkel, his son, along with a promise he had never kept. But he frowned when he took out the second item. A large golden cross, about the size of his hand and filled with gems. It had the largest ruby he had ever seen. But there was something about the marking under the ruby which tugged at his memory. He felt like he had seen it before, but his ale-muddled mind could not drag up the memory. It was like Thor trying to pull Jörmungandr out of the sea. And just like Thor had failed, so did Sven's memory.

He looked up at the small boy and saw the desperation in his eyes. He saw something else as well, something that irritated him. Disappointment. Sven ground his teeth and put the Mjöllnir and the cross back into the pouch, but he did not hand them back. 'I'm sorry, lad. I don't know what your father told you, but I'm not your grandfather.' Thora was about to say something, but Sven glared at her and she kept quiet.

The boy, however, did not. 'But you must be! My father did not lie to me!' Fresh tears ran down his face, reminding Sven again of the last time he saw his son. But this boy was not trying to be brave like Torkel. And that irritated Sven even more.

He struggled to his feet, feeling the pain in his joints, and staggered towards the boy. The thrall took a step closer, his hand on the knife in his belt. Sven caught himself praying to Odin that the bastard would use the knife and end his miserable life before he turned back to the crying boy. 'I'm not the person you're looking for. Go home, leave me in peace.'

'I have no home!' the boy cried, and ran off. The thrall glared at Sven before spitting at his feet and running after the red-headed boy.

'You really are a boar-headed bastard.' Thora rubbed her forehead, but Sven ignored her as he walked away. 'Where are you going?'

'Mind your own business.'

'Gods!' Thora said, and stormed off after the boy.

Sven turned and watched her go, and then he looked at the pouch still in his hand. He might not have remembered where he had seen that cross before, but he knew what to do with it. He looked around, trying to get his bearings, and then headed to his favourite tavern, muttering the old war song again.

It did not take him long to get there. It was close to Thora's house, which used to be her father's. He stumbled into the tavern and paused for a heartbeat as he allowed his eyes to get used to the dim light inside. The tavern was like a small hall, much smaller than the one he had in Ribe. It had a hearth fire in the centre, where they cooked the food the tavern sold, and a few burning torches along the walls. But it was always dark in here, and that was one of the reasons Sven liked it. Benches and tables were spread out across the tavern, giving a person just enough space to move past without knocking someone's drink over. He made his way to a bench in the far corner and sat down with his back to the wall. The tavern owner, a round man with grey hair and stern eyes, glared at him and made a point of not going to him until Sven threw the pouch on the table. The loud *thunk* made the tavern owner raise an eyebrow and after a few heartbeats, he filled up a jug with ale and walked towards Sven.

'Don't even think about it!' Thora's voice stopped the tavern owner in his tracks. Sven shook his head as the man shrugged and went back to his bar. 'By Thor, I can't believe you were about to use the boy's things to buy ale.'

'Why not? He doesn't need them.' Sven crossed his arms across his chest.

'Argh, I feel like punching you right now!'

'Somebody already beat you to it.' He pointed to the bruise on his face.

Thora sat down and signalled for the tavern owner to bring two cups of ale. The man frowned at her and only did what Thora asked when she took two coins out of her pouch and threw them on the table. While they waited, she stared at the bloodstained pouch. 'He looks just like Torkel.' Sven felt his heart skip a beat. His son's name had not been spoken out loud for a long time. He grabbed the cup of ale from the tavern owner and drank it in one gulp. Thora took hers and drank from it before she stared at him. 'You really going to say that boy is not your grandson?'

'My son died a long time ago.'

Thora grimaced at the comment and took another sip of her ale. 'Your son died a few days ago, and he sent his son to you. Your grandson, Sven. Your own flesh and blood. And like you, he has no one left.'

'My son died a long time ago,' Sven repeated, feeling a small spark of anger in his stomach. 'He died when he took their faith and abandoned our gods.' He still remembered the day the trader he had paid to keep an eye out for his son had told him the news. That was the beginning of the end for him.

'No, Sven. He did what he had to to survive, especially after you abandoned him to live with the Christians.'

Her words stung more than any wound he had ever taken and Sven clenched his teeth as the spark turned to fire, but what Thora said next killed his anger.

'Would Eydis want you to abandon your grandson as well?'

Sven saw Eydis, his wife, in his mind, her eyes wide with shock as she held out a hand to him. 'Eydis would want to be alive.'

'Not if she saw what you had become.'

Thora's words stung again, but he knew they were true. Like her father, she was not afraid to say what needed to be said.

Sven took a deep breath and eyed the cup of ale in Thora's hand. 'Helping the boy will not bring her back, or my son.'

Thora handed him the rest of her ale. 'No, but perhaps the gods have given you a chance at redemption.'

He took the cup and drank deeply. 'The gods don't care about me, so why would they offer me redemption?'

'How can you say that? They brought your grandson to you.'

'He's not—'

'Say that one more time and I will punch you.' Thora stood up and grabbed the cup from Sven's hand and downed what was left of it. 'Now, you're going to help that boy, or I swear by the All-Father, I'll kill you myself.'

Sven stared at the empty cup, but only so he didn't have to look at Thora. He thought back to the storm five days ago; him lying on his back on the deck of the fishing boat, the lightning bolt coming towards him. But then it twisted away at the last moment and struck the mast. The mast had caught fire and so had the sail. The sailors panicked, but the captain was an experienced man. He had rushed to the mast and cut the ropes of the sail loose so the wind could take it away from them. The storm had been a message from the gods and as soon as it was delivered, the weather calmed, and the men were forced to row back to the shore. Sven did not know what the message was, but he now wondered if it had anything to do with the boy. He sighed as he stood up. 'Fine. Let's go find the boy and get out of here.'

'He's waiting outside.' Thora smiled when she saw him frown. 'I had a good idea of where he was going and he doesn't know these streets as well as I do.'

Sven shook his head as Thora turned and walked out of the tavern. He glanced at the empty cup and then the tavern owner before following her. Outside, Sven had to blink a few times until his eyes adjusted to the bright light. Thora and the two boys were waiting for him, the young boy looking at him before glancing at his feet and the thrall glaring at him. A few of the townspeople stopped and glanced at them as if expecting some confrontation, but Sven paid no attention to them.

'What's your name, boy?'

'Ch... Charles,' the boy responded while looking at his feet.

Sven grunted, disappointed his son had not given the boy a Danish name. He was about to say that when he saw something that made his blood go cold. He almost heard the gods laugh in the voices of the people as they walked past.

'Thora!' Thora's young warrior friend waved his arm in the air as he approached them with the two warriors who had attacked Sven at his side. Sven took a step back and paled when he saw the grins on their faces.

'We need to go.' He turned to walk away, but Thora and the boys only frowned at him.

'Why?' Thora asked. 'You know Sigge.'

He glanced over his shoulder at the two warriors. 'Aye, and I also know them.'

Thora looked at the three warriors, still frowning. 'Who? Amund and Egil?' Her eyes widened as she looked at Sven's bruised face again. 'They're the ones who attacked you?'

'What's going on?' Charles asked, the fear obvious in his voice. Sven wanted to be annoyed by it but had to stop his knees from trembling first.

'Nothing, but stay behind me, and whatever happens, don't run,' Thora responded as she placed herself between Sven and the approaching men. The boy said something to the thrall in Frankish, and the thrall glanced at the warriors before responding. Charles shook his head, and the thrall sighed, but grabbed the knife tucked into his belt. Sven wondered what he thought he would achieve with that.

Sigge, Thora's friend, raised an eyebrow when he saw the scowl on Thora's face.

'Well, if it isn't Thora the shield maiden,' Amund, the brown-eyed warrior, said, grinning viciously at her, before Sigge could say anything.

'Aye, but she's not been a shield maiden for a long time,' Egil, the other warrior, added. 'Not since poor old Steinar got skewered by a Frank's sword. Now, it seems, she looks after the poor.' He sneered at the boy and the thrall before turning his attention back to Sven, whose heart was racing. He glanced at one of the side streets and wondered if he could get away from them.

'What do you two idiots want?'

'Nothing.' Egil tilted his head as he stared at Sven. 'We just want to talk to the drunk.'

'And not just us. We hear there are a few who want to hang the fat man.'

'We don't have a tree strong enough for him.' Egil scratched his head as he thought about it. Sven glanced down the street again, but then he caught the fear in the eyes of the young boy, and his feet refused to move.

'No, that's true. I guess we'll just have to drown him.'

'Leave them be.' Sigge tried to intervene.

Amund turned to Sigge, the scowl on his face making him take a step back. He was younger and smaller than the two warriors and Sven knew he would never stand up to them. Satisfied that Sigge wouldn't stop them, the two warriors turned and sneered at Sven and Thora, one of them pressing his fist into the palm of his hand. The surrounding people saw what was happening and quickly disappeared into their houses or ran down the streets to get out of the way. One boy wanted to watch and complained as his mother dragged him away.

'You take one step towards Sven and I swear by Thor you will regret it,' Thora threatened the two warriors, her fists clenched at her side. Sven's mouth went dry as his eyes darted around, looking for an escape.

Young Charles glanced at the thrall, who had his hand on his knife, his face grim as he too understood what was about to happen.

'Guys?' Sigge tried again, but everyone ignored him. Charles yelped as Amund shot forward and swung his fist at Thora. She twisted out of the way and elbowed the man in the side of his head.

Sven took a step back, his heart racing in his chest, as the man's head snapped to the side.

Egil roared as he charged and tried to tackle Thora to the ground, but she moved out of the way and kicked him in the leg. As he fell to the ground, the other one grabbed Thora from behind. The young boy looked at Sven, his eyes imploring him to do something, but Sven could not. He just stood there, his hands shaking as he willed his old legs to take him away from danger. Thora did not need his help though, as she stamped down on Amund's foot and elbowed him in the side. Egil got to his feet and threw a punch at Thora who twisted out of the way and the man punched Amund in the face. As he stood there, stunned by what had just happened, Thora kicked him hard between the legs. Egil's eyes almost popped out of his head and as he dropped to his knees, Thora kneed him in the face, knocking him out. But she did not see Amund behind her recover and could do nothing as he punched her in the back of her head. Thora stumbled forward and turned in time to twist out of the way of the follow-up punch, but Sven saw she was disorientated. He struggled to breathe as he anticipated what might happen next.

Thora stayed on her feet though, shaking her head to regain her bearings while the brown-eyed warrior wiped the blood from his nose.

Sigge, who had stood frozen to the spot as the warriors attacked Thora, had had enough and tackled Amund to the ground before he could attack Thora again. He sat on top of the man and punched him in the face three times before Amund stopped moving. The young warrior stood up and shook his hand, his face grimacing.

'You killed him!' the tavern owner, who had come out of his tavern to see what the commotion was, shouted.

Sigge paled and shook his head. 'No, I didn't. I swear by Odin.'

Sven looked at the warrior on the ground. His face was bloody from Sigge punching him, and Sven could not see if he was breathing or not. Not that it mattered as the tavern owner sent a boy running towards the jarl's hall.

'I didn't kill him!' Sigge protested again, but the townspeople who saw the fight did not believe him.

'You did! We saw you!' a man shouted, waving his fist at Sigge. Sven felt the anger coming from the townspeople and trembled.

Thora grabbed Sigge by his tunic. 'Sigge, you need to leave, now!'

Sigge shook his head, his eyes wide. 'I'll go to my uncle Ketil. Tell him everything.' Sven raised his brows. He never knew the young warrior was Ketil's nephew.

Thora shook her head. 'Ketil can't protect you from murder. You know that.'

Sigge nodded as he stared at the body of Amund before he turned to Sven, his face creased. 'By Odin, you're nothing but bad luck!' Sven looked away, not wanting to face the young warrior's anger.

'Don't blame him.' Thora turned to the boys. 'Let's go, I need to go to my house and grab a few things. Sigge, get them out and wait for me by Frey's Stone.' Sigge nodded and Thora turned to the boy, who had been struggling to keep up with what they were saying. 'My friend will get you out of the city.'

The thrall, his tone urgent, said something to Charles, who nodded and turned to Thora. 'What about our horse and the rest of our things?'

'There's no time, we need to leave before more warriors turn up.'

'Or the people find their courage,' Sven commented, but Thora ignored him as she put her hand on the young boy's shoulder. 'Go with my friend and everything will be fine.'

'What about you?' Charles asked, unable to hide his fear. The townspeople were getting louder and increasingly confident as more people came out of their houses. Angry voices demanded that Sigge be captured and punished for killing one of the jarl's warriors. Someone threw a stone at the young warrior but missed as Sigge saw it and ducked.

'It's time to go,' Sven said, his coward's instinct telling him their time was up.

Thora nodded and then turned to the boy. 'I'll be with you soon.' She looked at Sven and at Sigge. 'Now go!' Before waiting for a response, she lifted her skirt and ran towards her house. Sigge turned to Sven, scowling at him before he led them out of the city.

'Do not let them get away!' the tavern owner shouted, but none of the townspeople seemed eager to chase after them.

Sven squeezed the leather pouch still in his hands, feeling the Mjöllnir which had belonged to him once as he heard Odin laughing in his ears.

11

'Are you sure that's your grandfather?' Gerold asked when they were a safe distance away from the town. No one dared to speak as the young warrior led them out of the town, constantly rushing them as if the devil were on their heels. Perhaps he was. It was the only way Charles could explain what had just happened.

Charles looked at the short, fat man limping ahead of them. It was hard to match that man with the fearful image he had conjured in his mind. The most feared Danish warrior who had terrorised the Franks and who ate Christian children. That's what he had been told. Charles almost expected flames to be burning in his eyes. The old man ahead of them, though, was nothing like that. He was... Charles frowned. He was a coward. Charles knew he was not one to call someone else that, but there was no other word he could think of as he stared at the man his father had thought would keep him safe. 'I don't know,' he said at last. 'I expected something different from what everyone had told me.' Charles glanced at Gerold. 'He didn't fight.'

'No,' Gerold agreed. 'He hid behind the woman.'

'He did. She fought like a man and beat those two men.' Charles frowned as he relived the fight in his mind. He had never seen a woman fight like that. He had never seen a woman fight. Women could not fight. That's what the priests always said. A woman's role was to serve her husband, not fight other men as if she was one.

'I know. These Danes disgust me. We should not trust them, especially not her.'

Charles raised his eyebrows at Gerold. 'Why? She helped us. She took us to my grandfather, and she protected us.'

Gerold shook his head, his face sour. 'She followed us to the church, and waited for us. She took you to a man she claims is your grandfather. Apart from being very short, he looks nothing like you. And she did not protect us. She protected that fat bastard.'

Charles frowned. 'But he has the same name as my grandfather.'

'She heard you say the name when you spoke to the old men. She said so herself.' Gerold scratched his head, his eyes fixed on the back of the old man's head. The old man glanced over his shoulder at them, but quickly turned away. 'Besides, he still has your pouch, and we found him in a tavern. What do you think he was going to do with that fancy cross?'

Charles stopped and felt the blood drain from his face as he patted his tunic and realised that Gerold was right. The old man had never given him the pouch back. 'I thought I still had it.'

'Well, despite what the old man said, he recognised the Mjöllnir when he took it out.' Gerold swatted an insect away that was hovering near his face.

'How do you know?'

'I saw it in his face. He recognised it.'

'Why didn't he say anything?' Charles struggled to make sense of everything. He didn't understand why adults kept lying to him or only told him half the truth.

'I don't know. But I wouldn't trust them.'

Charles frowned again. He thought about the woman and felt like he could trust her. More than that, he felt God had sent her to help him. That was the only reason he could think of for her being outside the church and him running into her. And after, she had known how to find him. Charles had tried to find his way back to the church again, but soon after he had run away from them, he heard her voice calling after him. When he stopped and turned around, she was standing there, hands out like an angel come to protect him. He was not convinced about the old man, but he was sure about her. Yet he also knew he should listen to Gerold. Even though he was a slave, Gerold had kept him safe so far. During the fight outside the tavern, Gerold had stood in front of him, protecting him from the two angry warriors, just like he had protected him from the bandits. Charles looked up and saw the birds flying above his head. He wished he could be like them. So carefree and so close to heaven.

They walked in silence after that, both Charles and Gerold lost in their thoughts, until they reached a place which stunned them both. It was on the edge of a field and not too far from the town. Stones had marked out a large circle, and on each stone were the same markings as on the Mjöllnir pendant in the pouch. Runes, Gerold had called them, but that was not what stopped them in their tracks. Charles crossed himself as Gerold said, 'Barbarians.'

Sigge, the young warrior, turned. 'Welcome to Frey's...' His cheeks reddened when he saw Charles's wide eyes.

'Frey's Cock,' the old man said, shaking his head as he walked to the large oblong stone in the middle of the circle. There, he untied his trousers and pissed against the boulder. A raven landed on top of the stone and screamed at the old man before it flew away.

'What are you...?' Sigge's face paled as he put his hands on his head. 'Are you trying to anger the gods? We have enough trouble to deal with as it is.'

The old man finished and tied his trousers up again. 'The gods stopped caring about me a long time ago, lad. And they don't care about you either.' He hawked and spat at the stone before he found a spot to sit.

Charles studied the old man, while Gerold stared open-mouthed at the stone, his dull eyes reminding Charles of his father's. He then looked back at the stone and frowned. 'Why does it look like a...' Charles struggled to find the correct word. He wondered what Bishop Bernard would say about this.

'A cock,' the old man said, glancing at the stone. 'Because Frey thinks too much of himself.'

'Who's Frey?' Charles scratched his head as he glanced at Gerold, who had turned his back on the stone as if he was refusing to look at it.

'Frey is one of the Vanir and he does not think too much of himself.' Sigge scowled at the old man. 'He makes the lands and animals fertile so that we have plenty of food.'

'Not just the animals,' the old man added.

Charles frowned at the old man, not sure what he meant by that. 'So, he's like a spirit.'

Sigge shook his head. 'No, not a spirit.' He glanced at the stone, like a child hoping he wasn't heard saying something wrong. 'Frey is a god and a very important one. Without Frey's blessing, our crops would not grow, our animals would not have any young. We would starve.'

'Don't forget about the women,' the old man said, and Sigge scowled at him.

Charles looked around, seeing the many farms in the distance. A few houses built next to each other, the houses longer than those in Francia, and surrounded by fields where men and women were working. Cows and sheep roamed around, watched by one or two men, or perhaps boys. It was hard for Charles to tell from this distance, but in Francia it was usually the sons who were sent out to watch the livestock. 'How does the stone help the farmers?'

Sigge glanced at Hedeby in the distance, nervously rubbing his hands together before he responded. 'Every spring, the people gather around the stone, all of them bringing offerings to Frey. The jarl sacrifices a boar—'

'Or a thrall,' the old man interrupted, and Charles's mouth fell open.

'The jarl sacrifices a boar and asks Frey for his blessing.'

'And Frey answers?' Charles asked the young warrior.

'In a way.' Sigge scratched his short beard. 'If we have good crops and plenty of calves, then yes.'

'But then you have to wait until the end of summer to find out?'

Sigge nodded, not knowing how to respond.

'So, how do you know he's real?' Charles looked at the young warrior and saw him frown as he scratched his beard again.

'Does your god answer when you pray to him?' the old man asked, which surprised Charles.

'He...'

'So, how do you know he is real?'

'Thora!' Sigge shouted, and Charles was saved from having to answer the question. But he saw the spark in the old man's otherwise dull eyes and wondered about that.

'What is she wearing?' Gerold asked, his voice stunned. Charles turned and saw Thora rushing towards them with a small sack in her hand, and his mouth fell open again. When they had left her by the tavern, she was wearing a dress. It was different from the ones women wore in Francia, but it was a dress. Now she wore loose-fitting trousers, similar to the ones Sigge was wearing, and leather boots. She also had a leather jerkin, like the ones Charles had seen some warriors in Hügelburg wear – though hers was smaller, as if it was made for her. What stunned him more, though, was the sword on her hip. The only thing that was still the same was her hair, with its thick braid. 'Even the women are barbarians,' Gerold hissed.

'She looks like a warrior.' Charles thought about how she had fought those two men before. 'Women can't be warriors, can they?' he asked Gerold.

'Of course not. God forbids it, but what else can you expect from these godless people?' He looked at Charles, his eyes filled with venom. 'Remember, you can't trust them.'

Charles thought about it. He hadn't read the whole Bible, and the priests had said nothing about women as warriors, but Gerold was right. If God wanted women to be warriors, then they would be big and strong, like men.

'We need to leave now,' Thora said as she reached them. 'Egil came to and was talking to some of the jarl's captains.' She looked at Sigge. 'The jarl will send men after us before the sun goes down.'

'I didn't mean to kill him,' Sigge said, a pained expression on his face.

Thora looked at him. 'That doesn't matter, Sigge. You killed the bastard and the jarl will want to hang you for it.'

'By the gods!' Sigge turned to the old man, his fists clenched. 'This is all your fault, you drunk bastard. Now my life is ruined. Gods, I should have just let them kill you.'

'Sigge!' Thora grabbed the young warrior by his tunic and stared into his eyes. 'You can't blame Sven. You know as well as I do the Norns choose our fate and this is what they chose for us.'

The old man hawked and spat and then shook his head, while Sigge just dropped his. Charles watched, his eyes wide at how unconcerned Thora was, and then he wondered who the Norns were and how they chose their fates.

'There's no point in arguing now. We need to get away from here.' Thora looked back towards the large town. Charles followed her gaze and saw the countless birds flying above the wall and the smoke from the many houses filling the air like an enormous cloud.

'But where do we go?' Sigge asked.

Thora looked at the old man and then at the large stone. She frowned as she bit her lip. 'North, to Ribe. It's a three- or four-day walk from here. I still have kin there, they might help us and then there is...' She hesitated and looked at the old man again. 'Jarl Bjarni.'

'No,' the old man said, crossing his arms.

'Frigg knows I don't like it either, but there's nowhere else we can go,' Thora said.

'Who is Jarl Bjarni?' Sigge frowned at the old man.

Thora sighed. 'He is Sven's brother, and the one who took Ribe from him.'

Sigge laughed. 'So you don't want to face the brother who humiliated you.'

'Sigge!' Thora scowled.

'No, he's right.' Sven took a deep breath and got to his feet. 'I don't want my brother to see me like this. He thinks I'm dead. It's better it stays that way.'

Charles scratched his head as he struggled to make sense of everything and looked at Gerold, who shook his head.

'We should leave them, go back to Francia.'

The thought made Charles's heart skip a beat. 'I can't go back to Francia.' He rubbed his arm.

'Why not? We don't belong with these people, if you can even call them that.'

'What's he saying?' Thora asked, scowling at Gerold.

Charles was about to respond when he saw Gerold shaking his head, so he kept quiet.

Thora walked towards him and crouched down. 'Look, I know you don't trust us, and you have no reason to. But the gods brought you here, to your grandfather. Your father wanted you to find him. Whatever danger you are in, we will keep you safe, but you have to come with us.'

Charles hesitated and then said, 'Or perhaps God brought me here.'

Thora smiled. 'Perhaps he did.' She looked at the old man. 'Sven, give the boy his pouch back.' The old man looked confused for a heartbeat and then nodded. He took the pouch from his tunic and handed it to Charles, who grimaced at how warm and wet it felt. Thora smiled and then glanced at Gerold. 'And you can tell your friend to stop pretending. I know he can speak our tongue.'

Charles raised his eyebrows and looked at Gerold, who looked just as shocked.

'How did you know?' Gerold asked in Danish, although he had a bad accent.

Thora straightened up and smiled. 'It was obvious that you were following our conversations. You hid it well, but sometimes your reaction gave you away.'

Gerold smiled, but not a friendly smile. 'You're smart for a woman.'

'She is Thora the shield maiden and a great warrior.' Sigge stepped forward. 'You should show her some respect.'

'She's a woman.' Gerold clenched his fists.

'And you're a thrall,' Thora said, smiling at him. 'Who is more important to your god?' Gerold's eyes widened, and it was obvious he did not know how to respond. Thora turned back to Charles. 'You can go back to Francia, I guess that's what he was telling you, but I'm also guessing if your father told you to come to Denmark, then you are not safe there.'

Charles still hesitated and then thought about his father and his last message to him. *Find your grandfather. He will keep you safe.* He chewed on his lower lip as he looked at the short, fat man, seeing how he swayed on the spot. Charles did not feel like the old man could keep him safe, but he believed Thora could, despite what Gerold had said about her. So he nodded.

'Good, you're smart, just like your father.'

'You knew my father?'

'Aye, a long time ago, before...' she glanced at the old man, who turned away, 'he was taken.'

Charles looked at the old man and saw how he avoided eye contact. It was something his father never spoke about, and he wondered if his grandfather would tell him more about it. He glanced at the pouch in his hands, feeling the weight of the cross and the Mjöllnir. Two symbols of different fates together in the pouch, just like the five of them. 'We go north?'

Thora nodded. 'I think it's our best option.'

'Charles!' Gerold hissed, in Frankish. 'We shouldn't.'

Charles looked at him and shrugged. 'You go back to Francia if you want to, but I can't. I don't know who to trust there.'

'And you can trust these heathens?'

'Why do you care so much about what I do?' Charles scowled at Gerold, who seemed taken aback by the question.

Gerold looked away, his eyebrows drawn together as he wrestled with some thought before he looked at Charles again. 'You... you remind me of my brother.'

Charles raised his eyebrows. 'You have a brother?'

'I did.' Gerold sighed. 'He died before my father sold me. I couldn't protect him and... I guess I thought that if I can keep you safe, then perhaps I can make up for it.'

Charles looked at the Danes as he thought about what Gerold had just said. The old man was standing there, gazing at his own feet, while Thora watched him, her eyes patient and kind. Sigge was staring at the town, grimacing as he shook his head. 'God brought us here for a reason. He sent her to us for a reason. I think we can trust them.'

Gerold sighed and gripped the knife in his belt. 'I'll stay with you.' He glanced at the old drunk. 'But I guess I can forget about being paid for this.'

Charles's cheeks reddened as he remembered what he had told Gerold to convince him to help him. But he had not known that his grandfather was like this. He looked at Thora and in the Danish tongue said, 'We're ready.'

Thora smiled and then glanced at Gerold while raising an eyebrow at his hand on the hilt of his knife, before she turned. 'Let's go. We need to put as much ground as possible between us and Hedeby before nightfall.'

'Have we got any ale?' the old man asked, eyeing the sack Thora was holding.

Thora shook her head as she walked on. 'Only bread and cheese, Sven. There'll be no ale for a while.'

The old man sighed. 'The gods have cursed me yet again.'

Birds flew above them and insects around them, while small animals disappeared in the distance as they walked in silence. A dog was barking from one of the distant farmsteads as Charles looked at Thora walking ahead of them, dressed like a man. She had taken them off the main road and into the forest. The route would be more challenging, but it would keep them out of sight of those who would be hunting them soon, she had said. Somehow Thora had become the leader of their group, something the young Charles struggled to understand. Sigge, the younger warrior, was walking beside her, but he wore no armour and only an axe for a weapon. He kept glancing behind them, as if expecting someone to attack them from behind. It made Charles more nervous and caused him to glance over his shoulder as well. But all he saw was his grandfather staring at him, his face a grimace as he struggled to keep up with the pace that Thora had set. Charles's stomach rumbled, reminding him that he had not eaten all day. The realisation made him feel weak and he hoped they would stop soon.

'Why didn't you tell me you could speak the Danish tongue?' Charles asked Gerold to distract himself from his hunger.

Gerold shrugged. 'Didn't seem important. And besides, you speak it better than me so it made more sense to let you do the talking.'

Charles thought about that and decided that made sense. Then he glanced over his shoulder again. 'Do you think those men are chasing us?'

'They're not after us. They are after the old man and those two.' He pointed to Thora and Sigge ahead of them. 'If they catch us, then we just tell them they tricked us and they'll spare us.'

'You really think that will save you?' the old man asked in the Danish tongue from behind them. Both Gerold and Charles looked over their shoulders, surprised he had understood them. 'Those men are cruel bastards. Their jarl encourages them to be. They might not kill the boy, but you,' he looked at Gerold, 'they'll kill slowly so that your screams have time to reach the gods before you die.'

Gerold stopped and turned on the old man, his hand on the hilt of his knife. 'You better watch it, old man. I don't care if Charles thinks you're his grandfather.'

The old man looked at the slave, and Charles thought he saw his eyes harden before he looked away.

'I thought so. You're nothing but a coward.'

'Is there a problem?' Thora asked, and they all turned to see her standing there, glaring at them.

'No problem,' Gerold responded and then glanced at the old man, who shook his head.

'Good, we need to keep moving.'

'I'm hungry and tired. Can't we rest?' Charles asked. His legs felt weak, and he was struggling to stand straight.

'I wouldn't mind a rest as well. My old legs aren't used to this any more.'

'But you walk around all the time?' Thora said with a raised eyebrow.

'Aye, but I walk slow, rest often, and usually have some ale to drink.' He patted his side. 'We don't even have water.'

Charles realised his grandfather was right, but then Sigge smiled.

'There's a small stream not far from here. We can get water and perhaps rest there for the night.'

Thora looked at the darkening sky, frowning as she worked out how much daylight they had left. 'Fine, we'll head to the stream, and get some water, but we won't stay the night there.'

'Why?' Charles asked.

'Because if someone is hunting us, they'll just follow that and find us,' the old man said. Thora nodded to confirm and then turned to Sigge.

'Lead the way.'

Sigge gave one more glance in Hedeby's direction, before he led the way. Charles couldn't help himself and again looked behind them to see what the young warrior was looking at.

'Stop doing that,' Gerold said.

'But why does he keep doing that?'

Gerold shrugged. 'Because he's scared.'

'Scared?' Charles scratched his head. 'I thought the Danes knew no fear.'

'All men know fear. Doesn't matter where they come from or what gods they believe in,' the old man said as he walked past them. Charles looked at Gerold, who shrugged before they followed as thunder sounded in the distance.

12

It didn't take them long to reach the stream. Charles tried to distract himself by looking at the forest, something he had not really done before. The trees looked much like the trees in Francia and he even recognised the birds, their songs the same as the ones he would listen to back home. Deer tracks led to the stream and then away again, a single set which meant a stag. That was one of the few things he remembered from when his father took him hunting. Charles felt the heaviness in his chest and lowered his head as he thought of his father. He still struggled to understand why his father had to die and for the first time in his life, Charles found himself questioning God. The thought sent a shiver down his spine, which was not helped by a bird crying out from above him. Charles looked up, startled, and saw the large raven sitting on the branch above him, staring at him with its black, beady eyes.

'Odin's watching you.' Sigge rubbed the Mjöllnir around his neck.

Charles glanced at Gerold, who was scowling at the raven which was the size of a small dog. 'Is that a good thing?'

'No,' the old man said. 'When Odin has his eye on you, then you are about to be shat on.'

Sigge shook his head as the raven cried out again. 'That's not true. It means Odin has blessed you.'

Charles looked at the large bird again. He had heard of Odin, that was the only Norse god he knew of, but he knew very little about him.

'It's a sign of the devil,' Gerold said, and Charles frowned at him as he remembered something a priest had said about ravens.

'God used ravens to feed Elijah when he was a fugitive, so they can't be that bad.'

'Well, that raven belongs to Odin, so he won't be bringing any food or ale,' the old man said, glowering at the bird which screamed at him before it flew away.

'I wish you'd stop doing that.' Sigge rubbed the Mjöllnir around his neck as he watched the raven fly away.

'Doing what?'

'Upsetting the ravens. No good can come from it.'

The old man shrugged and walked away from them. Charles watched him when Gerold said, 'The Bible also says ravens are unclean.'

Charles looked at the dark-haired boy, realised how he almost looked like a raven and remembered the priests saying the same thing as well.

They filled up the only water flask they had, the one Thora had thought to bring with her. Charles copied Gerold and cupped some water from the brook into his hands and sipped from it. The water was chilly and Charles felt slightly more refreshed after he drank a few mouthfuls, but he still did not want to carry on walking. His feet ached and his legs were numb. And the brief respite also reminded him of how tired he was, as his eyelids suddenly felt heavy. The old man rinsed his face downstream from them and took a few mouthfuls of water before he sat down and smacked his lips.

'It's not ale, but it'll do for now.'

Thora frowned at him. 'Don't get too comfortable. We need to find a place to rest tonight, away from any brooks and paths.'

'Too late.' The old man lay down on his back, but before he could sleep, Thora walked up to him and kicked him in the side.

'Get up, Sven. The sun will set soon. You know more than most the need to hide.'

Sven opened his eyes and frowned before saying, 'Fine.' He struggled to his feet and Charles was glad to see him swaying less. Maybe a few days off the ale and the man his father had remembered might return. But then he wondered what had happened for that man to turn into this drunk.

'Perhaps the old man should stay here and clean himself up.' Sigge waved a hand in front of his grimacing face. 'Anyone chasing would just need to follow his stink to find us.'

Sven scowled at the young warrior as Thora responded, 'Better chance of Thor letting us use his chariot than Sven deciding to bathe himself.' She turned and walked off before Sven could say anything.

Charles rushed after her, forcing his tiredness and hunger out of his mind.

'What happened to him? My father told me he was a powerful leader and... the bishop said that many people feared him.' He glanced at Sven over his shoulder.

'Aye, Odin knows it's hard when reputation doesn't match what you see.'

Charles frowned and Thora smiled before she sighed.

'After Sven was forced to give up your father, the gods turned against him, and many others as well.'

'What do you mean? God would never abandon his flock.'

Thora smiled. 'Your god, perhaps not. Our gods are fickle. Their moods change like the weather. One moment they're behind you and you are unbeatable, the next they turn against you and nothing works out.'

'But why? Are your gods not there to protect you and guide you?'

She shook her head. 'No, our gods only do things that amuse themselves. If it's in their interest to help you, they will. If it is more entertaining to drown your men in a sea storm and leave you as the sole survivor, then that's what they do.'

Charles glanced over his shoulder again, seeing how Gerold watched him, his face unreadable. 'Is that what happened to him?'

Thora sighed again and rubbed the Mjöllnir around her neck. 'It's not my story to tell, but after he returned from that raid in Francia twenty winters ago, Sven tried to raise more men to return to Francia and get your father back. Many refused, and Sven spent most of his gold to pay for mercenaries. But that raid failed.'

Charles stopped in his tracks and scratched his head. 'He tried to get my father back?'

'Aye.' Thora looked at him but kept on walking. 'He swore an oath to your father that he would rescue him.'

Charles caught up with Thora again. 'He was beaten again on the second raid?'

She shook her head. 'He never made it to Francia. A storm struck, and he lost most of his men and ships.'

Charles thought about that and felt sorry for the old man. He also wondered if his father had known about this. 'Is that why he is like this?'

Thora smiled a sad smile. 'No, there's much more to his story. When he made it home, he found no one would go with him, not even mercenaries. They said he was cursed, that he had angered the gods. Although Sven always believed it was people against him, not the gods. Not yet.'

'What do you mean?'

'I don't really know, but Sven always said that the gods had nothing to do with it. But he bided his time, tried to raise more money and men and then...' she glanced at Charles and he struggled to make sense of the look in her eyes, 'the news came that your father became a Christian.'

Charles smiled. He believed that was good news, but then frowned when he saw Thora shaking her head again.

'It almost broke him and your grandmother. Sven started drinking more, became more withdrawn and then one night, something happened that did break him.' She glanced over her shoulder at old Sven limping behind them, his eyes vacant as he stared at his feet.

'What happened?' Charles's eyes were wide.

Thora shook her head. 'That is a story only he can tell.'

Charles lowered his head and then remembered something. 'You knew my father?'

Thora smiled a sad smile. 'Aye, we grew up together, although he was a few winters older than me. My father was one of Sven's hirdmen, so we spent a lot of time together.'

'What was he like?'

'Small, shy. The other boys always made fun of him because of his height, but Torkel was too...' She struggled to find the right word, but Charles thought he knew. It sounded a lot like him.

'Weak?'

'No, your father was never weak. He took his beatings and even fought back. Sven was a harsh father and would not accept his son running away from a fight. "You must always fight back, harder and faster than them."' She imitated Sven's voice. 'Your father was brave and smart, much like you, I suspect.'

Charles remembered his father saying the same words to him, and he glanced at Sven, struggling to match those words to the man he saw. 'I'm not brave. Not like my father was. When boys tried to fight me, I would run away and hide in the church. I could never fight, not like he could.'

'Your father was a good warrior?'

Charles nodded, forcing the image of the last time he had seen his father from his mind.

'You should tell Sven that. It'll make him happy.'

'You think he cares? He acts as if my father never existed.'

Thora sighed. 'He cares, although he won't admit to it. It hurt him more than you could imagine when your father rejected our gods.'

'But God is good. He guided my father and made him a brave warrior.'

Thora smiled. 'And I'm sure he will do the same for you.'

'No, I'm no warrior. I always felt more comfortable in the church, praying and listening to the priests.' He fell silent, remembering the conversation between the bishop and the duke. 'Or at least I did. Now I'm not so sure.'

Thora put a hand on his shoulder, which surprised him. 'We like to believe that our fate is not in our hands, that the gods and the Norns decide what becomes of us. I don't know what they have in store for you, but your story is far from finished. And I think you will learn much about yourself that you didn't know before.'

Charles smiled at Thora, finding a strange comfort in her words, although he felt Gerold's glare on the back of his head and remembered his warning.

Thora stopped and looked around. 'I think we can rest here for the night. Sigge, will you get a fire going?'

The old man just dropped to the ground. 'Thank the gods. Thought my feet were going to fall off.' And before anyone could respond, he closed his eyes and started snoring. Sigge shook his head and used his axe to chop some branches from the trees.

Gerold sat down by a tree and Charles caught him glancing his way as if summoning him. But Charles did not want to go to the morose boy. He was enjoying his conversation with Thora and there was so much he wanted to ask her.

Sigge got the fire going, rubbing his hands as he smiled at himself, but then he looked around and frowned. 'We need some food.' He looked at Thora, who opened the sack she had been carrying.

'I only had time to grab some bread and cheese.' She took a loaf of bread out of the sack and broke a piece off which she handed to Charles. Charles felt his stomach rumbling and devoured the bread, almost biting his fingers in his haste. 'Tomorrow we'll have to hunt for some meat,' Thora said, smiling at Charles. She offered some bread to Gerold, who after hesitating for a heartbeat took it and nodded his thanks to her.

'Gerold can hunt, he's really good at it,' Charles said without thinking, and lowered his head when he saw the dark-haired boy glaring at him while chewing on the bread.

'I don't have my bow. We left it in the barn with the rest of our stuff, remember?'

'Oh,' Charles said, glancing at Gerold and then away.

Gerold glanced at the bread in his hand and then sighed. 'I could set some traps in the morning. Maybe we'll get lucky.'

Thora thanked Gerold before handing Sigge some bread and cheese. She looked at the old man, but he seemed to be sleeping, so she shrugged and ate some cheese.

'He doesn't have any friends?' Charles asked, thinking of his own life in Francia.

Thora shook her head. 'He's never been an easy man to like. But my father remained his friend, even after we were forced to flee Ribe.'

'Why did you have to flee?' Charles raised an eyebrow.

'My father did not agree with what had happened to Sven and rejected Sven's younger brother, Bjarni, as the new jarl. Made him very unpopular, so we had to leave.'

'Where are your parents now?'

'My mother died many winters ago, my father not so long ago.' Thora bit her lower lip and then shook her head. 'Anyway, enough about me. I want to hear about your father. Tell me about his life in Francia.' She sat down near the fire and patted the ground next to her, inviting Charles to join her.

He sat down and, after a deep breath, told Thora what little he knew about his father. Charles told her about Bishop Bernard baptising him, and he was sure Sven's snoring briefly stopped there, but it quickly continued. He spoke of how his father became one of King Louis's personal guards and how after the civil war in Francia he had left the king's service and moved to Hügelburg, although Charles never knew why. Thora listened and didn't ask any questions, which he was glad about, because he knew little about that part of his father's life, only what the bishop had told him.

'Sounds like your father was a brave warrior.' Thora smiled as she stared into the fire.

'He was one of the best, that's what the bishop always said.'

'Tell me about his death,' Sven said, surprising Charles.

'Sven, that's not a good idea. The boy has been through enough.'

'No, it's fine,' Charles said, glad that Sven had asked. It meant that the old man did care. Charles told them of the night his father had died. He had to stop a few times to fight the tears and even shivered at the image of Lothar standing there with the flames behind him as if he had come from hell to take his father. Sigge moved closer, as if he too wanted to hear what Charles had to say, while Gerold made himself comfortable and seemed to fall asleep.

Sven smiled when he told them of his father's last stand. 'His mother always said that the boy was braver than Thor.' Sven cuffed a tear away, which surprised Charles. 'Why did they kill him?'

'I don't know.' Charles lowered his head. 'But I think it was my fault.'

Sven scowled. 'How?'

Charles did not want to answer, and then Thora placed a comforting hand on his shoulder. 'You can tell us.'

He took a deep breath and told them about the fight he had had with the group of boys earlier that day. 'Drogo is Lothar's son. I humiliated him and so he killed my father, but...'

'But what?' Thora asked as he trailed off.

'But I don't understand what the bishop and the duke had to do with it. They were his friends, or so I thought.'

There was silence for a short while as they all thought about what he had said before Sven spoke. 'Your father did not die because of you.'

'But I hurt Lothar's son.'

Sven smiled. 'Many boys hurt your father when he was a child. He was smaller and the son of the jarl. Many wanted to fight him. By Loki, I even told some boys to do it.' He laughed and then lowered his head when he saw Thora glare at him. 'But I never killed anyone because they hurt my boy. This Lothar will be the same. He was a warrior. He'd want his son to be strong and deal with his own problems. But this bishop and the duke, they might have something to do with it.'

Charles nodded and then looked at Sven. 'Why did you give my father away?'

Sven opened his mouth to respond, but then his face darkened and he turned around, not wanting to face them any more.

Charles frowned at Thora, not sure what had happened.

'It's a difficult story for him to tell. Give him some time and perhaps one day he will tell you.'

Charles looked at the old man as he lay down on his side and pretended to sleep and then thought of something else. 'Where's my grandmother?'

Thora looked at the flames as they danced away, her eyes misting over. 'That's another difficult tale only Sven can tell you.'

'Seems he has many difficult tales,' Sigge said, glancing at old Sven.

'Aye,' Thora agreed. 'There's a reason Sven believes that Odin betrayed him.'

* * *

Bishop Bernard sighed as he walked into the dark library of Duke Liudolf. They had been back in Ehresburg, the duke's capital, for two days, and so far the old bishop had barely had a moment's peace. It had taken them a few days to clean up the mess left behind by Lothar's foolishness, although neither the bishop nor the duke had any idea of why Lothar had decided to attack Torkel. They had tried to find this messenger they'd been told about, but the man was nowhere to be found, and neither was the warrior who had told Lothar of the messenger. After appointing a new chatelain, they had returned to Ehresburg, but there were still too many questions to answer. The most important of which was the whereabouts of Torkel's son, Charles. The bishop sighed again. He liked the boy and wished that his fate could be different.

Duke Liudolf looked up from the letter he was reading. 'Bishop?'

Bishop Bernard took a moment to compose his thoughts as he stared at the many bookshelves that lined the walls of the library, filled with more books than they had in his church in Paderborn, not far from Ehresburg – and with more weapons, he mused as he looked at the swords and axes which hung from the walls. The bishop finally turned his attention to the stern brown eyes of the duke. 'Any news?'

Duke Liudolf leaned back on his chair and put the letter he had been reading down on the desk. 'The boy is in Denmark.'

'Denmark?' The bishop raised an eyebrow. 'What would Charles be doing in Denmark?'

'We both know why, bishop. His grandfather.' The duke frowned as he stared at the letter again. Bishop Bernard wondered what else it said.

'Surely not. I've told the boy enough stories to make him fear that heathen. Why would he go to him?'

The duke shrugged his wide shoulders. 'Torkel must have told him to. That is the only thing I can think of.'

Bishop Bernard scratched his wrinkled cheek. 'This is not good. King Charles wants the boy. It's important that we find him and the cross, and soon.'

The duke picked up the letter again and read it. The bishop wondered how many times he had done that already. 'You don't need to remind me, bishop. I know what's at stake here.' He stared at the bishop, his face suddenly hard. 'I sent my best hunters out this morning. God willing they will find him and the cross before they are both out of our reach.'

The bishop crossed himself. He knew the hunters the duke was talking about. They were assassins who could hunt down any person in any kingdom and the bishop disliked them immensely. The devil's spawn was how he thought of them, but there were few men in Francia better than them at tracking a nine-year-old boy in Denmark. 'I pray they do,' the bishop said. 'For our sake and the kingdom's.'

13

Sven sat up and rubbed his left leg. The old wound he had taken many winters ago hurt more than usual, most likely from the long walk the previous day. The sun was still low in the cloudy sky, so the clearing they were in was mostly in the shade of the trees. Sven shivered as he felt the cold of the morning through his thin tunic, even though it was still midsummer. The forest was slowly waking up around him and he could hear the birds greeting the new day with their songs. A squirrel ran up a tree near him, too busy to pay any attention to them. Everyone else was still sleeping, apart from the thrall, who was lying near the boy, glaring at Sven. Sven looked away, not wanting to see those venomous eyes. Sven shook his head before looking around for some ale. His shoulders sagged when he remembered there was none. All they had was water, and he did not like drinking that stuff. It cleared his mind, which meant his memories became more vivid.

After struggling to his feet and grimacing at his stiff joints and aching back, he limped to the trees to have a piss. When he had finished, he turned and found Gerold standing there, his hand on the hilt of his knife. Sven looked at his feet to avoid seeing the anger in his eyes.

'Are you really his grandfather?'

Sven lifted his head, but kept his gaze down. 'So the boy says.'

'And what do you say?'

Sven briefly glanced up and saw Gerold's raised eyebrows. He shrugged. 'I guess I am.'

Gerold took a step closer, his hand still on his knife. 'Well, God knows, I don't really care. The only thing I care about is keeping him alive, so if you try anything, I'll gut you like the spineless worm you are. Do you understand me?' His strong accent made the threat sound more menacing.

Sven nodded and released the breath he had been holding when the thrall left. There was a time when Sven would have strangled a thrall with his own bare hands for speaking to him like that. But that Sven was no more, and he did not think he had the strength to kill again. A raven screamed from somewhere and, without looking up, Sven said, 'Fuck you.' He wasn't sure if it was at the bird or the All-Father, but he didn't care as he walked back to the camp. He guessed his grandson was lucky to have a friend who cared for him so much. The gods knew he could not. Not after that night. The image of his wife, staring at him, her eyes wide and the knife in her stomach, the blood staining her nightdress. Sven shook his head. 'Why is there no fucking ale?'

Everyone was awake when he walked back into the clearing. His grandson was talking to the thrall, who gave him a quick glance. Sigge was staring at Thora while she rubbed her eyes.

'Not much for breakfast.' She fished out a loaf of bread from the sack and broke it into portions for everyone.

'I'm not hungry,' Sven lied as she offered a piece. He sat down and rubbed his leg. Out of the corner of his eye, he saw the boy staring at him and Sven closed his eyes so he could ignore the boy, but he didn't get to sit for long.

'We need to go. If the gods smile on us, then we might reach Ribe by tomorrow.' Thora got up when everyone had finished their breakfasts, and sheathed her sword. Sigge got to his feet and stretched his back before he stamped on the embers of last night's fire and tucked his axe into his belt.

Sven sighed and looked around the small clearing before he got up and followed Thora and the others. He knew they would not reach Ribe so soon. He could not walk that fast and neither could the boy, but he kept quiet. Thora was their best chance of surviving anything that might come their way, and he did not want to anger her.

They walked in silence for a short while. Sven struggled to keep pace with everyone and was already sweating, even though the sun had barely moved. He shook his head, wishing Thora would slow down, but knew they had to keep the pace to avoid being caught by the men chasing them. Jarl Torgeir of Hedeby was not a forgiving man and did not tolerate anything that made him look weak. And killing one of his men in the streets of his town made him look weak. Sven glanced over his shoulder as he felt the hairs on the back of his neck stand on end.

'Why do you have so many gods?' the red-headed boy asked eventually. Sven noticed how the thrall ground his teeth at Charles's interest in the gods. Perhaps he feared Charles would abandon their god and follow *false idols*.

'Because we do,' Thora responded with a smile. 'And they all have their own roles.'

'Like what?'

'Well, Thor protects us from the giants and Loki's misdeeds. The Vanir provide us with food and children and Odin gave us runes and magic.'

'Exactly,' Sigge added. 'One god could not do it all.'

'Why not? God does.'

'What? Your god controls the weather, the seas, the lands and the animals. All of that?'

'Yes.' Charles puffed his chest out. 'God is Almighty. He made everything we see, including us.'

'No,' Sigge said. 'Odin and his brother did. They built Midgard with the corpse of Ymir. And they created men and women.' He shook his head. 'It's impossible for one god to do everything.'

'No, it isn't.'

Sven could see that Charles was trying to stay calm, but the boy was not used to people questioning his fate.

'So, your god defends you from the giants as well?' Sigge pointed to the sky.

'Giants aren't real,' Gerold said.

'Yes, they are! What do you think those mountains in the distance are?'

They could not see any mountains, but Sven decided not to point that out.

'Enough, Sigge,' Thora said, shaking her head. 'We're not here to fight over who is right or wrong.'

'There's no point. We are right,' Gerold said, which earned him a glare from Thora.

'What do the mountains have to do with giants? And who's Ymir?' Charles asked, not ready to give up on the conversation. Sven couldn't help but smile as Thora sighed.

'I'll tell you another time.'

Charles opened his mouth to respond, but then Gerold said something to him in Frankish. Charles nodded, and they walked in silence, listening to the birds singing above their heads.

A short while later, though, Sven felt the hair rise on his neck. He stopped and tilted his head. Thora did same as her hand went to her sword. Sigge stopped and looked at Thora, his brow furrowed.

'What?' the young warrior asked.

'Quiet,' Thora whispered, her face hard as she scanned the trees.

'What's going on?' Charles asked, and Sven noticed how the thrall put a hand on his shoulder and slowly pulled him away from the rest of the group.

'The birds, they're quiet.' Thora looked at Sven, but he just stood there, not sure what she expected him to do.

'Perhaps an animal? A wolf or a bear?' Sigge suggested, but Thora shook her head and crept forward. Sigge had no armour and only his axe, which he took from his belt and held in his hand as he followed Thora. The boy and the thrall glanced at each other before following as well. Sven stood where he was, his eyes darting between the trees, trying to spot the danger the tingling sensation in his stomach was warning him about. He might not have picked up a weapon for a long time, but his warrior's instincts had never left him. Although, these days, he used them to avoid fights. In the distance he heard a woodpecker, its constant hammering at the tree almost causing him to miss the low whistle. He glanced behind him, wondering if he could outrun the danger they faced, but then he sighed. He could never outrun anyone, and he had a better chance of surviving if he stayed with Thora. She was a great warrior, even if, like him, she refused to fight for her own reasons. So he followed the group, trying to move as quietly as his bulky frame allowed him to. But they did not get very far.

'Well, well, it seems Odin is with us today.' The cruel voice came from the trees.

'Shit.' Thora stepped in front of the young boy, her sword in her hand. The thrall glanced at her, but took his knife from his belt and stood beside her, both determined to protect Charles.

'Amund! You're alive!' Sigge, his eyes wide, lowered his axe as the brown-eyed warrior stepped out of the trees. His lip was busted and his face heavily bruised as he sneered at them. Egil stepped out from behind another tree, his face also bruised with a cut to his cheek. Sven almost enjoyed seeing them like that, considering how bruised his own face was because of them. But then he shook his head as six more men stepped out from the trees. Sven's hands trembled when he realised they had been waiting for them.

'You're in a lot of trouble, Sigge,' Amund said. 'Jarl Torgeir was very upset that you broke your oath to him.'

'I did not.' Sigge's face paled. To be an oath breaker was one of the worst things a man could be called.

'I don't know,' Egil said. 'First you attack us to defend this bitch,' he pointed his sword at Thora, 'and a worthless drunk. And then you run.' He grinned a vicious grin. 'Looks like an oath breaker to me.' The other men all grunted their agreement as Sigge stared at all of them, his eyes wide and mouth open.

'But... but I thought I killed you. I panicked,' he said.

'You're too weak to kill me,' Amund growled through clenched teeth.

'Why don't you boys just go back to Hedeby, tell the jarl you could not find us,' Thora said, her face grim. 'No one needs to get hurt.'

Amund laughed and then looked at his friend. 'She thinks she can hurt us, Egil.'

Egil rubbed the bruise on his cheek. 'Barely touched us.'

Thora glanced around, her brow creased, and Sven saw there was no way out for them. The eight warriors who surrounded them were all armed and wore *brynjas*. The only thing missing was their helmets, but then, they didn't really need them. 'I barely touched you, yet I left both of you on the ground,' Thora retorted. The other six warriors glanced at each other, while both Amund and Egil glared at her.

'You got lucky, and this worm,' Amund pointed his sword at Sigge, 'attacked me from behind.'

'I... I was just trying to stop the fight.' Sigge tried to defend himself, but Sven knew it was pointless. He saw the other warriors creep forward and glanced around as his hand went to his neck. But then he remembered he wore no Mjöllnir, had not done for a very long time. Now, though, he wished he had one, because he knew he was going to die. Sven glanced at his grandson, hoping that the thrall would somehow get the boy out of this, and that he would grow up to be a strong warrior, just like Torkel. More than anything, he wished he could have seen Torkel one more time to see the man he had become, even if he was a Christian.

'I know, Sigge,' Amund said. 'I'm not mad at you, I swear by Odin. I know you were just trying to help your friend. Why don't you come back with us, explain it to the jarl and your uncle? Ketil's very concerned about you.'

Sigge glanced at Thora, who shook her head. But Sven knew it was pointless. The young man was an idiot. 'They'll listen?'

'Of course,' Egil said. 'It was just a misunderstanding.'

'Aye. Nobody died, so the jarl will forgive you, Ketil will make sure of it,' Amund added while rubbing the bandage on his head.

'Sigge, don't listen to them,' Thora said. Sigge looked at her, his eyes filled with pain.

'I'm sorry, Thora. I'm not throwing my life away for that drunk.' He pointed at Sven, who shook his head.

'Sigge,' Thora tried again, her eyebrows pinched together.

But Sigge wasn't listening to her any more. He lowered his axe and walked towards Egil and Amund, both men grinning like wolves at an injured lamb.

'You won't hurt Thora?' Sigge asked as he reached them. Sven noticed how the other warriors still crept closer. The forest had gone quiet, as if the gods themselves were holding their breaths to see what would happen. Charles, his face pale and chin trembling, glanced at Sven, who stood away from them. The fear in his eyes was like a knife stab in his chest, but Sven knew there was nothing he could do. *Odin, protect my grandson. Do with me what you will, but do not let my grandson die here.*

Egil grinned. 'If you can convince her to put her sword down and come with us, then no one will get hurt.'

Sigge looked at the warrior and hesitated for a heartbeat, before he turned to face Thora. He opened his mouth to speak to her, but before any words could come out, a sword erupted from his chest. Charles screamed as Sigge stared at the bloody sword point with bulging eyes. He looked at Thora as tears ran down his cheeks before Amund pulled the sword free while grinning savagely.

'Sigge!' Thora cried, her eyes wide.

'Kill them all!' Amund roared before Sigge's body hit the floor.

What happened next reminded Sven of the sea storm from a few days before. He could almost hear the thunder in the sky as the other six warriors rushed at Thora and Gerold. The thrall stood his ground, but grabbed Charles by the tunic, so the boy could not run away. Thora turned and blocked an axe with her sword before kicking the man in the stomach. Another stabbed at her, but she twisted out of the way and sliced the man's throat open. Blood sprayed over Charles and Gerold, both too stunned to move.

One warrior rushed at Sven, but all he could do was stare open-mouthed at the man while hearing Odin laughing in his ears. The warrior struck Sven on the side of his head; the blow knocking Sven to the ground.

'Leave him!' Egil shouted as the man stood over Sven. The warrior looked at Egil, confused. 'He's ours to deal with.'

The warrior nodded and rushed at Thora as she stabbed another in the stomach.

'Watch out!' Charles screamed before the warrior reached her. Thora twisted out of the way, freeing her sword and slicing at her attacker at the same time. The man jumped back, avoiding her sword, and then stabbed at her. Thora turned out of the way, but before she could retaliate, another warrior shoulder-barged her from the side. Thora fell to the ground and quickly rolled to her feet as the man thrust his sword at her. Instead, his sword struck only dirt, and she kicked him in the face, knocking the man out.

But there were too many for her to fight, especially while she was trying to keep an eye on Charles. Sven glanced at his grandson and the thrall. Gerold was standing in front of Charles, his knife in his hand as he tried to protect the young boy, but so far the Danes weren't paying any attention to them as they tried to deal with Thora.

Thora deflected another sword strike, but she could do nothing as Amund rushed in and cut her leg. Thora cried out and collapsed as the brown-eyed turd stepped back. Sven heard the gods laughing as the bastard stood over her, leering at her body. He held his hand up as one of the other warriors wanted to kill her.

'No, we'll have some fun with her first and then we kill her. I want to make sure she doesn't get to go to Valhalla.'

If he expected to see fear in Thora's eyes, then he was disappointed. She glared at him as she spat at his feet, but Sven saw she knew the fight was over. She looked at Sven and shook her head, disgusted at him as he just lay on the ground. His face burnt with shame, but Sven could not fight these men.

'What about these two?' one man asked, pointing his sword at Charles and Gerold. Gerold glared at them, but Charles just stood there covered in blood, his eyes wide. He glanced at Sven, but Sven looked away. He did not want to see the fear in the boy's eyes. It reminded him too much of the son he had failed.

'Don't you touch them, or I swear by Odin I'll—' Thora started.

'Shut up, bitch!' Amund pointed his sword at her before turning his attention back to Charles and the thrall.

'Let us go,' Gerold said in his accented Danish. 'We have nothing to do with them.'

'Where are you from?' Amund asked, tilting his head.

'From Francia. We are travellers.'

'And why were you travelling with this lot, then?'

'They offered to guide us north. We don't know the land, so we accepted.'

Amund frowned and then glanced at Egil, who only shrugged. But then one of the other warriors' eyes lit up.

'Wait.' He stepped closer to get a better look at Charles. 'By Odin, I recognise this boy. They were bothering people in the market, asking questions. Even asked me.'

Gerold's eyes widened, and even Sven knew they had failed to fool the warriors.

'What did he ask you?' Egil looked at the man.

The warrior smiled. 'He was asking about his grandfather, Sve—'

Before the man could finish his sentence, Gerold lunged forward and stabbed him in the throat with his knife. The warrior's eyes bulged as he gripped his throat and tried to stem the blood flow.

'Charles, run!' Gerold roared as the warrior dropped to his knees, his eyes pleading Amund for help. But Amund turned and struck Gerold hard on the side of his head with the pommel of his sword. Gerold dropped to the ground, his eyes rolling in his head and, before Charles could run, one of the others grabbed him, his sword at the boy's throat.

'Be strong, Charles. Everything will be fine.' Thora clutched her leg, which was bleeding heavily. She looked at Sven, her pained expression begging him to do something.

'Shut up, you bitch!' Amund said again, before turning to Charles. 'Who is your grandfather?'

Charles kept his mouth shut, and Sven's heart raced as he prayed the boy would keep it that way. It was the only way he was going to survive this. He might be sold as a thrall, but he would live.

Amund grabbed Charles by the tunic and almost lifted him up, before screaming in his face. 'Who is your grandfather?'

Again, Charles kept quiet, but his eyes flickered towards Sven and Sven dropped his head, knowing what Amund was going to do now.

'Well, well, the gods do smile on us today, boys. This is Sven the Boar's grandson.'

The men laughed as Egil said, 'Never knew the bastard had any children. Feel sorry for his bitch of a wife, though. She must have suffered having to rut with him.'

'Aye, I bet he squealed like a pig while he fucked his whore of a wife,' Amund said, which made the men laugh even more.

Sven gritted his teeth, feeling the small spark in the pit of his stomach.

'I think you made him angry,' one warrior said, and the others laughed again.

'Well, let's kill the bastard and put him out of his misery. I'm getting bored with this and, besides, the bitch will bleed out soon and I still want to have some fun with her.' Egil freed his sword from its scabbard and walked towards Sven.

'No.' Amund smiled a cruel smile that made Sven's blood go cold. Even Thora knew what was about to happen as she shook her head. 'Why don't we add to his misery instead of putting an end to it?'

Amund stopped and frowned at him.

'Let the old bastard watch as we kill the boy and fuck Thora. Then we let him go and he can spend the rest of his pathetic life knowing he did nothing to stop us.'

Amund smiled and looked at the other men as they all nodded. 'I like that plan, but kill the boy slowly, make him scream to his god.'

'Oh, he will.' Amund turned to Charles and grinned savagely at him. Charles's face paled even more, and the boy pissed himself as his fear took over his bladder. Sven felt the pain in his chest, the pain so bad he thought his heart would stop. His hands trembled as he watched Amund put the point of his sword at the base of Charles's neck and knew that the bastard was going to push that sword in as slowly as he could so the boy would feel every agonising moment of it. His grandson stared at him, tears streaming down his cheeks and leaving white lines in their wake, his eyes begging Sven to do something. The men laughed as Sven saw himself standing on his ship and sailing away from the Frankish shoreline, watching as his son disappeared in the distance. He remembered the anger he had felt that day. He could almost feel it in his veins as his hands trembled. His son had tried to be brave, but he had still had the same terrified look in his eyes. Sven also remembered the promise he had made that day. The one he had never kept. He saw his wife, standing in front of him in their dark bedroom, the knife in her stomach, the blood leaking out. As she stared at him, her mouth opened and the words that came out erupted in his head like a thunderstorm.

Our son.

14

———

'What the—?' Amund asked when he heard the scream behind him, like a wild beast set free. He turned and saw Sven on his knees and screaming at the dark clouds.

Egil had just enough time to glance at Amund before Sven jumped to his feet and stormed at the scarred-lipped warrior. Taken aback by this sudden turn, Egil was too slow to lift his sword and could do nothing as Sven headbutted him in the chest and, as the warrior landed on his back, Sven stepped over him and grabbed his knife from his belt before stabbing him in the neck and cutting his throat open. Blood squirted up in the air like a volcano erupting and drenched Sven, but he ignored it as he rushed at the next warrior.

'Kill him!' Amund screamed.

Sven ducked under the sword of the nearest warrior, turned, and stabbed the man in the back. As the warrior arched backwards, Sven grabbed his long hair and pulled the knife free before he buried it in the man's neck. He turned to the warrior standing beside him, the man too shocked to move, and kicked him hard in the leg, just above the knee. There was a loud crack as the warrior's leg broke and bent in on itself. The warrior screamed as he collapsed, but was quickly silenced when Sven stamped down on his head, which exploded like a pumpkin and covered Sven's foot and leg in blood and brains.

Sven, his red face creased and teeth bared, turned and faced Amund, the only man still standing. He felt the bone splinters and brains between his toes, but ignored it as he panted heavily. The blood coursing through his veins was filled with a fire he had not felt in a long time. The anger and strength that came with it was intoxicating. A drink sweeter than any ale he had ever drunk. 'Let my grandson go.' The words came out strained, making him sound like a beast which had only just learnt how to speak.

Amund stared at him, his face as pale as Charles's, his hand trembling as he lowered the sword from the boy's neck. He glanced at Thora and saw the grin on her face.

'You're a dead man,' she said, and Amund looked at Sven again as he stalked closer.

Sven's senses were more alive than ever. His heart was hammering away in his chest as if about to break free. He felt the breeze on his skin and ignored Freya's attempt to calm him. The blood pounded in his ears, sounding like Odin laughing as Sven broke the oath to never touch a weapon again or spill the blood of another man he had made the night his wife had died. But Sven did not think of that now. All he thought about was ripping Amund's head off his shoulders. 'Fight me,' he growled, but Amund only backed away from the boy and him. 'Fight me!' He beat his chest with his fist.

Amund shook his head as he took a step back, his sword trembling in his hand.

'Fight me!' Sven roared and charged barehanded at Amund. Amund dropped his sword and fled through the trees, screaming to the gods for mercy. 'Argh!' Sven roared, his anger at not getting to kill the man who had threatened his grandson too much for him to control. He saw the warrior Thora had knocked out coming to. The man looked round, confused by what he saw, and then his face paled when Sven picked up Amund's sword and walked towards him. Eyes wide, he tried to crawl away, but Sven grabbed him and dragged him to the nearest tree before throwing him against it and stabbing the sword through the man's shoulder and into the tree. The man screamed as tears ran down his cheeks.

'Please, I beg you. I was only following orders.'

Sven knelt down and took the man's sax-knife from his belt. 'And what were your orders?'

'Sven?' Thora tried, but he ignored her.

'What were your orders?'

'T... to find you and bring you back to the jarl.'

'To find us and bring us back to the jarl,' Sven repeated. The man nodded. 'And yet you decided to kill us.'

The man shook his head, which angered Sven, and he stabbed the bastard in the leg with his own knife. The man screamed. 'Amund and Egil told us to kill you all. Said you were not worth the effort.' The man cried. 'Please. We could not go against them.'

Sven leaned in closer. He could smell the fear on the man, or perhaps that was his shit. The smell heightened his senses, and he saw the lice in the man's beard and the dirt in his pores. 'You tell Egil that when I get to Valhalla, I'll torture him every day. I'll rip him apart with my bare hands and do it again the next day and every day until Ragnarök. You tell him that for me. Will you?'

The man nodded, confused. Sven stood up and with a roar buried the knife in the man's skull. Letting go of the knife, he stepped back and stared up into the sky.

'Are you happy now, you one-eyed bastard?' He stood like that for a few heartbeats, waiting for something to happen, and then frowned when the trees remained silent. Sven looked down and saw Charles gaping at him and Thora smiling.

'Charles,' she said. 'Meet your grandfather, Sven the Boar.'

* * *

Charles gulped, but could not take his eyes off his grandfather who stood there, covered in blood and hands trembling. He was terrified of the man standing in front of him, even if that man had just saved his life. He struggled to make sense of the confusion he felt and wanted to pray, but realised he would not know what to say.

Sven sighed and then looked at the bleeding wound on Thora's leg. 'Boy, help her with that wound before she bleeds to death. Now!' he said when Charles just stood there. He nodded and rushed to Thora's side.

'And what about you?' she asked Sven.

Sven stared at the men he had killed, his hands shaking as his blood cooled. He turned and pulled the knife out of the man's skull. 'I'll be back.' The dead man's head fell forward as blood leaked from the hole on his head and reddened his hair.

Charles tore his eyes away from the sight and saw his grandfather disappear amongst the trees. 'Where's he going?'

Thora smiled, although her faced grimaced in pain. 'Don't worry, he'll be back. Now, find me something to stop this bleeding.'

Charles looked at the open wound in her leg. The cut was deep, and the sight of the blood oozing out made his head swim.

'Charles, look at me.' Thora sat up, grimacing, and took his head in both her hands. He smelt the blood on her hands which did not help. 'Look at me. Good boy, now take deep breaths. That's good.'

Charles breathed in deep and breathed out, feeling his head

clear. But the smell of blood, mixed with excrement, still made him nauseous and Charles thought he might vomit all over Thora.

'Good.' She looked around and then pointed to one of the bodies. 'Go to him. Do not look at the others. Take his tunic off and bring it to me.'

Charles nodded and rushed to the body she had pointed at. He passed Gerold and felt guilty for not checking on his friend, but a quick glance showed him the slave was still breathing. As soon as he dealt with Thora's leg, he would check up on Gerold, he told himself. He got to the body and saw why Thora had pointed him out. Of all the corpses he was the least sickening to look at as he lay there with Gerold's knife stuck in his throat and his eyes still open wide in shock. Charles's hands trembled as he struggled to get the tunic off the corpse. He was desecrating the dead which he knew was a sin, but wondered if God would forgive him because he was doing it to help a friend. When he finally managed to get the tunic of the dead man, he rushed back to Thora, who was looking very pale.

'Thank you,' she said as he handed her the tunic. Thora took her knife and cut the tunic into strips, which she tied around her leg. 'Good, that should help with the bleeding.'

'Will you live?' Charles was aware of the fear in his voice, but did not care. He had already pissed himself. They all knew he was terrified. Perhaps that was why his grandfather had left.

'That's up to the gods now.' She looked at Sigge, the young warrior lying dead not far from them, his face still surprised at his own death. 'Oh Sigge, you young fool.' Thora leaned back and closed her eyes as a tear ran down her cheek.

'He didn't deserve that,' Charles said, staring at Sigge and wondering why he had believed those warriors.

'No, he didn't. He was a good man, better than those bastards.'

Charles nodded, agreeing with her even if he hadn't known the young warrior well, and then rushed to check on his friend.

'Check his head for any cuts,' Thora said as he got to Gerold.

Charles checked his dark hair, but saw no cuts or blood. He sighed in relief and then struggled to roll his friend over. Gerold groaned and opened his eyes, blinking a few times until they could focus on him.

'What happened?'

'You got hit on the head.'

Gerold stared at him for a short while and then sat up and looked around him, seeing the dead and broken bodies. His eyes fell on Sigge and stayed there for a few moments. 'And what happened here? It looks like a wild beast tore through them.'

'Not a wild beast, but my grandfather.' Charles tried not to look at the bodies littered around him.

Gerold's eyes widened. 'That old coward did this?' He looked around again and shook his head, but grimaced at the pain that must have caused him. Charles handed him the flask of water which Gerold drank from before pouring the rest over his head.

'He was different, like something took over him,' Charles tried to explain. He still did not understand what had happened. One moment, the man was standing in front of him, his sword on his shoulder, his grandfather sitting on the ground, his eyes dull and filled with fear. And then, he just... Charles frowned. He did not know. He had thought his father's fight with the warriors of Hügelburg had been violent, but what he had seen here was something he had never known a man was capable of. Perhaps Gerold was right, perhaps a wild animal had killed all these men.

'What happened to your neck?'

Gerold's voice dragged him back and Charles touched the base of his neck where the man had put his sword. It surprised him to see the blood on his fingertips. 'The man was about to kill me.'

'And your grandfather saved you?'

Charles nodded.

'Perhaps God had come to him.'

'Or the devil.' Charles thought again of how his grandfather had killed the men. Three of them dead in the time it took his heart to beat once.

'Where's the old man?'

Charles looked in the direction his grandfather had gone. 'I don't know. He took a knife and left.'

Gerold nodded, but said nothing. Charles glanced at Thora. She was sitting by the tree, her injured leg in front of her, and watching them talk. Charles struggled to read her face and wondered what she was thinking about. They all sat like that for a while, each of them lost in their own thoughts, when there was a rustling noise from the trees. Charles's heart skipped a beat and Gerold jumped to his feet, although he swayed slightly. But then he dropped to the ground again as Sven walked into the clearing, still covered in the blood of the men he had killed, and pulling a horse behind him.

'Bastard cut the horses loose, but luckily for us, this one stayed behind.' Sven stopped and frowned at their reactions. 'What?'

'We thought Amund had come to finish the job.' Thora smiled.

'No, that coward's halfway back to Hedeby by now. Which is why we need to leave.' The old man glanced around the bodies. 'Won't be long before he returns with more men, or scavengers come looking for a meal.'

Charles's eyes widened as he scanned the trees. 'What kind of scavengers?'

'Bears, wolves. Most likely ravens and crows, but we don't want to stay here and find out.' He led the horse towards Thora. 'Now, help me get her on the horse.'

'I don't need a horse,' Thora said, her face defiant.

Charles got to his feet and looked at her. 'But you can't walk, not with your leg.'

'Yes, I can.' Thora struggled to her feet, grimacing as she leaned on the tree. 'See?'

Sven shook his head. 'The boy's right. You can't walk like that, and besides, we need to move fast.'

'Just leave her if she wants to be stubborn,' Gerold said as he got to his feet. Sven turned and glared at him.

'Boy, if you say something like that again, then I'll knock you out myself. If it weren't for Thora, you'd be dead.'

Gerold opened his mouth to say something, but wisely closed it again and nodded. He then helped Charles get Thora on the horse while Sven searched through the bodies.

'Grandfather, what are you doing?' Charles looked at his grandfather. Gone were the dull eyes and stooped figure with the slow, aimless gait. The old man stood straighter. His walk had more purpose, but the biggest change was his eyes. They were still red, but a fire that made his grandfather almost frightening to look at replaced the dull expression. Even Gerold was unsettled by his hard eyes. The blood-covered man Charles saw now reminded him more of the stories the bishop had told him.

'We need weapons. Your little knife will not help you in a real fight. And I need shoes. I can't visit my brother looking like a vagrant.'

'You are a vagrant,' Thora said from on top of the horse.

'Aye, but I don't need to look like one.'

Charles and Gerold watched as the old man went from body to body, pulling off a boot and measuring it to his feet.

'These will do.' He sat down and pulled the boots on.

'What about your tunic? Not much left of that one,' Thora said, smiling at the old man. Charles frowned, unsure of how they seemed so calm around the dead. Even Gerold kept glancing at them as if he expected the bodies to stand up and attack them.

Charles's grandfather shook his head. 'They're all covered in blood and I doubt any would fit me.' He got to his feet and walked to the body stuck to the tree with the sword in its shoulder. With a grunt, he pulled the sword free and took the belt from the body. After fastening the belt around his large waist, he cleaned the sword and put it in the scabbard. He collected another from one of the dead men and Sigge's axe. 'Let's go,' he said, and walked towards them, his limp less obvious.

Gerold bent down and picked up a sword from one of the dead Danes and tucked it into his belt, but decided against finding a pair of boots to wear. 'I don't understand these Danes,' he said in Frankish as Sven took the leash of the horse and guided it out of the clearing. Charles glanced around one more time, looking at the men his grandfather had killed to save his life. He couldn't help but wonder if they had unleashed the devil.

They walked in silence, Charles still too afraid to speak as he stared at the horse's legs in front of him. Thora, her face pale as her leg continued to bleed, swayed slightly on the horse and, if it wasn't for Gerold catching her, she would have fallen off the horse.

'Thank you,' she said, her face surprised. Gerold looked just as surprised and only shrugged. 'Sven, we need to stop. The sun will set soon and we need to rest.'

Sven stopped and looked around before nodding. 'Fine.' He turned to Gerold. 'Get a fire started. We need to deal with that wound.'

Thora nodded, understanding what the old man meant, but Charles was lost. 'How?'

'We need to cauterise it,' Sven said.

Charles's eyes widened as he looked at Thora. 'The old man is right. The bandage isn't working.'

Gerold got the fire started as Charles and his grandfather helped Thora off the horse. She stood unsteadily and had to lean on the old man as they went to one of the trees where she got to sit down. Charles watched as his grandfather took two large knives from his belt. He studied both of them and the cleanest one went into the flames. The other one he handed to Charles.

'Why?' Charles asked, his mouth suddenly dry.

'So that next time a man holds a sword to your throat, you can gut him and not have to wait for others who might not come to help you.' He saw the brief shame in Sven's eyes before it was replaced by the new hardness.

'B... but I'm not a warrior.' He felt his voice tremble and looked away from his grandfather.

His grandfather sighed. 'This is not about being a warrior. This is about not being killed. I broke my oath to Odin so that you could live. Next time, you might not be so lucky.'

Odin is not real, Charles wanted to say, but the fire in his grandfather's eyes kept his mouth shut.

'I can protect him,' Gerold said as he put another stick in the fire.

'Like you did today?'

'I killed one of them.'

'Aye, you did, but there were four of them left when they knocked you out.' Gerold bristled, but Sven ignored him as he looked at Charles again. 'I'm not asking you to look for fights. I'm asking you to protect yourself and not to rely on others.'

'Sven, he's just a boy.'

Sven looked at Thora and then back at Charles. Charles felt the weight of his stare on him and wanted the old drunk coward to return. 'In this world, that does not matter.' Sven held out the knife for Charles. 'Take the knife.'

'Your grandfather's right,' Gerold said in Frankish. 'You can't always rely on others to help you.'

Charles looked at his friend and then at the knife again, before he nodded and took the knife.

'Good, keep it safe and always have it near you. Even when you sleep.'

'Very touching, but can we deal with my leg now before I bleed to death?' Thora said.

Sven went to the fire and pulled the knife out. Charles stared at the blade as it glowed red and already felt his stomach tighten. He did not want to see what was about to happen, but knew he had no choice. He wanted to be a priest, and this was what a priest had to do.

'Ready?' Sven asked Thora. She nodded as she pulled her trousers down to reveal the deep cut on her thigh. Charles looked away, his face as red as the knife. 'This is no time to be shy, boy. You need to hold her legs.'

'What?' Charles was shocked and shook his head. 'I can't.'

'You have no choice,' Thora said. 'Don't worry, I'll be fine. This is not the first time I've had to do this.'

'Aye, me neither,' Sven said. 'Although some ale would be good.'

'Keep it together, old man. I need your hand to be steady.'

Sven nodded and then looked at Gerold. 'You, grab her shoulders, pin her to the tree. Charles, sit on her legs. You can turn your back to her if that helps.'

Charles nodded, glad he would not have to see what they were going to do, or look at Thora's exposed flesh.

Sven gave Thora a piece of wood, which she put between her teeth, and pulled the knife from the fire again. Charles felt the heat as his grandfather brought it near, hovering it just above the wound, which Thora had unbandaged and wiped as clean as she could. 'Ready?' Charles heard his grandfather ask Thora as he tried to control his stomach.

Then Thora screamed, the sound almost piercing his ears and ringing in his head. Charles screwed his eyes shut as the smell of burnt flesh reached his nostrils. His stomach convulsed, and when Thora's screams finally stopped, he bent over and emptied his guts.

15

Charles woke up to the sounds of birds singing above his head and a gentle breeze blowing over him, bringing with it the scent of the trees and the wild flowers that grew on the forest floor wherever they found enough sunlight. As he opened his eyes, he saw a small squirrel run along the branch which hung over his head. The squirrel stopped and looked at him before it rushed off, too busy to spend any time with Charles. For a few heartbeats, he lay there and wondered if this was what heaven looked like. Then he turned his head and saw the knife his grandfather had given him, and the forest darkened. Sitting up and rubbing his eyes, Charles saw Gerold sleeping nearby, his new sword in his hand and his face stern even in the depth of his dreams. Charles wondered about the life his new friend must have lived as a slave to a drunken and abusive owner. He looked at where Thora was sleeping, her trousers still down to her knees and exposing her thigh, although her tunic covered her private parts. Charles still turned away, though, his cheeks burning with embarrassment. He wondered what the bishop would have said and then wondered why he still cared. The bishop had something to do with his father's death. But it was difficult for Charles to understand what. The bishop had been a large part of his life, the reason he wanted to join the church and spread the word of God. Charles sighed and then glanced at Thora again, careful to look at only her face. She had passed out when his grandfather cauterised her leg and Charles lowered his head when he remembered how he had puked. His grandfather had said nothing about that. He had barely said anything as he put the knife back in the fire to clean it and lay Thora down, so she was more comfortable. Charles was surprised by the tenderness his grandfather showed towards Thora. It was not something he had expected from a man many had told him was a vicious monster. Afterwards, the old man just lay down near her and fell asleep, leaving Charles and Gerold to sit there, staring at each other with pale faces.

Gerold decided to take Charles to a small stream they had passed, so he could clean himself up. His trousers had reeked of piss and now his tunic was stained with vomit. When they had returned to the camp, Gerold followed the old man's example and found a spot on the opposite side of the fire before he too fell asleep. Charles had been uncertain of what to do as he sat by the fire in his wet clothes, so he prayed. He had asked God to heal Thora's wound and to guide them safely to their destination. But as he prayed, all he saw were the visions of his father, which then changed into his grandfather standing in the clearing, his eyes wild and covered in the blood of the men he had killed. Charles rubbed his eyes and looked around, his heart beating faster in his chest as he realised his grandfather was missing and so was their horse.

'He left a while ago.' Thora sat up, wincing at the pain.

'How are you feeling?' Charles asked, but avoided looking at her.

'I'm alive. I can thank the gods for that, at least. Although I won't be able to fight for a while.'

'I prayed over you last night,' Charles said, not wanting her false gods to get the credit.

Thora smiled. 'I know, I heard.' She hesitated for a heartbeat. 'Thank you.'

'Where did my grandfather go?'

Thora shrugged. 'Hopefully to find some food, but don't worry. He'll be back.'

'How do you know?' Charles frowned as he scanned the trees.

'The man broke his oath to the All-Father to keep you alive. He will not abandon you now.'

Charles smiled, but found no reassurance in those words. He wasn't sure why. Perhaps it was because she was talking about a god he knew was not real. 'Why don't you believe in God?'

'I'm not sure I believe in any gods at the moment.'

He frowned again. 'Why?'

Thora stared at him, her eyes turning glossy. 'After my husband died, it was hard to believe in anything.'

'How did he die?'

'Saving me.' Thora lowered her head and Charles kept quiet. 'We were fighting the Franks, and they pulled me out of the shield wall. My husband rushed in and took the blade that was meant for me.' She stared into the distance as she remembered that day. 'He died in my arms. That was the last time I picked up a weapon.'

'Something he would be very unhappy about.'

They both turned as Sven walked into the small clearing leading the horse behind him. Thora smiled as Charles's mouth fell open, his eyes fixed on his grandfather. The dirty hair was gone, leaving only a bald head, with a few fresh cuts and some old scars. The marking on his head looked more visible now, and Charles saw it was some kind of bird. But that was not the only change. Sven's face had been cleaned, his skin still red from where he had scrubbed the old dirt out of his pores. His bushy beard was clean as well, no more bits of old food and other things Charles could never identify. It seemed even bushier now and somehow brighter than it had been before.

'By Frigg!' Thora stared wide-eyed at Sven as he tied the horse's reins to a low-hanging branch. 'What happened? Did you fall into the water?'

Sven's cheeks turned red, but he quickly composed himself. 'You were right, Thora.' He looked at Charles. 'The boy is a chance for redemption, if not from the gods, then from Eydis. She'd want me to do everything I can to protect our grandson.' Charles felt his heart skip a beat as the old man called him his grandson. He looked at Gerold and saw that his friend was sitting up and rubbing his eyes as he too stared at Sven. 'But the only way I can do that is if I become the man I used to be.'

'Well, the gods must be having a great time laughing at you, but I must admit, it's good to see the old Sven back.'

Sven smiled broadly, revealing his stained teeth, with a few missing. 'How's the leg?'

Thora looked at it. 'Feels fine. Frigg willing, I'll be back on my feet in no time.'

'Good, we can rest here for the day, but tomorrow we will head for Ribe. We need my brother's help now more than ever.'

'Why?' Charles asked.

'The men we killed yesterday belonged to the jarl of Hedeby, and he's one of the most powerful men in Denmark, after the king. He will not be happy that we killed his men, so we need to get to Ribe before he finds us.'

'But how did they find us?' Thora frowned. She pulled her trousers up, much to Charles's relief, but grimaced at the effort.

His grandfather sighed. 'I found markers left behind by

someone.'

'Markers?' Gerold asked, walking over to join them.

Sven glanced at him. 'Aye, very subtle ones, but ones that a trained tracker would notice.'

'You mean someone left them a trail to follow?' Thora asked.

'Aye, looks like that.'

'You think Sigge? But why?'

Sven shrugged. 'Perhaps he was hoping the jarl would forgive him if he led them to us.'

'Well, Amund and Egil had other plans.'

The old man spat on the ground. 'Aye, vicious bastards.'

'So, what do we do now?' Gerold asked in his accented Danish.

'Like I said, we get to my brother in Ribe. But today we rest.' Gerold nodded, and Sven looked at Charles with a raised eyebrow. 'That pouch, give it to me.' He held out his hand.

Charles looked at his grandfather and then nodded before taking the pouch out of his tunic and handing it to him.

Sven opened the pouch and took the Mjöllnir from it. He held it up as he stared at it. 'It used to belong to my father.'

'He gave it to you?' Charles asked.

Sven shook his head. 'I took it from him after I killed him.'

Charles glanced at Gerold and saw how his friend grimaced as his grandfather continued.

'I was smaller than all my brothers, even though I am the oldest. My father never approved of me and always encouraged my brothers to pick on me, to bully me. I guess he hoped they would drive me away. Everything became a fight for me, even eating. My brothers were always stealing my food until one day I had enough.' He looked at Charles, who shivered at the fire in his grandfather's eyes. 'One night, we had a feast. I wasn't much older than you are now, I guess, and I was forced to sit as far from my father as I could. As we were about to eat, I saw my brother's hand move towards my plate. I don't know if he was going for my food, but I knew he normally would. So I grabbed my knife and pinned his hand to the table.'

Charles's eyes widened, and he saw Gerold had the same reaction.

'That was the last time any of my brothers tried to steal my food, although my father beat me bloody. But I learnt an important lesson that day.' He stared Charles in the eyes and Charles stood there rooted to the spot as his fear gripped him. 'People will always think they are better than us because we are smaller than them. I had to fight that my entire life, and so did your father. I'm sure even in Francia there were those who tried to knock him down because of it.' Charles nodded as he thought of Lothar. 'You ever go hunting, Charles?'

Charles nodded.

'The boar is smaller than the wolf, the bear and the deer. It is smaller than all men, yet it's one of the most feared creatures for any hunter. Why? Because of its aggression. That is what I learnt that day. To be more aggressive, to never give up. To hit my enemy before they even think of hitting me. In the end, my shortness became my strength. Do you understand what I'm saying, boy?'

Charles nodded. 'My father would tell me the same thing.'

Sven smiled. 'I'm glad he listened. I don't know what will happen next, but remember this. When the time comes, you must strike at your enemy before he can even think of doing it and you must strike harder than he ever will. That is the only way to survive what will come.'

'And what will come?' Charles asked, his voice trembling.

'I don't know.' Old Sven took the Mjöllnir and thread a leather thong through the hole before tying it around his neck. 'But Odin knows it won't be good.'

Charles felt his heart racing. He wasn't sure if it was because of what his grandfather said, or because the old man was slowly changing into the terrifying image he had had of him before he came to Denmark. He looked at Gerold and saw the frown on his face and then the smile on Thora's. Gerold seemed to agree with him, whereas Thora was happy to see the change in his grandfather. He remembered a sermon that the bishop had given once. He had said that God had a plan and provided His flock with the means to see out His plan. That was why He had sent His son to be sacrificed for man's sin. And perhaps that was why He had sent the devil to Charles's aid. To help him survive whatever would come next.

'What?' Thora's voice made Charles focus on his grandfather again. The old man had the large cross in his hand, his thumb rubbing over the symbol in the centre, below the large ruby.

'This symbol.' The old man's brow furrowed. 'I've seen it before, but can't remember where.'

'Is it important?' Thora asked.

Sven shrugged. 'It could explain why my son was killed and why he sent Charles to Denmark.' He looked at Charles. 'What do you know about your mother?'

Charles looked at his bare feet, seeing the dirt between his toes. 'Not much. My father never spoke of her.'

'She died?' Thora asked.

Charles kept his gaze lowered. 'That's what my father said.'

'So you don't know where she got this cross from?'

Charles shook his head. 'My father never told me.'

The old man frowned and then showed the cross to Charles. 'Do you know what this symbol is?'

Charles shook his head again, without looking up. But Gerold stepped forward.

'It's the symbol of the Carolingians, the line of Charlemagne.'

They all looked at the slave, their eyebrows raised. Even Charles looked up before he said, 'My father was a personal guard of King Louis.'

'King Louis?' Sven frowned.

'Grandson of Charlemagne,' Thora said. 'You don't know him?'

The old man shrugged. 'I don't know.' His eyes glazed over as he lost himself in a memory. 'The day I lost your father, there was a young prince. But I don't remember his name.' He looked at Charles. 'How long has this Louis been king?'

'I don't know. My whole life, I guess.'

'What are you thinking?' Thora asked, grimacing as she moved.

'That my son did something very dumb.'

'Well, he is your son.' Thora smiled and then looked at Charles. 'Does King Louis have any daughters?'

Charles shrugged, but Gerold responded.

'Three. But they've been locked up in monasteries for a long time.'

Sven and Thora frowned at him.

'What? My former master was a trader. We travelled all over the kingdom. You learn things as a slave.'

'Remind me to be more careful what I say around thralls then.' Sven looked at the cross again, frowning. 'Is one of King Louis's daughters old enough to be Charles's mother?'

'I think so,' Gerold said.

'You think he got one daughter with child?' Thora asked.

'Perhaps. Or perhaps a maidservant and the two of them ran away after stealing this cross. Torkel must have thought he could sell it.'

'Would he be that dumb?'

Sven shrugged. 'I don't know.' He looked at Charles. 'Would your father have been that dumb?'

Charles shook his head, but he didn't really know. If he had to be honest, he didn't really know much about his father. 'But then why hide the cross?'

'He hid the cross?'

Charles nodded. 'I've only ever seen it once, many years ago. I forgot about it until he gave it to me before...'

'Then how did they find out about it?' Thora asked, looking at his grandfather, who could only sigh.

'I don't know.' The old man sat down and put the cross back in the pouch. 'This is a mystery only Odin can solve, and he'd rather watch us struggle over it.'

'We should find something to eat,' Gerold said. Charles nodded as his stomach growled. He had not eaten since the previous morning and had puked out what remained of that meagre breakfast last night. Now that Gerold mentioned food, he suddenly felt weak with hunger.

Jesus went forty days with no food and the devil could not tempt him to turn stones into bread, Charles reminded himself. So he had to be strong. But then his stomach growled again, this time loud enough to make the others look at him.

'Gerold's right.' Thora smiled. 'The boy's stomach sounds like a wolf protecting her cubs.'

'I'll go set some traps,' Gerold offered, and left after Thora nodded.

Thora and the old man fell asleep, leaving Charles alone with his thoughts. He thought about the golden cross, but could not understand how that would lead to his father's death. He still believed that it had something to do with him hurting Lothar's son, but then that made no sense, either. Charles scratched his head, which was starting to hurt. A few days ago, everything was still normal. Now he found himself in a land that mocked his God and believed in false idols. A land of people who took pleasure in attacking his people. But then, were the Franks really his people? Charles's father was a Dane. Something they had always bullied him about. The Franks in his home town had never really accepted his father, and neither had they accepted him. Only Bishop Bernard had been a friend to him, but now he wondered if that had always been an act. Then there was Ribe, a place Charles knew nothing about. He still wasn't sure how he felt about living there, so he decided to do what he always did when he felt uncertain.

Charles sat on his knees and clasped his hands in front of him. Praying always calmed him down, but for the last few days he had not been able to think of the right prayer. None of the ones the bishop had taught him seemed right and, after learning the bishop might have been behind his father's death, those prayers felt dirty, like they were tainted by the hand of the devil. He took a deep breath and decided that perhaps a personal approach might be better.

Lord Almighty, I thank you for my life and for my health. I thank you for bringing Gerold into my life as a friend and protector and for sending your angel to me. I also thank you for helping me find my grandfather. He is a man with his own demons and I trust you will help him fight those, even if he doesn't believe in you. But God, he sighed, I am lost. My father sacrificed himself to save me from men we thought were friends, but as I sit here now, I feel unworthy. I know you have a plan and I understand it is not for me to question you. But I don't understand. My father was a good Christian. He prayed every day and always gave money to the church. He fought many battles to protect your flock from those who wish to harm them. So why did he have to die? And why did I have to come to the land of the Danes? A tear ran down his cheek as he took a deep breath. Lord, I am lost, but I trust you have a plan, even if I don't understand it. You have sent your angel to protect me and the devil to fight by her side. I will try to trust in your plan, but I ask you for the strength to get through this ordeal and to find the truth behind my father's death.

Amen.

16

Sven watched his grandson sitting on his knees, his eyes closed, and hands in front of him. He wondered what the boy was asking for when he saw the tear run down his cheek. It reminded Sven of the last day he had seen his son. Torkel had tried to be brave that day, but tears also ran down his cheeks. He wondered what life his son had lived, something he had never really done before. After he was forced to give his son up, all Sven had thought about was getting him back. But setback after setback had dimmed the flames of his fight and when the news came that his son had become a Christian, Sven decided it was better to believe he had died. It made it easier to deal with the pain, especially when Eydis died afterwards. The Christians believed that their god was all-loving, that he protected them from the evils of Midgard, but Sven had no illusions about who his gods were. They were cruel and malicious. The gods of Asgard only cared about themselves and had decided that men were there to amuse them. But he never understood how the death of his wife had amused the gods. Or perhaps that was a punishment for him giving up on saving his son. Sven had made an oath to Torkel, and he had failed. He felt his hands shake. What would the punishment be for breaking his oath never to fight again? He thought back to the storm on the fishing boat the day before his grandson appeared. Was that a sign from the gods of what was to come?

'We need to go!' the thrall cried in his accented Danish as he came rushing towards them, ducking under branches and jumping over roots.

Sven sat up, his eyebrows drawn together. 'Why?'

'I saw men, plenty of them, on horseback. The one who attacked us yesterday was with them.'

'Amund?' Thora asked, and looked at Sven.

Sven felt his heart beating hard in his chest. He should have killed the bastard, but the man had run away instead of fighting. Sven missed the warriors he had grown up with. They would never have run from a fight. Or betrayed their friends. 'Did they see you?'

'No.' Gerold shook his head. 'I was hiding in a tree, waiting for a rabbit to be caught in my trap when I saw them.'

'Which way are they going?'

'Away from us, but they have men searching for tracks.'

'That's good.' Sven looked at his grandson and saw the uncertainty in his eyes. Charles still had the sax-knife he had given him and Sven hoped the boy would not have to use it, but you never knew what would happen when the gods got bored.

'How is that good?' Charles asked, confused by his grandfather's smile.

'Because they're looking for us in the wrong place.' Thora looked at Sven. 'We can't stay here. They might still find us.'

Sven rubbed his freshly shaved head, still struggling to get used to not having his hair any more as he scanned the trees. He knew most of the Danish land well, having spent many winters wandering from place to place, always avoiding people. Then he smiled when he realised exactly where they were. 'There's an old trail not far from here. It'll take us north, but away from Ribe.'

'Do we have any choice?' Thora grimaced as she moved her leg.

Sven looked at Gerold. 'Did you see a large man, black hair with grey in it? Not much younger than me.'

Gerold thought for a short while and then nodded. 'I think I did. He was leading the group.'

Sven nodded and turned back to Thora. 'No, we don't. Ketil is leading them. He knows who I am, or who I was. He'll guess we're heading to Ribe.'

'Won't he be heading there then?'

'No, there's tension between Hedeby and Ribe. He'll want to get us before we get there.'

Thora frowned. 'How do you know that?'

'Nobody pays attention to the drunk sleeping in the street.'

'So we use the path and get around them?' Gerold asked. Sven glanced at Charles, who was sitting on his knees and following the conversation.

'Aye, the gods know it's our best chance.' He rubbed his head again, before he got to his feet and went to the horse. 'Help Thora onto the horse.'

Both Charles and Gerold nodded and helped Thora. She grimaced in pain, but said nothing as she made herself comfortable. Sven thought of her father. The man was one of the best warriors he had ever fought with, and Sven wished he was with them now. But then, the man had been old. Just like Sven. His body still ached from the fight, his leg almost unable to hold his weight. His shoulder screamed every time he moved his arm and his back was tight. Sven had never realised how much his body had aged, as the ale numbed most of the pain. But he could not show weakness now. Not in front of his grandson and Thora. For the first time in many winters, Sven rubbed a Mjöllnir pendant around his neck and asked Thor to protect his family.

'Let's go,' he said when he realised they were all staring at him. He led them past a large oak tree, his fingers rubbing a rune that someone had carved into the trunk a long time ago. Not far from the tree, he found the thin trail, mainly used by deer and hunters, and after spending a few heartbeats working out which way was north, he turned and led them away from danger. Or so he hoped. Ketil was a smart man. The two of them had fought against and with each other many times when he was still a young warrior, and Sven knew that if there was anyone who could figure out where they were going, then it was Ketil. He was just surprised the jarl had not sent the man out first. A raven cried from the trees above them, and Sven couldn't stop the shiver from running down his spine. Odin was planning something. He could feel it in his bones as he glanced over his shoulder. Thora sat on the horse, her eyes fixed on the trees as she avoided the low-hanging branches. Charles and Gerold were walking behind the horse, his grandson lost in his thoughts again, while the thrall was watching him.

They followed the trail in silence as the sun, hidden by the clouds, climbed into the sky and started its descent. Around them, the forest stopped and watched as they trudged along the path. Birds tilted their heads to stare at them before flying away. At one point, Sven spotted a deer through the trees, but the animal quickly turned and disappeared again. But Sven pushed on, ignoring the pain in his knees and lower back. Behind him, Charles sat on the horse with Thora. The boy had tripped at one point and everyone could see he was exhausted, so Thora suggested he ride on the horse with her. Charles had protested, but in the end, Thora had won. Now his head hung forward as she held on to him, but Sven could see she was struggling to stay awake as well. The only one still comfortable was the thrall. He moved as if they had just set off, his eyes watching everything around them. Sven had never really thought much about thralls. They had been part of his life, servants to take care of his every need, even those his wife was supposed to. But this one surprised him. He had a lot of strength and was even prepared to give his life to protect Charles. Sven wondered why. From what Charles had told him, he had only met the thrall a few days before, yet the two of them seemed to have a strong bond. It reminded him of all the friends he had had. All of them were dead now, either in battle or in their beds. Sven shook his head to chase the thoughts away, and then stopped as he took in his surroundings. 'There's a farm not far from here. The old man usually lets me sleep by his hearth fire and his wife feeds me.'

'And gives you ale?' Thora asked

'Aye, and gives me ale.' He rubbed the back of his neck, but it did nothing for the pain. 'If the gods are kind to us, then they'll let us sleep there for the night. From there, we can head west to Ribe.'

'We can trust them?'

Sven shrugged. 'I don't see why not. They've always been kind to me.' Without waiting for a response, he left the path and led them through the forest towards the farmstead he had passed through many times.

They stopped at the edge of the forest and, in the late afternoon light, Sven and Thora studied the farmstead in the distance. Smoke drifted into the sky from the roof as a few goats grazed in the fields near the longhouse. A boy was sitting on a stone near the house with a dog lying in the grass beside him. He remembered the dog. It was big and dark, and reminded him of Fenrir, but the animal liked him and would often sleep beside him when he passed through. He did not remember the boy, though, and wondered if it was a new thrall or perhaps a grandson.

'Will we sleep there tonight?' Charles asked.

Sven glanced at his grandson, seeing the dark rings under his eyes, and then back at the farmstead. He sensed no danger from what he saw and a quick glance at Thora showed she felt the same, so he nodded. 'Aye, if they let us.' He turned to his grandson and his friend. 'I suggest you hide your crosses. Christians are not much liked in this area. And try not to say anything. We don't want to draw attention.'

'You don't think you showing up with a woman and two children will draw attention?' Thora asked.

'Let me worry about that.' Sven scanned the skies, not really sure why, but he had learnt to be cautious. Life as a vagrant was sometimes more dangerous than that of a warrior. Seeing nothing to change his mind, he walked towards the farmstead. The others followed him. He heard the thrall asking Charles a question and hoped they would keep quiet when they got to the farm. His grandson spoke better Danish than the thrall, but he still had an accent that sounded strange. And people in these parts did not like strange.

The large dog lifted its head and jumped to its feet as it started barking at them. The boy turned to see what the dog was barking at and when he spotted them, he jumped off his rock and ran towards the house.

'Don't be afraid, it won't harm you,' Thora said on the horse behind Sven. At first, he thought she was talking to the horse, but then Charles responded.

'Dogs frighten me.'

Sven shook his head, but said nothing as he wondered how his son had raised the boy.

'Don't show it any fear and it'll leave you alone,' Thora said, but Sven felt her eyes boring into the back of his head. An old man walked out of the door as they neared the farmhouse and stood there leaning on a staff. He called to the dog which ran to him, its eyes never leaving Sven and its hackles raised. The boy was standing behind the old man, his head just visible as he stared at them.

'That you, you old drunk? Thought you were dead!' the old man shouted. Sven stopped about twenty paces away from the house, not wanting to get too close because of the dog. It had stopped barking and was sniffing the air, but it must not have liked what it smelt as it started growling.

'Aye, it's me.' Sven raised his hand. 'Although, I'm not sure who you are calling old.'

The old man hawked and spat as he studied his new arrivals. He looked the same as the last time Sven had seen him, although his back was more stooped and his hair was thinner. His clothes were too big for him as well: Sven realised the man was thinner. But his voice still sounded strong and his eyes still seemed sharp. 'You look different.'

Sven rubbed his head. 'Aye.'

The old man scowled, his eyes flicking to the people behind Sven. 'And who are they?' He patted the hound as it looked up at him, waiting for the signal to attack.

'A family heading north,' he lied.

'And why are they with you?' Sven heard the suspicion in the old man's voice.

'They're paying me to guide them.'

The old man barked a laugh. 'They must be fools to trust a drunk like you.'

'Not fools,' Thora said. 'Just low on coin and desperate. The old man said he knew the land well.'

'Aye, desperate you must be.' The old farmer stood in silence for a while, stroking his bearded chin. 'You want a place to stay, then?'

'Just for the night,' Sven responded. 'Don't want to be a burden on you or your wife.'

'You won't be a burden on her. She died a few winters back.'

'I'm sorry to hear that.'

The old man waved a hand at them. 'Don't be. I finally have some peace around here. Come on then, that boy looks like he's about to fall off the horse. You can put the horse in the field with the goats, the boy will look after it.' He turned and walked back inside his house. The hound stood where it was for a few heartbeats before it turned and followed its master into the house.

'You didn't know his wife was dead,' Thora scolded Sven.

Sven shrugged. 'I didn't even know he needed a staff to walk.'

'Do you even know his name?'

He opened his mouth to respond, then closed it again before he walked to the house.

'By the gods, Sven. You really have the people skills of a boar.'

Sven ignored Thora as the boy ran out of the house and towards the goats. Sven scowled but thought nothing of it as he walked in the direction of the house. He stopped at the doorway and tried to remember the last time he had been here, but his mind had been filled with ale and he remembered nothing. Thora grunted behind him as Gerold helped her off the horse. She leaned on the thin thrall as he helped her past Sven and into the house before Gerold came out again and took the horse towards the field where the goats were grazing. Charles, already off the horse, just stood there, his eyes fixed on the boy in the distance. 'You want to join him?' Sven asked.

His grandson shook his head and then said, 'I'm just surprised how similar the people in Denmark are to the Franks.'

Sven looked at the boy in the distance as he sat on his rock again, watching them and not the goats. 'What did you expect? Us running around naked, covered in blood as we kill and eat each other?'

Charles frowned, his head tilted as if he was picturing it in his mind. 'Yes.'

'Aye, well, that's the same image we have of you Christians.' Sven turned and walked into the house, leaving his grandson gaping behind him. Inside, it was dark. The hearth fire was mainly embers and a small flame was struggling to stay alive. There were no torches burning on the walls either, and Sven wondered how the old man saw anything. But the rest of the longhouse was like any other in Denmark. It was longer than it was wide and separated into two parts. The part they were in now was the living quarters, which consisted of the hearth fire, a table and some benches. At the back of the living space was an old bed with mouldy-looking furs on it and a few cups scattered on the floor. The second part of the house would be behind the partitioning and that was where the animals would stay during the winter. Sven creased his nose as the scent of goats reached his nostrils. It smelt like the old man had not cleaned that part out for a long time or the rest of the house, judging by the smell of piss coming from his bed. Sven could not remember much about this house, but he remembered it used to be much cleaner, or perhaps he had just been dirtier.

'What happened to her leg?' the old man asked as he sat on the bench opposite Thora, his large dog next to him and watching them.

'We were attacked by bandits,' Sven said as he sat down and sighed, glad to get off his feet.

'Bandits?' The old man scowled. 'Not many of them in these parts. Jarl Torgeir makes sure of that.'

'Aye, the gods weren't kind to us.' Sven rubbed his left leg.

'And why is she dressed like a warrior?'

'Because I need to protect my sons and this old drunk can't fight,' Thora responded, giving the old man a stern stare.

The old man nodded, but said nothing as he looked at Sven, his old eyes taking in Sven's shaved head and the large Mjöllnir around his neck. He glanced at the door as Gerold entered and then got to his feet, using the staff to help him. 'There's not much to eat. I've got some old bread and cheese somewhere, but you are welcome to stay for the night.' He walked to his bed and climbed in under the furs. The dog looked at Sven with a tilted head before it turned and followed its master. It jumped onto the bed and made itself comfortable.

Sven looked at Thora and saw her scowl at him. He knew she was right. Luckily, the bastard was too old to try something during the night, and they'd be gone as soon as the sun came up.

'It stinks in here,' Charles said, his fingers pinching his nose. Gerold grimaced as well, but said nothing, which Sven was happy about.

'Well, you can always sleep outside with the boy and the goats,' Sven said as he found somewhere on the ground where there were no dog shit or pee stains and made himself comfortable.

'Just don't pay any attention to it,' Thora said as Sven closed his eyes. In his mind, he saw his wife again, her eyes wide and mouth open, her nightdress stained with blood from the knife in her stomach. But she was not looking at him, she was staring at something behind him. Sven turned and saw a figure standing there, its shoulders shaking as it laughed.

17

'Sven! Come out, Sven! I know you're there!'

Sven sat up and rubbed his head, feeling the stubble as his hair was starting to grow back. He shook his head to clear the voice from his dreams, which sounded so real.

'Sven! Come out, you old drunk!'

Sven frowned and looked around the old man's house. Thora and Charles were sleeping on the table, the thrall sitting on the bench and leaning against the wall. He opened his eyes as Sven looked at him. The dog, still on the old man's bed, lifted its head and growled, but Sven saw no sign of the old man under the mouldy furs.

'Sven! If I have to ask one more time, then I'll burn the house down with you in it.'

'What... what is that?' Thora sat up. Charles groaned beside her, but kept his eyes closed.

Sven sighed and looked at the door. 'Ketil. He found us.' He recognised the man's voice. Sven scanned the house again, trying to find another way out, but knew it was pointless. Ketil would have the house surrounded.

'What do we do?' Thora asked, her hand on her injured leg, her trousers still stained from the blood.

Sven stared at the bed, wondering if the old man had somehow sneaked out and found the jarl's man. But then he saw the furs move and dismissed the thought. The bastard was much older than him, and there was no way that he would have run around outside trying to find Ketil. That meant only one thing. Sven ground his teeth as he heard Odin laughing at him.

'Sven!' The call came again, this time with more frustration in it.

'Keep your shirt on!' Sven shouted back. 'I'm coming!'

'You can't go out there,' Thora said, her eyebrows drawn together. Sven's grandson finally woke up and frowned as if he had forgotten where they were. He then stared at Sven, his eyes coming into focus, and must have seen the scowl on Sven's lightly bruised face.

'What's going on?'

'We have guests.' Sven grabbed his new sword and struggled to his feet, his body stiff and sore from sleeping on the ground. His shoulder was aching from the fight and his head hurt from not having had any ale for a few days now. He looked around the farm-house. 'Old man, you have any ale?'

'No.' The response came from under the furs and Sven grunted.

'This is no time to think about drinking!' Thora said, her face stern.

'There's always time to think about drinking,' Sven responded as he turned to the door.

'How did they find us?' Thora asked as she stared at the door.

The old man laughed from under his furs before Sven could respond. Sven shook his head. 'You sent the boy, didn't you, old man?'

'You think I'm a fool?' the old man responded, still hiding under his furs as if they could protect him. The hound stared at Sven, its teeth bared, but Sven was sure it wouldn't attack until the old man told it too. 'There are no bandits here. Jarl Torgeir's men often patrol this region. So yes, I sent the boy. I figured you'd done something dumb, and the jarl's men were chasing you.' He laughed again as Sven scowled.

Sven ground his teeth as he turned to the door. 'I'll deal with you after, old man.'

'What are you doing?' Charles asked, his eyes wide. He glanced at Thora, but she did not respond. She only stared at Sven.

Sven grimaced as he stretched his back before he looked at his grandson. 'Either I go out there, or they burn us alive in here.' Without waiting for a response, he turned and pushed the door open before stepping outside, sword in hand. The sun was just above the horizon, the air outside fresh, and Sven took a deep breath to chase the dirty air out of his lungs. It helped ease the pains in his ageing body, but not by much.

'Grandfather, wait!' Charles shouted behind him as he stepped outside and waited for his eyes to adjust. He heard the boy jump off the table and rush towards him, Thora shouting for him to stop.

Sven sensed his grandson behind him, but did not want to take his eyes off the ten warriors, all on horseback, in front of him. They all wore *brynjas*, with shields on their backs and swords or axes on their hips. They wore no helmets, which allowed Sven to see only the hostility in their eyes as they all glared at him. A few of the horses stomped the ground and one took a few steps forward, but was quickly pulled back in line with the rest. Ketil was in the centre, the old warrior looking tired and his dark hair lifting in the morning breeze. Next to him was Amund, the warrior scowling at seeing his sword in Sven's hand. But what really surprised Sven was the old farmer's boy standing behind the horses, smiling at him. *The gods are bastards*, he thought as Ketil frowned at something behind him. Sven glanced over his shoulder and saw Gerold helping Thora out of the house.

'Thora Haraldsdóttir. It surprises me to see you here.' Ketil glanced at Amund, who looked smug. 'I did not want to believe Amund when he said you were with the drunk.'

Sven hawked and spat as he tightened his grip on the sword. It had been a long time since he had held a sword in his hand and faced men intent on killing, and he had to admit, it felt good.

'Your men left me with no choice,' Thora responded, her voice strained.

'You could have come to me, you and Sigge.'

'No, we couldn't,' Thora said. 'Amund and Egil made sure of it.'

'She lies,' Amund said, his smug look replaced by a sneer. Sven wondered what the coward had told Ketil.

The jarl's man ignored the warrior and turned his attention to Sven, who was still staring at him. He glanced at the sword in his hand. 'Is the old Sven back?' Sven shrugged. He was not sure himself yet. Ketil nodded. 'Well, it's good to see him again.'

'We should just kill the bastards!' Amund said, still sneering at Sven and Thora, but again, Ketil ignored him.

'Who's the boy?'

Sven glanced at his red-headed grandson, again surprised at how much he looked like Torkel. 'He's my grandson, and that one's his friend.'

'I did not know you had a grandson.'

Sven shrugged. 'Neither did I, not until a few days ago.'

Ketil nodded. 'The gods work in strange ways.'

'Aye, they do.' Sven glanced at the men around Ketil. None of them had their weapons in their hands, and that meant that Ketil was not here to kill them. But it did not mean they would live. Birds flew overhead, chirping away and not paying any attention to them.

Somewhere in the distance, Sven heard a goat bleat, but he kept his eyes on Ketil as he waited for something to happen.

Ketil took a deep breath and then he asked, 'So, why did you have to kill my nephew?'

Sven took a step forward and glared at Amund. He felt his grandson tugging at his tunic, but ignored it. 'I did not kill the boy.'

Ketil scowled and glanced at Amund, who glared at Sven. 'He lies, Ketil! You really going to believe that old drunk?'

'Ketil, you know me. You knew my father. We did not kill Sigge,' Thora said. 'He was my friend. I would never harm him.'

'Friends have turned on each other before,' Amund said, his knuckles white as they gripped the reins of his horse.

'That man is a coward and a liar, Ketil.' Sven pointed at Amund with his own sword. 'He killed Sigge before your men tried to kill us all. And then dropped his sword and ran like a whipped dog when the fight turned against him.'

'I'm no coward!' Amund shouted, his face turning red.

'Quiet,' Ketil said, and then he looked at Sven again, his eyes hard. 'Who killed my men? You?'

Sven nodded. 'Thora killed a few, and the thrall killed one. I killed the rest.'

'So the old Sven is back then?' Ketil asked again, while stroking the scar on his cheek.

Sven shrugged again. 'That's for the gods to decide.'

Ketil nodded and looked up at the cloudy sky before he sighed. 'So what do we do? Amund tells me one story, you tell me another.'

'That old bastard's a drunk. You're not going to believe him over me? Ketil, I have fought for you for many winters.'

'Aye, you have,' Ketil said, before he turned his horse and punched Amund hard. Amund never saw the punch coming and fell off his horse, the animal skipping to the side. He cried out as he landed on his shield and then rubbed his cheek while staring at

Ketil with wide eyes. 'I will not believe a drunk, but I will believe the man who gave me this scar,' he pointed to the scar on his cheek, 'and let me live when he could have killed me. And Amund, I know exactly what type of man you are.' He glared at Amund, who was smart enough to keep quiet, before he turned his attention back to Sven and Thora. 'Jarl Torgeir wants me to deal with this situation quickly. My sister wants me to avenge her son's death, but I need to make sure I kill the right man. So, Sven, how do I decide who to kill?'

Sven scratched his stubbled scalp and looked up at the sky again and saw a small bird flying circles above their heads as it chased a fly. He was not sure if that was a sign from the gods, but he knew how he would have dealt with this situation. He glanced at Thora and saw her shake her head, before he looked at his grandson and saw the mark on his neck where Amund had placed his sword. Charles stared at him, his eyes wide as he tried to understand what was happening. Sven turned back to Ketil. 'There's only one way to decide this.' He tightened his grip on the sword. 'Trial by combat. Let the gods decide who speaks the truth.'

Ketil stroked his beard as his men looked at him and waited to see if he would agree. 'And who will fight Amund? You?'

Sven nodded.

'The man is scum, but he is a good fighter, Sven.'

Sven shrugged. 'So was I.'

'Aye, a long time ago.'

'Sven, don't do this,' Thora said behind him, but Sven ignored her. Just like he ignored the urge to rub the Mjöllnir around his neck. But the words had been spoken and they could not be undone. If Odin was going to punish him for breaking his oath, then this would be his chance.

'Are you sure you want to do this?' Ketil asked.

'I only ask one thing,' Sven said to Ketil, who tilted his head. 'If that coward kills me, make sure nothing happens to Thora and my grandson. The thrall as well. What happened was because of me, not them.'

Ketil nodded. 'You have my word. I'll leave them to go to Ribe.'

Sven nodded and then turned to his grandson, seeing how the tears were building up in his eyes. He would have knelt down, but his knees wouldn't have made it easy for him, and Sven did not want to look weak. 'No more tears, lad. Now you need to be strong.'

Charles nodded. 'But you will beat him, won't you? My father said you were a great warrior.'

Sven smiled. 'Aye, but that was a long time ago. It's up to the gods now.'

'You put your fate in false idols?' Gerold asked, unable to stop himself.

Sven looked at him and shrugged. 'I have put my fate in their hands more times than I can count, boy. And I still live.' With that, he turned and faced Ketil and his men again. Amund was on his feet and loosening his shoulders, but he could not hide the apprehension on his face as he must have remembered what had happened in the forest a few days before.

'Give me my sword back, old man, so I can kill you with it.'

'Like you tried to kill an unarmed young boy?' Sven asked. Ketil glared at Amund, but said nothing. 'If you want this sword back, then you'll have to kill me first, boy.'

Amund scowled as he pulled the sword out of its scabbard. It was not as beautiful as the one Sven had taken from him, but its blade glinted in the sun as Amund swung it in arcs after taking the shield from his back. Sven tested his shoulder, which was still sore from the fight a few days ago. There was not much movement in it, neither was there much movement in his old knees or his back. He just hoped it amused Odin more to let him win. *Týr, help me kill this bastard who insults you with his cowardice*, Sven prayed. It never hurt to rely on more than one god for your fate. He then looked at Ketil. 'I need a shield.'

Ketil looked at one of his men who walked his horse towards Sven and handed him his shield. 'I'd offer you my *brynja*, but I doubt it'll fit.' The warrior grinned before he turned and went back to his place. Sven ignored the comment as he felt the weight of the shield in his hand. It had been a long time since he had held one and he tried to remember if they had always been so heavy.

The men on horses spread out around them, forming a fighting square, with only Ketil staying where he was, his stern eyes watching Sven. Sven gripped the shield in his left hand and Amund's sword in his right. It had tasted blood by his hand before, and he hoped the sword would not let him down. He glanced over his shoulder at Thora and the boys one more time, aware that this might be the last time he saw them. Thora stared at him, her face grim, while his grandson's chin trembled as he stared at Amund. The thrall had his hand on Charles's shoulder while letting Thora lean on him as he stared at Sven, his face unreadable. Sven nodded and turned back to Amund, whose lips were pressed together in a slight grimace. It had been a long time since Sven had fought in a fight like this. He closed his eyes, feeling the morning breeze blowing over his skin, as he took a deep breath and tried to bring the memory of his son to his mind. Sven tried to remember the anger he had felt that day he was forced to leave his son behind. He felt the spark ignite in the pit of his stomach as he saw himself sailing away from the Frankish coast. He remembered how he had gripped the side of his ship, believing he could break it with his bare hands. But before the anger could take hold, he heard a roar and opened his eyes in time to see Amund charging at him.

Sven lifted the shield and grunted as Amund struck it, his arm almost collapsing from the force of the blow. Amund then struck out with his shield and caught Sven in the chest before he could react. Sven stumbled backwards, but stayed on his feet and Amund attacked again, this time swinging his sword at Sven's large stomach. Sven got his shield up and blocked the blow, and then stabbed with his sword. But it was a weak strike as his shoulder protested and Amund easily blocked it with his shield before taking a step back and grinning at him.

'This is it? This is the mighty Sven the Boar?' He hawked and spat. 'Pathetic.'

Sven rolled his shoulder, trying to warm it up as he gritted his teeth. 'That's not what you thought a few days ago.'

The grin disappeared from Amund's face. 'You got lucky. It won't happen again.' He charged again, but this time Sven was prepared as he ducked under Amund's attack, ignoring the pain in his knees and back. He turned and swung his sword at Amund's exposed back, but the blow was not strong to break through his *brynja*. Amund cried out as he arched backwards, before he turned to face Sven again, his nostrils flared. He launched himself at Sven, stabbing with his sword which Sven deflected before taking a step back to avoid the shield punch. Sven was already struggling to breathe, and knew that he would not survive a long fight. He needed to finish this quick. Amund rushed at him again. He chopped down with his sword, which Sven blocked with his shield, before stabbing at Amund's exposed midriff. Amund twisted out of the way and kicked at Sven's right leg, who grunted as the pain shot up his hip and fought hard to stay on his feet.

'Come on, Amund. Kill the old bastard!' one warrior shouted, which earned him a glare from Ketil.

Sven grimaced at the pain in his leg and forced it out of his mind as Amund came at him again. This time, he punched with his shield and as Sven stepped to the side, Amund stabbed at him. Sven almost saw the blade too late and twisted his head out of the way, but still felt it slicing his neck.

'No!' Charles shouted, and Gerold grabbed him before he could run towards Sven.

Sven paid no attention to his grandson as he touched the cut with his fingertips. It was not deep and, apart from stinging, it would not affect him. But his age would. He was getting tired now, his breathing was laboured and the shield in his left hand was getting too heavy. The anger he had tried to summon would not come and Sven glanced at the clouds, wondering if Odin was sitting there, watching him make a fool of himself. Amund roared as he charged again, cutting at Sven's face, and Sven ducked, his back protesting as he felt the sword slicing through the air just above his head. He gritted his teeth as he punched Amund in the stomach with his shield, and as the warrior bent over, punched him in the face with the pommel of his sword. Amund's head snapped back, his lip bleeding. Sven saw his chance and went on the attack, but Amund recovered and got his shield in the way of Sven's sword.

Amund took a step back and spat blood from his mouth. 'Not bad, old man.'

Sven glared at him. 'I'm not the same drunk you liked to pick on.'

Amund smiled as he shook his head to clear it. 'No, but you'll die all the same.' With a roar, he charged. He stabbed at Sven and then punched out with his shield. Sven twisted out of the way of the sword and used his shield to block Amund's. The blow rattled his arm and the shield dropped from his hand. Charles gasped and Sven knew that Odin wanted him dead. Amund grinned viciously as he kept on pressing, slicing and stabbing at Sven. Sven took the sword in both hands as Amund forced him back and did everything to block or deflect Amund's attacks. Amund chopped with his sword and Sven was forced to block with his, but the blow was harder than Sven expected and pushed his sword into his shoulder. Without a *brynja*, the blade cut into his skin and Sven clenched his teeth as he felt the blood running down his arm. Amund grinned at him, his eyes wide as he sensed the end of the fight was near.

Sven tried to push the pain out of his mind and punched Amund in the face. The blow was not hard, but it was enough to force the warrior back. Over the blood rushing in his ears, he heard his grandson's voice, speaking words he did not know. And when he glanced at Charles, he saw him on his knees, his eyes closed and his hands held in front of him. But Sven had little time to think about that, as Amund attacked again. He took a step back and felt a sharp pain in his left leg before he collapsed to the ground, screaming in pain. Amund stopped and smiled viciously as Sven tried to get up, but his left leg refused to respond, and the fight left him. Suddenly, Sven felt old and wondered what he was thinking, fighting a warrior almost half his age. His body was not as strong as it once was, his shoulders not able to lift the heavy shields any more. His body trembled as the pain took over, aching joints and bleeding cuts weakening him even further. This was his punishment for breaking his oath to Odin. A humiliating death in front of his grandson. Sven looked at the short boy and saw that he had stopped praying as he sat there, his wide eyes pleading for him to get up. Thora limped forward and put her hand on Charles's shoulder, her eyes red from the tears as she already mourned his death. Only the thrall was unconcerned by his fate. Sven sighed, remembering the words he had always spoken to his son. Fight harder and faster than them, be more aggressive than they ever will. The words rang in his head, mocking him for thinking he could kill Amund.

'See, Ketil, I told you I spoke the truth,' Amund said as he looked at the old warrior sitting on his horse. Ketil did not respond and Amund shrugged as he grinned at Sven. 'This time you will die.'

Sven curled his lips as he saw the smug smile on Amund's face. The same smug smile he had worn every time he beat Sven when

Sven was drunk. The same smile he had when he was about to kill his grandson. It was also the same smug smile the Frankish bastard had on his face when he had told Sven to leave his son behind. The image of the young Frankish prince mocking him came to Sven and he saw red. He screamed as the agony of those memories tore through him, overtaking the pain of his ageing body. Amund hesitated and had just enough time to see Ketil smile before Sven launched himself at the younger warrior, like a boar trapped by hunters and seeing no other way out. He lifted his shield as Sven shoulder-barged into him, but could do nothing as the force of the attack knocked him off his feet. Sven stood over him, his eyes bulging as he beat his chest with the flat side of the sword.

'On your feet,' Sven growled, his teeth bared. He gripped the sword tight in his hand and heard it whisper to him as he watched Amund get to his feet, his eyes filled with fear. But Amund could not run away this time. And as he glanced at the surrounding men, his eyes pleading, Sven charged, roaring his anger at the man who lifted his shield to block the blow. Sven struck the shield hard and forced Amund to take a step back, and before he could bring his own sword up to attack, Sven grabbed his shield with his free hand and pulled it down. Amund's eyes widened before Sven punched him in the face with the pommel of his sword.

Amund tried to keep hold of his shield as his head snapped back, but Sven ripped it from his grip and kicked the bastard in the side before throwing the shield at him. The shield struck Amund on the shoulder and, as the warrior collapsed, Sven limped towards him, his rage coursing through him, his pains forgotten and the sting of his cuts barely affecting him. Amund got to his knees and swung his sword at Sven, who batted it away with his sword and punched him in the face. He fell to the ground again as Sven glared at him, his neck muscles straining. His nose bleeding, Amund looked at his companions for help, but they only stared back, their faces impassive.

'Ketil, please spare me. I'll go into exile. I swear by Odin you'll never see me again,' Amund pleaded, but the old warrior said nothing.

'Not so brave now, are you, you little shit?' Sven said as he walked around Amund and kicked his sword away.

'No!' Amund cried, and before he could reach out for his sword, Sven grabbed a handful of his hair and pulled him to his knees. 'Ketil, please!'

'Stop your whining, boy,' Sven growled as he looked at the sword in his hands. The same one the coward had almost killed his grandson with. Sven looked at Ketil, who nodded.

'The gods have spoken, Sven. Do with him what you want.'

'Grandfather, spare him, please,' Charles shouted, and would have run towards him if it had not been for Gerold holding on to him. 'God says you must forgive your enemies.'

Sven looked at his grandson, outraged that the boy could be so naive, before he looked at the sword again. He smiled as the idea came to him and when he looked at Amund, he saw the fear in the man's eyes. 'I broke my oath to Odin because of you. So I send you to him to repay my debt.' Sven moved Amund's *brynja* to the side and placed the sword between his neck and collarbone. Amund's eyes bulged when he realised what Sven was going to do.

'No, please. I beg you, make it quick.'

Sven leaned forward and through gritted teeth, he growled, 'Like you were going to make it quick for my grandson.'

'Grandfather, please, I beg you. Do not kill him. Remember what God says!'

Sven looked at his grandson. 'I don't care what your god says, boy. You spare your enemy and he will come back to kill you when you are weak.' He pushed the sword down slowly, feeling Amund tense as he kept his eyes on his grandson, whose face paled before he turned away. Sven then looked at Amund as the man screamed. His eyes bulged as Sven pushed the sword into his chest, slowly cutting through his lungs and heart, taking his time so that Amund felt every agonising moment of it. Just like Amund had intended for Charles. The other warriors turned away as Amund screamed loud enough for the gods to hear him. And Sven hoped Odin was watching and listening. He wanted Odin to know that nothing would stop him from protecting his grandson.

Amund shuddered as the sword cut into his stomach and as soon as Sven saw the life leaving his eyes, he shoved the sword all the way in. 'There, now you can have your sword back.'

18

Charles shuddered as his grandfather slowly pushed the sword into the man's chest, whose face contorted in agony. His grandfather only glared back at the man, his face red from anger and effort. Charles wanted to look away as he brought his hand to his mouth to stop the bile rising in his stomach, but he could not. It wasn't because of Gerold's hand on his shoulder, neither was it because of the other warriors surrounding them. Charles didn't really know why he couldn't look away, only that he couldn't. The man shook and his grandfather said something to him before he drove the sword into the warrior that had tried to kill him a few days ago. Charles felt the bile rushing up as the man died, shocked by the viciousness of a man who, a few days ago, could barely stand straight. His grandfather took a step back as the dead warrior stayed on his knees as if he was just sitting there and preparing to pray, and looked at Ketil.

'He almost had you there,' the warrior said.

'No, he didn't. Not even close.'

The warriors surrounding them laughed as Charles's grandfather wiped the sweat from his forehead. Charles did not know how these men could laugh or how his grandfather could be so relaxed after what had just happened. His grandfather tilted his head.

'Now what?'

The old dark-haired warrior looked at the warriors surrounding them and then at his grandfather. Charles felt Gerold tense behind him, before the warrior said, 'Now, I go back to the jarl and tell him the issue has been resolved.'

'He won't ask how?' his grandfather asked, ignoring the cut on his shoulder which was bleeding badly. The blood ran down his arm like great rivers after heavy rain before dripping onto the ground from his fingertips.

Ketil shrugged. 'If he cared how, then he would have been here, not me. But he'll be glad the old Sven the Boar is not back, not yet at least.'

Charles's grandfather hawked and spat. 'Aye, age is a bitch that catches up to us all.'

The warrior smiled. 'Why do you think I get these bastards to do my fighting for me?'

'And what of Sigge?' Thora asked.

Ketil looked at her before he glanced at the body of Amund. 'Those responsible for his death are dead. That will be enough for my sister.'

'So, you'll let us go?' his grandfather asked. The dark-haired warrior nodded. 'You'll leave us the bastard's horse?'

This time Ketil barked a laugh. 'It's not his horse to give you. It belongs to Jarl Torgeir. May the gods be with you, old friend. Your path ahead will not be what you expect.' With that, he turned and galloped away, his warriors following him without a backward glance.

'Your shield!' his grandfather shouted at the warrior who had lent him his shield.

The man stopped and smiled at his grandfather. 'Keep it, old man. You might still need it.' He turned and followed his companions.

They stood there, watching as the warriors disappeared in the distance, none of them sure what to say or do. Charles felt his stomach settling, but his legs were suddenly weak and he just wanted to sit down. But then his grandfather turned around, his eyes cold and teeth bared.

'Where's the little shit that told Ketil we were here.'

'The one watching the goats?' Charles asked, and looked around, but saw no sign of the boy who couldn't have been much older than him. He remembered seeing the boy standing behind the warriors. The boy must have fled when his grandfather killed the man who had slain Sigge.

'Aye.' His grandfather walked up to the dead man, still on his knees, and pulled the sword out of him, the sound of it bringing a fresh wave of nausea to Charles, before his grandfather kicked the body over and walked towards the farmhouse, his neck muscles strained and the vein bulging on his forehead.

'What are you going to do?' Thora frowned.

'I'm going to thank the old bastard for his hospitality.'

Charles was about to rush after his grandfather, but then Gerold gripped his shoulder.

'It's best you don't see what's about to happen,' he said in Frankish.

Charles frowned and before he could respond, the dog inside yelped and went quiet. There was a crashing noise and then the old man's scream ended abruptly.

'Sven, you bastard.' Thora lowered her head.

'Did he...?' Charles looked towards the house, unable to finish the sentence. He heard his grandfather rummaging around and wondered what he was doing inside as he gripped the cross around his neck. 'I don't like the man my grandfather has become.'

Thora looked at him, her eyes sad. 'You might not like it, but what he is now is the only thing that will keep you alive.'

Charles thought about the golden cross in the pouch and his father's words when he had given it to him. Had his father known what his grandfather was like? Had he known he was sending his son to the devil? As if in response to his thoughts, old Sven limped out of the house, his face and tunic covered in fresh blood, and carrying a bag in his hands.

'Gerold, get the horse,' Thora said, and Gerold nodded before he rushed to get the horse they had left in the field with the goats. She put her hand on Charles's shoulder, partly to comfort him and partly to support herself.

Charles stared at his grandfather as the old man snatched the pouch tied to Amund's belt and threw it into the bag he was holding while Gerold returned with their horse and helped Thora onto it.

'Come on, lad. There's no point standing here,' she said to him as she led the horse past. Gerold stopped beside him and the two of them stared at his grandfather, who had stormed off without a word.

'Thora's right, there's no point in standing here.'

Charles nodded and then looked at his friend. 'Do you think God will forgive him for this?'

Gerold shrugged. 'Should God forgive him for this? He's a heathen, after all.'

Charles looked at the house again and thought about that. In the church, the priests had always said that God forgave all sinners if they prayed and asked for forgiveness. He frowned as he wondered how he was going to get his grandfather to do that.

His grandfather set a relentless pace as he led them west, through fields and over hills. Not once did he look back to see if they were behind him, but Charles saw his fists were clenched tightly and heard him muttering to himself. The cut on his shoulder did not seem to bother him as the blood dried on his arm. Thora was the only one who kept pace with him on the horse, and she kept glancing behind her to see if they were keeping up. Charles was out of breath as he forced his tired legs to move, and even Gerold seemed to struggle. Charles was also starving, his stomach rumbling to remind him they had not eaten yet that day. It was not even midday yet and so much had already happened that day and the dark clouds on the horizon seemed to warn him that more was going to come. As Charles watched the clouds, his foot got caught in a hole and he yelled as he fell.

'Charles!' Gerold shouted as he tried to grab him, but was too late.

Thora stopped the horse and turned around to see him lying on the ground and rubbing his knee. Charles felt the tears welling up in his eyes and took deep breaths to keep them away. His grandfather had told him to stop crying, and he was determined to do that. No matter how much the fall had hurt.

'Sven, stop!' Thora shouted at the old man.

Charles's grandfather turned, his nostrils flaring, but then he saw Charles on the ground, holding his knee and fighting back the tears. 'Are you hurt, boy?'

Charles shook his head and Thora said, 'We need to rest, Sven. The boy is tired.'

Sven scanned the open plain they were on before he nodded. 'Fine. But not for too long. We need to keep moving. It's too open to stay here for the night.'

Thora nodded and signalled for Gerold to help her off the horse. As his friend did so, Charles watched his grandfather stand near them, his hand on the hilt of the sword he had taken from the warrior he had killed, his head constantly swivelling around. His jaw muscles worked as if he was reliving the fight in his mind and

Charles wondered if he was. He also wondered how he could kill a defenceless old man in his bed. 'Why did you kill him?' Charles asked before he could stop himself.

His grandfather glared at him, the sight sending a shiver of fear down his spine, but Charles told himself he needed to be brave now. He had to confront his grandfather if he wanted him to atone for his sins. 'Kill who?' his grandfather asked.

Charles felt his hands tremble, but forced himself to sit up straight.

'Charles, leave it,' Thora said, but he ignored her. He wanted to know.

'The old man. Why did you kill him?'

His grandfather clenched his fists and walked towards him, his hard eyes making Charles's bladder feel full. Gerold tensed beside him and, in the corner of his eye, Charles saw his friend's hand on the hilt of the sword he had taken from the dead Dane in the forest. His grandfather stopped a few paces away from him, just enough to be out of reach. Through clenched teeth, he said, 'He sent the boy to find Ketil and to tell him where we were. That's why I had to kill him.'

'But you didn't have to kill him. God says we should forgive those who have wronged us, that we have to turn the other cheek,' Charles protested.

'Your god knows nothing of our world!' Charles's grandfather took a step forward, his face red. Gerold pulled the sword out slightly, and the old man's eyes darted towards him. 'Take your hand off that sword, thrall, or I swear by Odin I will cut it off.'

Gerold let go of the sword as Charles flinched at the threat of violence from a man who, only a few days ago, hid behind a woman to avoid a fight. Thora moved closer to him.

'Sven, calm down. The boy's only trying to understand.'

'He doesn't need to understand!' Sven exploded again. 'He

needs to listen and survive.' His grandfather looked at him, and Charles thought he saw the conflict behind his eyes. He tried to think of what the priests would say now, of what Bishop Bernard might say, but his mind was blank with fear. Fear at the man who was supposed to keep him alive. Charles thought of his father at that moment – not of the last time he had seen him, but of the way he usually was. Confident and calm, always aware of what he needed to do and always putting others before himself.

'My father would not have killed the old man.' He heard Thora sigh next to him and didn't understand why until his grandfather's anger erupted like a thunderstorm.

His face creased in anger, he jabbed a finger at Charles. 'Your father is....' The old man stopped mid-sentence, his mouth still open as he was about to say the word. Charles almost wanted him to say it. He did not know why, but as he felt his own anger bubbling inside him, he wanted his grandfather to say the word. But his grandfather only stared at him, his face still creased as he fought to control his anger.

'Dead.' Charles said the word for him. 'My father is dead.' He glared back at his grandfather, the anger inside him both frightening and exhilarating. It was the same anger he had felt that day that changed everything when he fought back against the boys who bullied him.

His grandfather took a step back as if he had been slapped in the face, his anger suddenly replaced by shock as his eyes widened. Charles jumped to his feet and faced his grandfather with his fist clenched at his side.

'Charles,' Gerold said, but Thora shook her head at him.

'My father is dead,' Charles said again, finding the courage to face his grandfather in his anger. 'Say it! My father is dead, and it's all my fault!' Tears streamed down his face, but Charles knew it was not from the pain of losing his father. The world around him went quiet as he stood there. It was as if the birds which had been flying above them had disappeared, like the wind which moments ago was cooling him down had stopped. 'My father is dead, and you almost died today!' As soon as he said that, something erupted inside of him and Charles launched himself at his grandfather, who dropped the bag he had been holding and took another step back, his eyes wide as Charles started punching him in the chest, again and again as he gave in to the anger flowing out of him. 'My father is dead, and you almost died today, and it would have all been my fault!' He kept on punching his grandfather's chest until powerful hands grabbed hold of him. Charles looked up and saw his grandfather scowling at him and he gritted his teeth, expecting his grandfather to react, but the old man wrapped his arm around him and Charles felt his anger being washed away with his tears.

'I... I...' his grandfather started, and then stopped. Charles felt the tension go out of the old man's body, like an invisible hand plucked it away, and the old man collapsed, dragging him down with him. 'My son is dead,' he heard his grandfather say, his voice so soft Charles almost missed it as he held on to his grandfather. 'I'm not going anywhere, Charles. Odin is not yet ready for me in Valhalla.'

Even though Charles knew his grandfather was talking about a place that was not real, he still felt comforted by the words as he nodded and then looked up and saw the tears running down his grandfather's cheeks and being soaked up by his beard.

'I'll get a fire going,' Gerold said, as if he wanted to get away from this moment, and Charles looked at him and Thora. Gerold looked uncomfortable, but Thora smiled at him. Charles released himself from his grandfather's grip and sat back. He took the pouch from his tunic and took the cross out. As he stared at it, he asked a question that had been bothering him for years.

'Why did you give my father up? How could you give your son to strangers?'

His grandfather sighed and then looked at the cross Charles held in his hands. 'I didn't have a choice.'

They sat in silence as Gerold found enough sticks to get a small fire going. Thora made herself comfortable and tended to her wound, content to give Charles a chance to speak to his grandfather.

'My father said we always have a choice. To fight or to run.'

His grandfather sighed again and when Charles looked up, he was surprised at how old the man suddenly looked. 'I raided those lands so many times and not once have I ever faced anyone other than a few farmers. But that raid...' He clenched his fist and Charles saw the anger returning.

'What happened on that raid?' he asked, still gripping the cross in his hands.

His grandfather looked at the sky as if he was checking to see who was listening. 'Odin fucked me. The raid started like any other. We attacked a few farmsteads and churches, a small town as well. Got plenty of plunder and captives to sell as thralls. The men were in good spirits and so was I. But then as we got to the ships where I had left your father with a few of my men, they were waiting for us.'

'Who?' Charles frowned.

'A young prince with more men than I had. I fought them, confident that Odin would grant me victory, but then they brought out my son on a horse with a knife at his throat. They had reached my ships before me, killed my men, and captured your father.' Charles's grandfather looked him in the eyes and Charles saw the anger those memories brought up. 'They gave me a choice. Fight and he dies. Leave and he lives, but he stays with them. So Charles. I had no choice. As long as my son lived, I could go back and find him again.'

'But you never did,' Charles said, and his grandfather's shoulders sagged.

'I didn't understand it at first, but as we sailed away, I knew I had been betrayed. Someone had told the Franks I was coming and where to find me.'

'Who betrayed you?'

'The king of Denmark, Horik. He had signed a peace treaty with the Frankish emperor that summer.'

'Louis the Pious?' Charles asked, and his grandfather nodded before continuing.

'This was soon after Louis had helped Harald Klak, a former Danish king, to attack Denmark so he could get his throne back. Horik won the battle and wanted peace with Francia. As part of that peace, we were told not to raid the Frankish coast any more.'

'But you still did?'

'I was young and arrogant. I thought Odin was by my side and that nobody could stop me. The king could not confront me, even when he was blamed for my raids. I was the jarl of an important trading town. I had as many men as he had. So he must have colluded with the Franks to ambush me.' Sven shrugged. 'Or perhaps that was part of the peace treaty, to give my son to the Franks as a hostage. That's the only thing that makes sense to me.'

'Not the only one,' Thora said, surprising Charles. He had almost forgotten about her and Gerold as he listened to his grandfather.

His grandfather looked at her and growled. 'Don't start that again.'

Charles frowned. 'Start what?'

'Your father was about your age when Sven took him on that raid. His first raid ever, and who convinced you to take him with?'

Charles looked at his grandfather, waiting for him to respond, but the old man didn't.

'Bjarni, your brother. He convinced you and Eydis that Torkel was old enough to go with.'

'Bjarni would never betray me.'

'How do you know?' Charles asked. What Thora said made sense to him.

'Because I gave him everything when I became jarl. He would have nothing without me.'

'Aye, and now he is jarl and most people don't even remember your name.'

19

Sven sat brooding as the sun lit up the horizon and illuminated the heavy clouds that had been following them since Hedeby. He wondered if that was an omen of things to come, or perhaps he was just seeing signs where there were none. With a wrinkled brow, he looked at the short, red-headed boy sleeping near the remains of the fire. *Why did you send him to me?* He wasn't sure whom the question was for. His son whom he had abandoned, the gods who liked to play their games, or his wife who had not deserved her fate. Sven closed his eyes and saw Eydis standing in front of him in their bedroom, her eyes wide and mouth open, the knife in her stomach as blood soaked her nightdress. He shook his head to clear the image and wished he had ale. Lots of it. This had been the longest he'd gone without a drink, and although his mind felt sharper, his body ached. Sven had never realised how old his body had become. The many winters of sleeping rough had taken their toll on him. Even now, sitting here, his whole body ached. He could barely move his arms after the fight, the cut on his left shoulder not helping him. His back was on fire and no matter how he sat or lay, it would hurt. His knees protested every time he stood up and walked. Sven wondered how he was still alive, but then remembered that Odin was punishing him. Making him suffer until he was ready to let Sven die. The previous day, after the conversation they had, his exhaustion had taken over and Sven had not been able to summon the strength to get back to his feet. So Gerold had started a fire and they had eaten the bread and cheese he had taken from the old man's house after he killed the bastard. He closed his eyes and again saw his wife standing there, her wide eyes staring at him, blaming him for everything.

'I'm sorry,' he said. 'But I swear I will do everything to keep the boy safe. I will not let you down again.'

'I think she knows that already.'

Sven opened his eyes and saw Thora sitting up and staring at him with a pained expression on her face. He wasn't sure if it was because of her leg or because of what she said.

'How's the leg?' he asked her, not wanting to have that conversation.

Thora looked at her right leg, her trousers stained by blood and ripped. Even the bandage which was wrapped around her leg was stained, but she seemed unconcerned as she shrugged. 'Stings, but feels better. There's no sign of rot, so gods willing, it will heal.'

Sven nodded, not knowing what else to say.

'You need to clean your shoulder.'

He looked at his left shoulder, seeing the deep gash made by the sword as he had tried to block the blow from Amund. The blood had dried, leaving a large, ugly scab, but he could still move his arm. He had poured some water over it the previous night to wash away any dirt trapped inside and to clean some of the blood off his arm. Sven glanced at the shield that Ketil's man had given to him, strapped to the horse, and wondered if he could lift it again. He hoped he would not have to find out as he rubbed the Mjöllnir around his neck.

Thora raised an eyebrow. 'You trust the gods again? After spending many winters cursing them and blaming them for your fate.'

Sven let go of the Mjöllnir and glanced at his sleeping grandson. 'They brought him to me, so why not give them one more chance?'

They went silent after that. Sven clenched his left hand, feeding off the pain in his shoulder as he listened to the sparrows singing and the tits chirping. Freya's song, they called it.

'You really don't think that Bjarni betrayed you?' Thora asked as she removed a stray hair from her face.

Sven growled, not wanting to have that conversation again, but he knew she would not let go. 'Why would he betray me? It was Horik, even if I don't know how.'

'But you told my father that Bjarni had convinced you to take Torkel with you and to beach your ships where you did.' She frowned at him. 'You really don't think that is strange?'

Sven looked away as he tried to stop the memories of that day from coming to him. But she was right. Bjarni had wanted to beach their ships at the same place they had done the previous summer. Sven never went to the same place twice. Every summer he would raid a different part of the coast, but Bjarni had convinced him to go back to the same place again. Sven shook his head. 'No, Bjarni would never betray me!'

Charles and Gerold woke up as Sven said that louder than he intended to. The boy rubbed his eyes and yawned while the thrall just got up and walked away to relieve himself. Thora looked at Sven and nodded to show that she would say no more.

'What's going on?' Charles asked, frowning as he saw Sven scowling at Thora.

'Nothing,' Sven said, and looked at the sun. It was sitting just above the horizon, and the dark clouds looked like they were planning on staying all day again. 'We need to go. If the gods smile on us, we can reach Ribe tomorrow.'

'But I need to pray,' Charles said.

'And I need to piss,' Thora said, raising an eyebrow at Sven.

Sven sighed and struggled to his feet, wincing at the pain he felt everywhere. 'I don't see why you need to pray. Your god can't hear you here.'

'Yes, he can.' Charles scowled and crossed his arms. 'He saved your life yesterday.'

Sven stopped and looked at Charles. 'No, he didn't.'

Charles nodded. 'Yes, he did. You were about to lose and I prayed, asking God to help you, and then you won the fight.'

Sven glanced at Thora and saw her hide her smile before he shook his head. 'I also prayed to Týr, and he was closer to us than your god.'

Thora got to her feet and hopped on one foot until she was far enough away to take a piss, but Sven could hear her laugh.

'Who is Týr?' Charles scratched his head as Gerold stamped out the embers from their small fire.

'Another of their pretend gods,' the thrall said, and Sven scowled at him.

'Týr is the god of war, amongst other things,' Sven responded.

'I thought Thor was the god of war?' Charles frowned.

'No, Thor is a warrior god, but he is not the god of war.'

'That makes no sense,' Charles said as Sven fetched the horse.

'I never said our gods make any sense,' Sven said, and was left scratching his own head.

'Ready,' Thora said as she hopped back towards them, rescuing Sven from having to explain about the gods. Sven held the horse as Gerold helped Thora mount it and then looked at the sun, peeking through the clouds, before he turned and walked the opposite way.

'I haven't prayed yet,' Charles said.

'Then pray as you walk. We need to move.' Sven grimaced as the pain in his left leg made it hard for him to walk and hoped his leg would warm up soon. He also hoped that it would rain ale, but he doubted that would happen.

They walked on for the rest of the day, only stopping so that Sven and Charles could relieve themselves. Charles was still young, his bladder not able to hold much, and Sven knew he was just old. Sven kept his eyes on the sun as he followed it west through the dark clouds, but also watched the birds as they flew overhead, trying to find any sign from the gods in their patterns or the direction they flew in.

'Thor's upset,' Thora said as thunder rolled over their heads.

'How do you know?' Charles asked, looking up at the dark clouds.

'The thunder,' Sven answered. The sun was fighting to be seen, but Sven did not think it would rain. He did not have the same ache in his joints he would normally have, but the constant dark clouds concerned him still. They were a warning from the gods, of that, he felt certain.

'I think we should have a break. The horse needs a rest, and so do you,' Thora said as she too stared at the clouds, her eyebrows drawn together.

Sven was about to protest, but then decided against it. The last few days had taken a toll on him and he was exhausted. He scanned the area, trying to understand where they were, as Gerold helped Thora off the horse.

'Do you know where we are?'

Sven turned his attention to the surrounding landscape, taking in the distant hills and the forest just to the north of them. To the south, he could see the small settlement he knew well and wondered if they still paid *landgilde*, a land tax, to Ribe like he had told them to so long ago. Farmsteads dotted around the small village, and even at this distance, Sven could see men working in the fields. Which meant the farmers could see them as well. 'Aye, we're about half a day's walk from Ribe.'

'How do you know?'

Sven pointed to two identical hills sitting next to each other. 'You see those two hills? We call them Freya's—'

'Sven!' Thora scowled at him as she hopped towards them. 'Do not!'

Charles frowned as Sven shook his head. 'Ribe is behind those hills.'

'But we have to go past those farms to get there,' Charles said, pointing to the farmsteads and the small village.

'Will that be a good idea?' Thora asked, leaning on Sven for support.

Sven winced at the pain in his shoulder. 'Probably not. I don't know who they're allied with.'

'Used to be with you,' Thora said.

'Aye, but Odin knows that was a long time ago.' Sven frowned as he scratched his bushy beard. He looked at the forest sitting just north of them. 'We'll go through there. We can hide from the farmers, and perhaps the thrall will find us something to eat.'

'Gerold,' Charles said, scowling at Sven for not saying his name.

Sven shrugged. 'Gerold.' The thrall was sitting behind them, but he seemed to pay no attention to their conversation. 'For now we rest, and,' he looked at his grandson, 'if you really think your god can hear you from here, you can pray. But make it quick. We don't want those farmers sending someone to find out who we are.'

Charles glanced at him before he turned and walked towards the thrall. He sat down on his knees and closed his eyes, his lips moving as he prayed. Sven ground his teeth, wondering why Christians felt the need to pray so much. 'It must drive their god crazy.'

'What must?' Thora asked, still watching the farmsteads in the distance.

'The constant praying. Every morning, every evening, in between.'

Thora shrugged. 'Perhaps he wants them to.'

Sven watched his grandson, wondering what he was saying to his god. 'Then that explains why Christians are so miserable.'

Thora laughed and then looked at him. 'And why are you so miserable, old man?'

'Because we have no ale.' Sven helped Thora sit down while doing his best to ignore the pain in his back.

'Plenty of ale down there.' She nodded towards the small village.

'Aye, plenty of nosey bastards as well.' He grimaced as he sat down and glanced at his grandson again, who was still praying.

'Something's bothering you, and it's not the boy praying,' Thora said with a raised eyebrow.

Sven was going to say nothing, but knew Thora would not let it go. She was like her father that way, and again he missed the sour bastard. 'I'm still trying to understand what Torkel did.'

Thora inspected her wound through the hole in her trousers made by the sword which had cut her. She lifted the bandage and seemed satisfied with what she saw. 'It's obvious. He got some maid pregnant, and they forced her to leave. No one wants a pregnant maid running around.'

'And my son gave up his cosy life as one of the king's royal guards to follow her?' Sven scratched his head. 'Feels like there's more to it than that.'

Thora shrugged. 'Only the gods will know that. Perhaps he loved her.'

Sven thought about it while tugging on his beard. He guessed it was possible, but then something else bothered him. 'Then what about the cross?'

'They needed to survive. One of them must have taken it.'

Sven frowned. Something about that still made no sense to him, but he could see no other explanation. 'Then why did Torkel hide it from everyone, including his own son?'

'I don't know, Sven. Perhaps it reminded him of the mother of his child, so he kept it, but had to hide it to keep them safe. Or he was waiting for Charles to be old enough and then give it to him.'

Sven grunted as he thought about what Thora had just said. 'Aye, I guess you're right. But I can't help feeling that my son was killed because of that cross.'

Thora shrugged. 'Gerold said that the symbol belonged to the kings of Francia. It could be an important heirloom.'

'Then why would the maid steal it? She must have known what it was.'

Thora smiled. 'Perhaps she was angry. She got with child, and they kicked her out.'

Sven rubbed his head, feeling how the hair was growing back. He would have to shave it again before they got to Ribe.

'You really think they kicked my mother out because she got pregnant?' Charles asked, surprising them both.

'Why not?' Sven responded.

'Because they are Christians, and Christians don't do things like that. They would have looked after her.'

Sven shook his head. 'Boy, it doesn't matter which god or gods you believe in. All men are the same, and they are all cruel. A maid with child is another mouth to feed and she will be distracted from her duties. Few people would want that.'

Charles frowned. 'Did you do that when your slaves got pregnant?'

Sven looked at the boy, not wanting to tell him the truth, but then Thora saved him from having to.

'We should go. We've been sitting here too long, and we want to get to the forest before the sun goes down.'

Sven looked at the sun through the clouds and saw it had moved little. But Thora was still right. At the pace they were walking, it would take them longer than usual to reach the forest. He got to his feet and stretched his back before he looked at his grandson. 'Tomorrow we reach Ribe and you'll be safe. Not even the king of Denmark would want to attack my brother's town.'

'It's not the king of Denmark you should be worried about,' Gerold said as he brought the horse for Thora.

Sven glanced at him. 'Aye, but the king of Francia does not know where we are.'

Thunder rumbled over their heads again, and Sven looked up, wondering what that meant.

20

Charles watched his grandfather and frowned, struggling to understand the man as he held on to the horse while Gerold helped Thora mount it. His face was still bruised from a fight he had before Charles met him, although the bruises were going away. The man was his guardian now, his protector, yet Charles knew nothing about him other than the stories he had been told. Charles turned his attention to his destination as he looked at the twin hills with the grey clouds hovering above them. Beyond those hills was his new home, and Charles wondered what it would be like. Would it have a church like in Hedeby? Would there be boys to pick on him like in Hügelburg or would they even accept him there like he never had been back home? Charles frowned as he struggled with all these questions and felt the weight of the pouch in his tunic as he wondered again why all this was happening to him.

'Charles, let's go,' his grandfather called, and Charles saw they had already started walking towards the forest before he rushed after them.

In the distance, an eagle cried and, when Charles looked up, he saw the large bird hovering in the sky above the forest.

'You think he always planned for you to come here?'

Charles looked at Gerold and frowned at the question. 'Who?'

'Your father? Maybe that's why he taught you the Danish tongue.'

Charles stared at the eagle while he thought about it. 'I don't know. He used to say that I could unite the Franks and the Danes, but I don't see how.'

Gerold smiled. 'I don't think that would ever happen.'

'Why?' Charles raised an eyebrow as he looked at his friend.

'My master always said they spent hundreds of years fighting each other and will spend hundreds more doing so.'

'But why?'

Gerold shrugged. 'They're heathens and they fear God, so they attack us. These people are simple. It's hard to understand how they think.'

Charles remembered Bishop Bernard saying something similar about the people of Hügelburg attacking him and hating his father because they feared the Danes. 'But if they believe in God, then there will be no more need for fear, and the fighting can stop.'

Gerold laughed, which caused Charles's grandfather and Thora to look at them. 'I don't think these heathens will ever believe in God.'

Charles watched the eagle in the distance again as he thought about what Gerold had said. The eagle screeched once more as it flapped its wings, climbing higher into the sky before it turned and soared away.

'We believe the gods turn themselves into eagles and falcons when they want to observe us,' Thora said, and when Charles looked at her, he saw she was watching him with her blue eyes.

Gerold scowled at that, but Charles asked, 'Which god is that, then?'

'Probably Odin,' his grandfather said. 'Wanting to see us so he can work out how to fuck us.'

'Sven,' Thora chided him, but then glanced at the eagle as it disappeared and frowned.

'Would Odin really do that?'

His grandfather stopped and looked at him. 'Trust me, Charles. The bastard would love nothing more than to spoil our day.'

Charles frowned and looked at Gerold.

'Don't look at me. You're the one who keeps asking about their gods.'

They walked on as more thunder resounded in the dark clouds, and Charles hoped it would not rain. But soon they reached the forest and Charles saw a rune carved into the trunk of the oak trees. He had seen that in every forest so far and it was always on oak trees, but this time the trunk of the tree was stained red and the stench of a dead animal hung in the air. Thora leaned forward so the low-hanging branches would not knock her off the horse, but then the animal stopped. It snorted as it stomped the ground with its front hooves.

'There now, there now,' Thora said as she rubbed the horse's neck, her eyebrows drawn together. But the animal was not having it. Its eyes widened as it tried to back out of the forest.

'What's the matter?' Charles asked, his hands sweating as he got infected by the horse's fear.

'Probably just a dead animal somewhere,' Thora said. 'That rune on the tree shows that hunters come here often.'

'How?' Charles glanced back at the tree with the rune.

'That rune is linked with Freya. It shows that this forest belongs to her, so the hunters will leave offerings by the tree to ask for her permission to hunt and sacrifices to thank her for a good hunt.' Her eyes darted around the trees as she spoke.

'Who's Freya?' Charles asked.

'She's the reason these trees grow strong,' Thora said. 'She also helps our crops grow so we have food and makes our livestock fertile so they produce plenty of young.'

'Is that not Frey?' Charles scratched his head while still staring at the rune carved into the tree.

'Aye, he as well. They are brother and sister,' Thora said.

'And lovers,' Sven added, which earned him a glare from Thora. Gerold pulled a face as if he had just stepped in something unpleasant.

'Barbaric.'

'Ignore the old fool,' Thora said to Charles, who nodded but still looked at him with wide eyes.

Charles's grandfather turned around and stroked the horse's nose to calm her. 'Perhaps a hunter injured an animal, and it died nearby. Either way, we should not stay here. We need to move.' He glanced around. 'Freya will be upset at the disrespect, and we don't want her to think it was us.' The horse seemed to calm down, and Charles's grandfather took the reins from Thora and led them into the forest.

Charles frowned, surprised his grandfather would believe something like that.

'Almost reminds me of stories my mother used to tell me about the forest near my home,' Gerold said, and Charles raised his eyebrows at him. 'She used to say that dark spirits haunted the forests, people who got lost on their way to heaven.'

'You think that is what the horse sensed?' Charles remembered hearing similar stories in Hügelburg, but his father had always dismissed them.

Gerold shrugged. 'These people don't know about heaven, so they would not know how to get there.' He gripped the sword in his belt and followed Charles's grandfather and Thora. Charles stood there for a few heartbeats until he heard a twig snapping somewhere and, with a racing heart, he rushed after them.

They walked silently through the forest, Charles fighting his fear as his hands trembled. He wasn't even sure why he was afraid, as even the horse seemed calm now. Birds sang from the branches and somewhere a woodpecker was busy pecking at a tree while a raven would call out as if it was following them. The air smelt earthy and damp as the leaves rustled in the breeze. But Charles still felt afraid so he gripped the cross around his neck and asked God to protect him. Gerold was walking beside him, his head down as he watched where he walked, not wanting to trip over a root, while Thora just swayed in time with the horse's gait. Charles couldn't really see his grandfather, but imagined the old man was tense as he limped ahead of them. He had been that way since the fight at the farmhouse, and Charles struggled to understand why. Charles felt closer to the man after the conversation they had after the fight, but there was still something about him that frightened Charles. His expression was no longer dull, and his eyes were no longer red. Even with the light bruising, his face was now tense and his eyes filled with violence. Charles shivered when he remembered the look in his grandfather's eyes after the fight.

'Are you cold?' Gerold asked, frowning at him.

Charles shook his head, but then didn't want to admit that he was afraid, so he said, 'Yes. It feels like the sun has not warmed these trees up for a long time.'

'It does.' Gerold agreed. He looked up, trying to see the sun through the clouds. 'It'll be getting dark soon. I'm sure the old man will call for a stop soon.'

Charles nodded as he too looked up. He could not see the sun, but even if he could, it would have made no difference. He never understood how to read it.

They walked for a while longer, Charles trying not to let every noise scare him, but what had happened as they entered the forest still played on his mind and he could not help but feel the evil spirits breathing down his neck.

'This seems like a good place,' the old man said after a while as he scanned the trees and the small open patch between them.

'Not much space,' Thora said, frowning.

'Aye, but the trees will give us suitable cover if it rains.'

Thora glanced up and shrugged. 'Gerold.'

Gerold nodded and helped her off the horse before he tied the animal to a branch. 'Shall I find us something to eat?'

'Aye, you do that. But don't be long. I'll get a fire going,' Charles's grandfather said as he broke some branches from the trees.

Thora made herself comfortable and leaned back against a tree. She signalled for Charles to sit with her and he rushed to do so. 'You don't need to be afraid, Charles. There's nothing in this forest that can hurt you.'

'Apart from the wolves and the bears. Perhaps some boar as well,' his grandfather said as he stacked the branches together for the fire.

Thora shook her head. 'Ignore the old fool. Even if any of those animals are here, they would not come near us.'

'But how do you know?' Charles asked, biting his lip.

'Because I feel Frigg watching us and she will protect us.'

Charles frowned. 'Or maybe God is watching us.'

Thora smiled. 'Perhaps both of them are.'

'But—'

'Say it, boy, and I'll feed you to the wolves myself,' his grandfather said as he got the fire going. 'Our gods are as real as your god. It doesn't matter how often you say they're not. And right now you're in their domain, so I would start showing them some respect.'

'Like you ever show them any respect,' Thora defended Charles. His grandfather looked up from the fire he had started and scowled.

'Aye, and look how well that turned out for me.'

Thora ruffled Charles's hair and smiled at him. 'He's a sour old bastard, isn't he?'

Charles smiled and nodded, again feeling like God had sent Thora to watch over him. Thora closed her eyes, and Charles looked at the scar on her eyebrow. 'How did you get that scar?'

Without opening her eyes, she responded, 'A battle a long time ago. Some bastard hit me with the head of his axe.'

'Did it hurt?'

She shrugged. 'I guess it must have done, but it was a long time ago.'

'My father had a lot of scars.' Charles remembered the scars that covered his father's arms and the big scar on his side.

'Aye, a sign of a good warrior,' his grandfather said as he sat down by the fire and rubbed his left leg.

Charles frowned. 'How?'

'Because he still lives while the bastard who gave him the scar is dead.'

Thora laughed. 'My father used to say the same.'

'Well, he had plenty of scars.' Charles's grandfather smiled.

They fell silent as Charles listened to the singing birds and the leaves rustling. A twig snapping somewhere and the sounds of the fire crackling away. He smiled, feeling safe as he sat next to Thora. The fair-haired woman's presence seemed to chase away all his concerns and fears.

'Did you have any children?' he asked her.

Thora opened her eyes and smiled at him, but he saw her brow crease. 'No. Freya never blessed me with a child.'

Charles nodded and felt bad for asking, but then Gerold walked into the forest with two dead rabbits.

'Well, at least Freya blessed this forest,' the old man said, smiling in anticipation.

Thora scowled at Charles's grandfather. 'You're lucky my leg's injured. I'd kill you otherwise.'

The old man held a hand up to apologise. 'When we get to Ribe you can, but first let's eat.'

They all watched as Gerold gutted and skinned the two rabbits before skewering them with branches and placing them over the fire. The flames sparked as the fat on the rabbits sizzled, the smell of the cooking meat making Charles's mouth water. He licked his lips and struggled to remember the last time they got to eat meat. He was sure they had eaten the previous day, but right now as he watched Gerold turn the two rabbits over the fire, the meat browning as the flames licked it, that felt like a long time ago. None of them spoke. It was like a spirit had enchanted them as they sat there, their eyes fixed on the rabbits as they cooked. Even Gerold was trembling in anticipation of the meal. And then Charles's stomach rumbled, and Thora laughed.

'At least we won't have to worry about bears trying to steal our food. Your stomach will scare them away.'

Charles smiled, too hungry to think that there might be bears in the forest. 'Are they ready yet?'

Gerold poked one rabbit with his knife. 'Soon.'

They waited in silence, all of them too hungry to speak. After a while, Gerold decided the rabbits were done and gave one to the old man, who ignored the heat of the meat as he bit large chunks off it. The other rabbit, Gerold brought to Charles and Thora. Thora took the rabbit from the slave, and with her sax-knife, cut pieces off for her and Charles. She left some for Gerold, who smiled his gratitude before he sat down and took a bite. Charles blew on his meat to cool it down and watched as his grandfather devoured the whole rabbit himself, his cheeks and beard shining in the fire-light from the grease. Charles frowned, wondering why his grandfather was so selfish.

'When you spent a long time without food, you tend to lose control,' Gerold said in the Danish tongue as he chewed.

Charles looked at him, not sure what he meant by that. His grandfather thumbed his chest and burped.

'Your friend is right. Old Sven would often go days without food, fuelled only by ale and his stubbornness. So don't be too harsh on him,' Thora said before she took a bite of her food.

'Then how is he so fat?' Charles couldn't help but ask.

Thora smiled. 'That would be the ale. Lots of it.'

His grandfather looked up from his meal as if he had heard them. He glanced away, his cheeks turning red as Thora laughed, and even Charles smiled. Gerold just focused on his meal. Luckily for them, the rabbits were well fed, so even though the three of them had to share one rabbit, it was enough to fill their stomachs. Charles's grandfather threw the stick his rabbit had been skewered with into the fire, which sent sparks flying. He burped once more and then laid down on his back, his eyes closed as he started snoring. Charles yawned and before he realised what he was doing, he leaned against Thora and fell asleep.

21

Loud noises woke Charles the following morning and when he opened his eyes, he frowned, unable to make sense of the scene in front of him. On the other side of the clearing was Gerold, his eyes wide, as a man stood behind him, his arm wrapped around the thin boy's neck and a knife in his other hand, which was pointed at Gerold's throat. Thora sat beside Charles with her sword drawn and a scowl on her face. His grandfather stood in front of them, his back towards them, and he too had his sword in his hand. 'What's happening?'

'Quiet now, Charles,' Thora said, the tension in her voice clear. 'Everything will be fine.'

His grandfather glanced over his shoulder. 'The boy's awake? Good. Charles, when I say run, you run faster than Ratatoskr. Head towards the coast. Understand?'

'No.' Charles shook his head, struggling to make sense of everything. But his grandfather's words reminded him of the last thing his father had told him before he died.

'Let the boy go!' Charles's grandfather ignored him and shouted at the man holding Gerold.

'Be quiet, you old fool! Give me the child and we'll make your death quick,' the man standing said in the Danish tongue, but with a strong accent. Charles's grandfather took a step back, his head turned to the side. Charles followed his gaze and saw more men, all of them armed with knives. They all wore green tunics and trousers, with thin shoes on their feet. Their dirt-covered cloaks were also green, and just like the man holding Gerold, their hair and beards were short. They all looked so alike, it was hard for Charles to tell them apart.

'Take your knife,' Thora whispered to Charles. 'If any of these men come near you, you stab them. Do not give them a chance to grab you.'

Charles nodded as his fear took over him and made it hard for him to think. His trembling hand gripped the knife his grandfather had given him, the one he had dutifully worn but never planned on using.

'Give us the boy. He's the one we want,' the man holding Gerold said. Gerold's eyes were fixed on the knife, his face ashen as his chin trembled. Charles had never seen his friend so afraid, not even when the bandits had attacked them.

'Why?' Charles's grandfather asked as he swivelled his sword from side to side, trying to keep their attackers at bay.

'That's not important.'

'What are you going to do with him?'

The man shrugged behind Gerold. 'That's not my concern. I was only told to find the boy.'

'And who told you to do that?'

'That is not your concern.'

Charles watched as the other men slowly crept closer while his grandfather spoke to the man holding Gerold, who was trying to pull his neck away from the sharp blade. He wanted to close his eyes and pray to God, to ask him for help, but he couldn't.

'He's my grandson. It is my concern.' Charles's grandfather crouched slightly, his sword in front of him. The back of his head was red, so Charles guessed his face was as well, but the men in the clearing seemed unconcerned.

'So, you are the famous Sven the Boar.' The man smiled a mocking smile. 'I expected more.'

'Let go of the thrall and let's see if I meet your expectations.'

The man laughed. 'Why do you care about the life of a slave?'

'You're right. I don't.' Charles's grandfather launched himself at one of the men who had been creeping towards him and had got too close. Charles watched with wide eyes as his grandfather sliced his sword across the man's face before he turned and lunged at the next one. The man his grandfather had cut fell to the ground, crying as he clutched his bloody face, but the second man was more prepared. He skipped to the side and Charles's grandfather missed before he stabbed at Sven. The old man batted the knife away with his thick forearm and punched his attacker in the face before ramming his sword into the bastard's stomach. The man grunted as his eyes bulged before old Sven pulled the sword free and the man fell to the ground. Charles turned to Gerold, willing his friend to use the distraction to escape, but Gerold just stood there, frozen in fear.

Thora struggled to her feet and pulled Charles behind her so she could protect him. One of their attackers saw this and charged at her, thinking that she was an easy kill with her injured leg. Thora waited until the man was close, and standing on one leg, stabbed at him with her sword. Their attacker jumped back, narrowly missing the sword point, and smiled at them.

'Think that bitch is going to save you?' he said to Charles in Frankish. Charles gaped at the man as his heart raced in his chest. They were Franks.

Thora gritted her teeth and kept her sword pointed at him,

waiting for him to attack again, but the man was more cautious now as he circled them, forcing Thora to twist her body to keep her sword pointed at him.

'Get ready to run,' she told Charles, and he felt his legs go weak. But before he could say anything, a sword erupted from the man's chest as Charles's grandfather stabbed him through the back. The Frank's eyes widened as the old man pulled the sword free and threw the dying Frank at one of his approaching companions. That man jumped to the side and glared at Charles's grandfather.

'You're going to die, old man!'

Sven placed himself between Charles and the remaining Franks, but his heavy breathing told Charles that he was tiring already. Thora noticed the same.

'There's too many of them, Sven.' She stood behind Charles's grandfather, her pale face contorted. His grandfather did not respond, but Charles saw fresh blood running down his left arm.

'Fine,' the Frank holding Gerold said, his knife still at Gerold's throat. 'I gave you a chance. Kill them all!'

The remaining Franks all smirked and rushed at them, when there was a twang from the trees. One of the Franks stopped and stared wide-eyed at the arrow in his chest. He frowned at his companions, who had also stopped, before he collapsed. Two more arrows flew from the trees in quick succession, killing one more Frank and hitting another's arm.

Gerold finally came to his senses and used the distraction to elbow the man holding him in the stomach and stamp down on his foot.

'You fuck!' the man screamed as Gerold freed himself and ran towards the trees, but before the Frank could chase after him, an arrow flew past his head.

He ducked and his eyes darted around the clearing as he tried to find their attacker, but then he shook his head and shouted at his men, 'Leave them! Let's get out of here!' The arrows stopped as the Franks turned and fled, but the leader stopped at the edge of the tree and looked back at them, smiling. 'This is far from over,' he said in the Danish tongue before he disappeared.

The silence that followed the violence sent a shiver of fear running down Charles's spine, and he prayed to God that he would not piss himself this time. Something he feared was a strong possibility, as his bladder felt very full. Neither his grandfather nor Thora said anything as they scanned the trees, unsure if the danger was gone. There was a rustling noise to their left, and Sven turned as a man with a bow stepped out of the trees.

'Easy now, old man. I'm a friend.' The man's long beard and hair marked him to be a Dane, and so did the Mjöllnir hanging from his neck. He wore drab colours to mix in with the forest and had a felt cap on his head.

'Who are you calling old?' Charles's grandfather said as he straightened up and lowered his sword.

The man smiled. 'Forgive me. It's obvious you still have many winters left in you.'

Charles's grandfather glared at the man before he lowered his sword. 'We thank you for your help.'

'Aye, you can thank the gods I was nearby.'

'You were hunting?' Thora asked, leaning against the tree to support herself, her face pale from the pain.

The hunter nodded. 'But Odin knows, this was not what I expected to find.'

'Aye, us neither.' Charles's grandfather rubbed his head and looked at the dead men. There were five of them, two killed by arrows and three by Sven. Even the man whose face he had cut was dead with a stab wound to his chest. Charles swayed as he stared at the dead men, but then he remembered his friend.

'Where's Gerold?'

Thora frowned. 'I don't know.'

'Did they take him?' Charles panicked when no one answered him.

'I'm here,' the voice came from the trees, and Gerold stepped into the clearing. The hunter pointed his bow at him, an arrow notched, and the string pulled back. Gerold quickly raised his hands to show he meant no harm.

'Stop, he's my friend!' Charles yelled at the hunter.

The hunter looked at them before lowering his bow. Gerold sighed and then rushed towards Charles.

'Charles, forgive me. Are you all right?'

Charles nodded, but then frowned. 'What happened?'

'That's what I'd like to know as well.' His grandfather scowled.

Thora sat down again and rubbed her leg as Gerold's cheeks turned red. 'Please, forgive me. I never saw them. I was setting my traps when they grabbed me from behind.'

'You could have yelled, tried to warn us somehow!' Charles's grandfather glared at Gerold, who lowered his head.

'I... I panicked. They appeared out of nowhere.'

'It's fine,' Thora said, her face still pale. 'We're all safe.'

'Did they say anything to you?' Charles's grandfather asked, still not happy with Gerold.

Gerold shook his head. 'Only asked how many we were. I refused to answer, and they struck me on the head.' Charles saw the light bruise on Gerold's temple and thanked God that his friend was still alive.

Charles's grandfather scanned the trees, his face creased. 'How did the bastards find us?'

'They must have followed us or tracked us somehow,' Thora responded.

'And avoided everyone, even Ketil and his men?'

Thora shrugged. 'It's possible.'

Charles's grandfather stared at Thora before he nodded and bent down to clean his sword on the tunic of one of the dead Franks, wincing as he did so.

The hunter looked at them with a wrinkled forehead. 'Where are you headed?'

'To Ribe. Are you from there?' Charles's grandfather asked the hunter.

The hunter shook his head. 'No, I'm from a small village a little south of here, but I can take you to Ribe. Make sure those men don't bother you again.'

Sven glanced at Thora, who shrugged. Charles thought it was a good idea. The hunter had chased the Franks off after all, so why not accept his help? He looked at his grandfather, seeing him frown as he thought about it.

'Well, Odin knows, if it weren't for you, we'd be feeding the ravens by now. We accept your offer.' The hunter smiled as Sven sheathed his sword. 'But we should get going. I want to be in Ribe by midday.'

'You been to Ribe before?' the hunter asked as he walked around and collected his arrows from the dead Franks. Charles watched, his stomach feeling unsettled as the hunter put his foot on one body and pulled his arrow out. He looked at the arrow before wiping it on his trousers and putting it in his quiver.

Charles's grandfather looked at the man before he responded. 'It was my home. A long time ago.'

The hunter nodded, perhaps sensing that Charles's grandfather did not want to talk more about it. They collected their things as Gerold went to get the horse. The animal whined and stomped her feet as she tried to back away from Gerold.

'The animal is spooked,' Thora said.

'Then just leave it,' the hunter said.

'And are you going to carry her?' Charles's grandfather asked the man.

The hunter frowned when he looked at her leg, seeing the stained trousers and the bandage. 'Looks like you had an eventful journey.'

'Aye,' Charles's grandfather said. 'The gods have been amusing themselves at our expense.'

The man rubbed the Mjöllnir around his neck. Sven saw that and smiled.

'You having second thoughts about helping us now?'

'No.' The hunter shook his head. He walked to the horse and held his hand out to calm the animal, similar to what Charles's grandfather had done before. After a few heartbeats, the horse was calm enough for the man to untie her from the tree. 'You sure you want to sit on this horse? She's still nervous.'

Thora struggled to her feet. 'I'll be fine. She won't throw me.'

'If you say so.' The man shrugged. He held on to the horse as Gerold helped Thora to mount it. Thora turned to Charles.

'Charles, come ride with me.'

'Good idea,' his grandfather said. 'If there are more of those bastards, then the two of you have a better chance of escaping.'

Charles hesitated, crossing his arms in front of his body as he bit on his lip.

'What's the matter?' Thora asked, frowning at him.

'I need to pee.'

'Then go, we don't have all day.'

'Sven, can't you see the boy's afraid? Go with him,' Thora said as Charles glanced towards the tree.

His grandfather sighed and then limped towards him. 'Come on, boy. My old bladder won't last much longer anyway.'

Charles followed his grandfather into the trees, and they found a spot to empty their bladders. Charles finished before his grandfather and waited for the old man. 'Grandfather?' Charles felt strange calling the old man that considering he had only met him a few days before. But the man was his grandfather and Charles did not know what else to call him.

'What?'

Charles hesitated, but then took a deep breath. 'Do you ever get afraid?'

He heard his grandfather finish, and then there was silence for a few moments. 'Every day, my boy.'

Charles raised his eyebrow at the response as his grandfather limped from behind the tree. 'But you never look afraid.'

'Doesn't mean I'm not. Just because you're afraid doesn't mean others need to see it.' His grandfather looked up at the branches above them.

Charles bit his lower lip. 'Do you think my father was afraid when he sacrificed himself to save me?'

His grandfather put his hand on his shoulder and looked at him. 'I'd give my right eye to Odin to say he was.'

Charles frowned, not sure what this grandfather meant by that. 'But he did it, anyway.'

His grandfather sighed. 'I don't know what kind of man my son became, but I guess it was his fear that gave him the courage to do what he needed to keep you safe.' He looked towards the clearing. 'Now, come. I'm afraid of what Thora might do if we waste any more time here.'

Charles nodded and thought back to the last time he had seen his father. The pouch in his tunic felt heavy as he remembered his father kneeling down in front of him, his body covered in blood and his face creased in pain. He looked at his grandfather as they walked back to the others. 'Were you afraid when you fought that man?'

'Aye, I was. But if you tell anyone, then I'll gut you.' His grandfather smiled and ruffled his hair as they walked into the clearing.

'Finally. I was about to ask Gerold to look for you.'

Charles's grandfather waved a hand at her. 'My bladder is old. It can't be rushed.' The hunter smiled as Thora shook her head. 'Now, let's go. It's smelling here.'

They all turned and walked toward Ribe, Charles's grandfather limping ahead with the hunter beside him. Charles sat on the horse with Thora, her arm around him, as Gerold walked behind them. Every time Charles glanced at his friend, he wondered about the scowl on his face. Charles guessed his friend felt guilty about what had happened and decided he would tell him it wasn't his fault when he got a chance.

Sven ground his teeth as they walked through the forest towards Ribe. His left leg sent a sharp pain shooting into his hip with every step, and his left shoulder stung from the cut that had reopened. And that was on top of all the usual pains and aches he had. But Sven did not care about that now. He was furious. They were so close to their destination and they had almost died, would have died if it hadn't been for the hunter. He thought back to when the first Frank had walked into the clearing with his knife at the thrall's throat. Gerold had gone to find them some breakfast, and Sven was about to look for a stream or puddle so he could shave his head and tidy his beard. He had wanted to look his best when he reached the town that had once belonged to him. But then the Franks had arrived. Luckily for Sven, he was already on his feet at that point; otherwise, he doubted he would have been able to get up. He had cursed the gods then. It had seemed like just the thing Odin would do. Give him hope of salvation, only to snatch it away at the last moment.

'What's Ribe like?' his grandson asked. Sven did not look back. He did not want the boy to see the anger in his eyes or his clenched jaw muscles.

'It's not as big as Hedeby, but it's still larger than most of the towns you will see in Denmark,' Thora responded.

'You come from Hedeby?' the hunter asked.

'I lived there for a long time, although I was born in Ribe,' Thora said.

'And now you're coming home again?'

'Something like that,' Thora said, and Sven understood what she meant as they left the forest and walked towards the twin hills.

'Tell me of Ribe, any news from there?' he asked the hunter to distract himself from his thoughts.

The hunter scratched his bearded chin. 'Not really sure what to tell you. It's calm and peaceful. Jarl Bjarni is tough on any who break his laws but kind to those who serve him.'

Sven looked at the man with a raised eyebrow. 'So Bjarni's a good jarl?'

The man nodded. 'Been good to us, unlike the previous bastard. Although Odin knows, I'm too young to remember him. Sven the Boar they called him, and my father used to say he was a cruel bastard.' Sven glanced over his shoulder and saw Thora smile at that last comment. 'Jarl Bjarni reduced the *landgilde* we have to pay, so living's easier for us. He also sends his men to protect us when raiders come.' The hunter followed the flight of a seabird. 'And Ribe has prospered. Trade has been good, they have traders from all over, men you wouldn't believe came from Midgard,' he glanced over his shoulder to Thora on the horse, 'although, I guess you see the same in Hedeby.'

They got to the top of the hill and Sven felt his heart skip a beat as he stared at the town his brother had taken from him.

'Was she this big the last time you saw her?' the hunter asked.

Sven shook his head. His former town had grown and although it was not as large as Hedeby, it was almost twice the size of what it had been when he was jarl. The town was half-moon shaped and had an outer wall. It was not as formidable as Hedeby's, but it would still make it almost impossible for anyone to take the town by land. In the middle of the town, he saw the large hall, the home he had shared with his wife, and where she had died. Sven took his eyes away from the hall and studied the docks. There were more wharves than he remembered, and each wharf had a ship or two attached to it. He recognised some ships as Danish ones, but there were a few from other parts of Midgard. He looked at the market, not surprised to see how busy it was. From where he stood, it looked like hundreds of ants scurrying around the many stalls. The market had been the source of his wealth. The taxes he got from the traders and farmers had kept his men fed and happy and the plunder he sold had kept his war chests full. Sven had always wondered how it would feel to go back to Ribe again. He had stood on this same hill many times in the past, looking at his home. But it was not his home. Not any more. For the first time, Sven wondered how his brother would react to seeing him alive. He also worried about how his brother would react to Charles. Would he protect his grandson, or see him as a threat? Bjarni had no sons, only daughters, but Sven didn't know if they had any children. He heard a raven and saw the large bird circling above them, like it was watching what they would do, before it turned and flew towards Ribe. He clenched his jaw and, without saying a word to anyone, followed the raven. It was time to tell his brother he still lived.

22

Sven's mouth went dry as they approached the gates of Ribe, the town that he had taken from his father's dead hands. The town the gods had decided he did not deserve. He clenched his fists so the others would not see his hands trembling as he kept his eyes fixed on the wooden walls. The hunter had kept on talking about how Bjarni was a good jarl, but Sven had stopped listening. He was not sure how he felt about seeing his brother again, not after all this time. And especially not after what Thora had said about the raid in Francia so long ago. Sven frowned. *Could Bjarni really have betrayed me?* He gritted his teeth at the thought but then decided that Bjarni wouldn't have betrayed him. Bjarni was the youngest of his siblings, and he did not share the same mother as Sven and his other two brothers. Something he had constantly been mocked about. Just like Sven had always been ridiculed because of his height. So the two of them had formed a strong bond, and when Sven made a move against his father and brothers, Bjarni had been there with him. So, no, Bjarni would not have betrayed him. Sven heard an eagle cry from the clouds but did not look up as he resisted the urge to hold the Mjöllnir pendant around his neck.

They stopped in front of the gates, and Sven took a deep breath to calm his trembling hands. *I need ale. Lots of it*, he thought, and not just to wet his dry mouth. These gates were not the same ones he had run out of that night, but the town had grown, and he guessed Bjarni had to build new ones. Sven was glad about that. He was not sure if he could walk through those same gates again.

'Impressive, isn't it?' the hunter said, mistaking Sven's apprehension for awe. 'The gods know, I've never seen Hedeby, but I still think this is the biggest town in all of Denmark.' Sven glanced at the man, but said nothing. Behind him, Thora sat on the horse, her frown showing her own internal struggles. Sven knew her father had left in disgrace after refusing to accept Bjarni as the new jarl. Sven had told the man many times to apologise to Bjarni and swear an oath to him, but he had refused. Charles just stared at the town, his eyes wide as he took in the place that would become his new home. Sven wondered if the people of Ribe would accept him. When he had been jarl, the town was not friendly to Christians, but that might have changed in the many winters since he had been here.

Sven glanced at the hunter and realised the man was waiting for a response. 'Aye.'

'How long since you were last here?' the man asked.

Sven looked at the gates again. 'Long before you had whiskers on your chin.' He took another deep breath and walked through the gates, muttering the old war song under his breath. Two warriors guarded the gate. One was leaning against the post with his arms crossed, while the other was picking at something in his teeth. Neither guard paid them any attention, even as the hunter greeted them. Sven's heart raced as he took the first steps into Ribe, and once past the threshold, he had to force himself to keep on walking. He kept his eyes fixed ahead of him, not wanting to see how the people stopped what they were doing to watch the newcomers.

Those old enough to remember him stared open-mouthed at the man they thought was dead, while those too young only frowned. One old man, his beard resting on his belly, grabbed hold of a young boy and after whispering something to him, sent the boy running towards the hall.

'Strange,' the hunter said. 'Folk here are usually friendlier than this.'

'Must be the weather,' Thora said behind them on the horse. Sven could hear the tension in her voice.

'Aye, must be.' The hunter scratched his ear as he glanced at the old folk who started following them.

Sven ignored them and their new followers as he stared at the hall his grandfather had built a long time ago. He had drunk his first ale in that hall, got into his first fight, fucked his first woman. His son Torkel was born in that hall and Sven had killed his own father in there too. But Eydis had also died in there. Her image came to him again, her eyes wide and mouth open. The knife in her stomach and her nightdress soaking up the blood. Sven gritted his teeth and pushed the image out of his mind as he kept putting one foot in front of the next, ignoring the pain in his leg and the many people behind him. The hall was the largest building in Ribe, large enough to fit more than two hundred men in there. The bowed roof looked like a giant upturned ship; the wooden beams supporting it were so thick, a grown man could not get his arms around them. Two large doors, taller than all the men, blocked the entrance and could keep out anything men or gods threw at the hall. Sven stopped in front of those doors, his legs weak as the weight of the history of the building almost crushed him. Sven straightened his back as the two men guarding the hall frowned at him. They looked too young to remember him, but both wore *brynjas* and held spears and shields, just like the warriors at the gate. One of the warriors, a large fair-haired man, was about to speak to them when three men walked out of the hall. All three had grey hair in their beards, although they were not fully grey yet. The men had broad shoulders and thick limbs, but fat covered the muscles that had not been used in a long time. Sven scowled as he stared at the man in the middle. He was slightly shorter than the men on either side of him, but he was still taller than Sven, and had the same red hair Sven once had and blue eyes. His beard was long and neat, with a thin braid in the middle of it, and his fingers were covered in gold and silver rings. Bjarni. A deep silence filled the square in front of the hall as the entire village held its breath.

'By the gods, it's true. The boy did not lie,' Jarl Bjarni said, his voice deep as he took a few steps towards Sven. Sven guessed he should say something, but his mouth was so dry, he doubted the words would come out. 'Everybody thought you were dead, killed by someone who held a grudge against you, but I always said you still lived.' He turned to one of the men who walked out of the hall with him. 'Didn't I, Oleg? Didn't I say the bastard is still alive?'

'You did, Jarl.'

Sven looked at Oleg and remembered that the large ginger-haired warrior had been part of his hirdmen, as was the other man. Perhaps that explained why neither man was prepared to look at him. 'Odin's not ready for me yet,' he said, his voice rough.

His brother laughed a deep, rumbling laugh. 'Aye, I doubt the All-Father ever will be.' They stared at each other for a while longer. The hunter beside Sven fidgeted, unsure of what was happening, as his eyes darted from Sven to his brother. But then Bjarni smiled. 'It's good to see you again, brother.'

The hunter's eyes widened and his face paled as he remembered what he had said before. 'Sven the Boar?' The townspeople came alive then, their voices humming as they all whispered to each other, the noise almost deafening after the silence of before.

'You too, Bjarni,' Sven said, and the two brothers embraced.

Sven swallowed back the tears, not wanting his brother to see him cry. They parted, and Sven's brother looked at Thora on the horse and frowned, until a smile separated his moustache from his beard. 'Thora Haraldsdóttir? Is that you?'

'It is,' she responded with a nod.

'By Freya, you have grown into a fine woman. How is your father? Is he well?'

'My father died not so long ago.'

'I am sorry to hear that. He was a fine man.' Jarl Bjarni lowered his head.

'It was his time.'

Bjarni nodded and then looked at the boy, frowning again. 'Is that your son?'

'No,' Sven said. 'He is my grandson.'

Bjarni squinted as he studied Charles and then whistled. 'By the gods, yes. I see it. He looks just like Torkel.' Sven gritted his teeth at the mention of his son's name. 'And is Torkel here as well?' his brother asked.

Sven shook his head as his heart pounded in his chest. 'We have much to discuss.'

His brother frowned and then nodded when he understood. 'Come into the hall. We can talk, and you look like you need a drink.'

Sven smiled for the first time all day. 'Aye.' He took a step forward and then stopped when he remembered the others. He turned to the hunter, who looked like he was about to faint. 'Thank you for your help, hunter. I owe you a debt I can never repay.'

Bjarni frowned. 'A debt?'

'We were attacked, and if it wasn't for the hunter and his bow, we would not be standing here now,' Sven explained.

'By Odin.' Bjarni turned to the hunter. 'Then I owe you a debt as well. You're not from Ribe?'

'No, Jarl,' the hunter responded, while looking at his feet. 'I come from Halstein's farm. He is my father.'

Jarl Bjarni smiled. 'Then your father shall also be rewarded.' Bjarni turned to one of the warriors who stood by the door. 'Take the son of Halstein to the tavern. Make sure he has more ale than he can drink.'

The hunter smiled and nodded at Sven before he turned and followed the warrior. Sven looked at his brother. 'Thora has a wound on her leg that needs to be seen to.'

'It's fine, Sven. I still have some kin here. They will help me.'

'Are you sure?' Bjarni asked with a raised eyebrow.

Thora nodded and then looked at Sven. 'I'll take Charles and Gerold with me. Get them cleaned up and fed, if that's fine with you?'

Sven looked at his grandson sitting on the horse with Thora, his wide eyes fixed on Bjarni, and nodded. He needed to talk to his brother and it would be easier if his grandson wasn't there to hear the conversation. 'Aye, you do that.'

Thora turned the horse and left them as the people crowded behind them parted to let her past. Many of them gave Charles and Gerold strange glances, and Sven wondered what his grandson was making of Ribe.

'People of Ribe! My brother, Sven the Boar, has returned to us. Tonight, we will hold a feast to celebrate!'

The people cheered, but Sven knew it was more for the feast than for his return. Most of them were still unsure about who he was and those old enough to remember him didn't seem too pleased to see him back. Sven ignored them as he followed Bjarni into the hall. Inside, he took a deep breath and savoured the smell of the smoky air mixed with the earthiness of the reeds and the thatch roof. As his eyes adjusted to the darkness inside, he saw that not much had changed. Shields and weapons, swords, axes and

spears hung on the walls, most from his grandfather's days, but a
few that he had hung up himself. He saw some shields he did not
recognise and guessed they were his brother's doing. Benches and
tables lined the walls of the hall, most of them filled with men who
all went quiet as they stared at him. Memories flushed his mind,
but one pushed them all away as his eyes fell on the door at the
back of the hall which led to the sleeping quarters he once shared
with his wife. Sven clenched his fists and forced himself to look at
the large chair on a raised platform near the back of the hall. A
chair he had sat in for a long time. Next to this chair was another
and a woman he did not recognise sat in it, her face like stone as she
stared at him.

'Meet Gunnr, my wife,' Bjarni said, smiling at the woman, who
only glared back.

'What happened to Astrid?' Sven asked about the wife Bjarni
had when he still lived here.

Bjarni lowered his head. 'She died. Illness took her about eleven
winters ago.'

Sven nodded but said nothing as Bjarni led him to one bench.
The two older warriors with Bjarni sat near them, but far enough
for the two brothers to have some privacy as a thrall brought a jug
of ale and two cups. Bjarni filled the cups and handed one to
Sven, who emptied his in one gulp. His brother smiled and filled
his cup again as Sven licked his lips, relishing the taste of the ale
on them. He took the second cup and drank half of it before he
looked at his brother. Deep lines and heavy bags under his eyes
marked his age and grey hair threatened to take over his head and
his beard. There was a scar on his cheek that Sven did not
remember and Sven wondered when he had got it. But Bjarni still
had the same quick smile as before, and judging by the many arm
rings he wore and scars on his arms and hands, he still loved to
fight.

'So tell me. What brings you back after all this time?' Bjarni asked, suddenly serious.

Sven looked at the ale in his cup before he emptied it. 'They killed my son.' His brother filled his cup again as Sven told him the story his grandson had told him and of their journey here.

Bjarni listened as he drank from his cup and when Sven finished his tale, he asked, 'Are you sure the men who attacked you near here were Franks?'

Sven scowled at his brother. 'Bjarni, I know a Frank when I see one. Those bastards were Franks.'

His brother frowned. 'Any idea why they want your grandson?'

Sven shook his head. 'Only Torkel knew.'

They sat in silence for a while as Sven filled his cup and emptied it again, savouring the flavour as it washed down his throat. Bjarni finished his ale and gripped Sven by the shoulder. 'Well, you're home now, brother, and so is your grandson. We'll do whatever we can to keep the boy safe.'

Sven nodded his thanks and glanced at the door at the back of the hall again as he fought to keep those memories away.

'We have a new bathhouse just outside the hall. I'll have a thrall warm some water for you. Get yourself cleaned up and ready for the feast. Tomorrow, we can discuss this properly.'

'Thank you, Bjarni,' Sven said, feeling like he could relax for the first time in days. His eyelids felt heavy, and he shook his head to clear it before he stood up and followed the thrall Bjarni had asked to take him to the bathhouse. Outside, Sven stood for a moment and took in the town. The houses near the hall looked the same as he remembered them. They were much smaller than the hall, but large enough for a family. They looked well kept, and the thatch on the roofs looked like it had been replaced not too long ago. Curious faces stared at him from the doors of those houses, but Sven ignored them as he turned to the market in front of the hall. The market was busy, the traders shouting over each other for the attention of potential buyers, but most of the townspeople were not interested in spending their money as they all stared at him. Sven grunted, wishing the people would mind their own business, and turned to follow the thrall when a warrior stopped him. The man towered over him, his broad shoulders almost blocking out the sun as it struggled through the clouds. He looked about twenty-five winters old with long blond hair and a thin beard. There was something familiar about him, but Sven could not place it.

'Are you really Sven the Boar?' the warrior asked, his voice soft for his size.

'Aye,' Sven said, frowning at the man.

'My name is Rollo Arnbjorgson.'

Sven raised an eyebrow at the warrior. 'Arnbjorgson?' He remembered his former champion, a giant of a man, bigger than the warrior standing in front of him now. 'You're his son?'

The warrior nodded. 'Aye. My father fought for you.'

'He did. The best warrior I knew,' Sven said. 'I still curse the gods for taking him.'

The warrior smiled and then said, 'Mother always said you were good to him. She would be happy to see you, I'm sure.'

Sven's eyes widened. 'Your mother still lives?'

'She does. Will you visit her?'

Sven wanted to say no. He had found it hard to face her after that raid. As he had most of the wives and mothers of the warriors he had lost that day. Many blamed him for the deaths of their husbands and sons, but Arnbjorg's wife did not, and that had made it harder to face her. 'I'll visit her tomorrow,' he said after a while.

The warrior smiled again. 'And perhaps tonight at the feast, you can tell me about my father?'

Sven glanced at the thrall waiting for him and then looked at the huge warrior again. 'Aye, lad. I'll tell you about your father.'

The warrior smiled. 'Thank you.' He turned and left Sven standing there.

Sven watched the warrior walk away and thought of his father. Arnbjorg had been a good friend, one of the first to join him when he plotted against his father. That and the fact the man was a giant and was unequalled in combat was the reason he had made Arnbjorg his champion. The man was also one of the few who could outdrink him. Sven smiled, but then his smile turned into a scowl as he remembered the other men he had lost on that raid. He sighed as he turned to follow the thrall to the bathhouse.

The new bathhouse was a small hut around the back of the hall with a fireplace next to it where two thralls were busy heating large stones. Inside was a large wooden tub filled with steaming water in one corner. On the other side was a small area where they would put the heated stones so a person could sweat out the dirt. Sven already felt himself sweating as he pulled his dirty tunic over his head. He was about to take his trousers off when he realised the thrall was still standing there. He found it strange that he was suddenly aware of her when most of his life he paid no attention to them. Perhaps Charles's friend had made him see thralls differently. 'Do you mind?'

The thrall looked shocked that Sven did not want to undress in front of her. 'I... I'll get you some new clothes,' she said before she turned to leave.

'Bring me a knife as well and make sure it's sharp.'

The thrall nodded and left the bathhouse. Sven shook his head and took his trousers off before he climbed into the warm water. He sat back and closed his eyes, feeling the aches in his body disappearing. Even his leg, which had been bothering him for many winters, felt less sore, the skin around the old wound seeming to relax. But the warm water did not have the same effect on his thoughts. He still struggled to understand how he felt about the death of his son. Sven never thought about what man his son had become, as it was easier not to think about him. Torkel had abandoned their gods and become a Christian, something Sven could not forgive. But seeing Charles, the short boy who reminded him so much of his Torkel, and hearing the stories of what his son had done, brought back memories he had forgotten he had.

That was not the only thought that made his chest feel heavy, though. He wiped the dried blood from his arm and shoulder, feeling the cut sting in the warm water as he thought about the last time he had been in Ribe. The night his beloved Eydis died. Sven closed his eyes and saw her again, the same way he always saw her. Just before she died. That night he had fled, leaving everything behind: his famed axe, his shield and his money. Wearing only his trousers and tunic, he had run out of the gates of the town he had fought so hard to get. That was when the old Sven the Boar died. His hands trembled as he struggled to make sense of the emotions rushing through him, and when he opened his eyes again, he saw fresh clothing had been brought to the bathhouse and the knife he had asked for. Sven took the knife and looked at the reflection of himself on the sharp blade. Old, wrinkled eyes stared back at him. His cheeks were reddened by the many winters of drinking, and thin red veins covered his nose. He had changed much since the last time he had been in Ribe, but now, after a lifetime of wandering around Denmark, he was finally back where he belonged. Sven sighed as he allowed himself to relax. He was home and, more importantly, his grandson was safe.

23

'*Skol!*' Jarl Bjarni lifted his cup of mead, the amber liquid spilling from the cup and wetting his fine tunic.

'*Skol!*' the men and women in the hall echoed.

Sven sat at the table to his brother's right as an honoured guest. It felt strange to him to be considered a guest in a town he used to be jarl of, but he did not think about that as he drank the first mead he had had in a very long time. The sweet drink made of honey brought back memories of a happier time for Sven, and he just wanted to enjoy the feast his brother had laid out for him. To Sven's right was Charles, the short boy's eyes as wide as the plates of food in front of him. And Sven could understand why. Even he was surprised by the amount of food they had prepared for the feast. Three hogs were being spit-roasted over the large hearth fire, while enormous platters of boiled meats and cooked fish filled the tables, along with rabbit stew and stuffed pigeons. There were also buttered turnips, parsnips, carrots and much more. The smell of the freshly baked bread mixed with the meat being prepared made Sven's mouth water and his stomach growled like an angry wolf. Bowls of different berries and nuts were also laid out for those wanting something sweet after they had their fill of the rich food. But all that was nothing compared to the mead Bjarni had given Sven. He could not remember the last time he had tasted anything so sweet. Sven took another sip of the mead and smacked his lips as he looked around the hall and wished that Thora was here as well. Charles had told him that her family had tended to her wound, and that she wanted to spend some time with them, although Sven wondered if she wasn't just avoiding the feast and Bjarni. He knew she resented him for the way he had treated her father. Charles and Gerold had been cleaned up and given new clothes to wear. Gerold, although a thrall, had been allowed to sit at the table with them and sat next to Charles, although the boy looked more uncomfortable than a young man about to fight in his first shield wall.

Charles nudged Sven's arm and said something, but with all the noise of the townspeople talking and laughing, it was hard to hear what he said, so Sven leaned in closer to him. 'What happened to your head?'

Sven rubbed his freshly shaved scalp, feeling the many minor cuts. 'I shaved my head.'

'You're not very good at it,' Charles said, smiling.

Sven smiled back at his grandson. 'Aye, I'm not.' He looked at the townspeople again and remembered the feasts he used to throw. Although none were as big as this one, he mused as the people enjoyed themselves. He saw the young warrior he had spoken to before, Arnbjorg's son. The man raised his cup at Sven, who did the same before he carried on talking to his companions. Thralls were scurrying around, making sure everyone had enough to drink and taking empty platters away, only to bring them back filled with more food. One thrall caught Sven's eye as she brought a new jug of mead to a table nearby. She was young and pretty, although her short, cropped hair made her look boyish. Her breasts, though, did not and Sven felt a stirring where he had felt nothing for a long time. He looked away from the thrall to the seat where his wife used to sit at these feasts. That spot was now taken by Bjarni's wife, who was busy talking to the woman beside her.

'Do you always eat so much here?' Charles asked, his eyes still wide and with fresh grease around his mouth as he chewed on a parsnip.

Sven smiled and then shook his head. 'No, only when we celebrate or want to impress someone.'

Gerold muttered something beside Charles, but Sven could not hear what he said and did not want to. He took another sip of his mead when the pretty thrall he had spotted before brought him some pork from the fire. Sven felt his cheeks burn as she smiled at him, and then his brother elbowed him in the side.

'She's a beauty, that one,' he said as he leered after the thrall. 'I can have her sent to you after the feast.'

Sven shook his head. 'Odin knows, I'm too old for that now.'

His brother laughed. 'Nonsense, brother. And besides, she'll make you feel young again.' Sven took another sip of his mead before he stuffed some of the hot pork into his mouth, which only made his brother laugh even more. 'Where is the *skald*?' Jarl Bjarni shouted, and a thin man stood up from one of the benches with a lyre in his hands.

'Jarl?'

'Sing us a song.' Bjarni frowned and rubbed his chin and then said, 'Tell us about Sven the Boar's first victorious battle as a jarl.' The men cheered and slammed their fists on the tables, the sound vibrating around the hall.

'Do you know this story?' Charles asked him, and Sven shook his head. He remembered his first victory as a jarl, but he did not remember any song written about it.

The *skald* took a sip from his cup as the hall fell silent and, after plucking at a few strings on his lyre, he started singing of a battle fought many winters ago. Sven remembered the battle well. It was after he had become jarl and another jarl, who had been good friends of his father, thought he could defeat Sven and take Ribe for himself. Sven's army had been outnumbered, but he had still won that battle and King Horik was forced to accept him as jarl of Ribe after that. As the *skald* sang, Sven recognised it as the song he always sang to himself as he wandered around Denmark. He pushed his food away, not wanting to eat any more. That battle had been one of the greatest moments of his life and six winters after that, he had lost it all. Sven glanced at the seat where his wife used to sit and saw Bjarni's wife staring at him. He looked away before he saw the glint in her eye and took another sip of his mead as the *skald* came to the end of the song. The part where Sven had broken the enemy's shield wall and cut their jarl's leg off before splitting his skull in two. The men in the hall sang along as they banged their fists on the tables, their deep voices almost ripping the roof of the hall, and when the song finished, the door of the hall swung open.

Four men stood at the door, and in the dim light, Sven couldn't make them out. The conversations in the hall stopped, and it was like all the life had been sucked out of the feast as the four men walked towards the jarl's table. Thralls disappeared and all the warriors turned towards the table where Sven sat beside his brother. Sven frowned, struggling to understand what was happening, but knew something wasn't right. He had drunk too much mead, forgetting how potent it was, and when the newcomers were close enough for Sven to recognise, he heard Charles scream.

'Grandfather!'

Sven turned, knocking his mead over, and saw Gerold dragging Charles away. At first, he thought that the thrall was taking his grandson to safety, but then he saw Charles's wide eyes and the knife at his throat. He looked at Gerold and saw his red face and teeth bared. The hall seemed to spin as Sven struggled to make sense of things and he heard the gods laughing at him in the silence. Or perhaps that was his brother's wife.

'Ah, Sven. Let me introduce you to our honoured guests,' his brother said, raising his cup to the four men as they stopped in front of the table.

Sven recognised the three men who had attacked them in the forest not far from Ribe. He did not recognise the fourth man, who wrinkled his nose as he glanced around the hall, but his fine tunic and his expensive leather boots told Sven this man was important. The other three, who still wore the same green outfits they had on when they attacked them earlier, grinned at him. Sven felt numb as he looked at Charles and saw the boy frozen with fear, his face pale and eyes red. He turned to his brother, frowning as he still struggled to understand.

'You still don't get it, do you?' His brother smirked at him.

'What?' Sven kept looking at his grandson and then at the Franks in front of him, not sure if what he was seeing was real. His brother laughed beside him, his wife and most of the people in the hall joining in. The sound ripped through his head like thunder, as if Thor had struck the truth into him with his mighty hammer. Time seemed to stop as Sven finally understood. Even the battle against the Franks so long ago. It all made sense, and Sven knew who had betrayed him. Thora had been right all along. Sven roared as he launched himself at his brother, and before anyone could react, he punched Bjarni on the side of his head. Bjarni's wife screamed and warriors jumped to their feet as Bjarni fell over the table. Sven saw nothing else, heard nothing else, but his brother. The bastard who had taken his son away from him. He grabbed Bjarni by his red hair and smashed his face into the table before throwing him to the ground. The Franks stood back as warriors rushed at Sven and before he could stomp on his brother's head, someone grabbed him from behind. Sven roared and struck the man with the back of his head. The warrior let go and stumbled back, and Sven turned and launched himself at the man. He tackled the warrior to the ground and punched him in the face, again and again, until two more warriors grabbed him and pulled him off the unconscious warrior. Sven screamed and kicked. Spit was flying from his mouth as he twisted and turned, doing everything he could to free himself from their grip, but they were too strong.

'Enough!' His brother's voice tore through the red fog in his mind and Sven's heart almost stopped when he saw Bjarni standing there, blood gushing out of his nose and with Charles in front of him. 'Stop, or I kill the little shit!'

Sven's bulging eyes darted around the hall, trying to find anything or anyone who could help him as he strained against the warriors holding him. He looked at the Franks and saw only the smirks on their faces.

'Please stop.' Sven heard the voice behind him and recognised it as Arnbjorg's son, Rollo.

He glanced over his shoulder and saw the huge warrior was one of the two men holding him. Sven ground his teeth as he looked at his brother again. 'Why?'

'You should never have come here,' his brother said, not really responding to his question.

'Why?' Sven growled again, straining against the two men holding him.

Jarl Bjarni shook his head. 'Because you are cursed, Sven. Because you ruin everything you touch!'

Sven roared as he surged forward, catching the two warriors by surprise as he freed himself from their grips. But before he reached his brother, Bjarni pulled a knife out and stuck it against Charles's throat. The boy whimpered and Sven stopped in his tracks, seeing the fear in the boy's eyes. It reminded him of the last time he saw his son, and Sven dropped to his knees as the fight left him. He looked at his grandson.

'Don't be afraid, Charles. I'll come for you.'

His brother laughed. 'You made that promise once and failed to keep it. What makes you think you will this time?'

Sven ground his teeth as he glared at his brother, but before he could say anything, Charles responded.

'Because he is Sven the Boar.' The boy looked at him and Sven saw him trying to be brave, just like Torkel had done that day.

Again, Bjarni laughed. 'Ah yes, Sven the Boar. The fiercest warrior on Midgard. A man even Odin is too afraid to have in Valhalla.' The warriors laughed as Bjarni pulled the knife back and knelt down so his mouth was by Charles's ear. Both of them stared at Sven, Charles looking afraid, but trying to be brave, whereas Bjarni's eyes glinted from the mead and the fun he was having. 'Let me tell you about the man your grandfather is.' He stared at Sven, who frowned. 'Did your grandfather tell you why he has spent the last eighteen winters wandering around Denmark and trying to drink himself to death?'

Sven shook his head when he saw where this was going. 'Bjarni, don't. Charles, don't listen to him.'

Bjarni smiled. 'Did he tell you about your grandmother? About how she died?'

Charles shook his head and frowned at Sven.

'Don't listen to him, boy.'

Bjarni leaned in closer to Charles and, with a lower voice, said, 'Did he tell you how he killed her?'

Charles's eyes widened, and he stared at Sven. 'Grandfather, is... is that... true?'

Sven lowered his head and closed his eyes. In his mind, he saw his wife standing in front of him, her eyes wide and mouth open. A knife in her stomach, the blood drenching her nightdress, and his hand on the hilt of the knife. 'Eydis, please forgive me.'

'See,' Bjarni said. 'And not just that. He fled afterwards. The thralls found her dead in their room, a knife in her gut. Your grandfather's not the man you think he is and he will not do anything to save you, just like he did nothing to save his own son.'

Sven opened his eyes and stared at his grandson. The tears running down his cheeks were like a stab in his chest. 'Charles?' But Charles only looked away from Sven as the shrill laughter of Bjarni's wife mocked him.

'I've had enough,' Bjarni said. He looked at the warriors behind Sven. 'Deal with him.'

Sven looked over his shoulder and said to Rollo, 'Your father was a better man than you, boy.'

'Perhaps,' Rollo said, and Sven just had enough time to look at his grandson again, to see the tears in his eyes, before Rollo knocked him out.

* * *

Charles stared at his grandfather, who lay unconscious on the ground, his scalp bleeding where the giant warrior had struck him. He felt cold as the words of his grandfather's brother rang in his ears. Had his grandfather really killed his wife? Charles did not want to believe that. He could not, but then his grandfather's reaction told him it was true. He knew his grandfather had sinned, but he had never realised he was so evil. All Charles wanted to do was free himself from the horrible man behind him and run until he could run no more, but his legs were too numb to move. The feast had stopped as everyone in the hall watched what was happening, as if this was part of their entertainment. The *skald* who had sung the strange song was sitting again and staring at his own feet. The only people on their feet were the warriors who had rushed to their jarl's aid and the Franks who stood exactly where they had been before, all of them glaring at him. Charles looked at Gerold, who was sneering at him, and felt his heart break.

'Should we kill him?' the giant warrior asked his grandfather's brother.

The jarl rubbed the side of his head where he had been struck, scowling at Charles's grandfather, but then shook his head. 'His death should be public. The bastard brought a lot of misery to this town. Throw him in the hut for now.' The two warriors nodded and dragged his grandfather away.

'Give me the boy,' the richly dressed Frank said in Danish, his dark eyes fixed on Charles.

Charles shivered and tried to take a step back, but the jarl still held on to him.

'Why?' the jarl asked. 'Why not just kill the runt?'

'Because those were not my orders.' The Frank scowled at the jarl.

The jarl shrugged. 'Fair enough. Just thought it'd be easier to kill him.'

'I agree,' the Frank said. 'But my master wants something from him.'

Charles felt like he was lost in a dark forest, unsure of which path to take to leave. He looked at Gerold, who was standing nearby, his knife still in his hand and glaring at him.

The jarl shrugged and pushed Charles towards the slave, who grabbed him and hissed in his ear, 'Don't you try anything now.'

Charles paled and shook his head as his eyes were fixed on the sharp knife pointing at him.

'Will you stay and enjoy the feast with us?' the jarl asked the Franks.

The leader of the group glanced around, taking in all the people staring at them. 'I thought the feast was finished.'

Jarl Bjarni laughed and rubbed the side of his face again. 'No,' he faced the people of Ribe and lifted his cup of mead, 'the real feast starts now!'

The warriors cheered, and those who could lifted their own cups, but Charles noticed the people were more subdued than before. The two warriors who took his grandfather returned, and Charles wondered what they had done to him. He then wondered why he cared. His grandfather was a monster who had killed his own wife. But he was also the only man who could save Charles. His hand went to the small wooden cross around his neck as he prayed to God for help.

'I told you before, that will not help you,' Gerold said.

'Why are you doing this?' Charles asked him. 'I thought you were my friend?'

But Gerold only laughed. 'I was never your friend. I'm a slave, remember? And thanks to you, that life is over for me.' Charles frowned as Gerold smirked at him.

'Is there somewhere we can keep the boy safe until we leave?' the richly dressed Frank asked the jarl.

Jarl Bjarni frowned and then nodded. 'You can keep him in my sleeping quarters for now.'

'But, husband, that is our room!' his wife hissed at him.

'And they are important guests,' he hissed back.

The leader of the Franks nodded towards Gerold, who dragged Charles towards the door at the end of the hall. Charles thought about running again, but even if he could get his legs to obey, he had nowhere to go. He thought about running to Thora, but then knew there was nothing she could do, not with her injury.

'Rollo, watch the door,' Charles heard the jarl tell the huge warrior.

Gerold took Charles into a dark room larger than the house Charles had shared with his father back in Hügelburg, which had an enormous bed covered in furs and three huge chests. The walls were adorned with shields and weapons, and in one corner was a large chain mail vest hanging on a wooden frame and a beautiful helmet on top of it. A handful of candles struggled to light the room and the smell of the candle wax mixed with a musty scent made both Charles and Gerold wrinkle their noses.

Gerold threw Charles onto the bed as the door behind them closed and he landed on the soft furs. He sat up and swallowed back his tears as he stared at Gerold, determined not to cry.

'Stop looking at me,' Gerold said, but Charles ignored him. Through the thick door, Charles could hear the feast going again as people talked and laughed. He looked around the room and saw another door by the back wall and wondered where that led to before he looked at Gerold again, who was leaning against the wall, his arms crossed and face creased.

'Please, Gerold. Let me go. I swear to God I won't tell anyone.'

Gerold laughed. 'You really are dumb, aren't you? If I let you go, then they'll kill me.'

'Then come with me.'

Again, Gerold laughed. 'Why in God's name would I do that?'

'Because we are friends.'

Gerold rushed forward and pointed his knife at Charles, causing him to flinch. 'We are not friends. We never were and I thank God this charade's finally over and I don't have to spend any more time with those filthy heathens. You don't know how many times I wanted to stab them while they were sleeping. Especially that bitch who pretended she could fight like a man.'

Charles frowned as his mind raced. 'Thora?'

'Yes! Thora, that dumb heathen bitch! By God, I wanted to kill her so much, and as for your drunken excuse of a grandfather. That man was infuriating.'

'B... but the... then why help me?' His head started hurting as he tried to make sense of everything.

Gerold shrugged as he leaned against the wall again. 'I had to.' He sighed when he saw Charles frown. 'My master told me to look out for a small boy with red hair. He's very important and must be found quickly. And there you were, hiding under an empty stall in the market as if God had placed you there for me to find.'

Charles frowned. 'Your master? The drunk trader?'

'Yes, although he was never really drunk. Only pretended so people would tell him things they shouldn't. He was a spy for Duke Liudolf.'

'The duke wanted you to kill me?' Charles's eyes widened, but Gerold shook his head.

'No, not to kill you. The duke wanted you alive, although I don't know why. I offered to kill you but my master said no. We were supposed to take you somewhere, hand you over to other men. My master said the duke was looking for something, but wouldn't tell me what. I'm guessing it's that pretty cross you have though.'

Charles's hand went to his tunic where he would normally keep the pouch with the cross as he struggled to make sense of Gerold's story. But he didn't have the cross on him. Thora had suggested that she look after it while Charles and Gerold came to the feast. Gerold didn't know that though. And then he thought of something else. 'So you're not a slave? Your father never sold you?'

Gerold sighed. 'No, that was all true. My father did sell me. But he never realised he sold me to the duke's spies. They use slaves as informants and spies all the time.' He laughed. 'It's clever, really. No one pays attention to slaves. You'd be amazed at what we hear. The old trader was my spymaster. He was teaching me how to be a good spy and, if necessary, a good assassin. I learnt a lot from the old man.'

'And what about the bandits?' There was a loud cheer in the hall, and Charles glanced at the door.

Gerold studied the knife he had taken from the bandit he had killed. 'That was just unfortunate, but we got out of that situation. I wanted to take you to the nearest town and try to complete my mission, but you refused. So I had to improvise. I left a note on the cart, hoping that they would send men to search for it when we didn't reach our destination. After that, it was just a case of finding time to leave a trail for whoever was following us. Luckily for me, your grandfather asked me to hunt for food. So I had all the time I needed.'

Charles frowned, his mind going crazy with all the different thoughts. But then he remembered something. 'The trail the Danes used to find us. Sigge did not leave it, you did?'

Gerold shrugged. 'Yes. I was worried your grandfather figured it out, but the man is too dumb. Must run in the family.'

Charles was about to ask another question when there was a loud crash in the hall and women screamed. Above the noise, Charles heard a voice that made his heart race.

'You fucking bastard!'

24

Sven groaned as he opened his eyes and saw nothing but darkness. His head ached and at first he thought he had drunk too much and passed out. But then he felt the warm liquid on his head. He touched it with his fingertips and winced at the sharp pain as he remembered what had happened. He had been betrayed. Again. Sven growled. 'How did I not see it?' he asked as he remembered that day long ago when they had fought the Franks on the beach. His brother had fallen as they charged, and Sven believed he had tripped. But the bastard had done that on purpose. He had not wanted to be part of that fight. 'How did I not see it?' he asked again.

Sven looked around the darkness as he tried to understand where he was. The last thing he remembered was seeing his grandson's face, his wide eyes filled with fear and disappointment. 'Eydis, I'm sorry. I have failed you. Again.' He felt the tears running down his cheeks and wondered why Odin insisted on torturing him so much. Was it because he had lost his son, or because he had killed his wife? But he had never meant to. He had not meant for any of that to happen. In the darkness of the hut, Sven remembered that night eighteen winters ago more clearly than he had in a very long time.

It was a dark and stormy night as thunder ripped through the clouds and lightning flashed in the sky. Sven had been drinking heavily again, as he had done so many times since he found out his son had turned to the Christian god. His wife was already sleeping as he stumbled into their sleeping quarters, a jug of ale in one hand and cursing the gods. Thunder rumbled over his roof, and Sven looked up.

'Shut up, you ginger bastard!' He waved a fist at his roof and nearly fell over.

'Sven!' his wife shouted, the first words she had spoken to him all day. They did not speak much any more, not since the day he returned without Torkel two summers ago.

Sven was about to respond when he sensed something in their room. He might have been drunk, but he was still a warrior, and his warrior instinct told him something was not right.

'Sven?' his wife said again, her voice uncertain.

'Quiet, woman,' he hissed as he tried to see what made him feel uncomfortable. All the candles were out, a voice whispered in his ale-fogged mind. Or perhaps that was Eydis telling him that, but before he could figure that out, he sensed movement behind. Sven turned, his warrior reflexes taking over, and he smashed the jug against the head of his attacker. He could not see who it was, but the man was bigger and knocked Sven off his feet as he stumbled into him. Eydis screamed as Sven jumped to his feet, his sax-knife in his hand, and swiped it at the shadowy figure he saw in front of him. A man hollered and fell away, but then Sven sensed another figure behind him. He turned and stabbed and heard the grunt as the knife found flesh. But it was not a man's voice he heard. Lightning flashed once more and he saw his wife, her eyes wide and her mouth open. Sven looked down and saw his knife in her stomach as he still held on to it, as blood stained her dress.

'Eydis?' he whimpered, and when lightning flashed once more, he saw

his wife looking at someone behind him. Sven turned and before the light from the lightning flash disappeared, he saw Bjarni standing there, sword in hand. He turned back to his wife as her body grew heavy. 'Eydis. No.' The words barely came out through his restricted throat and Sven struggled to breathe as his wife collapsed to the ground, his knife slipping out of his hand and staying stuck in her stomach.

'You killed her.' His brother's voice reached him over the thunder outside.

'N... no. It... it was an accident. You saw.' Sven suddenly felt cold and could not stop trembling.

'You killed her,' his brother said again. 'You need to run, Sven. Get away from here.'

'R... run?' Sven struggled to understand the words. 'W... why?'

'You killed Eydis. You can't stay here. Run, Sven. Run as far as you can and never come back.'

Sven looked at his wife, but could not see her in the darkness. His legs felt weak and would not obey him, but then thunder cracked over the roof of his hall, so loud it hurt his ears. It was like the thunder god himself was telling Sven to flee, and without a second thought, Sven turned and ran. As he fled through the gates of Ribe, Sven swore an oath to Odin that for as long as he lived, he would never fight or touch a weapon again.

Sven hugged himself as he sobbed. His body was numb and his chest tight as he struggled to breathe through the tears. 'I'm sorry, Eydis. I never meant for any of this to happen.' He lay down and curled into a ball, believing he deserved whatever punishment the gods gave him. Sven had killed his wife and now he had killed their grandson because he was too arrogant to see the obvious. 'I'm sorry, Eydis.'

The door of the hut opened, and a bright light shined on his face. 'Sven?'

Sven looked up but was blinded by the flames of the torch. 'Ey... Eydis?' She had come for him. She had been sent by the gods to avenge the deaths of all those who had died because he believed he was better than everyone. 'I'm sorry, Eydis.' He closed his eyes and cried.

'Sven?' The voice came again. 'It's me, Thora.' A hand touched his shoulder. 'It's Thora, Sven. Oh, Frigg, what did they do to you?'

'I killed her!' He cried. 'I killed my wife.'

The hand went away and then returned. 'I know, Sven. But you didn't mean to.'

'It doesn't matter. I killed her.' He curled up again to get away from the flames. 'I killed her.' His shoulders shook as he cried.

'What's this?' Another voice rang in his ears. Also a woman, but older. 'The mighty Sven the Boar, lying in a ball and crying like a baby. Eydis would be ashamed if she saw you now!'

'Oda, now's not the time,' Thora said to the old woman behind her. Sven looked up and saw Arnbjorg's wife standing in the door of the hut and then he frowned at Thora sitting beside him, holding a torch in her hand.

'Frigg's tits! What do you mean now's not the time? Fine, let's just sit here and cry all our pains away and by the time the tears have dried out, they'll be gone and you lose your grandson forever. Then Eydis will really be mad at you. And she already has plenty to be mad at you for.'

Sven looked away from them, his cheeks burning. 'I killed her. I do not deserve to have my grandson.'

'Well, your grandson does not deserve to have an oaf like you as his only chance of survival. But the gods are cruel.'

Thora leaned in closer. 'I don't know what happened that night, not many do, Sven. But Oda's right. You need to get yourself together and help Charles.'

Sven looked at Thora, seeing her blue eyes and the scar on her left eyebrow. 'What's the point? The gods took everything from me. I have nothing left to fight for.'

Oda pushed past Thora and grabbed Sven by his beard. He winced as he tried to avoid her hard stare. 'Enough of this pathetic nonsense.' She spat, almost hitting Sven in the face. 'To think my husband died for you. The gods know he'd be disappointed in the man you've become. The gods took nothing away from you. Your shit of a brother did.'

Sven frowned at her. 'Bjarni? But I killed Eydis.'

'Aye, you did. But did you ever wonder why Bjarni was there that night?'

Sven frowned again as he thought back to that night, his brother standing there in the darkness, telling him to run. He had never thought of that. Sven had always assumed his brother was there to protect him. 'He...?'

'Bjarni was behind everything,' Oda said, shaking Sven by his beard. 'He told the Franks where to find you. He told you to take your son on the raid. Bjarni wanted to humiliate you before he killed you and Eydis. I heard the drunken fool boast about it at a feast.'

Lightning flashed outside as Sven's frown turned into a scowl. He remembered hearing his brother's voice in the darkness the night Eydis died. There had been no shock or remorse in his voice. Sven remembered now. He remembered the joy in Bjarni's voice. Oda was right. Bjarni had tried to kill him, and in his drunken stupidity, Sven had done him a favour. And not just that, Sven had spent the last eighteen winters living with the guilt of what he had done, tormenting himself with the memories of that night. He wondered how he had never seen it. Sven had been so blinded by his guilt that he never saw the truth. But then the image of Eydis came to him and his head dropped. 'But I still killed Eydis. I should have protected her, but I killed her.'

'Sven,' Oda's voice softened, 'I will not tell you that everything is fine, that Eydis forgives you. I'm sure she doesn't. But your grandson needs you. You say that the gods have taken everything from you, but yet they gave you your grandson. Through all the odds, he found you. How could he have done that if not for the gods? Frigg guided him to you, and now you're going to spit in her face.'

Sven thought of Charles, seeing the boy's frightened face in his mind. 'Charles.'

'Aye, Sven. Charles. And who took Charles from you now?'

Sven frowned. 'Bjarni.'

Oda smiled. 'And who told you to take your son on a raid, even though he was too young?'

Sven felt the spark ignite inside him. 'Bjarni.'

'And who told the Franks where to find you?'

He clenched his fists as the spark turned into a fire and his heart beat harder in his chest. 'Bjarni.'

'Who wanted to kill you and your wife?'

His limbs started warming up, and the pain in his shoulder and back disappeared. 'Bjarni,' Sven growled.

'Who humiliated you? Took everything away from you?'

Sven could barely hear Oda through the pounding in his ears. 'Bjarni!'

'Who are you going to kill?'

Sven jumped to his feet. Through the open door of the hut, he saw the hall and nothing else. 'Bjarni!' He was about to rush out of the hut when Oda grabbed him.

'Wait, you idiot. That hall is full of drunken warriors. Sigmund, come here!'

Sven blinked when he saw a tall boy appear at the door of the hut, his face strained as he carried something in his arms.

Thora, leaning against the wall of the hut, shined the torch over the boy, and Sven saw he was carrying a *brynja* and helmet. He also saw a sword in the boy's hands and a shield on his back.

'It was Arnbjorg's spare *brynja*. If it fit him, then I'm sure it'll fit you now.'

Sven nodded his thanks as he took the *brynja* from the boy, who sighed in relief, and pulled it over his head. It had been a long time since Sven had worn a chain mail vest and he took comfort in its weight. He shook his head as the boy offered him the helmet and rubbed the faded raven tattoo on his scalp.

'Odin needs to see this.' His voice came out a growl, and Thora smiled as he took the sword from the boy. He unsheathed and admired its sharp edge in the firelight.

'Arnbjorg took good care of everything. It will not let you down,' Oda said. 'Now don't forget the shield.'

Sven shook his head. 'I don't need it.' But the truth was that he did not think his injured shoulder could lift it. He looked at Thora and Oda standing there and frowned. 'How did you know where to find me?'

'Rollo sent his son, Sigmund, to tell me what happened after he dumped you in here,' Oda explained. 'And I knew Thora was with her kin, so I sent the boy to fetch her. Although I didn't realise she could barely walk.'

Sven rubbed the back of his head where the large warrior had punched him. 'Rollo was the one who knocked me out.'

Oda shrugged. 'Well, he couldn't exactly defend you now, could he? Rollo did what he needed to protect you and himself.'

Sven thought about it and nodded. 'Thank you.'

'You can thank me by killing that worm.' Oda scowled. 'Make him pay for every Dane that died because of his treachery.'

'Not just his.' Sven looked at Thora. 'Gerold's as well. He was one of them all along.'

'I know,' Thora said. 'Sigmund told me. First, we save Charles, then, if the gods allow it, we deal with Gerold.'

Sven nodded and glared at the hall. He gripped the sword in his hand and felt anger surging through his limbs. Gritting his teeth, he thought of everything he had lost because of his brother. 'I lost my son,' he said as he limped towards the hall. 'I lost my men, my friends.' His ears pounded as the fiery blood coursed through him. 'I killed my wife, spent a lifetime living in disgrace.' He started jogging, not feeling the pain in his back or knees. Even his left leg did not bother him. 'But I will not lose my grandson. Odin!'

Two warriors were posted outside the hall to watch the door. Both men were bored and frustrated at not being able to join the feast. Both men had also been given plenty of ale during the night by their friends, so when Sven reached the doors, they were not prepared for him.

'What in Odin's—' one man said before Sven barrelled into him, knocking him to the side as his companion tried to reach for his sword. Sven kicked the second man in the stomach and then knocked him out with the pommel of his sword. He turned to the warrior on the ground and the man just shook his head, not sure what he was seeing.

Sven hawked and spat, keeping the image of his son, wife and grandson in his mind to feed his anger. 'Bjarni!' he screamed as he pushed the door of the hall open. Lightning flashed behind him as thunder silenced those in the hall. Thor was with him. A woman shrieked when she saw his short silhouette in the door looking like a dwarf from Svartalfheim, and one warrior spat out the ale in his mouth as all heads turned to him. Sven gripped his sword tightly as he glared at his brother, seeing his wide eyes and the slice of pork hovering in front of his open mouth. Sitting to his right, where Sven had sat before, was the richly dressed Frank, the man looking as shocked as everyone else.

A young warrior sitting near the door saw his moment to make a name for himself as he jumped to his feet and charged at Sven. But the youth had drunk too much and swayed as he reached for his sword, which was not there. He paled as he realised his mistake before Sven punched him in the face with his hand gripping his sword. The warrior stumbled back and Sven kicked him hard in the stomach, which sent the boy flying onto the table behind him. He landed on the table with a crash, causing the women there to scream. And then Odin laughed as chaos reigned.

'You fucking bastard!' Sven roared as he charged at his brother.

The Frank reacted first and rushed towards the door Rollo was guarding as other warriors rushed to defend their jarl. A large warrior swung a jug at Sven, who ducked under the man's arm and elbowed him in the ribs. As the warrior bent over, Sven struck him on the side of the head. Someone grabbed him from behind and pulled him back. Sven turned and sliced the man's leg open. As he dropped to the ground, Sven kneed him in the face, hearing the man's nose break as his head snapped back. Another lunged at Sven, stabbing at him with an eating knife. Sven tried to twist out of the way of the knife but was not fast enough. His borrowed *brynja* held, though, and the knife deflected off his shoulder. Sven sliced the man's stomach open and jumped back to avoid another attack from the side. He ducked under the man's punch and shouldered him in the stomach. As the warrior bent over, Sven headbutted him and dropped him to the ground. Sven panted through clenched teeth as he watched the remaining warriors form a wall between him and his brother, who was still sitting in his chair, glaring at him. He glanced at the door and saw Arnbjorg's son fighting the four Franks, who were trying to get past him and into the bedroom. But then Sven turned his attention back to the wall of warriors preventing him from getting to his brother.

He started pacing as he frothed at the mouth. 'I lost my son. I lost my men, my friends. I killed my wife and spent a lifetime living in disgrace.' He shook his head, seeing the frowns on the faces of the warriors in front of him, before he roared, 'But I will not lose my grandson!'

The warriors were taken aback at Sven's sudden attack and could do nothing as he lowered his head, like a rampaging wild boar, and crashed into them. The man in the centre grunted as Sven headbutted him in the chest, crushing his chest and lungs. Before Sven was past the first man, he turned and sliced another warrior's neck open, the blood spraying out of the wound drenching him, before the warrior collapsed and gripped his neck to stop the bleeding. The other warriors hesitated, and this gave Sven the chance he needed as he launched himself at his brother.

Bjarni jumped to his feet, pulling a sword from under the table, and blocked Sven's strike. The sound of the two swords clashing rang around the hall as the women fled the hall and the warriors rushed to their jarl's aid. Bjarni lifted the table he had been sitting at, his wife screaming as she was cowering under it, and tried to crush Sven with it. But Sven jumped back as food and drink spilled all over the floor. He sensed movement behind him and ducked as one warrior tried to stab him in the back with a knife. Sven clove the man's chest open, the blood spraying over him as looked for his brother while the other warriors backed off.

'Bjarni!'

'You shouldn't have come back, Sven!' his brother shouted at him. Sven saw him walking past the upturned table. He also saw Rollo on the ground, and the door to the sleeping quarters open.

'Where's my grandson?'

Bjarni smiled as he glanced at the door. 'Gone by now.'

Sven gripped his sword, feeding on the anger still coursing through him, which was strengthened by his brother's smug smile. The warriors of Ribe made a circle around him, most of them unarmed and some armed only with eating knives. 'I'm going to kill you, Bjarni. I'm going to kill you and leave your corpse in the forest for the boars to eat.'

His brother laughed. 'Sven the Boar, making threats when he's too old to fight and surrounded by warriors.'

Sven ground his teeth as he glanced at the few dead warriors on the ground. Men he did not want to kill, but they had got in his way. 'Tell that to your men who are too afraid to fight me.'

Bjarni raised an eyebrow as he looked at his men, seeing their hesitation, and then he smiled. 'You really think you can kill all of them?'

'I'll slaughter anyone who tries to stop me from killing you.' Sven hawked and spat as he clenched his free fist. He felt the sting in his shoulder from the cut he was sure was bleeding again and used that pain to feed his rage. 'Why did you do it, Bjarni? Why did you betray me? Betray their fathers?' He pointed his sword at the men surrounding him, knowing that many of them were the sons of men he had lost that day. Some men frowned, and one glanced at his jarl.

Bjarni smiled, knowing he could not deny the truth. 'I had no choice.'

Sven glared at him. 'No choice? I gave you everything!'

'You were going to ruin everything!' His brother took a step forward and pointed his sword at Sven, his face flushed with anger. 'You, with your arrogance, were going to lose everything. I had to do it to protect Ribe from you!'

'You did it because you got greedy!' Sven shouted back. 'Because you wanted to be jarl!'

'I never wanted to be jarl! I never wanted to be the leader of this town, of these men! But you had to keep attacking the Franks, even after Horik demanded you stop. You were so arrogant that you thought no one would stop you. That no one could!'

Sven was stunned by what he was hearing. 'Then why, brother? Why take everything from me?'

Bjarni shook his head. 'Not everything. It was only ever meant to be your son. That was the deal. I made sure you brought Torkel with you and went raiding the same place as before. They knew he was your only son, your only child. They thought you'd never attack again if they had him. But they didn't understand how stubborn you were.'

Sven ground his teeth as his brother confessed. But he was angrier at himself for never seeing the obvious. 'Then why try to kill me and Eydis?'

'You killed Eydis!'

Sven felt his blood pumping through him and heard it throbbing in his ears. 'But you wanted to! That's why you were in my bedroom that night!' More men glanced at Bjarni. Even the two older ones Sven recognised as his former hirdmen were frowning. But Bjarni saw none of this.

'Because you had to be stopped! You were drinking yourself and Ribe into ruin! This town was one of the richest in Denmark and you were willing to piss it all away. That's why I decided to kill you. Eydis was never meant to get hurt. I was going to let her live, but then you killed her and I saw my chance. The gods gave me a way to punish you for everything, and so I took it!'

Thunder roared over their heads, bringing with it a flashback of that night. Sven saw his wife standing in front of him, his knife in her stomach, but her face was not one of shock. Her eyes were creased in anger, her mouth an ugly snarl.

Kill him!

25

Charles sat on the bed, listening to the fighting in the hall as his heart raced. He wanted it to be Thora in there, fighting to save him, but he knew it was not her. He had heard his grandfather's voice. Charles closed his eyes and prayed to God that his grandfather would save him and then hesitated before he asked God to forgive his grandfather for his sins. He knew his grandfather had to be the one asking for forgiveness, but he doubted the old man would and if he died trying to save Charles, then Charles wanted him to have a chance of getting to heaven.

Gerold glanced at him, but then looked back at the door, his knuckles white as he gripped his knife. He was about to say something to Charles when there was a loud thud outside the door and it burst open. Charles jumped to his feet as his heart leapt in his chest, but his elation was short-lived when he realised it was not his grandfather who rushed into the room.

'We need to leave now!' the leader of the Franks said, his fine tunic stained with mead.

Before Gerold could react, the huge warrior who had knocked Charles's grandfather out stumbled through the door, his arm bleeding and his tunic stained with blood on his side. Charles thought the man was there to help the Franks, but then the Dane grabbed one of them and threw him against the wall. The wall shook as the man struck it and he slid down, his eyes rolling in his head.

The Franks turned, their faces pale, as they saw the snarling warrior.

'Give me the boy!' the Dane said through gritted teeth, his face creased in pain.

The richly dressed Frank stepped back and grabbed hold of Charles. 'Kill the heathen!'

Gerold hesitated for a heartbeat as he glanced at the man, but then he joined the other two as they circled the huge Dane, armed with only an eating knife, but his size was enough to slow the Franks down.

'Kill him!' the Frank holding on to Charles screamed as he took a step back.

Charles spotted the knife with a large gem on the hilt in the Frank's belt and as he stared at it, his grandfather's words came to him.

So that next time a man holds a sword to your throat, you can gut him and not have to wait for others who might not come to help you.

Charles's hands trembled at the words. *Take the knife and stab the man*, the words came to him. But he did not want to. That was not who he was. *How do you know?* The words came to him again and Charles was convinced they were the words of the devil, even if they sounded like his grandfather. He glanced at the huge Dane, hoping the man had defeated the Franks, but they were keeping him at bay. The richly dressed Frank started pulling Charles towards the door at the back of the room, and his heart thudded hard in his chest as he looked at the knife again. His father's voice came to him then. *Never hesitate in a fight, son. In*

battle, that will kill you. Charles looked at the Dane and understood the man could not save him. His trousers were soaked with
blood, his face pale and he was struggling to stay on his feet. The
Frank holding him was too preoccupied with the huge Dane to
notice Charles reaching for the knife at his belt. *God, forgive me,*
Charles thought as he grabbed the knife and pulled it out of its
sheath. Before the Frank could react, Charles screamed and
stabbed him in the stomach. He felt the knife slicing through the
man's tunic and burying itself deep in his gut. The Frank grunted
as his eyes bulged.

'You...' The man struggled to get the words out as he let go of
Charles and dropped to his knees.

'Run, boy!' the Dane bellowed.

Charles didn't hesitate. He turned and rushed to the door at the
back of the room, but as he reached for it, thunder sounded outside
and the door swung open.

* * *

'Eydis!' Sven charged at his brother, his sword arm pulled back.

Bjarni smirked and stood his ground, his sword in front of him.
He twisted out of the way of Sven's attack and punched him on the
side of the head. But Sven did not react to the punch as he turned
and stabbed at his brother, who deflected the sword with his own.
He threw another punch at Sven, but this time Sven ducked under
it and threw his own which caught his taller brother in the ribs.
Bjarni bent to the side and Sven grabbed him by his beard before
headbutting him and punching him in the face with the pommel of
his sword. He let go of Bjarni's beard and his brother stumbled
backwards, his eyes dazed. Sven did not want to give him time to
recover and attacked again, swinging his sword at Bjarni's head.
Bjarni got his sword up to block the blow, but could do nothing as

Sven kicked him in the chest and he fell onto his back near the hearth fire. Sven strode towards him, his temples throbbing.

Sven was about to stab his brother when Bjarni grabbed a log from the fire and jabbed it in Sven's face. Sven tried to twist his head out of the way but still felt the burning log searing his skin as his bushy beard burst into flames. Sven screamed as he dropped his sword and patted the flames out while Bjarni struggled to his feet and turned to his men, who watched in stunned silence.

'What are you waiting for? Kill the swine!'

Sven gritted his teeth against the pain as he glared at the warriors of Ribe, waiting for them to attack. He had no sword now, but that would not stop him. One warrior, a brown-haired man about the age Torkel would have been, stepped forward, armed with a knife.

'Stop!' All heads turned to the door of the hall where Oleg stood holding a Dane axe in his hands. Sven gasped as he saw the familiar swirls and the boar head engraved into the head of the axe. 'This is a fight between Jarl Bjarni and Sven the Boar.' He walked towards Sven, who tensed. 'This is a family matter, and none of you will interfere.'

'Oleg, you bastard! What are you doing?' Bjarni screamed at his hirdman, his face bright red. 'You are my man. You swore an oath to me!'

Oleg stopped next to Sven, towering over him. 'Aye, but Odin also knows that I swore an oath to your brother to protect him and his family.' He turned to face Sven. 'I failed that oath, and I hope I can make amends for it.' He handed Sven his old Dane axe, the one which had brought him many victories. The weapon he had killed his father with to become the jarl of Ribe.

Sven took the axe, his fingers wrapping around the haft and feeling the grooves worn into the wood from all the times he had used the weapon. The axe was heavier than he remembered, or perhaps he was not as strong any more, but Sven still smiled as he held her in his hands. He looked at Oleg and nodded his thanks before he turned to face his brother again. He gripped the haft of his Dane axe, his hands twisting around the wood, his knuckles white. 'You betrayed me, brother. Betrayed my family. And today, Bjarni, I will kill you for it.'

Bjarni hawked and spat as he glared at his men. 'Fucking cowards.' He then looked at his brother. 'Let's see what the Norns decide for us, brother.' He roared as he charged at Sven.

Sven thought of his son, his wife and his men, all of them lost because of his brother, because of Bjarni's betrayal. He felt his rage at their deaths surge through him as he lifted his axe and swung it at his brother. Bjarni twisted to avoid the axe and stabbed at Sven's side as the axe struck the ground. Sven turned, not having the strength to bring the axe around. He felt the sword grate along the *brynja*, but the links held as he let go of the axe and grabbed Bjarni's sword arm with his left hand. The cut on his shoulder protested, but Sven ignored it as he punched Bjarni in the face. As Bjarni stumbled to the side, Sven grabbed his axe again with both hands and chopped at Bjarni, who deflected the axe with his sword and then kicked Sven in the stomach. Sven bent over from the blow and his brother kneed him in the face. Sparks flashed in his eyes as his nose crunched and, as he stumbled back, Bjarni stabbed at his exposed chest. Sven sensed the attack rather than felt it. He knocked the sword point away from him and struck Bjarni on the side of the head with the haft of his axe. Bjarni reeled from the blow but stayed on his feet as both men took a step back and shook their heads to clear them. The hall was so silent that Sven could hear his laboured breathing and the blood pumping in his ears. The thunder outside sounded so loud that Sven could have believed the storm was inside the hall.

'Thor is with me,' Bjarni said as Sven spat blood onto the

ground. His nose stung and his eyes were blurred, but he ignored all that as he glared at his younger brother. 'The Thunderer is on my side, brother. You cannot win.'

Sven shook his head one time before he gripped his axe in both hands. 'I don't need to win. I just need to kill you.' He lifted his axe above his head and charged at his brother, who crouched as he prepared to defend himself. Sven chopped down with his axe, but Bjarni jumped to the side and swung his sword at Sven's head. Sven ducked and as the sword went over his head, he brought his axe around to cut his brother in half. But Bjarni expected the move and stepped towards him. The haft of the axe struck him in the side, but he took the blow on his large hip and punched Sven in the face with his sword hand. Sven's head snapped back, and his brother shoved him hard. Sven fell on his back and rolled to his feet, as he expected his brother to stab him on the ground. But Bjarni had other ideas as he waited for Sven to get to his feet, wincing, before he shoulder-barged Sven to the ground again. Sven lay on his back and coughed as he struggled to get the air back into his lungs. The hall spun around him as he could just about make out the warriors surrounding him and his brother.

'You really thought you could kill me!' his brother shouted at him. 'I am Jarl Bjarni! This is my town!' He walked past Sven and kicked him in the side. Sven bent over, clutching his side as the air was driven out of him again. 'You really thought you could use your usual tricks on me? You forget, Sven, I have trained against you enough times to understand how you fight.' He walked around and kicked Sven again. Sven grunted as he lay on the ground and stared at the ceiling of the hall. He remembered, as a child, how he would climb up there and hide in the roof when he needed to get away from his brothers and father. He also remembered catching his son doing the same thing.

'Torkel,' he said, his voice faint.

'Torkel?' Bjarni frowned and then laughed. 'Your son who betrayed your gods. That is who you think of before I kill you?'

Sven saw his son on the beach as his ship sailed away, surrounded by the Franks while trying to look brave. But then his son's face changed, and he saw his grandson on the beach. And not just on the beach, but in the forest with Amund's sword at his neck. The fear he saw in the boy's eyes had made him break his oath to Odin. An oath he had made after he killed his wife. And Eydis would never forgive him if he died now after breaking that oath. 'I'm coming for you, boy,' he whispered.

'What are you muttering now?' Bjarni leaned in closer to hear what his brother was saying.

Thunder roared again outside as Sven grabbed his brother's beard. Bjarni's eyes widened and Sven struck him on the side of the head with the haft of his Dane axe. The blow was not hard, but it was enough to force his brother back so that Sven could get to his feet. He gripped his axe in both hands, gritting his teeth as his hot blood pumped through him. In his mind, Sven saw only his grandson, the frightened little boy who needed him. And Sven would not let his grandson down. Not even the gods could stop him. He lifted his Dane axe above his head and screamed as he charged at his brother again. 'Charles!'

His brother grinned as he lifted his sword and prepared to deal with the same attack again, but this time, as Sven reached him, he let go of the axe. Bjarni barely had enough time to frown as the axe fell to the ground before Sven tackled him. Sven's shoulder struck Bjarni in his rotund stomach, and he grunted as Sven lifted him up and pushed him backwards. The warriors behind them moved out of the way before Sven drove Bjarni into the tables lined up against the wall. Bjarni cried out as he dropped his sword and fell to his knees. Sven took a step back and punched Bjarni hard in the face, and as his head snapped to the side, Sven punched him again. He grabbed Bjarni by his tunic and screamed in his face before head-butting him. Blood sprayed everywhere as his nose broke. Sven took half a step back and wiped the blood from his forehead, not caring if it was his or his brother's, as he trembled with his rage. He stepped in again and punched Bjarni before he grabbed him by the tunic again.

'I gave you everything, and you took everything away from me!' Blood and spit landed on Bjarni's face, but Sven's brother was too dazed to react. Sven screamed in his face again before he took a step back. 'Why, Bjarni? I trusted you more than anyone.'

Bjarni coughed and said something, but it was too soft for Sven to hear so he came closer and leaned forward. 'I told you, I had no choice. I had to help King Horik stop you from attacking the Franks. If you didn't, they would have attacked Denmark. The king tried to warn you, but you were too stubborn to listen.'

'But all our men who died, their fathers left dead on the beach!' Sven pointed at the men standing around them.

But Bjarni only shook his head. 'They did not die because of me. I didn't tell you to fight the Franks that day. You did that. They died because of you.'

Sven growled as he grabbed Bjarni's hair and lifted his head so he could look him in the eyes. 'You took everything from me that day, Bjarni. I'm not letting you take my grandson as well.'

Bjarni smiled, revealing his blood-covered teeth. 'Too late.'

Sven looked at the door at the end of the wall, wanting to run to the room to see if his grandson was still there, but there was one more thing to do. He let go of his brother's hair and walked to his axe. He winced as he bent to pick it up and, gripping it tightly, he walked back to where his brother was still on his knees. None of the warriors in the hall moved to stop him. Nothing else seemed to exist other than Sven and his brother. Thunder rolled outside again when Sven lifted his Dane axe above his head, like Thor was encouraging him. Bjarni looked up at him and smiled.

'The mighty Sven the Boar. You don't know the storm coming your way.'

'Give my regards to our father.' Sven ignored his brother's words, and chopped down with the axe. Blood and brain splattered Sven as the axe crushed his brother's skull and sliced his head in two before it stopped in his chest. Sven stepped back and stared at his brother's corpse, hearing nothing but the thunder outside and the flames of the hearth fire. He became aware of the men around him as he heard their stunned breathing, but he paid no attention to them. His legs felt weak at that moment and his body ached, while his face burnt where his brother had struck him with the burning log. All Sven wanted to do was collapse and close his eyes, but he knew he could not. Sven turned to the door to the sleeping quarters and limped towards it as the warriors stepped out of his way. He saw his brother's wife cowering by the wall near the door, her condescending stare replaced by terror. Sven reached the door and stopped as he remembered what had happened the last time he was there. But then he took a deep breath and forced himself to enter the bedroom where he had killed his wife.

Inside, Sven felt his heart skip. His nose wrinkled when he smelt death in the room as the metallic smell of the blood overtook all other scents. He scanned the room, trying to find any sign of his grandson. One Frank was slouched against the wall, his head covered in blood, and another, the richly dressed bastard, lay on the ground near the back door. There was blood against the wall and all over the floor and as Sven tried to understand what had happened, the Frank on the ground moved. Sven grimaced and limped towards him. He dropped to his knees, doing his best to keep the pain off his face.

'Where is my grandson?' he asked the Frank in Danish.

'Fuck you,' the Frank responded, his face pale and sweaty.

Sven looked at the man while trying to control his anger. He glanced down and saw the knife in the Frank's stomach and, before the man could react, he grabbed the knife and twisted it. 'Where is my grandson?'

The Frank screamed and swore at him in Frankish so Sven twisted the knife again. Again the Frank cried out as fresh tears ran down his cheeks and he pointed at the door.

Sven looked out into the darkness and frowned. Then he turned to the Frank again. 'Why are you after him?'

The Frank shook his head, and Sven twisted the knife again as fresh blood soaked his hand. The Frank started praying, asking his god for forgiveness and mercy, but he refused to answer Sven's question.

Sven looked at Oleg, who was in the room with a few of the warriors of Ribe. 'Why do the Franks want my grandson?'

'I don't know. We didn't even know you had a grandson until a few days ago.' Sven frowned, so Oleg explained. 'This bastard arrived with his ship, spoke only to Bjarni, but your brother told me that your son was dead and that the Franks were after his son. They'd sent some men after him, but believed he was coming here.' Oleg shrugged. 'That's all I know.'

Sven looked at the Frank again, his hand still on the knife as the man prayed. He grabbed the Frank's hair with his other hand and brought his face close to his. 'Your god can't hear you here. Thor is making sure of that.' As he said that, more thunder boomed outside. 'So he can't give you mercy, but I can. I can kill you quickly, and end your pain. Is that what you want?' The Frank nodded and Sven smiled. 'Good. Now tell me, why do you want to kill my grandson?'

The Frank hesitated, and Sven twisted the knife. The man

grimaced and then he nodded before saying, 'We don't want to kill the boy. We were trying to rescue him.'

Sven's eyes widened. 'Rescue him from who?'

'King Charles of West Francia. He wants the boy and not just the boy, but something he has.'

Sven frowned. 'The cross?'

The Frank's face twisted in agony as he nodded.

'Why?'

'The cross... used to belong to Ch... Charlemagne. They say it helped him build... his empire. Charles believes your son and the cross will protect him from his brother, Louis. Maybe even help him build his own empire.'

None of this made any sense to Sven, so he twisted the knife. 'You're lying to me, Frank. Why did you kill my son?'

The Frank shook his head as tears streamed down his cheeks. 'That wasn't us. The man who killed your son was a spy for Charles. We did not know. That's why we were sent to find the boy, before they do.'

'And Gerold, what about that snake?' Sven growled.

'The boy is one of ours. He kept an eye on your grandson and left a trail for us to follow. He and his master were supposed to take the boy somewhere safe, where the West could not get him. But something went wrong.'

'Then why attack us?'

The Frank lifted his head and stared at Sven. 'You were in the way of my mission.'

Sven glared at the man. 'I was protecting my grandson.'

'It doesn't matter. My master does not want the boy to be raised by heathens. She never wanted him to come to this godless place.'

Sven frowned, struggling to make sense of everything. 'Who is your master? Who wants the boy?'

The Frank stared at Sven as if he was debating whether he

should respond or not. Sven decided to encourage him by twisting the knife again. The man cried out before he replied, 'Reverend Mother Hildegard. Daughter of King Louis and,' the Frank stared at Sven for a heartbeat, 'the boy's mother.'

Thunder ripped through the sky as Sven almost collapsed. He thought of the cross, with its huge ruby and the symbol of Charlemagne, a name all Danes knew and hated, and finally understood why his son had it. Sven pulled the knife out and stabbed the Frank in the chest. The man tensed and then his body went limp as Sven stared out of the door.

'What did he say?' Oleg asked.

Without looking back, Sven just said, 'Find my grandson.'

'What?' Oleg frowned.

'Find my grandson!' Sven turned to face him, his face red. The warriors behind Oleg rushed past him and out of the hall as Sven struggled to his feet and limped out of the door.

'There, on the wharf!' one man shouted.

Sven strained his eyes as he struggled to see in the dark night. In the dim light cast by the torches on the wharf, he saw what looked like a body. A large body. 'Charles,' Sven muttered, his eyes scanning the sea. In the distance, he thought he saw a pinprick of light, but then it disappeared. Other warriors ran past him when Oleg shouted, 'Sven! There!'

Sven looked to where his former hirdman pointed and as he squinted into the night, he saw four figures appearing out of the shade of one house near the hall. Oleg held up a torch he found on the ground.

'Charles?' Sven asked as Oda came into the light with Thora behind her, helped by Sigmund, Rollo's son. And behind Thora was Charles, the short red-headed boy holding on to Thora's hand as he stared back at Sven. Sven felt the knot in his throat when he saw his grandson. He took a step towards them, but then stopped as Charles took a step back.

Thora looked at Charles and then at Sven. 'Well, you can't blame the boy. You're covered in blood and you stink.'

Sven looked at his large stomach and saw his tunic red with blood in the torchlight. 'How?' he asked Thora as he looked at his grandson, knowing it was more than the blood that kept him away.

'Oda wanted to watch you kill your brother,' Thora said, and the old lady just shrugged. 'She led me to the back door and as we opened it, Charles crashed into us.'

'Knocked all of us over,' Oda said, and looked at Charles with a smile. Sven guessed that explained the torch on the ground. Charles looked away, but Sven saw the blood on his hand and raised an eyebrow.

Sven looked back towards the wharf. 'Then who is that?' In the dim light, he saw some warriors had reached the wharf and were helping the huge man to his feet.

'Rollo. Those bastards came after your grandson and Rollo drove them away.' Oda scowled.

'And the Franks? Gerold?'

'Gone. They got on their ship and sailed away. Gerold went with them. Must have been desperate to get away if they risked sailing at night.'

Sven scowled. 'Hopefully Rán will do us a favour and drown the bastards.'

'We can only pray,' Thora agreed, and then it was her turn to frown. 'Bjarni?'

Sven looked at her and sighed. His body ached and his face still burnt. 'Dead. You were right, Thora, you and your father. The bastard betrayed me. Sold me out to the Franks.'

Thora shook her head, which confused Sven. 'Not to the Franks. To King Horik. Soon after you left here, my father found a chest full of gold coins with Horik's face on them. Horik gave your son to the Franks to save his peace treaty and he used Bjarni to do it. I tried to tell you, Sven, for so many winters, and so did my father, but you always refused to listen.'

'He used that money to rebuild Ribe, make her bigger and wealthier than before so people here wouldn't ask too many questions,' Oda added. 'You were never a popular jarl, Sven, but you were still jarl and Bjarni understood he had to keep the people of Ribe happy.'

Sven nodded, not really knowing what to say, and then he looked out to sea again.

'But I still don't understand what any of this has to do with Charles?' Thora asked.

Sven looked at Charles, seeing how the boy hid behind Thora. 'Because of his mother.'

'His mother?' Thora asked.

Charles frowned as he looked at Sven. 'Because she stole the cross?'

Sven shook his head as he stared at his grandson, wondering how he was going to tell the boy the truth. But that, he decided, could wait until the next day, as the clouds finally released the rain they had been holding for so long. Sven gripped the Mjöllnir around his neck as the fat raindrops washed the blood of his brother from his skin and as lightning arched across the night sky, he made a new oath to the All-Father.

Mighty Odin, this oath I make to you now. For as long as I have a breath in me, I will do all I can to protect my grandson, the last of my line. No man, woman or kingdom will harm him or take him from me. This, I swear to you, Odin Raven God.

ACKNOWLEDGMENTS

First of all, I would like to thank Caroline for sending the email which chained the course of my writing career and for believing in me and my story. Also, to the team at Boldwood Books for their warm welcome and for making me feel part of the family even before I finished writing this novel.

To my wife, Anna, who has to live with my constant talk of battles and Norse gods.

And most importantly, to my readers. This journey would never have got this far without your continued support.

MORE FROM DONOVAN COOK

We hope you enjoyed reading *Odin's Betrayal*. If you did, please leave a review.

If you'd like to gift a copy, this book is also available as an ebook, large print, hardback, digital audio download and audiobook CD.

Sign up to Donovan Cook's mailing list for news, competitions and updates on future books.

https://bit.ly/DonovanCookNews

ABOUT THE AUTHOR

Donovan Cook is the author of the well-received *Ormstunga Saga* series which combines fast-paced narrative with meticulously researched history of the Viking world, and is inspired by his interest in Norse Mythology. He lives in Lancashire.

Visit Donovan's website: www.donovancook.net

Follow Donovan on social media:

 twitter.com/DonovanCook20
 facebook.com/DonovanCookAuthor
 bookbub.com/authors/donovan-cook

Boldwood

Boldwood Books is an award-winning fiction publishing company seeking out the best stories from around the world.

Find out more at www.boldwoodbooks.com

Join our reader community for brilliant books, competitions and offers!

Follow us
@BoldwoodBooks
@BookandTonic

Sign up to our weekly deals newsletter

https://bit.ly/BoldwoodBNewsletter